BY SUSAN ELIA MacNEAL

Mr. Churchill's Secretary
Princess Elizabeth's Spy
His Majesty's Hope
The Prime Minister's Secret Agent
Mrs. Roosevelt's Confidante
The Queen's Accomplice
The Paris Spy

THE QUEEN'S ACCOMPLICE

The Queen's Accomplice

A Maggie Hope Mystery

SUSAN ELIA MacNEAL

BANTAM BOOKS

NEW YORK

A Bantam Books Trade Paperback Original

Published in the United States by Bantam Books,
an imprint of Random House, a division of
Penguin Random House LLC, New York.

BANTAM BOOKS and the HOUSE colophon are registered
trademarks of Penguin Random House LLC.

This book contains an excerpt from the forthcoming book *The Paris Spy* by Susan Elia MacNeal. This excerpt has been set for this edition only and may not reflect the final content of the forthcoming edition.

LIBRARY OF CONGRESS CATALOGING-IN-PUBLICATION DATA
Names: MacNeal, Susan Elia, author.
Title: The queen's accomplice: a Maggie Hope mystery / Susan Elia MacNeal.
Description: New York: Bantam Books, 2016. | Series: A Maggie Hope mystery
Identifiers: LCCN 2016009035 (print) | LCCN 2016015739 (ebook) |
ISBN 9780804178723 (softcover) | ISBN 9780804178730 (ebook)
Subjects: LCSH: Women spies—Fiction. | Cryptographers—Fiction. | Americans—
England—London—Fiction. | Serial murder investigation—Fiction. | World War,
1939–1945—England—Fiction. | BISAC: FICTION / Mystery & Detective / Women
Sleuths. | FICTION / Mystery & Detective / Traditional British. | FICTION /
Historical. | GSAFD: Historical fiction. | Mystery fiction. | Spy stories.
Classification: LCC PS3613.A2774 Q44 2016 (print) | LCC PS3613.A2774 (ebook) |
DDC 813/.6—dc23 LC record available at https://lccn.loc.gov/2016009035

Printed in the United States of America on acid-free paper

randomhousebooks.com

8 9 7 6

Book design by Dana Leigh Blanchette
Title-page image: © iStockphoto.com

In memory of Violette Szabo
June 26, 1921–February 5, 1945

Posthumously awarded the George Cross
and the Croix de Guerre, and among the
117 SOE agents who did not survive
their missions to France

Little girls, this seems to say,
Never stop upon your way,
Never trust a stranger-friend;
No one knows how it will end.

—CHARLES PERRAULT,
"LITTLE RED RIDING HOOD"

AS A WARNING TO FEMALE VIRTUE,
This Monument
Is erected over the remains of
MARY ASHFORD,
a young Woman, chaste as she was beautiful,
Who, in the 20th year of her age,
having incautiously repaired to a Scene of Amusement,
without proper Protection,
was brutally violated and murdered
on the 27th of May, 1817,
in the Parish of Aston.

—PROPOSED EPITAPH FROM *A MORAL REVIEW
OF THE CONDUCT AND CASE OF MARY ASHFORD*

THE QUEEN'S ACCOMPLICE

Prologue

The winds were changing.

They were blowing in from the east now, Vera Baines noted, from the East End. Even though the air raids had stopped for the moment in London—as Hitler turned his attentions toward Russia—the docks, railroads, and factories were still burning.

Through her open bedroom window, she could smell cold wind scented with smoke and destruction. She watched as it ruffled the bare black branches of the trees of Regent's Park, rustling dead ivy. Since the war had begun, the park had become a desolate expanse of meandering walkways, overgrown shrubbery, and long air-raid trenches—an ideal location for crime. But not on her watch.

As an ARP warden for her section in Marylebone, Vera Baines knew not only the winds but the intricacies of light and dark. Sunset in London in late March 1942 arrived after six, but the violet shadows began to lengthen at least an hour earlier. This evening's sunset was extraordinary—bright red, with crepuscular rays piercing wispy clouds.

Despite barely clearing the five-foot mark and a slight figure, at eighty-three, Vera was a redoubtable woman. She was more wiry than frail, her energy giving the impression of her being much taller than she actually was. She had impeccable posture and moved with a force and confidence her friends and family hadn't seen since her husband had died ten years ago. And her face, with its high cheekbones and clear blue eyes that missed nothing, radiated strength.

Vera hated the war, hated the loss of innocent lives—but she couldn't deny it had brought a certain clarity to her existence. As an ARP warden, she now felt she had a purpose: She would protect her own. As she surveyed the park's deepening shadows from the window of her bone-colored Georgian terraced house, Vera felt responsibility, plus a fierce sense of love and pride. This was her London. These were her people. Nothing would happen to them on her sentry.

It was time to begin her shift. Vera took one last look at the fading light, listening to the forlorn cries of the birds, then picked her way downstairs, leaning on the railing. At her door, she put on her ARP tin hat, dark blue wool overcoat, and gloves, and reached for her walking stick—with a silver British bulldog on the handle. Then she went down the outside stairs and onto the icy flagstone pavement, bracing herself against the wind. She paced the street with her usual vigor, the pale symmetrical Nash architecture reflecting the last light of the dying sunset. The temperature was dropping and the air smelled of imminent storms.

A passing white-haired man tipped his black bowler hat, and she nodded in return. "Oh, Mr. Saunders—" she called after him, her breath making clouds in the chill air.

The man stopped and turned. "Yes, Mrs. Baines?"

"I noticed a chink in your blackout curtain on the second floor last night. Please see to it no light is visible from now on."

He took a few steps forward and frowned down at her. "We haven't had an air raid in months, dearie."

Vera was not deterred by his bulk, his height, or his condescending tone. "And the Luftwaffe might be choosing tonight for a return visit, Mr. Saunders. Let's not give them any light to guide them to us, shall we?"

She strode on, chin high, taking her usual route past the charred remains of Regent's Park's brick wall. The last of the sun's light melted away, but Vera didn't mind the dark; she liked being out alone at night. Without electric lights to pierce the darkness, the nighttime took on a new beauty in the icy bright moonlight. Her shuttered flashlight illuminated the strips of white paint on the curbs and tree trunks, giving off a ghostly glow.

In the distance, she could hear the sounds of the city: the faint rumble of motor traffic, the *clip-clop* of horses' hooves on cobblestones, the screeches and flaps of bats off to their night's hunt. The wind picked up once again, causing the ancient tree branches to sway and creak, the dead leaves and lipstick-stained cigarette butts in the gutters to dance.

Without artificial light, Regent's Park at night could have been any era in London—from the time when ancient Britons painted themselves blue, to the reign of Queen Elizabeth I, to the period of Victoria and Albert. Even the clocks obliged: When the Nazi bombs exploded, all nearby timepieces ceased to function, paralyzed at whatever time they were at the instant of impact. These comatose clocks were another reason Vera could imagine time telescoping—the suspended present creating an atmosphere where time travel seemed no mere fantasy. Really, anything seemed possible, especially in the shadows of night. It even smelled as it could have hundreds of years ago—the same stink of urine against the crumbling brick walls as there would have been in Pepys's day.

In the darkness, Vera tripped and nearly fell, saved only by her trusty walking stick. "What the—?" she muttered, her grip in leather gloves tight on the silver handle. She righted herself, glad Mr. Saunders hadn't been there to see.

She looked down at a long blanket-wrapped bundle. Leaning over, flashlight in one hand, she lifted and pulled back the wool covering with the tip of her cane.

Vera gave a sharp inhale, but didn't cry out when she saw the butchered body of a young woman. The corpse looked to have belonged to a girl in her early twenties—healthy and athletic, hair curled. Her throat had been slashed so savagely her head was nearly severed from her body. Her belly had been slit through her ATS uniform, which was soaked through with blood.

Vera felt as if she'd been struck dumb. But she swallowed and braced her shoulders, gathering her strength. "Murder!" she managed to croak. *"Murder!"* she cried, louder this time. "Someone— someone fetch the police!"

A blond boy in a tweed cap walking past stopped and stared. "What the devil's going on? Are you all right, ma'am?"

Vera lifted her chin, squared her shoulders, and deployed the stiff upper lip she'd perfected over a lifetime of practice. "Yes, yes, of course *I* am," she reassured him. "But I'm afraid *she* isn't," she added, pointing to the woman's mutilated body with the silver tip of her walking stick.

The boy squinted in the darkness, eyes following the flashlight's beam. When he realized what he was seeing, he tore off his cap and crossed himself, whispering, "Bloody hell." He looked from the body back to Vera. "She's been ripped, ma'am." He shook his head, his hands worrying at his hat. "Looks like she's been done in by Jack the Bloody Ripper himself."

"What are you going on about, young man?" Despite her occasional daydreams—or night dreams—Vera had no patience for macabre nonsense. But the boy was looking past her to the park's brick wall, gaping at the lettering.

With a shaking hand, Vera raised her flashlight. The words scrawled across the wall were in the same ghostly, glowing white paint as the curbs.

They read, JACK IS BACK.

Chapter One

Something was wrong. Maggie Hope was sure, but she couldn't yet put her finger on it. *What could it be?* Frowning, she went over the encoded document yet again.

Maggie was working as a girl Friday in a dim reception room at 64 Baker Street, at the Special Operations Executive's offices. It was in an anonymous gray limestone building down the street from Sherlock Holmes's fictional address and Regent's Park, only one of the many unremarkable SOE offices scattered around the Marylebone area of central London. Because of lack of space in Whitehall, Baker Street and its surrounding area had become home for SOE, and several buildings had been fitted with discreet plaques reading INTER-SERVICES RESEARCH BUREAU. The staff and those in the know called it the Firm, the Org, or the Racket, and its employees were known as the Baker Street Irregulars, in honor of Holmes's young informants.

The atmosphere in the shabby third-floor offices of 64 Baker Street was informal, with almost everyone sipping mugs of hot tea and smoking Gauloises, men and women passing through speaking perfect French. The icy reception room was small and narrow, with only one window and a low ceiling. A fire extinguisher and a notice pointing out the direction of the air-raid shelter decorated one wall, while a tacked-up postcard of the Arc de Triomphe covered the cracks of another.

Maggie wore an old skirt, a white blouse, and a thick navy-blue wool cardigan patched at the elbows. She was never without her pearl stud earrings, a graduation gift from her Aunt Edith, and her long coppery hair was up in a bun that had begun the day tidy but was now slipping, tendrils springing free around her face and neck. She sat at a dented metal desk with a Remington typewriter, behind a line of telephones in assorted colors, and an overflowing wooden inbox.

Only twenty-seven, Maggie had already performed any number of missions as an agent for SOE, but had taken a desk job in London while she was waiting for the arrival of her German half sister, Elise Hess, a Resistance worker in Berlin. Her rescue to London, ordered by Prime Minister Winston Churchill himself, was taking longer than expected—but Maggie knew all too well these missions never went exactly as planned.

And so she waited, and while she did, she made herself useful at the SOE offices. When she wasn't greeting prospective agents arriving for their various interviews, she was checking coded messages transmitted by F-Section agents. After all, she'd been secretary to the P.M. himself—as well as saving the life of the Princess Elizabeth, parachuting into Nazi Berlin, teaching at a paramilitary camp, and keeping the First Lady of the United States of America safe from scandal. How hard could managing an office be? And it was only temporary, until her half sister arrived in London and settled in.

On this Saturday afternoon, as the light from the grimy window began to fade, Maggie was performing a task known as "code check," going over an agent's transmission from the field, making sure all was in order. Maggie—a mathematics prodigy who'd graduated summa cum laude from Wellesley College, with a special aptitude for codes and ciphers—liked to try her hand at transposing the worst of the garbled messages. As she worked, she rubbed absently at an ink stain on her blouse's cuff and then buttoned up her sweater against the office's chill.

Maggie knew the Morse coding systems intimately, knew how to "unscramble the indecipherable." What looked to be problems in a given message might occur simply because an agent had transposed two letters, or misspelled a word. Each agent had a characteristic set of mistakes, and Maggie had quickly come to learn each one's unique style of communication. For example, some agents routinely misspelled certain words—bad habits from childhood. Then there were the trademark sign-offs; a few liked to end with a simple *Goodbye,* while others sent *Lots of Love,* and yet another's was *Tallyho!*

Maggie was worried about this particular message, from agent Erica Calvert, a young geologist who'd made a midnight boat landing on the beach near Normandy a few weeks before. Something was . . . not right. Calvert had studied earth science at St. Hilda's at Oxford and was considered an expert on sand grains. But this particular message from her—well, Maggie had never seen anything like it. It was what they called "mutilated," which might have been caused by atmospheric conditions. But Erica's writing was also uncharacteristically clipped.

Most troubling was that Calvert hadn't included her secret security check, carried by each agent, which gave SOE contacts back in Britain absolute confirmation the wireless operator was transmitting freely. Before leaving for a mission, each agent was assigned both a bluff check and a true check, which he or she had to insert into every message. These took the form of spelling mistakes or secret signals, agreed on with SOE, to show the sender had been captured.

All right, stay calm, Maggie thought as fear prickled up her spine. *Let's look at this logically.* She could see four explanations for the oddities of Erica Calvert's message.

One: The message had been transmitted by someone else in Erica's network, but on Calvert's set—and had left off the security code.

Two: Calvert was on the run and operating in difficult circumstances, which changed her fist, and she didn't have time for the security code.

Then, three: Calvert had been captured. She was operating under German control and so had deliberately omitted the security code to alert SOE she'd been compromised.

And there was four—the worst-case scenario: Calvert was dead and the Germans were using her radio and codes with impunity.

When Maggie went to the overflowing file cabinet and looked up Calvert's former messages, she found not only that Calvert had sent more than a dozen near-perfect ones since arriving in France, but also that she'd never forgotten her security check before. Not once. *Damn,* Maggie swore. *What's going on over there, Agent Calvert? Tout va bien?*

There was the click of heels on the scratched parquet floor, and then a woman's sweet, breathy voice inflected with a Welsh accent. "Excuse me? Miss Hope?"

Maggie slipped Calvert's message into a manila folder, then looked up, into the eyes of a petite, curly-haired brunette named Bronwyn Parry, kitted out in an ATS uniform. A gap between her two front teeth and a sprinkling of freckles across her nose only added to her charm. Bronwyn had been one of Maggie's best students at the SOE paramilitary training camp, near the town of Arisaig on the western coast of Scotland; she'd excelled at jujitsu, Fairbairn-Sykes knife fighting, and detonating explosives. Maggie had always liked Brynn.

"Just Maggie is fine now. How did the interview go?" Bronwyn had finished interviewing with Miss Lynd, one of the final hurdles before being sent to Beaulieu, the "Finishing School" for all SOE agents.

"It went well," the young woman replied in her broad Cardiff accent, "but I don't have a place to stay in London." Her usually open face was troubled. "All these posh girls can book a room at Claridge's or stay at Daddy's pied-à-terre." She rolled her eyes. "Meanwhile, the rest of us have to scrum for a place. . . ."

Maggie nodded. She knew firsthand how SOE was a curious cross section of social class and privilege.

Brynn shrugged. "And Miss Lynd insists I come in again tomorrow—for yet another interview."

"I wish I could help you, Brynn," Maggie offered with sincerity. "I'd ask you to stay with me, but my own flat was smashed in a raid—I'm bunking with friends myself."

Brynn opened her handbag and pulled out a Woodbine cigarette and enamel lighter. She stuck the cigarette between her lips, lit it, and inhaled. "What should I do, sleep on a bench in Regent's Park?" She puffed out a series of blue smoke rings.

"Well, that option might prove a bit nippy. Alas, SOE doesn't provide temporary lodging—but here's a place to try." Maggie rummaged through the left-hand desk drawer, through an old bottle of clear nail polish for stocking runs, two rationed sugar cubes saved in an envelope, and a battered box of paper clips, until she found a business card: *THE CASTLE HOTEL FOR WOMEN: Temporary Lodging for Ladies* and the address in heavy black ink.

She handed it to Brynn. "You can call from here to see if there are any vacancies for tonight. Miss Lynd tells me a number of SOE interviewees have stayed there. Here, use this phone," she said, pushing a green one toward the Welsh girl.

As Brynn came around the desk, they both heard a bellow. "Meggie!" a gruff male voice boomed from behind a thick wooden office door. *"Meggie!"*

Maggie sighed, then picked up Calvert's file and rose. She walked the strip of threadbare carpet through the dim passageway, then pushed at the half-closed office door.

"It's *Maggie*, sir," she reminded him gently. Although the men in the office were referred to by their rank and wore uniforms, the women were called by their first names and expected to dress in civilian clothes.

Colonel Harry Gaskell was in his late forties, a short, rotund man with yellow hair and a fleshy, shining face. The beginnings of rosacea pinked his nose and cheeks. Although he'd served in the British Army's Intelligence Corps as a doctor at the outbreak of the war, he'd been evacuated from Dunkirk and stayed in Britain. What concerned Maggie most was he had no firsthand knowledge of, or training in, guerrilla warfare, despite the fact he was in charge of F-Section.

Gaskell blinked pale eyes. "Meeting's at five-thirty. We'll jolly well need tea, and some of those oatmeal biscuits Miss Cooper made—hard as rocks, but if you dunk them, they're not so bad."

"Colonel—" Maggie began, handing him Erica Calvert's file. Gaskell accepted it with a brisk movement, then flicked his eyes over the document and Maggie's notes. He handed it back to her. "Jolly good job, young lady."

"No," Maggie persisted, "I believe something's wrong, sir."

"There's only one explanation for Miss Calvert's mistakes—carelessness," the Colonel admonished. "The next time the girl's schedule comes up, tell her she's forgotten her security check. And remind her to be more vigilant!" He chortled. "Give that girl a rap on the knuckles!"

Maggie braced her shoulders. "Colonel Gaskell, Erica Calvert didn't only forget the security check. Her fist was also out of character—unusually hesitant, not her style at all. I don't like to be negative, but I believe it's possible she's been captured and her radio's now in the hands of the Germans."

Outside the window, she could see cars passing on Baker Street dusted by a light snow shower. The side of one red-brick building was painted with the advertisement TAKE BOVRIL TO RESIST FLU. There was the screech of brakes, a loud crash, and then a torrent of swearing as one car hit another on the slippery pavement.

"Fiddlesticks, Meggie! Er, Maggie. When you hear hooves, think horses, not unicorns! You're doing jolly good work here and I know you're concerned about the agents in the field, my dear, but let's not let drama override duty, yes?"

As she turned and stalked away, Gaskell called after her: "And don't let the tea steep too long this time!" Maggie could easily make out his grumbled complaint, *"Damn Yanks . . ."*

Gritting her teeth, Maggie put the file back in her desk drawer, then braved the frigid corridor to the dingy kitchenette to put the kettle on.

Officially, she was part of the Auxiliary Territorial Service, a major in the women's branch of the Army, known as ATS—but for her, that rank was actually a cover for work with SOE. When she'd arrived in London from Boston, four years ago, all she'd wanted to do was settle her grandmother's estate, then return to the United States to pursue doctoral studies in mathematics at MIT, one of the few top universities to allow women as graduate students.

But then war had been declared, the Blitz began, and she'd convinced herself to stay in London and help—which had led to working for Prime Minister Winston Churchill. When given the opportunity to work for SOE as an agent, she grabbed it. She loved Britain and wanted to do "her bit."

As the kettle boiled, Colonel Frank Brody, second in command of F-Section, entered on wooden crutches, the left leg of his uniform trousers pinned around the stump. Brody hopped up on the rickety wooden table, his one leg swinging, whistling "Green Eyes."

"My aunt used to say 'whistling calls the Devil,'" Maggie teased. "Perhaps Satan's a fan of Jimmy Dorsey?"

Unlike Colonel Gaskell, Brody had trained to be an SOE agent, and been sent to France as part of F-Section. However, a leg injury on a mission led to an amputation that made short work of his career abroad. He'd returned to the London offices to be promoted.

As he slipped a bit on the table, then used his hands to right himself, he gave her a rueful smile. It lit up his plain, broad features, compensating for his upturned nose and overly large ears. "You should see my *Giselle*," he joked, finally settling his lanky frame. "I can pirouette better than Margot Fonteyn."

Maggie liked Brody. He never complained, and was always good for a witty rejoinder and a smile. She turned off the gas. "Any news on the leg?" she asked, using a pot holder to lift the kettle.

"The *peg*? No, still in the works, I'm afraid. With the amount of time they're taking, I'm hoping it comes with any number of additional features—a corkscrew, a dagger, even a flask. A whole Swiss Army knife of tricks." Brody had been fitted for a prosthetic leg, but because of high demand, its creation and delivery were delayed. "But, really, just the flask would be lovely."

He picked up a newspaper lying on the table. "Have you seen this yet?" he asked, glancing down the front page of *The Times*. "A murder last night, not too far from us. A girl—they say she was an ATS."

Maggie stopped fiddling with the tea things and looked up. "Do they say who it was?"

"Joanna Metcalf."

Maggie knew the name; she'd met the young woman in the

SOE office three days ago. Joanna had been another of her trainees at Arisaig. "Joanna Metcalf?" she managed. "Joanna's not just any ATS—she's one of ours—tapped by SOE and supposed to be sent to France. She was here for an interview just a few days ago."

"Bloody hell." Profanity, even in front of ladies, was as common in the office as French. "Poor thing."

Maggie turned away and bit her lip: She didn't want Brody to see the shocked expression on her face. When the tea was prepared, she put the Denby stoneware pot, mugs, and chipped plate piled high with biscuits on a tray, and carried it into a windowless conference room. Present were Gaskell and two other high-ranking SOE men in uniform, Colonel Bernard Higgs—with a neatly trimmed iron-gray mustache, and Colonel Rupert Shaw—with brilliantined, bushy hair that stuck straight up, like porcupine quills.

The walls were thin and Maggie's and Brody's voices had been overheard. "One of our girls murdered, you say?" Gaskell asked as Maggie walked in carrying the tea things, Brody on his crutches behind her. The Colonel shook his head in dismay. "I may be old-fashioned, but in my opinion, these girls should stay at home and listen to their mothers—war or no war, what ho? Certainly not gallivanting around London at all hours of the night, going to bars and dance clubs, listening to jazz . . ."

Maggie set the tray down on the trestle table covered in green baize as Brody took a seat, leaning his crutches against the wall. "That's a good girl," Gaskell muttered absently as he watched her pour. "Jolly good. Not too much tannin in the tea this way."

"What took you so long, my dear?" Colonel Higgs asked. "Powdering your nose in the ladies' loo?"

"You could use a little powder—and a little lipstick, too," Colonel Shaw added. " 'Beauty for Duty'—am I right, gentlemen?"

Maggie bit her tongue and passed out the agenda for the meet-

ing, the title of which was "The Woman Problem"—about the alleged knotty conundrum of female SOE agents—then perched on
a rickety wooden chair.

When SOE had been created by Minister of Economic Warfare
Hugh Dalton on July 22, 1940, Colonel Colin McVean Gubbins
had first secured authority, albeit unofficially, to send women behind enemy lines. Colonel Gubbins saw no reason why women
couldn't do the job of secret agent as well as the men. Gubbins had
met fierce opposition, but was ultimately supported by Prime Minister Churchill, who'd approved the deployment of women as SOE
agents.

Colonel Gaskell, Gubbins's successor at SOE, was far less enthusiastic about the "women situation." Although SOE employed
scores of women—as typists, drivers, and clerks—all were officially barred from armed combat, and there was no legal authority
for servicewomen to carry out the kind of guerrilla work SOE desperately wanted them to perform. The 1929 Geneva Convention
and the 1907 Hague Convention on Land Warfare, the main legal
instruments offering protection to prisoners of war, made no pro-
vision for women—as they were never considered, in anyone's
wildest imagination, to be combatants.

And so, although all SOE agents, both male and female, were
performing undercover missions, because of the Geneva Convention, women agents were at a higher risk. Men would be treated as
prisoners of war. Women, on the other hand, had far less legal
protection. They could be tortured for information and then executed as spies.

"We're already using women in the field to great advantage,"
Brody reminded Gaskell. "Nowadays, more and more Frenchmen
are being sent to Russia and the East—and any able-bodied man
left behind is looked on with suspicion. Whereas women can still
travel freely—generally underestimated by the Nazis, you know."

Gaskell looked to Maggie. "Would you be mother, my dear?"

Maggie poured the scalding, fragrant tea, passing out mugs to the men.

Gaskell blew noisily on the steaming liquid. "I'm still not in favor of sending our ladies abroad. And of course, if our use of girls as guerrillas leaks out, the policy will have to be denied."

"Sorry I'm late——" came a woman's high-pitched, warbling voice in a tone suggesting she was anything but sorry. Diana Lynd was the last to arrive for any meeting. Maggie was never sure if it was because she was legitimately busy or because she enjoyed making a grand entrance in a cloud of smoke and Jicky perfume. Miss Diana Lynd was a statuesque woman in her late thirties, with a quintessentially English sense of style—always dressed in impeccably tailored tweed suits in shades of brown and caramel and soft suede court shoes, her tawny hair rolled up at the nape of her neck. She had a distinctive accent—Benenden and Kensington, Maggie guessed, spoken in tones of cream and honey.

She'd informally been assigned not only responsibility for overseeing the women recruits but also the task of intelligence officer, which largely meant sifting through all information about life on the ground in France.

Gaskell stood, as did the other men. "Until we can shut down sending women agents to France, we can't have this policy of using females get out," Gaskell said, taking his seat once again. "If the Germans ever learn we're using women to fight, we'd be an international disgrace." He gave a nervous chortle.

"I believe," Maggie said, raising one eyebrow, "that the welfare and safety of our women in the field—as well as their well-being after they return—should be our highest concern. Not what the Germans may or may not think."

Brody cleared his throat. "I agree with you in principle, Maggie, but we cannot, under any circumstances, let the use of women as combatants become public knowledge—Goebbels would use it for the most horrific propaganda. If anything ever were to come to light, the policy of dropping women behind enemy lines would have to be denied."

"The problem is," Maggie interjected, pouring a mug of tea for Miss Lynd, "if the War Office won't take official responsibility for our female agents, they can't be treated as prisoners of war under the Geneva Convention—we're allowing them to be tortured, raped, and killed with impunity."

She handed the steaming mug to the older woman. "Also, if they die while serving their country, what are we going to tell their husbands, their children, the parents of these women when they don't return? They'll never know what their wives and mothers and daughters did for Britain."

"Plenty of us labor in obscurity, Miss Hope," intoned Miss Lynd as she accepted her tea, pursing moist, red-painted lips.

Maggie was undeterred. "And what of the female agents' pensions?"

Gaskell startled. "Pensions?"

"Yes, *pensions*," Maggie insisted. "Female operatives are already making only one-third the salary of the men—which I've said again and again is hardly fair, as we're doing the same jobs and in the same danger. But what if they return and need disability?" She looked to Brody, who had the grace to redden.

"And what if they're killed? What happens to their dependents?" Maggie cupped her numb hands around her own mug, using it for both warmth and strength. "The families of the male agents are well cared for—but what do the families of the women get? As of now—*nothing*."

"The female agents have fathers and husbands to take care of them, of course," reassured Colonel Shaw.

"No, sir, not all of them do. Only this morning I filed paperwork for Miss Audrey Thomas." Maggie looked to Colonel Gaskell. "You may recall she's part of F-Section's Prosper network, in Paris. She was captured by the Gestapo and sent to Ravensbrück. She's divorced, with one child—who's now in the care of an aunt, a retired schoolteacher, who's also taking care of their mother."

"Shouldn't have gotten divorced then," joked Colonel Higgs, lighting a cigarette.

"A little late for that bit of advice now, I think. What about her five-year-old daughter? What are we going to tell her? What sort of pension will she receive? The aunt is already taking care of the mother—how is she supposed to care for a child as well? If there were a pension in place, as the men have, it would be an invaluable help."

Gaskell ran his hands through what was left of his hair. "Miss Lynd."

"Yes, sir."

"In addition to your other roles, I'm making you responsible for this"—he waved a hand—"*female problem*. Report back to me next week."

"Yes, sir."

"Jolly good, Miss Lynd. Thank you. All right, we're done here. Carry on!"

Once again, Maggie ground her teeth and left for her desk. *It's like bloody Sisyphus pushing the bloody boulder up the bloody mountain—only to have it slide right back, rolling over you on its way down just for good measure. No wonder Aunt Edith's so bitter,* she fumed. *And has those deep frown lines between her eyebrows.*

She caught Brody looking at her. "I'm fine."

"It's not you, it's him," he said, leaning on her desk. "You must realize he lost his mind during the Dunkirk evacuation. Shell shock, they call it—startles at loud noises and all that. I've seen your file, you know," Brody continued softly. "You served bravely in Berlin. You're a credit to England."

"Thank you." She rose and walked the length of the icy hall to Miss Lynd's office. It was smaller than Colonel Gaskell's, the window with slatted blinds looking out on a red-brick wall across an alley, a lone bare sapling's branches whipped by the rising wind. It was tidy, though, with papers, pens, and reference books rigidly organized. At her elbow, Miss Lynd had a row of flip-flop card indexes, an inventory of names, addresses, and aliases of every F-Section agent, each with a small photograph attached. If she wanted to confirm a detail of an agent, she could run a fingernail along the top of the index, and little faces would appear, flipping over on the roller. The office's only decoration was a silver-framed photograph of the King.

Miss Lynd settled herself at her desk, scrutinizing a document, underlining a word here and there with a black fountain pen. It was almost six, and most of the staff were leaving or had already left—only the occasional clatter of a typewriter could be heard, and the intermittent call of "Good night!"

Maggie didn't like Miss Lynd. She found the older woman abrasive and tiresome, with a "what are you doing here, young upstart?" tone and a "don't bother me" attitude. Unearned, in Maggie's opinion, because Miss Lynd had never trained for the SOE or been on a mission. But as Miss Lynd was now in charge of so-called women's issues, she was the only one for Maggie to talk to.

Miss Lynd looked up as Maggie entered. "You're getting quite the reputation around here, you know." Her jeweled rings flashed as she plucked a cigarette from an engraved silver box. "Do you know what they call you? 'That talky redheaded bitch.'"

A fine, fine line between "plucky" and "bitchy," isn't there? Maggie knew she wasn't necessarily popular in the office, especially with Colonel Gaskell—but she wasn't about to let it stop her.

"Miss Lynd," she began, choosing her words carefully, "I don't give a flying fig what 'they' say about me—I'm concerned about the safety of the women. They—we—deserve the same protections as the men over there. Not to mention the same pay. And a pension, when this war's over."

"Close the door, Miss Hope." Maggie obeyed. The older woman stared at the redhead, then gazed over her head, through the small window behind, as she lit her cigarette. "I know you're concerned. And I am, as well," she admitted finally. "I'm doing the best I can."

"But more and more female agents are being sent over now, especially to France!" Maggie exploded. "Those are our own over there. We can't just drop them by parachute, cross our fingers for luck, then look the other way when something goes wrong. Britain has a responsibility to them! To their families!"

"I agree." Miss Lynd exhaled a mouthful of smoke and gestured in the direction of the conference room. "But you see what we're up against."

"Bad enough we have to fight against the Nazis, but our own agency, too? Why don't we go higher?" Maggie suggested. "Appeal to Sir Frank Nelson or Lord Wolmer? Sir Charles Hambro? Major Gubbins has always advocated for women agents—as has Mr. Churchill! Why not go to the P.M.?"

"Perhaps I'll bring it up the next time I take tea with the King." Miss Lynd blew smoke from her two nostrils like a dragon, then flicked the ashes of her cigarette into a cut-glass ashtray.

Maggie hated her, truly hated her, in that moment.

"Not a bad idea," was all she allowed herself to say, but she thought, *Maybe not the King, but perhaps the Queen? Queen Eliza-*

*beth does owe me a favor, after all—and I know after everything that
happened at Windsor Castle, she'd at least hear me out. . . .*

Without warning, the rumble of an explosion rocked the office.
The filthy window cracked, and dust from the plaster ceiling sifted
down on them. Maggie put a hand to the wooden doorframe until
it was over. Outside was deathly silent, then sirens began to wail in
the distance.

Miss Lynd blinked. "Well, it's either the Nazis or the IRA."
Unruffled, she looked back to the memo. "Regardless, Miss Hope,
I suggest you get back to work." She waved one bejeweled hand.
"Off with you!"

"Hankering Hades! What the devil was that?" demanded a young
man in front of the receptionist's desk in the antechamber, brushing snowflakes off the lapels of his double-breasted cashmere coat.

Maggie smiled. It was her friend David Greene; they'd worked
together in Mr. Churchill's office at Number 10 during the summer
of '40 and become close friends. "David! What are you doing
here?"

"Apparently, taking my life in my hands," he said, straightening his polka-dot silk bow tie. He was thirty, slender and fair, with
owlish eyes behind silver spectacles.

"It was probably an unexploded bomb randomly detonating.
Wouldn't be the first. Won't be the last."

"Fantastic," David said, walking over to give Maggie a broth-
erly peck on the cheek. "Now that bombs have stopped falling
from the sky, we need to worry about the unexploded ones left on
the ground?"

"Not a lot of manpower left for that sort of thing—womanpower
either . . ."

"I have something to distract you! A surprise!"

Maggie was on guard. "I don't like surprises."

"You'll like this one." He sat on the edge of the reception desk as his smile widened into a grin. "Now, now, don't be spiky, Mags. You'll love it, I promise."

Maggie eyed the folders on her desk.

"Oh, it's after six—surely Smaug will let you go?"

"David!" Smaug—the dragon of Tolkien's Lonely Mountain—was their private nickname for the incessantly smoking Miss Lynd.

David stood and offered his arm in a sweeping gesture. "Come, my dear Maggie—you can't win the war tonight. I have something quite special, quite special, for you up my sleeve. And I can't wait for you to see it!"

Chapter Two

Not far from Baker Street in Marylebone, there was a row of what used to be handsome houses, now shabby and worn. Most of those that had survived the Blitz had been converted to flats and rooms catering to war workers and an influx of Polish, Canadian, and, more recently, U.S. soldiers.

In the early spring of 1942, it was a quiet street. But to those who could remember, the bomb-pitted pavements, damaged buildings, and burned brick walls painted a story of the worst of the Blitz—bombs exploding night after night, fires raging, cars and buses tossed about like toys, broken bodies dragged from rubble. In the mornings after the raids, firemen swept ash, broken glass, and severed limbs from the gutters.

This wasn't Brynn Parry's first wartime excursion to London. She thought back to trips the year before, and recalled nights of bombing when the East End was blazing and the sky glowed red, and mornings when ugly clouds of black smoke filtered the light of the rising sun, bathing the city in a depressing gray smog.

Tonight, though, the air was clear and cold, the sirens were distant, and the searchlights dimmed. Still, it felt like more of an intermission than an end.

Halfway down the block, the row of brick houses was broken by the entry to a courtyard. Set back in the shadows was a massive turreted and crenellated building, six stories tall, covered with carved stone gargoyles and grotesques.

The bitter east wind blew harder, causing the few falling snow-flakes to whirl and eddy. Brynn clapped one hand on her hat to keep it from flying away as she peered up at the hulking building, its gables black against the setting sun. She could see a small sign: THE CASTLE HOTEL FOR WOMEN: TEMPORARY LODGING FOR LADIES. Her heart sank. Although it was called a castle, the hotel looked drab and hopelessly dilapidated. She rang the buzzer and then pushed open the etched-glass doors.

Inside, the lobby was hushed. There was a mahogany hat-and-umbrella stand to the right of the door, and a long dark-red drug-get runner, which matched the velvet flock paper on the walls. The shabby Victorian button-back parlor chairs turned to the fireplace were empty. The fire itself had burned down to a bed of glowing coals behind the cast-iron andirons, decorated with goblin talons with sharp claws.

"It's not safe to leave doors open in London."

Brynn looked up. She saw a dour young woman behind the reception desk, an open book in front of her. For a moment, their eyes locked.

"Please close them behind you. It's far too easy for anyone to slip in." The receptionist was no more than twenty, sallow and sickly, with limp hair and too much lipstick, sitting behind an ornate desk. "May I help you?"

Brynn crossed the black-and-white marble chessboard floor. "I rang earlier, but there was no answer. I need a room, please. Do you have any vacancies?"

The girl pushed aside her novel, *The Picture of Dorian Gray*. Brynn noticed she had a maroon port-wine stain on her right cheek. "How many nights?"

"Just one."

She looked through a binder. "We happen to have an opening for tonight."

"Fantastic," Brynn said. "I'll take it."

"How did you hear of us?"

"I was given one of your business cards."

"Where?"

"Special Operations Executive offices—on Baker Street."

"Ah, yes—the SOE. I dropped those cards off myself. Now, we do have a few rules here at the Castle Hotel." She spoke by rote: "No smoking, no drinking, no swearing, and, most importantly, no men beyond the lobby."

"That's fine," Brynn said, staring up at the immense ebony clock mounted on the wall behind the desk. Its black pendulum swung back and forth with a weighty *click* and *clack;* when it chimed the hour, both women startled.

The girl gave a short laugh at her own nervousness. "You'd think I'd get used to it by now—but no. My fiancé loves it, though—says it makes him think of Edgar Allan Poe."

As the girl pushed forward a large leather registry book to sign, Brynn caught the twinkle of a diamond and gold ring on the girl's left hand. "Congratulations on your engagement." Brynn smiled as she wrote, the nib of the pen scratching at the thin paper. "Or is it best wishes? I'm never sure."

"Thank you." The girl flushed. She gestured to a silver-framed photo of an ordinary-looking man, short, with medium-brown hair and small eyes. His features were undefined, as though the cartilage had never hardened properly. "That's my fiancé, Nicholas Reitter. He studied engineering and architecture—and helped redesign and renovate this place, for my father. He's going to be sent to the Mideast soon. War work, you know." She turned to grasp a key from the rack behind her. "All right then, Miss—"

"Brynn is fine."

"Brynn. My name is May, May Frank." She smiled, revealing a dead front tooth turned gray. "My father's in charge of the hotel. He's a practicing psychoanalyst—trained in Vienna and everything—his office is over there." She jutted her chin at glossy black double doors adorned with an engraved bronze nameplate, then came around the desk and picked up Brynn's suitcase. "Let me show you to your room."

"Oh, I can manage—"

"Nonsense! I'm delighted to help! Plus, I get to stretch my legs a bit." Suitcase in hand, May led the way to the birdcage elevator. She pressed an ivory button and they waited as gears and levers began to click and grind. When the ornate cage arrived, they stepped in—and it sank noticeably under their weight.

"Safe as houses," May stated with confidence. "Nick assures me, and he'd know—he's an architect and he's done all of the repairs and new additions to my father's buildings." She slid the rickety gate shut with a *bang*. "Back in the old days, there were men in white gloves to open and close the doors and press the buttons." She jabbed at the scratched knob marked 5. "Now they're all off fighting—and we're left to do it ourselves."

For a long moment there was no movement. The elevator was frozen. " 'Abandon hope all ye who enter,' " Brynn joked. "Maybe we should take the stairs?"

But with a jolt and a whine, the lift began to rise, shaking and shuddering. Brynn bit her lip and stared up at the wavering hand of the indicator, with a vision of being trapped between floors without anyone finding them for days. Finally, the elevator screeched to a stop. May retracted the gate and opened the door.

The birdcage was still six inches below floor level. "You can make the step, yes?" she asked, hoisting Brynn's valise out first.

"Of—of course."

"This way, please!" Scrambling up and following May on the faded Persian runner, Brynn surveyed the shadowy hall. It was awkward and narrow, and smelled of new construction and something vaguely chemical. The air was freezing, even colder than outside. The wallpaper was a faded red silk, while lights contrived to look like Victorian gas lamps lined the corridor. As the two women walked the twisting and turning halls in the gloom, Brynn had the sudden image of the Minotaur's labyrinth.

May stopped. "Ta-da!" she announced, opening one of the doors.

Except the door opened onto a brick wall. "Oops," she apologized. "Er, not *that* one."

Brynn was confused. "What *is*—?"

"Oh, they're always building and rebuilding here, especially after the Blitz took out so much." May shrugged. "I can scarcely find my way around these days. Only Nicholas has the master plan."

Across the hall was the correct room. May fumbled with the heavy key, but eventually forced the door open. It was small, with a high water-stained ceiling. The walls were covered in faded wallpaper with blowsy blue roses against a crimson background, the pockmarked floor mostly hidden beneath a fussy floral rug. The room itself was outfitted with mismatched furniture—a twin bed, a washbasin, a chest of drawers, a chair, and a tiny desk with a gooseneck reading lamp. From the walls, a series of engravings, portraits of early Victorian belles clad in lace and tarlatan gowns, frowned down at them.

Like the hallway, the room was freezing.

May set down Brynn's bag. "I'll let you get settled."

Brynn closed the door firmly, then twisted the dead-bolt lock. The loose windows rattled in the wind, and she walked over to cover them with the heavy blackout curtains. She hesitated.

A man in the building directly across the darkening street stared at her, lit by his desk lamp. Slim and dark-haired, he held a paper and pencil, and gazed at her intently, as though she were a specimen under a microscope.

Brynn yanked the blackout curtains closed, her hands shaking, then flipped on the overhead light. She took a book from her bag and curled herself up on the bed under the covers, shivering. *It's only one night,* she thought, trying to reassure herself. *Just one night.*

Maggie Hope was blindfolded.

"I don't like this, you know, not one little bit," she told David, leaning on his arm as he helped her up a short flight of steps. Her heart was beating fast, and the freezing wind whipped hard, icy snowflakes against her face. She knew they were still in Marylebone, but that was all. She thought back to her training in Arisaig and how she'd learned to rely on all her senses, not just sight. Listening for any ambient noise, she heard only branches tossed in the wind, a creaky bicycle going by, and a dog's howl in the distance.

"Oh, just you wait, Mags!"

There was the sound of a doorknob turning and then the exhaling squeak of hinges as a door opened and he led her forward. It sounded familiar. It smelled familiar.

And, best of all, it was blessedly warm.

"Surprise!"

As David tugged off Maggie's blindfold, she gasped. A crowd of faces beamed at her through arched double doors. A white sheet came down from the wall to reveal a hand-painted mural of the Union Jack and the Stars and Stripes, side by side in brilliant colors.

Maggie stiffened, her heart pounding. *This is not the sort of thing one does to an agent, even for fun.* She stepped forward, still bewildered. An ornate curved wooden staircase dominated the foyer, with a grand dining room to the left, parlor to the right. And there were people, lots and lots of people.

"Oh, come on, Mags! Don't you recognize it?" David prodded, his hand still guiding her. "Don't you know where you are?"

Yes, yes, she did—it was . . . *home*. Her grandmother's house and now hers—although she hadn't been back in ages.

The crowd broke into applause. "Welcome back!" a woman from the back called. Maggie recognized Mrs. Tinsley from the Prime Minister's office and managed a smile.

"Satan's whiskers," David whispered in her ear, poking her in the ribs as they walked through clouds of blue smoke, "I thought you'd be over the moon!"

"Just . . . shocked, is all," she whispered, giving him a peck on the cheek. She gazed around, trying to take it all in. At first glance, under the dim lights, the pressed-together bodies looked like a Doré etching from Dante's *Inferno*—but no, on closer look, she realized she recognized many of the faces. Friends from her first days in London: Mr. Churchill's office, the Vic-Wells Ballet, SOE. There was David's Freddie Wright, of course—with Maggie's dancer friend Sarah Sanderson, ensconced in a window seat—then Richard Snodgrass, Mrs. Tinsley, and Miss Stewart from the offices at Number 10 and the underground War Rooms. The rest of the pale faces looked more or less familiar under the veil of cigarette smoke, speaking loudly with pantomime-like animation.

The old pile looks good. Miraculously, the wood paneling and the medallions on the plaster ceiling seemed to have survived the bombing. *From out of the wreckage of stars . . .* Maggie shivered despite the warmth, overwhelmed by memories and conflicting emotions, as David led her through the crowd. Sidestepping, she smiled until her jaw ached, mouthed greetings, and kissed proffered cheeks as the low rumble of happy conversation resumed, along with the throaty tones of a tenor saxophone emanating from the gramophone in the corner. Maggie thought she could pick out the melody of Coleman Hawkins's "How Strange."

"Let me take your coat and hat," someone was saying, and Maggie relinquished them. She realized in her office clothes she was underdressed and rubbed at the ink spot on her blouse. "I do wish you'd warned me, David. I would have at least put on lipstick." The room was warm from the press of people, and so she peeled off her cardigan and took two yellow pencils out of her coppery bun so it tumbled down her shoulders and swung free.

"You look lovely as always, my dear," David reassured her as the conversations around them swirled and crescendoed. "Let me give you a tour," he said, as someone pressed a pink gin in her hand. She took a sip, hoping it would help ease her sense of shock.

"It's all structurally sound," David was saying. "Safe as houses, as they say. Safe as houses—ha!

"Had both an architect and an engineer give their approval after the bombing—the top floor took quite a hit, but luckily the bomb fell on a diagonal, not straight down," he prattled on. "Garden's still a mess, I'm afraid. Did a little redecorating as well—hope you don't mind. A few of my parents' pieces from the country house—tried to bring a breath of modernity to all the moldy Victoriana—no offense to your sainted grandmother, of course. And we moved all your things and set you up in the master bedroom." He gave her shoulders a squeeze. "Don't worry, Mags, it looks completely different now. You won't even recognize it."

"I—I can't believe it," Maggie managed finally. "Thank you—thank you so much." Then, realizing, "How can I ever repay you?"

"Your insurance money took care of everything, actually—you'd already started the paperwork for government compensation before we left for Washington. You'll have to wait until after the war's over for the full amount, but I was able to claim enough of an advance on your behalf for structural repairs." He waved a hand. "The rest is cosmetic."

"Well, gorblimey and God save the King!" Maggie managed, taking another sip of her gin. Someone was passing a plate of cheap sausage rolls, and she snagged one. "And the Queen and the Princesses, while we're at it." She and David exchanged a knowing look, remembering their perilous time at Windsor Castle with the Royals.

David puffed out his chest. "I set everything up while you were in Scotland, and then the overhaul was done while we were all in Washington. . . ."

Maggie was half-listening as they wandered through the house and David pointed out changes. Walking through the parlor and library felt like returning to a half-remembered dream. It was the same, but different. Or was *she* what was different now?

She tried to look objectively at the library, lit by silk-shaded lamps. The gloomy wallpaper had been stripped. The walls were freshly painted. Some of the heavy Victorian furniture had been removed and replaced with sleek deco pieces, upholstered in bright blue moiré. The murky oil paintings had been replaced in their gilt frames with colorful reproductions of works by Matisse, Dalí, and Magritte.

"A modern space for today's modern woman," David enthused. "We kept all the books we could salvage, of course—as well as all your back issues of *American Journal of Mathematics* and your grandmother's back issues of *Minotaure*—there's a lovely Picasso cover of a bullfight you might think of framing. Did you know you have some first editions of Sherlock Holmes here? Although, I must say your dear old granny had fairly gothic taste"—he gestured to the tall shelves—"translations of Dante,

Dracula, The Maiden Tribute of Modern Babylon, The Complete History of Jack the Ripper . . . even a few old penny dreadfuls." He quirked an eyebrow. "Have you ever realized Dante was the first to think of hell as a planned space in an urban environment? Ha! Must have visited London."

That made Maggie smile again. "I never had time to read much beyond math journals, but perhaps I should revisit Dante."

"Careful not to read too much—you'll never get married," cautioned a man with a shiny, bald head in passing.

Then David's "roommate," Freddie Wright, approached, tumbler in hand. He was a handsome man, tall, with dark hair and eyes. A handful who were extremely close to them knew David and Freddie were a couple, but kept it quiet, for obvious reasons: arrest, imprisonment, chemical castration would be their fate if their relationship were revealed.

"Thank you, David," Maggie murmured, blinking back tears of gratitude. "And you, too, Freddie. You must have had a hand in all this, while David and I were in Washington."

Freddie beamed. "I rather enjoyed having a project to work on while His Nibs was away." He looked to David. "You know, we might think about a country house when this blasted war is over."

"The *country*?" David looked appalled. "Why would anyone want to leave London?"

"Nature? Trees? Fresh air?"

"Spiders."

"Flowers?"

"Snakes."

"Hunting? Fishing? Riding?"

"Dirt, dirt, and more dirt, plus mud. I prefer theater, the ballet, and galleries. My idea of a trip into nature is a suite at the Ritz and a book of Audubon prints, thank you very much, old thing."

Freddie raised his hands in mock surrender. Maggie laughed.

"Wait here—we have one more surprise for you." David flashed his impish grin and tugged Freddie away.

Maggie caught sight of Sarah again, now in the doorway, and waved. Once upon a time, she and Sarah had been flatmates in this house, when she'd first worked for Prime Minister Winston Churchill and Sarah had danced with the Vic-Wells Ballet. *So much has changed*, Maggie realized, *and yet Sarah's as beautiful as ever*. Her friend was dark-haired and olive-skinned, tall, and slender, the sharp points of her hip bones jutting through the flowered silk of her dress. The ballet dancer made her way over.

"Sarah!" Maggie cried over the din, giving her friend a hug, feeling the hard, ropy muscles of her back.

"Hello, kitten!" Sarah's voice, too, was unchanged: low, raspy, and quite sexy.

"How are you? Did you end up staying in Arisaig?" The last time Maggie had seen Sarah was at the SOE paramilitary training camp.

"Made it through, believe it or not." Sarah took a sip from her glass of beer. "And I have a meeting with some people at an office on Baker Street tomorrow."

"Ah, the Baker Street Irregulars. I'm working there now—a little job while I wait for my sister to arrive. We'll have to pretend not to know each other, you and I, if we should bump into one another."

Sarah laughed. "Oh, I know the drill now," she assured Maggie. "And I'm sorry, but did you say—your sister?"

"Half sister. From Berlin." Maggie sipped her gin. "It's, well—it's a long story."

"It always is, isn't it?"

"That's another reason we had the place fixed up," Freddie interjected, catching the last bit. "David told me about your sister.

We wanted you two to have a place of your own—while you get reacquainted."

Maggie blinked back prickly, hot tears and swallowed the rest of her gin, her throat burning. "Acquainted is more like it. We don't exactly know each other yet." She looked around at the party guests, who were now rolling up the rug for dancing. "My word, it's been quite a while since we were all here together!"

"So much has changed—and not only the décor." Sarah gave a coquettish smile. "By the way, I too have something new in my life."

Maggie was desperate for some good news. "Really? Do tell!"

"I met someone. At Arisaig. After you left for London."

"Instructor? Or fellow trainee?"

"Trainee." Sarah's face glowed. "He's quite the bee's knees."

"Why, Sarah Sanderson!" Maggie exclaimed. She'd known Sarah to have relationships with men over the years, but no one she'd spoken about like this. "I do believe you're positively radiant!"

When Sarah blushed prettily and refused to say more, Maggie scrutinized the faces of the party guests. "I don't see Chuck," she said, referring to another of their old flatmates: Charlotte McCaffrey, always and forever known by her nickname, Chuck. She'd married Nigel Ludlow and they'd had a son, Griffin, who was now six months old. While Nigel was serving in the RAF, Chuck was taking care of their son at their flat in Pimlico.

"Chuck's coming," David insisted. "Invited her myself. She promised she'd be here, and you know she's always true to her word. But she's a mother now—and time and space seem to work in mysterious ways for new mums."

"I can't believe John isn't here with us," Sarah added. "And living in Los Angeles of all places!" She leaned in toward Maggie and lowered her voice. "Did you two ever—you know—sort things out?"

"Alas, not really," Maggie admitted. A pang of loss echoed through her. "Our time in Washington was, shall we say, chaotic. And then, when he had the offer to work for Mr. Disney in L.A.—"

"—it was too good to pass up," David finished. "He's living at the Beverly Hills Hotel, can you believe? Eating oranges and taking telephone calls poolside." He made a face. "Prat."

"Flirting with horse-faced American divorcées," Maggie added, not without bitterness.

"Nothing happened there," David protested. "I told you—that was a misunderstanding—"

Freddie called out, "And here's your other surprise!" A broad-shouldered young man appeared at her elbow, holding a ball of squirming fur. David took the animal from the man's arms and pressed him to Maggie. "And here we have His Eminence—"

"K! Mr. K!" Maggie squealed, handing her glass to Sarah and holding the squirming marmalade cat close.

"—back safe and sound from his tenure at Number Ten. I'm sorry to say he absolutely terrified Nelson while he was there—Rufus, too," David added, referring to Mr. and Mrs. Churchill's black cat and standard poodle. "They're not exactly sad to see him go. But now he can live here, too, with you and Elise."

"Darling K," Maggie exclaimed, rubbing the top of his head. She'd adopted K—Mr. K for special occasions—during her time in Scotland. The cat had stayed at Number 10 while she was in Washington, D.C., as Freddie was allergic. She pressed him even closer.

"*Meh,*" he meowed in his peculiar way, then bumped her forehead with his and rubbed his cheek on her face. She cuddled him close and stroked him, her nose in his soft fur, inhaling his warm, sweet scent.

"Yes, I missed you, too," she murmured as he jumped out of her arms to groom his fur on a reupholstered wing chair.

"We'll take you on a tour of the upstairs later. It's completely rebuilt. I do hope Elise likes yellow—it's what we decided on for her room."

"I'm sure she'll love it. And she'll adore you."

"Well, that goes without saying," David concurred. When Freddie elbowed him, he protested, "Well, you know it's true!"

The man who'd appeared carrying the cat was short, but built on muscular lines, with chiseled features and sleek dark hair— with a tense jaw, darting eyes, and a cigarette dangling from his lips. He cleared his throat pointedly, and David looked over.

"By the way, Maggie, meet Maximilian Thornton," David said. "Max, this is Maggie Hope."

"The infamous Maggie Hope," Max articulated through his cigarette, crushing her hand as he shook it. "I've heard a lot about you at Number Ten."

Maggie extricated her fingers. "Really?"

"He's the new John Sterling," David explained. "While John's away."

Maggie saw a flicker of annoyance in Max's eyes. "I'm my own man," he corrected, his English public school boy features hardening. "Did you hear about the big explosion?"

"Hear *about* it? I *felt* it," Maggie replied. "We figured it was another buried, undetonated bomb going off."

"They say it was a gas pipe explosion." Max's eyes were more vacant than horrified. "Landlord or someone working for him was trying to siphon off some for himself, it leaked and—*boom*."

"Where?"

"Somewhere in Pimlico."

"Oh my goodness—" Maggie looked to David with wide eyes. "Chuck—Chuck and the baby are in Pimlico. . . ."

David patted her hand. "Oh, they're fine. They're practically in Westminster, after all."

"She's coming tonight, right? Do you think we should telephone now? Just to make sure?"

"Stop worrying, Mags! Shouldn't you go make the rounds, darling? Say hello to all your guests?"

As Maggie left, Freddie whispered to David, "I still don't understand why she let this place out and came to live with us for so long."

"Well, there were some—shall we say—'issues,'" David admitted, "with one of the flatmates. A woman named Paige. It's . . . complicated."

"So you've said. I mean, I didn't always get along with my suitemates at Trinity, but . . ."

David glanced to Sarah, who'd been involved with all of the contretemps that had happened in the house almost two years ago. "No, not simply roommate squabbles," Sarah clarified. Then realization hit. "Oh, David. You mean—you haven't told him?"

"Not the full story." David shrugged. "You tell him."

"No, you!"

"Tell me *what*?" Freddie insisted. "In the name of King and Country, spill!"

Sarah rolled her eyes at David, then slipped her arm through Freddie's. "Take a turn around the room with me, love, and I'll fill you in on all the gory details."

After meeting and greeting more of the guests, Maggie retreated to the kitchen on the pretext of getting another drink—but really, she needed to collect her thoughts. She glanced around: The room looked unchanged. The floor was tiled with a chessboard of black and white squares, and blackout curtains protected the windows. It had been in this very room that Maggie had first begun to feel at home in London, waiting for her coffee to brew and listening to the wireless or eating and reading a book at the wooden table. Now, as she stood at the counter, adding bitters to another glass of gin, Max Thornton entered.

"Here, let me do it for you." He'd rolled up his sleeves, revealing thick wrists covered in dark, matted hair.

"It's fine, I have it," Maggie replied, setting the bottle down. She took a swallow of her drink. *It's not helping,* she noticed with irritation.

"You may have heard of me," Max was saying. "I was a war correspondent in Spain, then Berlin. Fought in Norway back in 'forty, but was transferred to Intelligence, then referred to Churchill." He gave Maggie a significant look as he moved closer, pinning her against the counter. "I can pinch-hit for John Sterling in any number of situations."

"Good for you." Maggie moved away. "And also, no thank you."

"Are you sure?" He sounded genuinely surprised.

"Quite."

"Well, well, well—how did you become such an independent young woman?"

Maggie gave a tight smile. "I went to Wellesley College."

His forehead creased. "What's that?"

"Like Paradise Island for the Amazons."

He looked even more confused. *Obviously he hasn't read Wonder Woman.* "It's like St. Hilda's at Oxford—but in the U.S.," she explained.

Max shook his head and poured himself the last of the gin. "Devil take you modern overeducated women," he chided, shaking a finger, "a bunch of whining radical spinster tartlets, the lot of you. Speaking of which, have you heard about this new Ripper?"

Maggie thought she'd misheard him. "What?" Then she remembered the article Brody had mentioned at the office. An SOE agent had been murdered.

"Rumor has it there's a killer loose in London—and he's aping Jack the Ripper, butchering young girls." Max leaned against the counter as if it were a bar in a pub. "The press is trying to keep it quiet for now, but of course we hear everything in the P.M.'s office. The papers have dubbed him the 'Blackout Beast.'"

Maggie felt a chill and swallowed yet more gin. It still wasn't helping.

"May I pour you another?"

"No." Maggie knew from unfortunate personal experience that too much gin, too fast, was an extremely bad idea.

He looked disappointed. "Then why don't we dance?"

Dancing was the last thing she wanted to do, especially with him. "No." Then, trying to be polite, "Thank you."

He stepped over and pulled her close, close enough that they were eye to eye and she could smell the alcohol on his breath. "Then how about a kiss?"

Maggie pushed off his arm and backed away. "No!"

He shrugged. "You say no now, but we'll see by the end of the night."

Maggie had endured enough. "You need to leave." She strode to the swinging kitchen door, then turned to face him. "Let me be quite clear—this is my house and you're not welcome here. I'm going back to the party and you're going to say your goodbyes. The next time I look around, you'll be gone. Do you understand?"

She left without waiting for his answer.

"Your new friend's a real charmer," Maggie remarked to David. "And by *charmer*, I mean snake charmer."

"Well . . ." David shrugged. "He works hard at the office and the Boss likes him well enough. Went to Harrow with Max's father—the old-boy network."

"Seems a bit hairy at the heel. And I'm going to have to needle-point the moniker 'Spinster Tartlet' on a pillow someday. Speaking of Number Ten, any news from—" *John*.

"Mags, I'm not the best letter writer," David admitted, "as you well know. But I've had a few postcards from our man in L.A.— cartoons mostly. He sounds well enough. You're not in touch?"

Maggie gnawed her lower lip, recalling their breakup over the telephone in Washington. "We left things with a full stop this time."

"Well, with you in London and him still in L.A., I can understand. Still, I always thought the two of you . . ."

Maggie's smile was wan. "Like Jo and Laurie?" She'd given David a copy of *Little Women* for Christmas.

"Indeed! And not the horrible Mr. Bhaer. I *shudder* at the very thought. And while we're on the topic of the shudders, are you still in touch with your American mick?"

Maggie poked his shoulder. "I've told you not to call him that! Tom O'Brian is quite well, thank you. And yes, we do write, occasionally. He's stationed at Fort Bragg, in North Carolina, now. He says his unit will be shipped off soon."

"Atlantic or Pacific?"

"Don't know. I don't even think they tell the boys until they're on board ship."

Sarah and Freddie reappeared, walking arm in arm. "That's horrible!" Freddie was saying. "No wonder she couldn't come back here—" He stopped when he saw Maggie. "Sarah told me why you didn't return—" He gave a small bow. "You're both extraordinary women."

"I helped, too!" David interjected, taking two sausage rolls from a Vic-Wells dancer passing by with a plate. "I was downright heroic, you know!"

"Yes, you were," Maggie agreed, patting his arm. "But you know, it's getting late—where's Chuck?"

"I told you, she's a mother now," David said, chewing his roll. "The minders of the tiny humans are never on time."

"Chuck's the most punctual person I know," Maggie rejoined. "She's never late. Ever. I'll ring."

"I already did, Mags, with the intention of telling her to buck up. But there's no answer—she must be on her way."

"Well, let's try again, just in case." But they didn't have to. The doors opened, and there stood Chuck in her wool coat, holding baby Griffin in her arms, her chestnut hair windblown.

"Chuck!" chorused the group.

Her eyes were wild and her usually rosy cheeks ashen. She took a few wobbling steps forward.

Alarmed, Maggie ran to her. "Chuck! What's wrong?"

The brunette couldn't speak.

"All right, come sit down," Maggie urged, leading the mother and child to the sofa in the library. She locked eyes with David. "A glass of water, please? And a cool cloth?"

David sprang into action: "Righty-o!"

"Here, let me take the baby." Sarah reached for Griffin. He gave a gummy grin and grabbed for her dangling gold earring. "Oh, no, my young friend," she chided, pulling away. She looked, and tucked in his blanket were two dolls—Mr. Punch and his wife, Judy. "I think these are much better playthings than Auntie Sarah's earrings," she cajoled, handing them to him.

When David returned with the water and cloth, Chuck stirred. "I don't suppose you have any whiskey?" she managed. "Jameson's, not that bloody Protestant stuff." Chuck was Irish, and Catholic, and proud of it. And inordinately fond of profanity.

"I'll see what we have." David raced back to the kitchen.

"Gone." Chuck fought back her tears. "Our home is gone," she whispered. "Gone."

"What do you mean, 'gone'?" Maggie was confused. The bombings were over, at least for the moment. What Chuck was saying didn't make sense.

Chuck worried at the damp cloth with her fingers. "When we got home from the park this afternoon, there was smoke and we could see flames. There were fire trucks everywhere—and ambulances. Gawkers and reporters with cameras. There was such a crowd, I couldn't see what happened at first. Then I realized—there was nothing to see. Our building is gone, just—gone. As in—*poof*.

"I never trusted our building's owner," Chuck muttered. "Always having problems with the gas. There were always inspections, and then his son, or whoever it was, would go down into the basement and 'fix things.' We knew something was a bit off. But with housing so dear nowadays—"

"What happened, Chuck?" Maggie demanded.

"Gone!" her friend repeated. "Aren't you bloody well listening? I keep telling you—everything's gone. We would be 'gone,' too, except"—her hands trembled as they twisted the cloth—"we were at the park this afternoon. Griffin wasn't going down for his nap, so I thought I'd take him outside for some fresh air and push him in the pram until he dropped off—"

"Oh, God." Maggie put her arms around her friend, realizing how close she'd been to death. And little Griffin, too. "You're safe. You're both safe now."

David arrived with a glass of whiskey, and Chuck gulped it. "We don't even have a change of clothes!" She shook her head in disbelief. "Everything we own, you see. Oh, I left the pram outside—but if someone pinches it, at this point, does it even matter?" She looked to Maggie. "How are we supposed to get letters

from Nigel? If he writes us—the address doesn't even exist anymore!"

"We'll write to Nigel tonight and tell him you're staying here.
With me."

"Griffin's baby pictures," Chuck moaned. "My engagement
ring . . ."

Gently, Maggie said, "Chuck, you're alive. Griffin's alive. And
you're here, safe, and with us. Everything else can be replaced.
Now, sip your drink."

Chuck did as she was told.

"Good girl. Now, you can borrow my clothes and things, and
tomorrow we'll pool all of our coupons and go shopping. We'll be
flatmates, just like old times."

"And Griffin?"

"And Griffin will be a flatmate, too. Small in body, but large in
spirit."

"Large in lungs. He cries at night, you know. Sometimes *all*
bloody night."

"I cry all night myself once in a while, dearest girl. Not to
worry."

"I think there are some baby things in the cellar," David interjected.

Chuck laid her head on Maggie's shoulder. "I don't think we
have a choice. But only for tonight—"

"Nonsense," Maggie interrupted firmly. "Do you know how
grateful I am to have some company in this big old manse? You'll
be doing me the favor—stay for as long as you'd like. Yes, and
you, too, young sir," she told Griffin, still in Aunt Sarah's lap. He
waved a chubby pink fist holding his Judy doll in reply. K had
emerged from underneath the armchair and was up on his hind
legs, sniffing delicately at the baby's tiny feet.

"Surely there must be paperwork to file . . ." Chuck thought out loud, trying to put the pieces together. "And our bank account—that's still untouched—"

"We can worry about it tomorrow," Maggie declared.

Freddie nodded. "I'll ring my solicitor first thing. He's a predatory hyena of a man, and I loathe him with all my heart and soul—but he'll get you what you deserve."

David returned, his arms full of antique toys. "Look, Master Griffin," he said, setting them down. There was an old-fashioned rocking horse, a puppet stage, and the board game Snakes and Ladders.

"He's not old enough yet," Chuck told them.

"Well, they'll be standing by for when he is. In the meantime, let's get you both upstairs. Is everything ready?" Maggie asked David.

"Absolutely."

As Maggie, Chuck, and Sarah made their way up the heavy oak staircase, Sarah chimed in, "Just like old times."

Maggie had Chuck hold on to her arm for support. "But you know what really gets my goat?" Chuck said. "After all we've been through—after *everything* we've been through—it wasn't the Nazis who took us out. It was one of our bloody own. Some devil of an Englishman."

"Not on purpose, surely," Maggie said.

"Oh, the owner of our building would skin a flea for a halfpenny, that one," Chuck muttered, "and his young minion, as well. *Go ndéana an diabhal dréimire de cnámh do dhroma ag piocadh úll i ngairdín Ifrinn,* as my sainted grandmother used to say—'May the Devil make a ladder of your backbones while picking apples in the garden of hell!' "

They reached Chuck's old room. It was lovely—plain but clean, repainted in pale green. "Here you go," Maggie said, leading Chuck to the bed. "Just like old times. I'll run you a bath, and you can take your drink and sip it in the tub. Like Joan Crawford."

As Maggie went into the bathroom, Chuck lowered herself onto the edge of the bed. "It's gone," she repeated absently. "Our home—it was there this morning—and now it's . . ."

There was the sound of the tap running and then Chuck gave a whoop of hysterical laughter. "Be careful! You'll fill it past the five-inch line!"

"Sod the silly five-inch line," Sarah said, hugging Griffin close and kissing the top of his fuzzy head. "You deserve a decent soak."

Maggie returned holding a nightgown, a dressing gown, and a hairbrush. "We'll figure everything else out tomorrow," she decided. "But, for now, I think a bath and a good night's sleep are in order."

Sarah turned to Maggie. "I know this is terrible timing, kitten," she said. "But may I stay here too? Just for the night. . . . I have the meeting tomorrow. I was going to stay at some women's residence hotel nearby—I put the card somewhere—but—"

"No! No—you *must* stay here, of course!" Maggie agreed. "See, Chuck, Sarah will be here as well. Just like old times. And then when Elise arrives, she can have the fourth bedroom." Maggie turned wistful. "Do you think she'll like it?"

"That one was Paige's room, wasn't it?"

Maggie nodded, eyes melancholy. "Time moves on, I guess. Everything changes."

Sarah handed Griffin back to Chuck. The baby's eyes drooped shut. "Well, I have no doubt Elise will love it," she whispered. "She's lucky to have you. And David and Freddie, of course."

Chuck began to sing in an alto voice that was tender and true:

"I'll tell me ma, when I get home.
The boys won't leave the girls alone.
Pulled me hair, stolen me comb.
But that's all right till I get home.

Let the wind and the rain and the hail blow high.
And the snow come travelin' through the sky.
She's as sweet as apple pie.
She'll get her own right by and by . . ."

Griffin had fallen fast asleep, snoring lightly. As Chuck held him and continued to rock and hum, Maggie murmured to Sarah, "My half sister Elise and I didn't exactly part on the best of terms."

"Well, you'll have plenty of time—and space—to become re-acquainted when she arrives."

Chuck looked up, distracted, and whispered, "Who the bloody hell's Elise?"

"Elise Hess—Maggie's German half sister. Keep up!"

Chapter Three

Elise Hess was being hanged from a tree.

At least, that's what the guards at the all-female Ravensbrück camp named the tall wooden cross they'd built to punish prisoners—the Tree. Mock crucifixion was one of the most common camp punishments for the religious political prisoners, Resistance fighters like Elise.

The guards would tie the prisoner's hands behind her back, palms facing out. Then they'd turn her hands in, tie a chain around her wrists, and raise her up onto the cross.

Elise's tormentors had added a crown of thorns—barbed wire left over from building the camp's high walls. They'd twisted it into a circlet and placed it on the young woman's head, shaved after lice inspection. Her light hair, once so thick and lustrous, had grown in only an inch or so, and was dull and straw-like. Where once she had been all sparkling eyes—blue as Novalis's mysterious Blaue Blume—with plump cheeks, a narrow waist, and womanly curves, there was nothing left.

The barbed wire dug into the bare skin of her scalp. Blood trickled down her forehead, stinging her eyes. She felt frozen to the marrow of her bones. She struggled to focus on the faint outline of the sun behind the sullen clouds. But the winter weather in Fürstenberg was unpredictable. It was already the coldest on record. Elise watched, her consciousness receding, as fat, lacy flakes began to fall.

Snow was loathed by the prisoners of Ravensbrück, for the guards had devised an exhausting way for them to dispense with it. The inmates were given boards for scraping, shovels, and wheelbarrows. The work had to be done at a quick pace, so the warmth of the sun couldn't melt the snow prematurely and spoil the guards' fun. The prisoners wore their winter clothing—dresses of the same blue and gray striped material as the summer uniforms, but slightly heavier, and "coats" of the same material. Although there were always rumors of gloves and socks to be distributed, none ever came.

Emaciated and mostly bald, all the prisoners looked identical. But an insider could recognize subtle variations on the uniforms. An inmate's number was sewn onto the left breast, and above the number was a colored triangle. Like Elise, the women below wore mostly red triangles—they were political prisoners, brought to Ravensbrück because of work with their country's resistance movements.

Up on the cross, Elise looked for anything to distract her from the pain. But the sheer ugliness of the camp was inescapable, even draped in freshly fallen snow. Rows upon rows of wooden barrack huts disappeared into the distance. Smokestacks choked out black funeral wreaths.

Even with her eyes closed, Elise couldn't escape the horror. She couldn't tune out the thuds of the prisoners' wooden clogs on the frozen ground, the harsh shouts of the guards, the snarling of the dogs.

But despite the pain, she had no regret for what she had done. There had been a young Polish girl named Karolina in the camp's infirmary, where Elise had been working as a nurse, a girl not yet ten, with sea-blue eyes. When Karolina died, the victim of one too many medical experiments, Elise had gone to find her body. It lay naked on a gurney in a narrow corridor.

Elise had used two fingers to close the girl's eyes and fold her hands over her chest. She straightened the legs, too, disfigured as they were by vertical scars and cut muscle tissue taken during the Nazi doctors' experiments. Elise prayed over the girl, who she knew was Catholic but had not received the last rites, then prayed for her soul. Surely, after all Karolina had been through, God would welcome this little one to heaven? A guard had found Elise making the sign of the cross over the body, and had shouted and dragged her away for punishment.

Elise was beginning to hallucinate. In her mind's eye, she could see angels with soaring, feathery wings; she could see saints with sorrowful faces. St. Teresa bent and whispered in her ear: "With words, it is true, a soul can be instructed. But it can only be saved through suffering." *And only in hell can one prove oneself*, Elise thought.

She swore she could hear heavenly voices in polyphony, singing Palestrina's hymn "Sicut cervus." *In the camp, I've thirsted for God just as the deer thirsts for water—and finally I found Him*, she realized, *as God stands out so much clearer in misfortune. Perhaps the Almighty sent me here so I could learn the essence of things and teach it to others. I do not see torture, I see a proving ground for my soul. In this godless world, I see Christ. In my faith, I can help others see Christ. My being here in the camp, even my death, is a victory for God. . . .*

Father, into Your hands I commit my spirit.

She was suffused with a feeling of peace, and swore she could smell the faint scent of spicy evergreen. From a great distance she heard shouting, taunting.

Do you really believe there's a God?

Then where is He now?

God is dead, you Jew-lover—the Übermensch has killed him!
Satan rules here!

And then, without warning, the pain stopped. She opened her eyes and looked around at the camp's high walls covered with charged barbed wire, the guard towers with rifles and searchlights, the rows and rows of barracks, the thin, broken women bent over their work, the guards screaming and kicking them, dogs on leather leashes lunging and growling, their fangs bared.

I'm dying, she thought as she began to lose consciousness. *Thy will be done. . . .*

"Get her down! *Schnell!*" the guard ordered. "Warden says she must be kept alive!"

"Will she make it?" she heard, as though from miles away.

"Doubtful."

That night, her first back in her old house, Maggie dreamed about numbers.

She sorely missed math—its order, logic, and elegance. In her dream, she was in the library, a dusty chalkboard full of equations in front of her. *Ah yes,* she thought as she wrote down the formulae in a notebook, *how beautiful, how graceful, how inevitable.*

Her former flatmate Paige was there, just like in the old days, when they'd all roomed together in the house. In the logic of dreams, it wasn't strange at all she'd be there, looking exactly as she had during the summer the Blitz began—cornflower eyes sparkling, blond waves impeccably coiffed. "Welcome home, Maggie," she said.

She put a dainty hand with polished red nails to the chalkboard, and the lines of equations Maggie revered were suddenly the walls of her house, black against shadows. Then the numbers began to tip over and quiver, growing and morphing into huge insects, black flies with iridescent wings flashing green and purple. They came together in the form of a huge beast, with the head of a goat—with sharp, pointed horns—the legs of a bull, and the body of a man.

It bellowed and snorted, pawing the ground with cloven hooves. "Here," Paige said, holding out an ancient-looking spear, carved with runes and strange symbols. "You'll need this."

Maggie accepted the spear; it was heavy in her hand. The beast circled, snorting and pawing the ground. As it charged her, roaring, she feinted to one side and stuck the point of the spear into its flank as it raced by. The beast bellowed in pain.

And then flies were everywhere, surging over dead bodies and shattered glass in a street that looked like London after a brutal night of bombing. The flies gathered in a swarm and lit on the body of a woman, her throat slashed and her abdomen mutilated, wet blood pooling on the pavement.

Kneeling on the rough bricks, Maggie saw the woman's face. It was Brynn, with her brown curls and freckles, the gap between her front teeth.

In panic, Maggie looked up at Paige. "Help me!" she pleaded.

The blonde smiled sweetly. "You're on your own now."

Something moved in the shadows. As Maggie watched, helpless, the Minotaur turned and lowered its head, snorting. The massive beast saw her watching, and its face became animated with sadistic joy. As it ran toward her, the ground shaking, she tried to scream—but nothing came out. The beast charged at her, hooves thundering.

Maggie picked up her spear and stood, braced and ready. As the beast ran, in the long moment of the charge, she asked Paige: "Am I the hunter or the prey?"

The other woman's smile was cryptic. "You must decide."

Maggie woke with a gasp and jumped bolt upright, the bed-clothes coiled around her like adders. She sat, panting, chilled by the horrific images of her dream.

She had once stared into the abyss—and the abyss, through the blue eyes of the young man she'd killed in Berlin, had stared back at her. *To defend what they love, people allow themselves to become what they hate, like a hall of mirrors, folding in on itself. . . .* But to look into the eyes of a beast?

At the touch of a velvety-soft paw on her cheek, she turned her head. K stared at her with glowing green eyes, pupils huge in the morning light filtering through the edges of the blackout curtains.

It's the house, Maggie realized. *Being back in this house where it all began. Where Chuck and Sarah and I lived with Paige. It's the re-minders of Paige, just that, nothing more. . . .*

She regarded the sleepy cat. "Why, hello there, K. You never told me—how was your sabbatical at Number Ten? Did Rufus and Nelson behave? Or the more important question is—did *you?* "

K blinked. *"Meh, "* he meowed in his odd way and dropped his paw. Then he marched toward the foot of the bed and turned his back on her.

"What? Wait—where are you going? Didn't you miss me?"

When Maggie reached over to pet him, he wheeled with ears pinned back and hissed. Then he went a bit farther across the bed to turn his back on her once again.

"I *am* sorry I left you, K," she offered in a small voice.

There was only silence and his sleek silhouette against the shadows.

"I had no choice—they wouldn't let me take you to America. You would only have been seasick on the voyage over, anyway."

He ignored her and began grooming, his pink tongue rasping against orange fur.

"And I missed you desperately, you know," Maggie persisted. "There's even a street named for you in Washington—K Street. I thought of you every time I crossed it—which was every day."

At this he stopped, turned, and met her eyes again, his expression suspicious.

"It's true. I missed you terribly, Fur Face." At this admission, the ice melted and he began to purr. Low at first, but growing into a loud rumble. He stalked toward her, deigned to sniff her outstretched hand, then allowed her to pet him. He then paraded onto her chest, and once again, they bumped foreheads.

"We're together again now, K," Maggie murmured, cuddling him close, his glossy fur fragrant and warm. "And we're home. I solemnly promise not to leave again unless it's absolutely necessary."

She looked around, taking in the details of her old bedroom. Same walls, same fireplace, same furniture—but the dark Victorian wallpaper had been stripped away and the walls were now painted in a bright blue. Gilded picture frames that once held gloomy hunt scenes now displayed recent covers of *Vogue*, *Look*, and even the *Wonder Woman* comic Tom O'Brian had given her in Washington. *Ah, David—thank you. All the bad memories cleared away.*

It was good to be back in London, and she had to admit it was also good to be back in her grandmother's—*her*—house again. Months earlier, when she'd left for the United States, she knew she could have stayed there—doing war work but enjoying more safety and less deprivation—but her heart was in Britain. She'd started the war with the Brits and she'd end with them.

She wanted to be like Dante and go into her own private hell and emerge, victorious—maybe that way, by gazing unflinching at her inner demons, she might escape them, conquer them. But the more she tried to sort out her past and make some sense of it, the more she felt trapped in a web of unwelcome questions no one could or would answer for her.

What if, for instance, she had grown up like most people, with two parents? Why had she been led to believe they were dead? What had made her mother embrace Nazi ideology? Why had her father abruptly disappeared when she was born? Was it because of her father she hadn't truly given John a chance in Washington, D.C.? Was that why she'd turned to Tom O'Brian, a soldier about to be shipped off? *Do I have problems with men? Abandonment issues, as a psychoanalyst might say?*

And, if she did, who could she talk to about it? What if her Aunt Edith had been a warm and maternal figure, who could have advised her on such things, instead of cold and authoritative? What if she'd had a sister to confide in? Speaking of sisters, would her half sister Elise ever forgive her for what had happened in Berlin? Would—

A soft knock at the door interrupted these questions. "Maggie? Are you up?"

Maggie lifted her head and released K. "Yes, come in."

It was Chuck, deep shadows under her eyes, her brown hair flattened by sleep, her borrowed tartan flannel dressing gown straining across her impressive breasts.

The horrors of what had happened to her friend the day before came rushing back to Maggie. "Were you able to get any sleep at all?" she asked, sitting up and crossing her legs. K jumped in and settled himself in her lap.

Chuck went to open the blackout curtains. Outside, the sun was beginning to rise and the horizon was gunmetal gray. "Some. I nursed Griffin and put him down for his nap, so I suppose I could try to sleep now. But I just can't. In shock, I suppose—it's how our minds protect us from horrible news, isn't it?" She tried to finger-comb the snarls out of her hair, then gave up. "I'm trying to look on the fucking bright side—Griffin's here, you're here—we'll post a letter to Nigel today, and to my parents as well. . . ." Chuck's lip trembled. "Sorry," she said.

"It's impossible to have a stiff upper lip before tea and breakfast," Maggie said lightly. K leapt off her lap and then off the bed to take a sunbath in the slanted rectangle of light on the threadbare carpet. "I'll talk to Sarah when she gets up. Between us, we'll get you and Griffin everything you need."

Chuck rolled her eyes and took a seat in a tattered wing chair. "First of all, I won't take your clothes—and second, they wouldn't fit me anyway. Although you did put on a bit of weight in the U.S."

"The food there . . ." Maggie tried unsuccessfully to dispel memories of real coffee, hamburgers, French fries, and chocolate bars. "Look, we'll pool our rations, so we can get you and Griffin the basics. And there must be something in place for the people from your building. . . . You're not the only one who's affected, after all." It had been a horrible event, but the British excelled at surviving. And organizing. "Certainly your ARP warden must know something by now. We can check in today."

Chuck slumped. "I'm dreading finding out about the neighbors," she confessed, avoiding Maggie's eyes. Her alto voice trembled. "I'm not sure all of them made it."

"Don't give up before you know the facts."

"Well, you're right: That's something to do today, stop by the block. I still have the pram and I'll take Griffin and we'll go by and see if there's anyone to speak with about . . . well, anything." Chuck straightened and scrubbed at her eyes with her fists.

"Knock knock!" called a raspy voice. Sarah was at the door in her red satin dressing gown, mouth open wide in a yawn, graceful hands stretching up to the ceiling. Her long dark hair was tangled, and there were black smudges under her eyes and a rose stain on her lips—remains of the previous evening's makeup.

"I thought I heard voices. . . ." she mumbled as she swept in, still half asleep. "Hello, Sir K, remember me?" she asked, bending down and offering her hand.

K raised his head to sniff her fingers and allowed her to pet him, then curled back up in a regal circle to continue his nap.

"Goodness gracious, Sarah!" Maggie gasped. "I'd forgotten about your feet!" Sarah's toes were distended by bunions and disfigured with calluses.

"Bloody hell, girl!" For a moment, Chuck was her old self. "Did you put your tootsies through a meat grinder?"

"Once a dancer, always a dancer." The brunette shrugged. "I don't care about my feet as long as my derriere's in decent shape." She smiled and turned to wiggle her bottom, then plopped down on the bed next to Maggie.

"What time's your meeting today, Sarah?"

"Nine sharp. And I'm hoping my friend will be there, too."

"Do you mean the one who's the bee's knees?"

Sarah gave a girlish smile, one Maggie had never seen before. "One and the same!"

"Oh, my," Maggie said, trying not to tease. "Nine's when I'm due in, too. Let's have some tea here, then we can walk over together. And I'll give Mr. Knees the once-over."

"You two go on," Chuck said wearily, leaning back on the chair and closing her eyes. "While Master Griffin is sleeping, I'll try to catch a few winks as well."

Even though the nightly bombings had stopped, the trappings of war were everywhere. Barrage balloons—massive zeppelin-shaped bulks—hovered over the city. Canvas sandbags were piled around building entrances. Emergency pontoon bridges stretched across the Thames, and brick bomb shelters cluttered the icy pavement. The Victoria Embankment bristled with pillboxes, while government buildings and other vital targets were tangled in barbed wire.

The newspaper stands trumpeted the latest: British forces were slugging it out in a back-and-forth campaign against the Germans and Italians in North Africa. The influx of American troops to Great Britain was ongoing in the wake of Pearl Harbor and the German declaration of war upon the United States. The Japanese were threatening to invade Australia, but descending first on small Pacific islands like locusts. Meanwhile, despite the bitter cold in the East, the Russians fought on.

"Wait a moment," Maggie said, catching a glimpse of a smaller article. She gave a few coins to the newspaper boy. "Look," she said to Sarah, pointing at a story titled *Pimlico Explosion Ignites Fire, Fells Buildings and Injures at Least 19.* As they walked through the stinging cold, Maggie read aloud: *"A powerful gas pipe explosion yesterday in Pimlico caused a building to collapse and ignited a large fire that quickly spread to neighboring buildings, leaving at least 19 people injured and 5 dead. At least one person was reported missing. The building is one of many in the area owned by Dr. Iain Frank, a practicing psychoanalyst."*

Sarah shook her head. "Chuck and Griffin were lucky."

Maggie continued to walk and read: *"'Based on records, the building has had some work done inside; new gas service pipes; a lot of things, piping and such, Mr. Clendenin from Westminster Gas Light and Coke Company said.'"* Maggie looked up from the newspaper. "Didn't Chuck say she saw some dodgy people siphoning off the gas lines? Sounds a bit iffy. And now we'll probably never know the truth."

The previous night's snow had melted and then refrozen, leaving the pavement slick with ice. All the windows they passed were taped to prevent breakage, the iron railings removed for munitions, leaving dangerous gaps. The two jumped aside as they heard a ringing bell, stepping out of the way as a woman in a Wren uniform and bright lipstick sped by on her bicycle.

At last they arrived at the sandbagged entrance of the SOE office on Baker Street. "Probably best if we don't go up together," Maggie whispered as two U.S. officers passed. Both doffed their caps.

"I'm early anyway." Sarah looked across the street and spotted a café. "I'll have another cuppa and a ciggie first, then come up. Sound good?"

Maggie nodded, then pushed open the heavy door and went upstairs. It was still early and Miss Lynd was the only other person in the office—Maggie could hear the *click clack* of typing behind her closed door. The air, as usual, was numbingly cold.

The first thing she did was check on Erica Calvert's latest dispatch. Like the last, it was missing both safety checks, and her tone seemed stilted and off. *Oh, Erica—what's going on over there?*

With a nervous knot in her stomach, Maggie looked over the other agent's file. Calvert had studied geology, specializing in sand eroded from sedimentary rocks, like those found on the coast of northwest France. She'd trained with SOE and had been sent over to investigate the beaches in that area for possible invasion landing places.

Her mission was to collect sand and soil samples, to be brought back to England for examination, so the Allies could plan the proper equipment for the terrain. While old French geological reports showed the coastal land had clay underneath the sand, which could bog down tanks and other military vehicles, Churchill demanded fresh samples and a modern analysis. If Calvert had been compromised, the Germans would know Normandy was being considered as an invasion point.

Maggie looked again at the message in Morse code:

.... . . - .. -..—— # / . ...- . ..-.—-.... .. -.—. /—.——-
-.. / ....-. .-.-.- / .-.. ..- - / .-.—- .. -. .-.-.- / .—.
.-... .-.. ..-. / .-. .—.—.——-.... . .-. /——- -.... . .-. # ... / -.... .
-. -.... -.. . - -.—.-.-.- /—.. ... . ——-. / —.—- .. .-.. /
.—-. .-.. .-...-.- / . .-. .. ..-.-. - / -.-.. .-. .-. ....- . .-. .-.-.-

Translated, it read:

Hello!
　Everything good here. Left Rouen. Please remember
mother's birthday with gift. Mission going well.
　　　　　　　　　　　　Erica Calvert

And Erica's not even using her code name, Josephine. How strange.
Maggie had a sudden thought: Agents dropped behind enemy lines
always left the names and contact information for next of kin.
Maggie checked through Erica's list—her husband, her father, her
sister. No mention of a mother.

Erica's husband was in the Navy and not able to be reached, but
her father was a professor of geoscience at the University of Dur-
ham, in the northeast of England, south of Newcastle upon Tyne.
Maggie called the number in the file and asked for Professor Stephen Calvert.

He wasn't there, and Maggie left a message with his secretary,
requesting him to return her call. She drummed on the desk with
her fingers, reading and rereading the message,

"Colonel—" she began when Gaskell arrived.

"Not now, Meggie," he snapped, taking off his hat and coat,
and thrusting them at her. His coat's collar sported a gold Man-
chester United pin, with its red devil and pitchfork emblem.

Maggie was undeterred. "It's about Agent Erica Calvert, sir.

She left off her security checks again, and her fist is still irregular. I have serious concerns about her safety."

Gaskell sneezed. He pulled a rumpled handkerchief from his breast pocket and wiped his nose. "What we do here is not an exact science, Meggie." He glared at her. "When she gets back, you can nag her about Baker Street protocol all you'd like."

Gritting her teeth, Maggie hung his things on the coatrack. They reeked of smoke. She returned to her desk and looked down at the book, then up at the clock. It was ten past nine. "Sir, your first appointment today is with Miss Bronwyn Parry."

"Yes, yes," he mumbled, putting the handkerchief back in his uniform's jacket pocket. "Jolly good." He glanced around the reception room. "And just where *is* our Miss Parry? Her appointment was at nine."

"She hasn't arrived yet, sir."

Gaskell walked to his office, tread heavy. "If that girl can't make a simple appointment on time, how can we expect her to . . ." He sighed and rubbed his temples. "Did she at least ring to say she'd be late?"

Maggie knew she hadn't, but sorted through last evening's message slips anyway, to appease him. "No, sir."

"Well then, as far as I'm concerned, she's a dud. We can't risk F-Section on some chit who can't even make her appointment on time." As he turned the doorknob to his office, he stopped and looked heavenward. "Girls!" He strode in, grumbling. "Their vanity knows no bounds! Keeping grown men waiting!" The door slammed.

Maggie was too concerned about Brynn to be annoyed with Gaskell. She knew Brynn: knew she was a hard worker, conscientious, never absent for drills and lessons at Arisaig House. Always responsible in her assignments. Good-natured. Quick with a joke. She'd never be late for an appointment.

She was planning on spending the night at a hotel, Maggie remembered, rummaging in her top drawer, looking for another one of the cards she'd given Brynn. *Damn.* The prospective agent had taken the last one with her. *Damn, damn, damn . . .*

The telephone warbled. It was Professor Stephen Calvert. "What's this regarding?" he asked in a low, brusque voice.

"This is Miss Hope, with the Inter-Services Research Bureau. Sir, I've received a message from your daughter Erica, and she mentioned sending a birthday gift to her mother. Since she's . . . working . . . I can pick up and post the gift for Erica. I was wondering what sort of present her mother would like, and where I can send it?"

There was a series of hisses and crackles on the telephone line. "Her mother's been dead for over ten years" was the curt reply.

Dead? It didn't sound that way in the message, at least. "Is— is there something Erica did on the anniversary of her mother's birthday? A gift she might have left at the cemetery, perhaps? Flowers?"

"No, no—nothing of the sort. Erica's not a sentimental girl, not at all. And her mother left us without so much as a goodbye, year before she did us the favor of dying. No gift necessary!" He slammed down the telephone.

Maggie winced and pulled the receiver away from her ear. *Something's wrong.*

But before she could get any further, Sarah opened the door and stepped inside, poised as any *Vogue* model.

As she did, Gaskell opened his door, folder in hand. He froze, slack-jawed, gazing at Sarah in what could only be described as awe and perhaps even terror.

Maggie tried not to laugh as she saw Gaskell react to Sarah's beauty. He stared, opening and closing his mouth like a hooked fish.

Finally he managed in his gruff voice, "And are you Miss Parry?"

"*Non, monsieur,*" Sarah replied in a cloud of clove cigarette smoke and L'Heure Bleue.

"Well, then—who are you, young lady?"

"Sarah Sanderson," she replied coolly, with a mischievous side wink to Maggie. "Here to be interviewed by Miss Lynd."

"Of course, of course," the colonel backtracked, hastily retreating to his office. "*Bonne chance,* Miss Sanderson."

"Welcome." Maggie grinned up at her friend. But the smile faded from her lips as soon as she caught sight of the man coming through the door. Hugh Thompson, her former MI-5 partner, looked the same: tall, with green eyes and a high forehead—perhaps a bit higher now as his hairline was beginning to recede—but handsome as ever. It had been a long time since she'd seen him last, at least. Her heart turned over, and she had no idea what to do with her hands.

"Maggie!" Hugh exclaimed, whipping off his hat and twisting the brim in his hands. "Er, I mean, Miss Hope."

"Mr. Thompson."

"Let me guess." Sarah angled a plucked eyebrow. "You two know each other." She did not look pleased.

"We—worked together once," Maggie admitted. "A long time ago."

Sarah would not be distracted. "When?" she demanded.

Maggie was startled by her tone. "The less information we all have, the better," she said, falling back on the standard SOE answer.

"Well." Sarah's eyes narrowed. "I bet it's 'a long story.'"

"We, ah—" Hugh cleared his throat. "That is, Miss Sanderson and I, have an appointment to see Miss Lynd."

"Of course," Maggie replied. She scooped up the telephone receiver and dialed the extension. "Miss Sanderson and Mr. Thompson to see you, ma'am." Maggie listened, then replaced the receiver. "Miss Lynd is ready for you now. Second door on the right."

"Thanks," Hugh said to Maggie. "It's . . . er, good to see you again, Miss Hope."

Sarah began to walk down the hall. "Come on!" she called back to Hugh. "Miss Lynd is waiting!"

"Don't mention it." Maggie did her best not to blush. "It's good to see you again, too, Mr. Thompson."

Miss Lynd rose and proffered a heavily ringed hand to both Sarah and Hugh, then settled herself back behind her desk, glowing in the thin strips of feeble sunlight allowed in by the wooden venetian blinds. She lit a cigarette, eyes fixed upon the new recruits as they removed their coats—Hugh helping Sarah with hers—and then took seats across from her. Sarah tried to rub some warmth into her hands through her gloves.

"You've been training in Arisaig?" Miss Lynd asked, already knowing the answer.

"Yes," Sarah answered for both of them.

"Well, you might as well know each other's real names now. Sarah Sanderson, meet—officially now—Hugh Thompson."

"A pleasure," Hugh said.

Sarah colored. "Likewise."

"Miss Sanderson," Miss Lynd said, "according to your file, you've spent a lot of time in France, Paris, on the Île St.-Louis specifically."

"Yes. My grandmother lived there. We would visit her every summer when I was younger."

"You speak French well?"

"Je suis bilingue, Madame. Ma grand-mère m'a tout appris."

Miss Lynd opened a folder. "Your reports are good," she stated, paging through. "Your physicals, your psychological examinations." She looked to Hugh. "And how is *your* French, Mr. Thompson?"

"J'ai passé deux ans à la Sorbonne, Madame. Ca, c'est à vous de me dire."

Miss Lynd gave a slow nod. "Not bad, not bad at all." She contemplated them, as if trying to make up her mind. Finally, she spoke. "Miss Sanderson and Mr. Thompson. You each did assessment and training at Wanborough Manor, then paramilitary work in Scotland. You completed your parachute training at Ringway airfield, then continued on to our so-called Finishing School at Beaulieu in Hampshire." Miss Lynd pronounced it the English way—*Bew-lee*.

"Yes, ma'am," Hugh answered.

"You both also have special skills—Miss Sanderson, you as a ballet dancer, and Mr. Thompson, you as a cellist." Though she rarely visited the training schools herself, Miss Lynd received regular reports from instructors as each agent progressed. She looked down again at the file on Sarah Sanderson. *Too beautiful,* one instructor had noted. *Will only draw attention. Too headstrong. Too used to getting her own way. DO NOT recommend.*

But Miss Lynd ignored the comments. She'd become quite used to the skeptical, if not downright damning, comments that came back to her about the women trainees from the men in charge. The male staff at the schools appeared awestruck by the "feminine" qualities of the women, who were "painstaking," "lacking in guile," and "innocent." Either that, or they were "too fast," "devious," and "slatternly." What the men really meant, in Miss Lynd's opinion, was that women shouldn't be serving behind enemy lines at all.

Sarah reached into her handbag and pulled out a cloisonné cigarette case. Hugh pulled out his lighter and flicked it for her.

Miss Lynd shook her head. "No smoking, Miss Sanderson."

Both looked to her, and one of Sarah's perfectly angled eyebrows shot up as Hugh's flame went out.

Miss Lynd held up a hand, her rings sparking in the light. "In France, women do not smoke. Only the men receive cigarette rations now. And women smoking is forbidden by the Nazis—it's not considered 'ladylike' and might not be healthy for any children of the Reich." She leaned forward. "It's not only the language you must perfect but all the *details.*"

"Is that it? The big news? We're going to France?" Sarah put her cigarette case away and snapped the bag closed.

"This has all been rather hush-hush, you know," Hugh added.

Miss Lynd leaned back in her chair before replying. "What is it you *think* you're going to be asked to do? Any clues from your training? Your interviews?"

"Commando work, I'd say," guessed Hugh. "At least given the curriculum—parachute jumping, stealth shore landings at night, blowing up bridges and roads, using intermediaries, *boîtes aux lettres,* Morse code, and the like. And somewhere in France, I'd guess by the language classes. But—"

"Yes?"

"But there were—ah—women training alongside men. And Miss Sanderson is a . . . a woman." He cleared his throat. "Obviously."

Sarah smiled. "I'm glad you noticed, darling. Those jumpsuits we wore weren't at all flattering."

Miss Lynd suppressed a smile. "Actually, Mr. Thompson, women are our secret weapon here at SOE. We women are underestimated by the Germans. And while most men of fighting age are being shipped off to the East, women may still travel freely." She looked directly at Hugh. "Do you have a problem with working with female agents, Mr. Thompson?"

"No, no, I've worked with female agents before, that is, *a* female agent in particular, but not—"

Sarah blinked. "Do you mean Maggie?"

"Miss Sanderson!" Miss Lynd barked, and Sarah jumped in her seat. "The less you know about your fellow agents in this business, the better."

"Sorry," Sarah amended.

"Back to the subject at hand," Miss Lynd chastised. "We'd like you both to go to occupied France."

Sarah and Hugh exchanged looks. "What would our mission be?" the dancer asked.

"First, are you amenable?"

Both nodded.

"I need verbal confirmation."

"Yes," they replied in unison.

"When would we leave?" Sarah asked.

"All in good time, Miss Sanderson. You both have one last training session, in a house called Blackbridge, in Beaulieu, on the estate of Lord Montagu. You'll be given French identities—names, backgrounds, everything. All your papers for your new identities will be in order. During your time in Hampshire, you will speak only French. And you must stay 'in character' for your entire stay."

"And then?" Hugh asked.

"And then, after a final evaluation—*if* you prove ready—you'll be sent to France."

"To do what exactly?"

"I can only paint in the broadest strokes—your mission will be to help organize resistance and serve as liaisons to London. You'll be told specifics if and when you pass the final tests of the Finishing School."

Sarah looked to Hugh with a broad smile. "So, we're to work together, then?"

"Yes, it will be part of your cover story. You'll be filled in on all the details when you reach Beaulieu. Do you agree?"

"I do," the two said.

"You will leave today. You'll take the train from Waterloo to Brockenhurst this afternoon, and you'll be met at the station by an SOE agent."

"And, if all goes well, when would we leave for France?"

"That's unclear at the moment. If you're approved, there are other variables—what's going on there, what's needed, the phases of the moon . . . They will let you know if and when you're ready. Do you have any questions?"

"What should I tell my mother?" Sarah asked.

"Yes, mine's wondering, too. I've been vague so far, but I can't put her off forever," Hugh added.

"You must continue to be evasive, I'm afraid," Miss Lynd answered, "but you might now begin to give vague hints about 'going away.' You've done tours with the Vic-Wells Ballet, Miss Sanderson—it's similar. One more thing before you go—why do you want to do this? It's undeniably dangerous."

"The Nazis killed my grandmother," Sarah responded bluntly. "I hate the Germans. I hate them for killing her, for taking Paris, for invading France, for bombing us. The list is endless, really. I hate them, I hate them with all of my soul. And I want to get a bit of my own back."

Miss Lynd's face remained impassive. "And you, Mr. Thompson?"

"Everyone's doing something. I want to do my duty as well."

"A rather bland response, Mr. Thompson."

"Well, then, because of God."

Miss Lynd's impassive mask wavered. "Excuse me?"

"At university, I studied religion. Almost became an Anglican priest, if you can believe it. I believe in God, and I believe in Satan, and I also believe we are called on to fight evil wherever we may find it. Working for the SOE seems like a good way to do my part."

"And, if necessary, are you prepared to kill in the line of duty, Mr. Thompson? Would that action square with your beliefs?"

Hugh nodded. "Yes, I'm prepared to kill, although of course I'd prefer not to. If given the option."

"You might not have an option." Miss Lynd took one last look at the couple, then rummaged through a desk drawer. "Here you go." She pulled out an envelope and handed it to Hugh. "These are tickets back to Brockenhurst. You're approved for the next stage of your training. Good luck to you both."

They all stood, and Miss Lynd showed the two interviewees out. In the front room, Hugh waved goodbye while Sarah avoided Maggie's eyes.

Maggie gave a small wave, but as soon as the door closed behind them, her face fell. Was Sarah angry with her? Had she accidentally done something wrong?

If Miss Lynd noticed how pale Maggie had become, she gave no sign. "I'm going to make a cup of tea to try to warm up—would you like one?" she asked the younger woman.

"No. Thank you." But Maggie followed Miss Lynd into the kitchenette. "Miss Sanderson and Mr. Thompson are doing the exact same job, but she's making two-thirds of what he is. If they're caught overseas, he'll be held as a POW, while she'll be executed as a spy. And they both have single, aging mothers. If they die in the line of duty, Mr. Thompson's mother will receive his pension, while Miss Sanderson's will receive—nothing."

"Yes," Miss Lynd said, tapping a foot as she waited for the kettle to boil.

"And you're all right with this?" Maggie persisted, pulling her sweater around her.

Miss Lynd turned to face her. "One war at a time, Miss Hope." The kettle whistled and she turned off the gas.

Maggie wouldn't give up. "Speaking of war," she continued, "I've gone over all of Agent Calvert's communiqués again. There's every reason to believe she's been compromised—things just aren't adding up. If she's in enemy hands and our team goes in for the extraction—well, not only is she already in danger, but they're likely to be taken out as well."

"What does Colonel Gaskell have to say about all this?"

"The colonel doesn't seem at all concerned."

There was a long pause. "Then you shouldn't be, either." On the reception desk down the hall, the telephone rang with a shrill bleat. "I believe that's your cue," Miss Lynd pointed out.

Maggie ran to pick up the telephone receiver. "Good morning. You've reached Inter-Services Research Bureau—may I help you?"

"Director General Peter Frain for Miss Margaret Hope," shrilled a woman's voice.

"This is she."

There was a series of clicks as Peter Frain, head of MI-5, got on the line. There was a pause, then, "Hello, Maggie."

"Hello, Peter." Even years later, it felt odd to be on a first-name basis with the director general of MI-5. The man who'd gotten Maggie involved with SOE in the first place.

"You must come to my office. Immediately."

She wound the telephone cord around her hand. "I—I'm at work, sir."

Frain was undeterred. "Yes, I know where you are—obviously. Tell them it's MI-Five. They'll understand."

Maggie looked up at Miss Lynd, who was retreating to her office with her steaming mug of tea.

"Yes, sir." Maggie hung up the receiver. She knocked on Colonel Gaskell's door.

"What is it, Meggie?"

"I need to leave, sir."

"Leave?" He arched one eyebrow. "*Leave?* May I ask where you need to be that's so important? A hairdressing appointment, perhaps? A dress fitting? An engagement party?"

Maggie really, really, *really* wanted to roll her eyes—but refrained. "Director General Peter Frain wants to see me as soon as possible, sir." She was gratified to see the Colonel startle and his pale eyes widen.

"But—but we need you here! Who will make our tea?"

"Mr. Frain said to tell you it's MI-Five business and you'd understand, sir."

Once again, Gaskell's mouth opened and closed like a fish's. Finally, he managed, "Women! Flibbertigibbets! All of you!"

"Yes, sir." Maggie gave him her best noncommittal look. "It's important, sir."

"Of course it is," he spluttered. "Well, then, go! *Go!*"

"Sir, about Agent Calvert—" Maggie took a deep breath. "In her latest communiqué, she mentioned something about a birthday gift for her mother. But her mother's been dead for over ten years. And when I spoke with her father—"

"Blast Agent Calvert!" He flushed red. "Blast her mother! And blast her father! Off with you to MI-Five, then!" he managed, waving his hands. "And bring me back a Sally Lunn roll when you return!"

"Yes, sir." Before Maggie put on her coat, hat, and gloves, she made sure to lock the latest transmissions back in the filing cabinet. *Hang in there, Erica. . . .*

And Brynn, where are you?

All Brynn Parry knew was she had the worst headache of her life. Her temples throbbed. She cracked open her eyes.

Then she started. The room she was in was not the room she'd gone to sleep in.

Something was wrong. She looked around. The room itself was small and narrow, with no windows and a low ceiling. Shadows from a candle on a battered campaign bureau danced over rough stone walls. It smelled of must, damp, and old brick.

She knew she had to get out.

As she struggled to sit up in her hard, narrow bed, her head spun and she feared she might vomit. When she kicked off the coarse, faded coverlet and swung her legs over the side, her muscles ached, as if she'd been through battle. She stood with effort, shaky on her feet, then took a few tentative steps on the cold, bare floor toward the door.

It was locked. She jiggled the knob and twisted and pulled at it. Then she beat upon the thick pine and called for help until her throat was raw.

You're a trained agent, she reminded herself. *Act like one.* In the dresser drawers were all of the things she'd had crammed in her suitcase—all the things she hadn't bothered to unpack the night before.

Her suitcase was gone. Someone had taken her suitcase.

There was a chipped jug of water and a bowl on a dressing table, along with her hairbrush and tube of lipstick. The bed's frame was made of white ceramic, like a hospital bed, and the mattress was thin. A reproduction of Henry Fuseli's *The Nightmare* hung on one wall, the incubus staring back at her with a malevolent expression. There was a deep chill in the air—like in her parents' cellar. Wherever she was, she was underground, she was certain of it.

The candle's flame flickered. Her book on the bedside table, *The Strange Case of Dr. Jekyll and Mr. Hyde,* mocked her.

She didn't know where she was.

She didn't know what time it was.

Or even what day.

For a moment, the wave of terror and shock was so overwhelming she feared she might faint, but she sat on the bed's edge and bent to put her head between her legs, as she'd been taught, taking deep breaths.

When the dizziness and nausea began to subside, she lifted her head. She'd been trained to withstand capture, imprisonment, even torture. And although her training was supposed to be of use in Nazi-infested Europe, in London—assuming she was still in London—it was the same principle.

She swallowed hard.

She was still alive.

And—somehow—she would get out.

Chapter Four

On St. James's Street, past Boodle's and White's and the other exclusive men's clubs, between Park Place and Jermyn Street, stood the headquarters of MI-5. It was officially known as the Imperial Security Intelligence Service. Its mission: countering any and all threats to national safety.

Maggie hadn't been back recently, but she still remembered where to go, resolutely making her way through marble hallways lined with rows of Corinthian pillars and past various security checkpoints, up in a polished brass elevator, until she reached the director general's office.

A secretary with grayish white hair that didn't quite match the fake white braid on her headband greeted her, then picked up the telephone receiver. "Miss Hope is here, sir." She looked up to Maggie. "Go in."

Maggie opened the heavy paneled door.

Behind his massive mahogany desk, Frain stood. "Thank you for coming, Maggie." Peter Frain had been made director under Mr. Churchill during the dark days of the summer of 1940, which was when Maggie had first met him. Then a tall man with slicked-back hair and cold gray eyes, he still looked the same—elegant, sophisticated, debonair—although Maggie could see he had more silver hair at his temples. *It suits him,* she decided as she shook his hand.

"Please sit down." He regarded her from across the desk, piles of folders, papers, and notes stacked neatly under brass paperweights. Not a salacious look, but intense—the kind one might give a particularly interesting crossword clue or a game of Chinese Go in progress.

"How's your father?" he asked, sitting back and making a steeple with his fingers.

"Still in the hospital, I'm afraid. I've been visiting once a week, although he's usually asleep or groggy. The doctors have him on a high dose of morphine."

Earlier in the winter, Edmund Hope, Maggie's estranged father, had been burned in an "accident" that revealed terrible abscesses on his feet, due to untreated diabetes. Both legs had to be amputated above the knee.

"I should go and visit, I know—but it's been, shall we say, busy here."

" 'There's a war on, you know.' " She quoted their oft-repeated line. "Next time I see him, I'll let him know you asked after him."

"I knew he'd been drinking, but I had no idea things were so bad."

Maggie didn't want to discuss it. "And any news of"—she didn't know what to call her estranged mother—"Clara Hess?"

"You know as much as we do. Either she died in the fire that night—or she somehow made it out of Chatswell House and she's out there." He waved a manicured hand in the direction of the window, with a view to Hyde Park and the rest of London. "Somewhere."

Terrific, Maggie thought. *Nazi agent Clara Hess could possibly be at large in London—now that's just bloody well terrific, isn't it?*

"By the way, I have something for you." Frain reached into a desk drawer.

"For me?"

He pulled out a brown paper envelope. *To Miss Margaret Hope c/o MI-5* was written in calligraphy on the front. Maggie flipped it over before slipping it into her handbag.

"You're not going to open it?"

It was the rarest of moments for Maggie to see Frain surprised. She rather liked it. "Later. I assume you asked me here for something more important than to pick up my mail."

There was a rap at the door; it opened to reveal Mark Standish, Maggie's former colleague. They'd worked together before, and while they hadn't always gotten along, they'd developed a begrudging professional respect.

However, the Mark Standish who stood in front of her was a different man from the one she'd known in Scotland last fall. He wore the same style double-breasted suit, but now it hung loosely on him. Where he'd once been charitably called robust, he was alarmingly gaunt and wan. His formerly doughy face was angular, and a startling streak of white cut through his dark hair.

"Hello, Maggie. Welcome back to MI-Five."

Maggie wondered if she would have recognized Mark if she'd passed him on the street. And when she shook his hand, she noticed it had a slight tremor. "Hello, Mark. Good to see you again."

"Let's go to your office, Mr. Standish," Frain said, standing.

"Yes, sir."

They walked down a corridor, and Mark opened a door. "Welcome." He stepped aside to let them enter.

Maggie fought the urge to whistle. "Spiffy," she said instead. It was spacious, with several good-size windows overlooking the street. There was a large desk with a green banker's lamp and a leather chair, overlooked by the official photograph of the King. On the desk was a typewriter, hole punch, a TOP SECRET red stamp, several telephones, and a metal inbox.

On one wall of the office, a corkboard had been set up. Photographs of a dead girl, clearly taken at a crime scene, were tacked up. Opposite was a green chalkboard, recently cleaned, fresh chalk and erasers at the ready.

Maggie couldn't help but think back to when Mark and Hugh had dented metal desks in MI-5's windowless basement, with all the other junior agents. She wished she could say she'd seen Hugh in the morning, but it was against all rules to mention it. Anyway, Frain probably knew—he somehow made it a point to know everything.

"Sit, both of you," the director ordered, gesturing to a sofa and a side chair. It might have been Mark's office, but it was clear who was running the show.

The secretary with the white braid came in with the tea things and set them on a low table, then poured. Once the door closed again, Frain took a seat and turned to Maggie. "We want to borrow you."

"Borrow me, sir? For what?"

Frain chose a cup of tea and took a sip. "There have been a number of girls vanishing around London. With the Blitz, it's been hard to keep track of the dead, of course, but it seems there's a definite pattern emerging in the Marylebone area. There are too many young professional women disappearing for it to be only the bombings. Which have ceased for the moment in London, at any rate."

Mark continued to stir his tea, his eyes not leaving the cup and saucer in his hand.

"Vanishing women?" Maggie asked, her thoughts instantly turning to Brynn Parry. "But that would be a case for Scotland Yard, surely. Why MI-Five?"

"Many of the missing young women were with the ATS and tapped for SOE duties. They were here for their interviews."

Joanna Metcalf, she thought. Then, with a shudder, *Brynn.* "Someone's targeting SOE agents?" she managed.

"It could be simple coincidence. Or it could be a Nazi plot to take our agents out before we can even get them off the ground. Or it could be something else entirely. The truth is we don't know, but when there's SOE involved, it makes sense for MI-Five to handle it. We'll have a liaison with Scotland Yard, of course, but this investigation is top secret, and under my supervision." Frain put down his cup and saucer with a *clink.* "I want you in particular on the case, Maggie, since it has to do with the murder of female SOE agents."

Mark rose and handed her a thick manila accordion folder from his desk. Maggie thumbed through page after page of the files of young women missing and presumed dead. In addition to Joanna Metcalf, she recognized more names—women she'd either trained with back in the day or trained herself when she'd been an instructor at Arisaig. All fit the same profile—women in their late teens to early thirties wanting to "do their bit." All from different corners of Britain. All social classes. All passing through London to interview with SOE. She felt sick.

"These are disappearances, sir. Are there any witnesses to these alleged abductions?"

Frain didn't blink. "No."

"And no one's found any bodies?"

"No. That is—not until now. A woman, Joanna Metcalf, who fit the profile, was found murdered outside Regent's Park—you might have read about it in the papers."

Maggie glanced at the corkboard, with its array of gruesome photographs. She remembered Brody's mentioning Joanna's murder at the office, and then Max Thornton bringing it up at the party. "Yes, I did hear something about a so-called Jack the Ripper–

inspired murder. Figured it was the London press gone mad, as usual. I hear they've dubbed him the Blackout Beast."

"We've done our best to shut the whole thing down while we investigate," Frain informed her. "The last thing we need now is a citywide panic."

Mark leaned on the edge of his desk and cleared his throat. "The particular young woman in question, Joanna Metcalf, was set to leave for France during the next full moon. What we managed to keep out of the press was that her body was mutilated, in a manner reminiscent of Jack the Ripper's murder of Mary Ann Nichols, his first victim. Not just reminiscent. A *re-creation,* down to the last detail."

He handed Maggie another file. Her eyes widened when she saw photographs of the body, along with the painted statement on the brick wall, JACK IS BACK.

"Was she killed there, by the wall?"

"We don't think so," Mark explained. "We believe she was killed somewhere else. And the corpse was placed there afterward."

"Any witnesses?"

"None. But we're interviewing people who were in the area that night. We've put up signs—you know, 'Did you see anything on the night of—call us' sort of thing."

Maggie went back to the report. "It says here the body was found by a Mrs. Vera Baines, the neighborhood's ARP warden."

"Yes, we've spoken to Mrs. Baines. She says she didn't hear or see anything unusual that evening. Literally tripped over the body, wrapped in a blanket and placed by the wall, as the photographs show."

"It also says here the cuts were made with surgical precision." Maggie was frowning.

"Which means we're looking for someone with skills. A doctor? A nurse? A veterinarian?" She tried not to wince. "A butcher?"

Mark crossed his arms. "The exact occupations the original Jack the Ripper was theorized to be."

"Or someone with a lot of experience with murder," Frain speculated.

Maggie flipped through to the last page. "There's no mention of rape."

"With the extensive injuries, it's impossible to tell. However, the coroner found no evidence."

"So," Maggie said, "there are missing SOE women. This particular murder scene had a message allegedly written by someone calling himself Jack, perhaps referring to the Ripper. The method of killing is the same as with Mary Ann Nichols. But what is there to link Joanna Metcalf's murder with the disappearances? And weren't the historic Ripper's victims all prostitutes? And from Whitechapel? These women aren't."

"Our Jack isn't murdering prostitutes, but they are 'working women,' nonetheless," Frain said. "The twentieth century's working women—out in the public sphere, doing so-called men's work, while the men are fighting overseas. The cuts to the lower abdomen show an intense anger toward women."

"Of course . . ." Maggie murmured, flipping through the pages again. She could see a pattern. Young women from out of town. All in the Women's Auxiliary services, all somehow connected to SOE. Women like Brynn. Like Sarah.

Like herself.

She shifted uncomfortably as she remembered her dream, the beast of crawling black flies.

"You fit the profile, Maggie," Frain stated, seeming to read her mind. "And you have experience solving—shall we say—*unusual* cases. You're also a female SOE agent—you have insider knowledge. Help us figure this out. We need to catch this monster before he kills again."

"But why do you think the SOE women's disappearances and Joanna Metcalf's murder are connected? Women can go off—elope, decide to work in a factory instead of the WAAF, go to Scotland to be Land Girls. . . ."

Frain nodded. "That's the piece we need to figure out."

There was a rap at the door. "Excuse me, Mr. Frain," the secretary said, ducking her head in, "but Detective Chief Inspector James Durgin from Scotland Yard's on the line. They've found another body. In Regent's Park. And, yes, he's keeping the press away—so far, at least."

The three exchanged grim looks.

Maggie was first to stand, smoothing down her skirt. "Well, what are we waiting for, gentlemen? Let's go and catch ourselves a Blackout Beast."

The black metal gates of Regent's Park had been removed and melted down for munitions, but John Nash's graceful rolling greens and bench-lined gravel paths remained. Still, it felt all too open and exposed, the thick grass covered in frost and speckled with dead leaves. While slanting sunlight pierced through the thick clouds, birds—sparrows, crows, ravens—chirped warnings of squalls to come, and pairs of black and white swans glided across the lake. The day was wintry and raw, and the air smelled of ozone and approaching storms. A bitterly cold east wind whispered its way through bare tree branches, making them shiver.

There were people walking the gravel paths: a few Polish soldiers on leave, a thickly mustached businessman in a black bowler hat, and women—everywhere women. Women in ATS uniforms, WAAF uniforms, FANY uniforms. Women in the uniforms of bus conductors, crossing guards, and shop assistants. Women in trousers on their way to their shifts at factory jobs, their hair pulled back in head scarves, swinging tin lunch pails as they walked. Women clutching their handbags, gas masks, and hats against the wind.

Maggie was amused to see people in matching uniforms keeping to their own, just like the park's pigeons, ducks, and geese. Under an ancient oak tree in the distance, a busking violinist played the melody of Berlioz's *Symphonie fantastique*, while a man being pushed in a wheelchair by a nurse tossed coins into his case.

"Ah, there he is," Frain said, catching sight of a man in a gray mackintosh pacing the walk near the park's entrance, causing a flock of strutting pigeons to scatter. "Detective!" he called. Then, to Maggie and Mark, "Detective Chief Inspector James Durgin, to be precise."

The detective whirled, then strode toward them in thick-soled shoes, pigeons startling and taking flight in his wake. Durgin was tall and lean, like a distance runner, Maggie thought, and his gray-blue eyes burned with an intense, almost maniacal energy. His full curly brown hair was clipped, his eyebrows were bushy, and the diagonals of his widow's peak only emphasized the severe lines of his forehead and sharp cheekbones. Maggie guessed he was in his mid to late thirties. He was certainly not the reedy, tweedy, upper-class sort of man, such as those in Mr. Churchill's office, whom she was used to.

"He's a pioneer in fingerprinting," Frain continued over the flaps of pigeon wings. "A legend at the Yard. You'll learn a lot from him."

Durgin called, "Glad you could join us, Director General," in a thick Glasgow burr. He took in Frain's and Mark's polished shoes and camel-hair coats, and Maggie's handbag and pumps with a withering squint. "*This* is your crack team—here to save the day?"

But Frain was unflappable. "This is Mr. Standish, one of MI-Five's senior agents," he replied, introducing Mark, "and our associate, Miss Hope, who will be . . . consulting."

Durgin didn't greet them. Instead, the policeman turned on his heel and walked at a terrific pace down one of the paths, past a red-and-white proscenium for a Punch and Judy show, past an empty band shell, and a row of box-trimmed holly bushes. "I've told you how I feel about this, Frain," Durgin threw over his shoulder. "I'm not pleased, not pleased at all. This case should be the Yard's—"

"It's sensitive," Frain countered easily, matching the detective's stride, while Maggie and Mark hastened to keep up.

"Just because we don't all wear Cleverley shoes—" Durgin shot back.

"I understand, Detective, and I respect your and your department's expertise. However—"

"I know, I know—'there's a war on, you know.'" The Detective Chief Inspector gave Frain a piercing glance from beneath his remarkable eyebrows. "Believe me, I know. Thing is, you think the war started in 'thirty-nine—whereas we at the Yard know the war never, *ever* begins or ends."

As they walked farther into the park, the hum of traffic faded and the birds' chirping grew louder. On the battered grass near one of the lakes was a cordoned-off area with a canvas tent where bobbies in uniform were turning away gawkers. One officer strong-armed a journalist, pinning his arms behind him and cuffing him, while another smashed his camera.

Detective Durgin stopped, turned, and shot them a warning glare. "Prepare yourself." He gave Maggie a particularly hard stare. "And absolutely no vomiting on my crime scene, young lady. I must insist."

"No, sir," Maggie replied. "No vomiting. Of course not, sir."

As they walked past more officers and then ducked into the tent,

Durgin closed his eyes and made the sign of the cross. Then he gestured to a woman's prone body, lying on a makeshift cot and splattered with dried blood. The victim was a slender woman in her twenties, with black hair and high cheekbones. She wore a gray flannel skirt, blouse, and Fair Isle sweater. Her head was turned to the left, her colorful scarf lying loosely around her slashed throat. In the shadows of the tent, Maggie could see not only was the woman's abdomen ripped open but her intestines had been deliberately placed over her right shoulder.

Oh, God. Maggie recoiled in horror, but fought the instinctive urge to turn away, to close her eyes, to run from the tent and throw up the morning's tea and roll now churning in her stomach.

Instead, she forced her gaze to the woman's innocent-looking face. *You were so young,* Maggie thought, her heart heavy. *So very young.* A surge of anger cut through her. *And someone killed you deliberately. Murdered you. But why?*

"As you can see," Durgin said softly, "she wasn't merely killed—she's been slaughtered." The rusty, thick scent of blood was overwhelming.

"Our victim, Miss Doreen Leighton, was found early this morning by the neighborhood's ARP warden. She alerted the police." Durgin noted Maggie's pallor. "You all right?" he asked. "Would you like to return to your Swiss boarding school now?"

"I didn't come down with the last shower, Detective Durgin," she countered, squaring her shoulders. There was no time for being emotional. Feelings would come later, in private. "I know my way around blood and bodies."

"Believe me," Mark interposed. "Miss Hope has earned her stripes."

Detective Durgin shrugged, his face still skeptical. "Steady on then, Tiger."

Maggie found anger helped quell her grief and horror. "That's Miss Tiger to you, Detective."

Durgin looked to Frain. "The victim was dead when we arrived. Looks to have been dead for some time, at least twelve hours." He pointed to the girl's neck. "Here you can see the first incision, and then the second cuts. . . ." From his inside jacket pocket, Detective Durgin withdrew a magnifying glass and bent low over the woman. He looked through the thick glass at the bruises on her throat.

"Killer wore gloves." Durgin's face was stone.

"There's not much blood."

"She was killed somewhere else and then moved here. She's not wearing a coat—she was killed indoors."

"No signs of a struggle."

"No, she's clean," Durgin agreed. "She didn't put up a fight."

"She knew her attacker then?" Maggie asked.

"Possibly. I believe we're looking for a man. Single. Young. Sadistic tendencies. Wishing he could be doing more with his life. He's enraged with the cards life's dealt him. And he despises women—probably had an abusive or absent mother. Look how he carefully arranged her body, her organs. Like she's a doll. Like she's a prop. Like she's a, a *thing* to him." Durgin said it softly.

Maggie was baffled. "How could you possibly know all that— just from looking at a body?"

Durgin continued to stare down at the corpse. "He's arrogant. He's young, but he's experienced. This isn't his first, or his second, murder. But now something's set him off."

"But how do you know that?" Maggie insisted.

"I get inside their heads. I think like them, create what I call a profile. It's a new way to look at perpetrators." He turned back to the body. "Look at his confidence. He's been doing this for a while.

His cuts are fearless. Even cocky. Only a young man cuts with that sort of arrogance."

"Any witnesses?"

"I have my men canvassing the area, asking questions. Ah," he said, as an older woman ducked into the tent to join them. "And this is the ARP warden I mentioned, Mrs. Baines. She has a few things to add."

Although she had one hand on the head of her silver bulldog walking stick, the woman's spine was ramrod straight and Maggie could see a lifetime of discipline in her posture. "I was on my patrol at around one this morning, when I saw a man come out of the park, onto the Outer Circle."

"What did he look like, Mrs. Baines?" Mark asked, taking out a Moleskine notebook and fountain pen from his breast pocket.

"He was big—a big man. Bald," she explained. "No hat. And he was wearing an apron."

"An apron?"

"The kind a butcher wears. White, but with stains. Bloodstains, I'd imagine."

Mark blinked. "And what did he do?"

"I saw him walk to a van and get in, and then he took off in the direction of Park Square. I was close enough to use my torch—the license plate started with an *E.*"

"Are you sure about the plate, ma'am?" Mark asked.

"I may be *old,* young man," the woman snapped, "but I'm not blind and deaf. Nor dumb in either sense, thank you very much."

"No, ma'am." Mark had the grace to look embarrassed. "Of course not. Sorry, ma'am."

"You're Mrs. Vera Baines," Maggie exclaimed, remembering the file she'd read in Mark's office. "You found the other young woman, too—Miss Joanna Metcalf."

Vera Baines appraised the redhead. "I did."

"And you know this area well."

"I do. I've lived here all my life. Raised my children here. And I'm taking it personally that this sort of horrible thing is happening on my streets, in my neighborhood, on my watch. Two poor dead girls! We need to catch whoever's doing this—before anyone else gets hurt."

Durgin stared down at her. "We're doing everything we can, Mrs. Baines. Please let me know if you remember anything else." He handed her his card.

She took it, then placed it in her handbag for safekeeping. She looked shrewdly at Maggie. "So many girls coming and going now, what with the war on." She sighed. "So many girls—who can keep track of them all? I don't know them the way I might have a few years ago. It's not like the old days, you know."

"These girls," Maggie asked, thinking hard, "the ones new to the neighborhood—where do they stay?"

"Anywhere. Everywhere. Anyone with a spare bedroom can rent it out these days, and most do. Some of the larger old houses have been turned into efficiency flats. There are women's hotels, boardinghouses. . . . Everyone's trying to turn a profit from this war, it seems."

"I like your cane," Maggie offered impulsively, admiring its silver bulldog's head and silver tip.

"Young lady, it is *not* a cane—it's a walking stick. There's a vast difference, you know."

"My apologies," Maggie said hastily. "Of course it's a walking stick. And a handsome one at that. Does he have a name?"

At this, Vera smiled. "*Her* name is Lady. Named after my beloved childhood pet. She was a good dog. But enough about walking sticks—go catch this monster!"

"Thank you, Mrs. Baines," Maggie called as the older woman was escorted out.

Mark murmured to Frain, "This second victim's injuries parallel the wounds made to Jack the Ripper's second victim."

Maggie started. *How would Mark know that?*

Mark caught her look of surprise. "Bit of a Ripperologist in my spare time," he said with a crooked smile.

"Our Jack seems to have left a calling card." Durgin pointed to a piece of bark removed from a tree trunk and brought into the tent. The writing in white paint read: *Catch me if you can! Yours, Jack the R.*

"Take the bark to the lab," Frain ordered the officers surrounding them. "And get the body to the coroner's."

They went outside. Maggie took a deep breath, grateful for the fresh air. "I have other business to attend to," she heard Frain tell Mark. "You two and Detective Durgin will take it from here. The three of you will use Standish's office at MI-Five as a home base for the duration of the case." He strode back to the street, the tails of his long coat flapping in the wind.

Durgin looked down at the two MI-5 agents. "We can meet them at the coroner's for the postmortem. I'll show you Metcalf's body and then we'll go over Leighton's." His gaze raked over Maggie. "Unless you have a tea party or a debutante ball to go to? Or perhaps an office with a desk, for that matter?"

She wasn't about to let him affect her. "I've checked in with my ladies-in-waiting and apparently I have the all-clear for today." She gave a grim smile. "Lead on, please, DCI Durgin."

The sky might have been gray and the wind chill, but to the man it was a beautiful morning.

He wore green sunglasses in a tortoiseshell frame and a Burberry coat as he walked down the stairs. As he reached the pavement, a red ball bounced across his path. He bent to pick it up, then looked into the face of a four-year-old—smiling when he saw the toddler's bright eyes and light locks. "Is this yours?" he asked, offering the ball.

The boy held out mitten-covered hands gravely. Behind him stood his mother, a heavyset woman with a patched wool coat and a strained smile.

"Well, here you go, son!" He handed the ball to the child, then straightened, noticing the woman was carrying willow baskets on each arm, heavy with onions and potatoes. "May I help you with those, ma'am?" he asked with a tip of his hat.

"Thank you." She gave a grunt of relief as she handed them over.

As they all walked together, he asked the woman, "Long queues at the shops today?"

"And not much left when you get to the front of them." At a drab yellow-brick building, she stopped. "This is us. Thank you so much for your help."

The boy hung behind his mother's skirt, shy.

"My pleasure," he replied with sincerity. "A boy with his mum—it's a lovely sight to behold." He looked down to the child. "You be good for your mother, young man—do you hear? She's making incredible sacrifices for you. You're a lucky, lucky boy."

He gave the lad a pat on the head and was off, whistling the tune of "Who's Afraid of the Big Bad Wolf?" as he made his way through the Marylebone streets to Regent's Park. The wind picked up, and he bent against it, pulling down the brim of his hat so it wouldn't blow away.

When he reached the entrance to the park, he was pleased to see the police had already set up a tent. He took some bread crumbs wrapped in a handkerchief in his pocket and found a bench—not too near and not too far from the flurry of activity—where he could feed the pigeons as well as watch the proceedings.

He put his gloved middle finger to his mouth and began chewing on it, savoring the rusty tang of the blood that had collected in the leather's seam. The taste reminded him of his previous night's adventure, the way he'd ripped the girl—slain her, annihilated her. For years, women had treated him like a mouse—well, who were the animals now? When he had gone to the hunting shop to buy a knife, he'd told the salesman he was after "small prey."

As the man in the green sunglasses gnawed at his fingertips, he thought with joy of Brynn Parry—the animal still down in the basement, awaiting him. One of the police officers nodded to him as he passed. With a thrill of adrenaline, the man realized he could sit on his bench and feed the pigeons as long as he wanted, and no one would suspect a thing. He liked that. He liked feeling powerful, being the man who knew the most. He was the hunter, lying in wait.

He recognized Detective Chief Inspector James Durgin as he strode up the path, as well as MI-5's Peter Frain, from the newspapers. But who was the man with the white streak in his hair? And who was the redheaded girl? His eyes narrowed. That hair! Even in the overcast, the slut's coppery hair glowed like Little Red Riding Hood's cape, like a matador's mantle, like fresh red blood. His lip curled. The arrogant whore must like the attention her hair brought her or she'd cover it up or cut it off. Flaunting it, that's what she was doing. Flaunting.

Things must be pretty dire if MI-5 and Scotland Yard were letting girls play in their sandbox. Another woman, stealing a job away from a man. It wasn't fair, he thought, muscles bunching under his jaw. It just wasn't fair.

As she passed him, she looked at him directly. As if she could look right through him, despite the glasses. Disconcerted, he looked away, then tossed more crumbs to the birds, pitiful creatures with molting feathers who fought over the meager morsels.

But in his peripheral vision, he followed her movements. He waited, feeding the pigeons and biding his time. And when the whore left with Durgin and the other man, he rose, the collar of his coat hiding the ghost of a smile. *She could be my redheaded Mary Kelly, my last victim in tribute to Jack,* he decided, bringing his gloved finger back to his lips and worrying once again at the dried blood on the tip. *But later.*

Now it's time to hunt.

Hugh and Sarah left the Baker Street office to take the Tube to Waterloo, where they caught the train back to Brockenhurst. As the train pulled out from the station, heading south with a shrieking whistle and clouds of steam, Sarah sank back in her seat with a sigh of relief. The air inside was stuffy, but at least they had the carriage to themselves.

"Not a big fan of London?" Hugh asked, putting their suitcases in the overhead rack.

"Love London." Sarah smoothed her gloves and settled her handbag in her lap. "Adore London. But I just want to get on with it—whatever 'it' is." She was excited, a little scared, but altogether eager to begin whatever it was they'd been training for.

"Agreed. Remember how they'd say it in Scotland? *Jess get oan wea it!*"

"And I suppose we should now say, *Juste passer à autre chose!*"

It was an overcast afternoon, the grass green laced with snow, the sky heavy and leaden. Sarah and Hugh sat opposite each other on the worn seats and looked out silently as the train sped past fences and haystacks and horses munching away at rough patches of grass. Sarah struggled to open the dirty window to let in some fresh air. As Hugh reached over to help her, their hands touched and they both burst out laughing.

"There will always be an England. . . ." Hugh sang in a decent tenor.

Sarah poked his arm. "I was thinking that, too!"

The two smiled, then became solemn as they remembered what they had pledged to do for their country, what they might be called on to sacrifice. Even though they didn't know the particulars yet, there was no question their mission would be dangerous.

On and on the train sped, past glossy black crows on telephone lines and small villages where little boys ran alongside the carriages for as long as their legs could hold out, waving their caps gleefully at the passengers. Sarah and Hugh bought tea from a plump young girl with a heart-shaped locket around her neck, wheeling a cart. They drank it and shared a cheese and apple sandwich, then did the *Times* crossword puzzle together.

"So really," Sarah said, "how do you know Maggie?"

"We worked together." A shadow passed over Hugh's face. "A long time ago."

"Just work?"

"You're observant," he noted. "You'll make a good spy."

"Oh, ha ha—hilarious. But I notice you didn't answer my question."

"We were . . . involved . . . for a time, you might say." Hugh tugged at his Tattersall collar, as if it were suddenly too tight.

"And you ended it with her?"

"She ended it with me."

"And broke your heart. Are you over her?"

"Are we ever over the people we've loved?"

"End of the line!" the conductor bellowed as the train slowed and lurched into the Brockenhurst station, its whistle piercing the air. Hugh reached for Sarah's suitcase.

"I can get my bag," she said.

"No, really," he insisted, smiling, swinging it down easily. "I've got it."

Stepping off the train into the fresh country air, they were met on the platform by a man in a gray suit with a dark red tie and pocket square. "Ah! Mr. Philby!" Hugh called, recognizing the man who had recruited him.

"Hello, Hugh, good to see you again!" The man in the red tie raised a hand in greeting. "And it's Kim, remember? We don't stand on ceremony here." Walking closer, Kim Philby smiled. "And you must be Miss Sanderson."

She held out her hand. "Sarah."

He shook it, smiling warmly. "Welcome back to Beaulieu. The car's this way, please. And let me help you with those bags."

Philby drove them in his russet Lagonda through winding hills, passing cow pastures, braking frequently for wild ponies and donkeys meandering across the road. At one juncture, while a shaggy brown horse seemed to deliberate which way to go, he made a full stop in the middle of the road. "They rule the roads here, and they know it," Philby told Sarah and Hugh. "The land is theirs—we're all merely passing through."

"When I was here last, I learned to give them a wide berth," Sarah agreed, staring out the car's passenger window as a line of silvery gray donkeys with dark, limpid eyes and large ears passed by the car without so much as a sideways glance.

"Of course, they've been here for over a thousand years or thereabouts, so I suppose seniority does confer certain rights."

"They're quite handsome," Sarah remarked as Philby shifted the car into third gear, and they continued on their way in the slanting afternoon sunlight.

"They are, but they're wild creatures."

"I know—I tried to pet one of the donkeys once, and he nearly bit my hand off. So, you two know each other?" Sarah asked. "From London?"

Philby and Hugh exchanged a look. "Right, right—" said Sarah. " 'Ask me no questions, I'll tell you no lies.' "

"Indeed," Philby agreed, "as we all learn how 'to stoop to conquer.' " He pulled the car into the gravel drive of a thatched-roof cottage and stopped, turning off the engine. "Here we are! A regular chocolate box, isn't it?"

The house did look like something out of a storybook, with diamond-paned windows, thorny vines of climbing roses, whitewashed cob walls, and a red-brick chimney. A shaggy tan and cream pony nibbled on the grass of the front garden. The only indication of a military training camp nearby was the sound of Range Rovers backfiring and gunshots in the distance.

"I thought we'd be back at the dormitories?" Sarah asked.

"We've requisitioned lots of the houses around here. Most of the trainees stay in the big houses on the Beaulieu estate, as you did—but since you two will be working closely together, we thought we'd give you some privacy."

"Privacy? Why on earth would we need privacy?" Sarah's pumps crunched on the gravel driveway as she sidestepped a mound of horse excrement.

"Miss Lynd didn't tell you?" Philby grinned. "You're being sent over as a married couple."

Sarah and Hugh exchanged an astonished look.

"You didn't know? Well, you do now. Think of this as your honeymoon cottage." Philby winked at Hugh. "Of course, what goes on behind closed doors is up to you."

Chapter Five

The rest of the day and a night passed before Elise Hess woke.

When she did, she thought she might be in heaven.

She was warm.

No one was screaming at her, no dogs snarling at her.

She could think of—nothing.

In fact, words seemed to have left her completely. She looked around at what she would have, in another lifetime, called a bed, a pitcher, a glass. She knew the objects—the thing people sleep on, that which holds water, the thing we drink from—but the words wouldn't come. *Maybe I've died and I'm in eternity?* she thought. *Limbo?*

Or maybe I've lost my mind.

She considered her hands. They were mottled with bruises, the nails filthy and torn. Pain radiated from her shoulders.

She looked to the wall next to the narrow cot. The wood was scarred with initials, full names, and occasional phrases. *Eva, my child, you are 9 years old, who will tell you the truth? Try to grow up the way I hoped* was scratched in tiny letters and dated June 1939. A heart with initials and an arrow slashing through. A crooked single word: REVENGE.

Out the window, the sunrise was incandescent. In her other life, the one before camp, Elise had slept through sunrises or, if she was up, didn't take the time to notice their beauty. *We miss so much,* she thought, watching the sun change from red to rose to gold. *I have missed so much.*

The word came to her: *infirmary*. She was in the infirmary. The pressure of her bladder made her move. *Ach! The pain!* But she managed to stand on her bloody and swollen feet, and shuffle down the row of beds to the toilet she glimpsed through an open door. Afterward, she cleaned and washed herself the best she could, shoulders, arms, and hands burning with pain.

She shuffled back, blocking out the wails and moans of the other prisoners. Back at her cot, she eased her aching body down, and once again slipped out of consciousness.

Minutes passed, or maybe hours. A nurse came, a fellow political prisoner with a red triangle, who brought her food and helped her sit up. Elise tasted the first spoonful of lukewarm soup—turnip broth with a bruised potato floating to the top—and thought nothing could be more delicious.

She had swallowed one spoonful when one of the guards entered.

"Attention!" the guard called.

Elise knew her—Hilda Jaeger. In reality, she was quite an average-looking middle-aged woman, with tightly braided light hair, the black buttons of her gray uniform straining against her ever-increasing bulk. But in the eyes of the prisoners, her actions had transformed her into a creature neither human nor animal, more like a she-devil in a painting by Hieronymus Bosch.

"25487! You will come with me!" Jaeger commanded. *"Now!"*

It took Elise a moment to remember her number. Jaeger was calling *her*. She handed her soup to the prisoner next to her, who bolted it ravenously. Next to her cot were her cap, coat, and clogs. She reached for them.

"Schnell!" Jaeger roared. Rage mottled her complexion.

Elise walked, stumbled, and slid with Jaeger out of the infirmary down icy paths, to Ravensbrück's administration building. It was an innocuous-looking yellow-brick structure. Nothing about it betrayed its true purpose.

Himmler and his cronies had worked out the ratio of the cost of keeping a slave alive to profit off her labor—to keep her working as long as possible, and then to liquidate her as cheaply as possible, chiefly through the principle of "extermination through labor"—working all the prisoners to death. The profit motive drove everything. When the mathematical equation proved it cost more to house and feed a slave than the worth of the work she produced, the worker was killed.

But each woman was ostensibly at Ravensbrück for a specific "crime." Elise, along with the other political prisoners, wore a red triangle sewn onto her jacket, above her number. So-called race defilers wore red triangles with black borders. Common criminals wore green. Homosexuals, pink; Jehovah's Witnesses, violet. The Gypsies wore brown. All others wore one yellow. Jews wore two yellow triangles, making a facsimile of the Star of David.

Of course, categories overlapped, so a Jewish woman who'd fought for the French Resistance wore both a yellow triangle and a red. A prostitute who spied for the German Resistance wore a green triangle and a red. "It's easier in America, with the colored people," the woman overseeing her sewing on her own red patch had said. "With their black skin, they don't need anything else, the way we do here. Although I pride myself on the fact I can always spot a Jew."

Now, Elise's curiosity finally overcame her fear. "What's this about?" she managed to ask Jaeger, taking off her shoes and shuffling barefoot on the icy path to keep up. "Where are you taking me?"

"Don't you know?" The guard laughed, a humorless yap. "You're to see the Commandant."

Everything had still seemed distant and removed to Elise, but that word, *Commandant,* brought her back to reality with a blow.

Jens Foth, the Commandant of Ravensbrück, was infamous, even among the thugs and villains he'd hired for guard duty. Under Foth's rule, canings were distributed arbitrarily. He liked to hear the prisoners howl. "Start screaming, you pig!" he'd cry, often making another prisoner—usually a friend—beat one of her own. But often the prisoner being beaten stayed mute—at least as long as possible. Self-control was the only form of rebellion.

As they walked up the slippery steps to the main building, Elise wondered if she'd have been better off dying on the cross.

Inside Commandant Foth's office, it was excessively warm, a fire burning red in a cast-iron stove across from his massive desk. In a place of honor was the ubiquitous official framed photograph of Hitler.

Elise's heart was beating wildly. She knew what it meant to be sent away. To be "transported"—sent to Auschwitz or one of the other camps, where no one was ever heard from again. But why was she here in the office then? The Commandant must have another fate in mind for her. What would they do to her first?

"How much money do you have?" Foth barked at Elise without preamble. He was an older man, with silver-gray hair and a chin as wide as his forehead. His once-trim figure had run to fat, and a hunch ruined what must have once been impeccable posture. There was an open bottle of schnapps on his desk, and the office reeked of alcohol.

Elise stared at him, shock freezing her tongue.

"How. Much. Money," he repeated, his chewed fingernails starting to tap in agitation. "Do. You. Have?"

She thought back to the wallet she'd surrendered when she first arrived. "Thirty marks," she replied. "Sir."

"Is it enough to get to Berlin?"

Berlin? Go to Berlin? "Yes," Elise managed, bewildered. Berlin? The city was as real as a kingdom in a fairy tale. "Yes, sir, it is."

Foth grunted, then thrust a form at her. Bold black letters spelled out: RELEASE.

The letters danced in front of her eyes, tantalizing her with their elusive meaning.

Then Foth snatched the paper back, slashed RELEASE with a black pen, and wrote below, 9 DAYS LEAVE.

Elise stared at the piece of paper. The letters seemed to float. She couldn't recall the meaning of the number 9, or the words *release* or *leave*. They were black squiggles on white paper.

"Well, what are you waiting for, Fräulein Hess? Don't you want to go?"

All Elise could comprehend was, for the first time in months, she was being called her name once again. A name, instead of a number. It sounded almost indecently intimate coming from his lips.

Foth turned to Frau Jaeger with a sneer. "Look, she wants to stay! I'm sure we can accommodate that. . . ." The two sniggered.

But Elise had grabbed at the paper. To be warm, to eat, to sleep in a bed. To go to church and receive the Blessed Sacrament. No more endless roll call in the freezing darkness, no more barking and biting dogs, no more screamed abuse . . .

Foth put his palms together. "Elise Hess, you are released." Then, "Well, get ready! *Schnell!* In ten minutes, I want you out of here! Take her! Get her cleaned up!"

Frau Jaeger led Elise to the warehouse where all the prisoners' clothing was stored, sorted, and meticulously labeled. When Elise saw her old clothes—her underthings, a floral linen dress and cotton sweater and high-heeled sandals—she thought once again she was in a dream. She remembered them, and yet did not—so much had happened since the summer and it seemed so long ago—although in reality it had been less than a year since she'd arrived at Ravensbrück.

Her fingers fumbled with the buttons on her uniform, but they were too swollen, too bruised. When Frau Jaeger saw, she helped Elise undress, as though she were now a small child instead of a prisoner. Elise stood very still, frightened by the change in Frau Jaeger's demeanor. The summer dress, once tight, hung off her gaunt frame.

"Before the war, my parents took me to Berlin," Frau Jaeger said in a kind, low voice. She was hunting for something—and procured a silk scarf with a smile, the like of which Elise had never seen from her before. "This will cover your head until your hair grows out," she added. "And here's a pair of thick tights. And a wool coat."

"Thank you," Elise responded, accepting the items, trying not to imagine what had happened to their former owner.

Frau Jaeger continued to help her dress, as if she were a doll. Not gentle, but not rough, either. "We lived in Dortmund," she prattled, "but my family and I went to the opera in Berlin once, when I was thirteen. Such a grand occasion!" She paused, savoring the memory. "We saw your mother in the role of Isolde—oh, she was so beautiful! And your father conducted. So romantic!"

Elise didn't know what to say. She managed "Oh."

It was impossible for her to put her old shoes on—not only

were they strappy sandals but her feet were too swollen for them to fit.

And so Frau Jaeger found her large-size men's bedroom slippers, which would have to do. "When I heard the famous opera star Clara Hess was your mother, you can bet I wrote and told everyone in my family!" Frau Jaeger eased Elise's feet into the black slippers. "They were impressed, let me tell you."

"Oh."

Frau Jaeger's face fell. "I was so sorry to hear of her death."

"What?"

"Don't you know? She died, from wounds she received while protecting Germans on a train to Switzerland. Your mother is a national hero. That's why you're being released—to attend the memorial service."

Elise was silent. She'd wondered what happened to Clara on the train they'd all taken—she, Clara, and her father—from Berlin to Zurich, and now her suspicions were confirmed. Clara was dead.

"I'm sorry." Frau Jaeger's brows were knit with concern. "I thought you knew. I thought they'd told you."

"It's all right," Elise assured her, although she felt nothing inside. *How odd, to be comforting this Nazi creature when it's my mother who has died.* "Really—it's fine." And, for the moment, it was. She was too numb to take the thought in.

Frau Jaeger blinked back tears and sniffed. "Now we must go back. There are many forms for you to sign."

Back at the camp's main office, Elise struggled to write with her damaged hand. One of the forms she signed stated, *The released inmate is never allowed to talk about camp life, the setup of the camp, camp punishments, and other events.* Frau Jaeger was happy to explain: "If we discover you've said or written anything about the events in the camp, you will be immediately transported back by the Gestapo and receive fifty to a hundred lashes. You wouldn't want that, would you?

"In Berlin, you will be able to attend the memorial service planned for your mother. You will also go to the office of the Gestapo. There, you will sign official documents to denounce Father Licht and exonerate the doctors of Charité Mitte, including Dr. Brandt."

Like hell I will, Elise thought.

The last form she signed stated she *had been released from the camp in good health* and would lay *claims of no kind upon the state in regard to possible future sicknesses.* As a trained nurse, she knew all too well the damage her body had suffered, and what it boded for her health in the future—should she even live to see the future. But she signed the paper anyway.

In the office, Elise saw another political prisoner, not more than thirty, as tangible as a ghost. The two exchanged glances for a brief moment, but didn't dare speak. The other woman gave the slightest nod.

Elise smiled back.

And then, in less than ten minutes' time, Elise found herself being walked by Frau Jaeger to Ravensbrück's high guarded gates. There, Frau Jaeger exchanged a few words with the SS guard on duty. "I'll take you to the station," she informed Elise.

Elise wanted nothing more than to walk alone, and certainly not to be accompanied by the guard—but she acquiesced, mute. Frau Jaeger began walking, and Elise followed, the borrowed black slippers sliding through the slippery white snowflakes. She had a suitcase of the things she'd arrived with in one hand and her papers in the other. She was leaving.

Alsatian dogs barked as they went through the black metal gates, and Elise let out a soft sigh of relief as they finally left the sinister walls. As she walked behind Frau Jaeger, she saw, on the other side of the road, beautiful houses, gardens, and even two chubby little children playing and laughing in the snow.

One, a boy about seven, ran up to the chain-link fence to stare at her. Elise tried her best to smile, her dry lips cracking in the cold. She was aware that her bald head, even under the scarf, marked her as a prisoner. *What do they know about us? What do any of them know? They're so close, and yet a universe away.*

She and the young boy locked eyes, blue to gray. Even in her time at the camp, she had never seen such a vicious glint, such a brutal expression. The boy bent down and scooped up a stone.

He threw it.

It struck her on the face, hard, causing her to flinch and take a step back.

Elise raised one hand to her face, a red mark already blooming on her pale skin. As the boy ran off, she stood still, watching. She'd become accustomed to random cruelty during her time at Ravensbrück, but it was still startling to see it from a mere child.

"Schnell!" Frau Jaeger ordered, seeing only that Elise had stopped. Then, in a milder tone, realizing she wasn't talking to a number anymore, but Fräulein Elise Hess: "Come, please. You don't want to miss your train."

Elise looked wide-eyed at everything as they trod over the slithery snow to the station. She'd never seen it; she'd come to Ravensbrück in a van with black-painted windows.

On the platform, people stared at them—such an unlikely couple, a prison guard in her gray uniform and a former prisoner. The train arrived in a cloud of steam and a shriek of brakes. "Here," an older woman urged, pressing bread and butter wrapped in a coarse cloth into Elise's hand. Elise gasped at the woman, speechless, as she disappeared into one of the cars.

Frau Jaeger raised an eyebrow but decided to ignore the transaction. Instead she asked, "Now, do you know where you're going in Berlin?"

"I still know where I live," Elise stated flatly.

"No." Frau Jaeger pulled out even more papers. "Your family's home in Grunewald has been requisitioned and taken over for official Party business. You will be joining your father, who has been set up in the Adlon Hotel. The address is here."

Elise knew the hotel, a short distance from the Brandenburg Gate. "Thank you," she managed.

Frau Jaeger's face turned red, and she spoke quickly. "Would you mind very much inscribing something in my album?" she asked, pulling out a small leather notebook. "Just a few lines? In remembrance of our meeting?"

Is the woman mad? Elise could not process the request. Once again, reality seemed to float away and she tried hard to remember names for things before they left her. *Book, pen, guard,* she made herself think.

Frau Jaeger continued, "For instance, a few lines from the *Liebestod,* in the last act of *Tristan and Isolde?* It's just—your mother was so wonderful. I have such fond memories of her."

Elise wrote as though it were someone else performing the task:

Do you not see?
How he shines
Ever brighter.

Star-haloed
Rising higher
Do you not see?

Then she wrote, underneath, *Tristan and Isolde by Richard Wagner*. And then, *Clara Hess, soprano*. Under her mother's name, she added her own: *Elise Hess*. She handed the book back to Frau Jaeger, who took it with a shy smile.

"Good luck, Fräulein," the guard said, as Elise struggled with her suitcase up the steps of the train car.

"Frau Jaeger—" Elise tried to decide what to say. So many things went through her brain, from profanity to prayers.

Then, finally, she called back, "There's no need of luck where there's faith."

Freedom.

Elise nearly fell onto one of the worn upholstered seats. *What a feeling! Life! Vita nuova!*

With a screech and snorts of steam, the train pulled away from the station. Elise, grateful to sit on soft cushions, gazed out the window. The sky was the purest blue, and not even a gentle breeze stirred the naked branches. This was Germany, forests and lakes and ancient trees, as it could have looked during any period of history. *Germany's story is long,* she thought. *I pray this is but a short black mark on the totality of it, not the end. . . .*

Up in the clouds, Elise glimpsed a bird, a crane. Now it soared above a lake, then over the forest, flapping its wings, flying higher, faster. *Birds have the most precious gift in the world—freedom!* Her eyes tracked its flight. *All of the wretched people, robbed of their freedom in prisons, penitentiaries, and concentration camps, envy you, little bird. I'm ecstatic to be free—and grieving for my fellow prisoners, whom I left behind in hell.*

She closed her eyes and recited the Lord's Prayer. That is, until she reached the line *As we forgive those who trespass against us.*

The words stuck in Elise's throat.

To forgive those who trespass against us—unimaginable.

To forgive was an impossibility. Elise couldn't lie to herself or to her God, and so she was silent during that line.

Chapter Six

"We always go to the loveliest places, Mark," Maggie deadpanned as they hurried into the Paddington Mortuary, following in DCI Durgin's long-legged wake.

Durgin didn't stop his mad pace to sign in at the front desk; he merely glared at the elderly guard on duty from beneath his eyebrows.

"We're, ah, with *him*," Maggie told the half-asleep guard, a bald man with a barrel-shaped chest, who blinked heavy-lidded eyes at them before settling back into his reverie.

They trailed Durgin down a cement staircase to the building's chilly basement, then down a long gray linoleum hall until they reached the morgue. "*'Abandon all hope . . . '*Well, you posh types know the rest," the detective muttered, holding the thick metal door open for Maggie and Mark.

Inside was a white-tiled room illuminated by fluorescent pendant lights, a room even colder than the hall. The floor was concrete, with a drain in the middle. A porcelain sink stood in one corner, while a human skeleton posed in another. On various shelves were scales, glass jars of organs, and containers of swabs and cotton balls.

A short, round man was working on a body, whistling the melody to "Heart and Soul." Despite his small stature, his nose was long, his ears were long, and his eyes were wide, red, and drooping, giving the impression of an old hound dog. "Hmph," he snorted, hands deep inside the abdomen of a dead body. "Imagine meeting *you* here."

"Ah, Collins—light of my life." Durgin spread his arms wide in abject surrender. "And where else would I be? I can't seem to tear myself away from you and your odiferous basement."

"You likes me for my corpses is all." Collins flicked his eyes to Maggie and Mark. "Who're they?"

"MI-Five," Durgin replied, seating himself in a rolling chair. He pushed with his feet to glide across the rough floor, ending up next to Collins. He looked back to Maggie and Mark and gestured. "Mr. Standish and Miss Hope, this is Mr. Alfred Collins—best coroner in the business."

Collins pulled out bloody gloved hands from the corpse. "Forgive me if I don't shake." He gave Mark the once-over, then looked to Maggie. His eyes lingered on her figure. "You don't look like no agent I've ever met."

"Perhaps, Mr. Collins," Maggie proffered, "you might try expanding your horizons."

They locked eyes for a moment, then all turned to the body. Maggie did her best not to gasp.

It lay on a white enamel autopsy table, nearly obscuring the drain grooves, which led to a circular hole drilled between the ankles for fluids. Next to the table was a steel tray, and on it was a leather instrument kit, lined in velvet, the ivory-handled instruments glinting in the overhead light.

Durgin stood and made the sign of the cross, then removed his magnifying glass from his jacket's breast pocket and leaned in to peer at the corpse. "So, what do we have here?"

"Arrived just before you did—a Miss Doreen Leighton." Collins jabbed a bloody thumb at a sheet-draped body on a table next to the one he was working on. "But here's your first. Joanna Metcalf."

Maggie cleared her throat. "Think it could be the work of a butcher?"

"Maybe," Collins admitted. "Look here—cut all the way to the bone."

Durgin turned his penetrating gaze to the body. "He certainly knows his way around the human body."

"Any thoughts as to the weapon?" Mark asked.

Collins shrugged. "These cuts were all made with something extremely sharp—but it's hard to know exactly what—hunting knife, a shoemaker's knife, penknife, stiletto. . . . But the cuts themselves are assured, confident. Our killer's got style, the bastard does."

"Long blade or short?" Mark asked.

"Can't tell. Human flesh is soft—it keeps its secrets."

"What's this?" Maggie asked, going to a muslin bag on the counter.

"Her clothes," Collins said. "Smell them."

Maggie braced herself, then took a whiff. There was a strange smell, like a dentist's office or an operating theater. "Nitrous oxide?"

"That—or ether or chloroform."

"So"—Maggie pondered—"since she shows no signs of a struggle, it's possible she was drugged, then killed. And then her body was moved."

Durgin looked up, his blue-gray eye through the magnifying glass huge, almost surreal. "Not a bad hypothesis."

No call for sarcasm, Detective.

Collins moved on to the body of the most recent victim, pulling off the sheet.

Durgin drummed his fingers on the table. "Well?"

An explosive exhale. "Jesus Christ."

"Any fibers or hairs?"

"No. She's clean. But—" Collins crooked a finger at Maggie; she approached warily. "Give 'er a sniff."

Maggie mustered every ounce of self-control she had and forced herself to inhale. Beyond the coppery smell of blood, there was also the odor of gas. "It smells the same as Joanna Metcalf's clothes. Some kind of drug?"

"I'm wagering yes."

"I'll check to see if she has family, then, if not, cross-check missing persons and SOE to identify the body, as well," Maggie added. *Our Jack is playing a game with us.* She thought of her nightmare. *You want to play? All right, then, Jack—let's go.*

"Excuse me, Detective!" The police officer who appeared at the door was at least seventy, an enormous belly protruding over his leather belt. He struggled to catch his breath. "They found . . . a man with a white . . . van!" he panted. "Fits the description and there's . . . blood on his clothes! He's been . . . taken into custody!"

Durgin gave a wolfish grin. "Good job." He glanced at Mark. "Let's go—holding cell's on the second floor."

He squinted at Maggie. "Don't you have tea with the Queen to go to? Crumpets and jam? Scones with marmalade?" He tapped absently at his chin, now sporting a dark shadow. "You look like the sort of girl who likes marmalade."

"I *do* like marmalade," Maggie answered evenly, "but only when this case is over. Detective Durgin, I want to catch this monster as much as you do. Maybe even more."

He trained his hooded eyes on her. "More? And why is that, Miss Hope?"

Maggie raised her chin. "The victims are all women, all young, all working for SOE. Let's just say for some of us—for me—it's personal."

He gave her a long look, then began walking. "Chunky or fine?" he tossed back over his shoulder.

"What?" Maggie asked, rushing to keep in step as he started his lope, leaving Mark to find an elevator.

"Marmalade. How do you like it?"

"Chunky," she replied, catching up with him.

"Bitter or sweet?"

She matched him, step for step. "Bitter. Dark and bitter, Detective Chief Inspector."

Mark had caught up by the time they reached the second floor. Outside the large taped windows, the wind had picked up and the snow was beginning to fall in earnest.

"I'm going in alone," Durgin announced.

"Detective," Mark said as a flunky handed Durgin a file. "I don't know if you realize this, but I've been catching domestic terrorists—IRA as well as Nazi—for years. And it's also how Miss Hope started off in this crazy business. The details of her most recent cases are classified to the likes of me, but I wager she's seen more action than you could ever imagine."

Durgin paged through the file, eyebrows drawn together. "Mr. Standish, Miss Hope." He made an astonishingly graceful courtly bow. "I don't want a woman in there. That is all." He turned to enter the interrogation room.

"What?" Maggie called after him. "This is my case too!"

"Sorry, Miss Tiger, no skirts allowed. You"—he jabbed his chin toward Mark—"if you insist, you may sit in."

"I want to show you something." Maggie began to pull her blouse out of her skirt's waistband.

Durgin drew himself up to his full height, looking aghast. "Miss Hope—that's neither appropriate *nor* necessary."

Maggie didn't stop until she'd uncovered her ribs. "See this scar?" she hissed, pointing to the still-raw bullet gash on her side.

Durgin's eyes were steely. "Hard to miss."

"I lived through that." She dropped her blouse and tucked it back in.

"And what happened to the person who shot you?"

Maggie met his eyes. "I killed him. He's dead." It was a simple statement of fact. "I'd like you both to keep that in mind as we conduct this inquiry. I have strengths and experience you may not anticipate. Don't make assumptions."

"She's good on a motorcycle, too, Detective, if it comes to it. Can make those big jumps." Mark made a soaring movement with his fingers, whistling through his teeth.

"Here's what's going to happen," Durgin stated, unsmiling. "I'm going to take Standish in with me—and you, Miss Tiger, will remain outside."

"But—"

"I do not doubt your expertise, Miss Hope, but I know men like this. And all my hard-won knowledge informs me he'll be more forthcoming without a lady present. That's my experience of more than twenty years. It's not personal—just my ken. Now, are you going to make this about the case? Or are you going to make it all about you?"

"Fine," Maggie muttered. "Have it your way."

"But, please, watch through the one-way mirror. And listen." Maggie got the distinct feeling Durgin wasn't the sort of man who said *please* often. "I want to hear what you think when we're done."

"Of course."

As Durgin took a seat and Mark entered the room, the Detective Chief Inspector told the MI-5 agent, "And when we're in there, take my lead. We're doing this *my* way."

The interview room was small, with a scratched wooden table and three dented metal folding chairs. Durgin and Mark both sat on one side.

They waited as two officers led in a large man with his hands cuffed behind him. The suspect had sloping shoulders, a shiny, bald head, and a prominent Roman nose. His shirtsleeves were rolled up, revealing forearms with protruding veins. He slumped into the chair on the opposite side, appraising the two men through slit eyes. The police officers departed, leaving behind a folder and a pen. From behind the thick mirrored glass, Maggie watched.

"I'm Detective Chief Inspector Durgin and this is MI-Five Agent Standish. Please state your name and your date of birth."

"Billy Fishman," the man said in a low rumble. "Born six of February, eighteen ninety-nine."

"Where were you last night, Mr. Fishman?" Mark asked, as he leafed through the file.

There was only silence and the creak of the chairs. It was cold in the room and Mark's nose began to drip. He pulled out a hand-kerchief and blew hard.

Detective Durgin took the file from him and flipped through it, pen in hand. "We have a witness who says she saw you coming out of Regent's Park at one A.M. She said you got into a van. Mr. Fishman, what were you doing in Regent's Park in the dead of night?"

Fishman looked straight into the mirrored window with flat, expressionless eyes; Maggie could feel her skin crawl. "I was takin' a piss."

"When you were arrested," Durgin continued, still looking at the file, "our officer reports you had blood on your hands. Underneath your fingernails."

Fishman glared. "I work with meat."

"What do you do?" Mark asked. "Are you a butcher?"

"No," the man snapped. "I transport the meat from the slaughterhouses to the shops. That's why I got me a van."

Durgin finally looked up. "Do you often urinate in Regent's Park?"

The man shrugged powerful shoulders. "Sometimes."

"And where did you go exactly?"

"I dunno. The Queen Mary Garden, maybe."

"Ah," Durgin mused, as though trying to picture it. "You stopped your van, and you went all the way into the park, at night, to take a piss in the Queen Mary Garden? May I ask why the wall wasn't good enough for you?"

Silence.

Mark leaned in. "A girl was murdered and her body was dumped in the park last night. What do you know about it?"

"Nothing! I don't know nothing about no girl!"

"Wait—who *do* you know, then?" Durgin appraised him from beneath his eyebrows. "Come on, tell the truth and shame the devil."

Agitated now, Fishman shook his head. "Can't tell you—but I didn't kill no girl. Didn't even *see* no girl."

Durgin rose, walked to the door, and opened it. "Guards!" he thundered.

Fishman's heavy-lidded eyes widened. "Wait!"

The detective waved the guards off. He closed the door, turning back to the suspect.

Fishman looked down at the metal table. "There weren't no girl—but there was a—well, a man."

Durgin leaned back against the wall, waiting. He folded his arms theatrically.

"Men—men like me—we go in the park at night. Hoping to . . . you know . . . find a bloke." Fishman glared up at them. "You gonna arrest me now?"

"Who's the bloke?" Mark asked impassively, making notes.

"Hell if I know! We didn't exactly go courtin'."

"What did this man you met look like?"

"Small—'bout five foot six, thin, posh. Maybe sixty. Wearing a real nice coat. Tweed. A toff."

Durgin banged on the door. "Let him go," he ordered the guards. "And check out his story about meeting up with a man—small, thin, upper-crust."

"Are you going to arrest *him*?" Fishman grumbled. "You never arrest the posh fellas."

"We'll bring him in for questioning, too. Unlike most of my fellow officers, I don't give a damn what you do, or when, or with whom. But I do care about murder." Durgin locked eyes with the manacled man. "And if you're holding anything back about that, I swear to you, there's going to be hell to pay."

Philby, Sarah, and Hugh entered the tiny cottage, Hugh ducking to get through the front door. The main room had a low ceiling with rough-hewn beams, an open stone fireplace, worn but clean wide-plank floors covered with colorful braided rugs, and plain, sturdy furniture. A few framed pictures and a shelf of books gave the place a homey air.

"There's a bedroom upstairs," Philby explained.

"I'll sleep on the sofa down here," Hugh said, while Sarah suppressed a smile.

"Let's sit down first," Philby suggested, and they did, in over-stuffed armchairs. "Your new identities." He opened his briefcase and handed each agent a thick file. "I want you to memorize these and then burn them." Philby looked first to Hugh, speaking in perfect French, "From now on, you will be known as Hubert Taillier. And you will speak only French."

He fixed his eyes on Sarah. "And your new identity is Sabine Severin."

"Yes, sir," she replied in Parisian-accented French.

Philby contemplated the duo. "Hubert Taillier and Sabine Severin," he intoned, "I now pronounce you man and wife."

Sarah and Hugh gave each other shy smiles.

"Let me clarify," Philby stated. "Your mission is to go to Paris. You will pose as a married couple. We've been working on your cover story for quite some time. Madame Severin—yes, you use your stage name, not your married name—you are a French ballerina who's been dancing in Monte Carlo. There will be an opening at the Paris Opéra Ballet, and you will join the company."

"There will 'happen' to be an opening?" Sarah asked.

Philby raised a hand. "Let us worry about that part. And Monsieur Taillier—you are Madame's husband, a cellist, exempt from military service because of a heart defect. You will play the cello in the Opéra's orchestra. You are both noted Nazi sympathizers."

"But the dance world is small." Sarah knit her brows. "Whether it's Britain or France. They'd know us, know of us—at least by reputation."

Hugh nodded. "The music world is small, too. If we're supposed to be good enough to perform with the Paris Opéra Ballet, they would at least have heard of us already."

"We're taking care of this. Our contact at the Opéra is Émile Charron. He's been talking you both up to the artistic directors and the management. We've created some false newspaper reviews of your performances from Monte Carlo, so he can show them your photographs and your reviews. We'll take care of all the details."

"Except—I haven't been practicing," Sarah admitted. "I haven't been dancing. Running, jumping, shooting, throwing hand grenades, yes—ballet, no."

Philby leaned back in his chair and eyed her. "Isn't it like riding a bicycle?"

"There's a saying in ballet—Miss one class, you know. Miss two classes, your fellow dancers know. Miss three classes, the audience knows." She sighed. "And I have missed months and *months* of class."

Hugh looked down at his hands. "And I haven't played the cello seriously in years."

Philby quirked an eyebrow. "Then I suggest you both get to work."

As Hugh blanched, Sarah asked, "And, once we're there, in Paris?"

"We will let you know your mission when we're sure you're going. Oh, and there's one more thing."

They waited.

"Remember, you're a married couple—you're going to have to practice relating as man and wife as well. You must be convincing."

Sarah and Hugh looked to each other, then both dropped their eyes. Hugh flushed.

"How much time do we have?" Sarah asked.

"We'll let you know," Philby replied, handing Hugh a heavy iron key. "In the meantime, I'll let you two lovebirds settle in."

———

Elise reached Berlin, the train's brakes screeching and steam hissing. It was still daylight, and weak winter sun shone through the arched glass skylights of the terminal's roof.

Elise summoned every shred of her remaining strength, took her suitcase, and walked from the train to the platform. Swarming everywhere were men in uniform, infinite variations on brown, gray, and black. The crumpled front page of the *Völkischer Beobachter* blew by; if her feet hadn't hurt so much, she would have stomped on it.

Outside, she made her way to the S-Bahn. A long black Opel Admiral, with curving fenders, chrome headlights, and stiff Nazi flags on the hood glided in front of her, blocking her path. The passenger door opened, and a man in a black SS uniform got out. He was young, certainly not older than thirty, with light brown hair, hazel eyes, and the short but powerful build of a wrestler. He was carrying a bouquet of forced narcissus blooms.

Elise tried to step around him.

To her astonishment, he snapped the heels of his polished black leather boots together and bowed. "Fräulein Hess? Fräulein Elise Hess?"

Elise was wary. ". . . Yes."

"My name is Captain Alexander Fausten," he told her, trying to hand her the flowers. "I am to be your liaison here in Berlin. I am to escort you to the Adlon Hotel, where your father is waiting for you."

Else waved away the blooms. She wanted nothing from anyone in a Nazi uniform. And she certainly didn't want to get into a Nazi car. Where would it take her? What horrors awaited? She clenched her jaw and started to walk. "I can get there myself, thank you."

He stepped in front of her. "Please, Fräulein, get in the car." His face was serious, but not cruel.

"No." Elise walked past him, through the dirty slush around the car. The cold wet seeped into her slippers. Her feet burned.

He followed with long steps. "Fräulein Hess, if you don't come with me"—he stepped ahead of her and into her way once again—"I'm afraid my superiors will send me to Russia. And I hear it's very cold there, this winter." He gave a winning grin. "You wouldn't want my frostbitten toes on your conscience, would you?"

As if I care.

But she was exhausted. Her feet were numb. Was there any use in arguing? She was in Berlin. She turned and limped back to the car.

He savored his victory with a smile, then took the suitcase from her hand.

Elise gasped with pain as the weight was removed. Fausten looked down at her hands, and his face paled. "I'll have a doctor come and look at you."

"No!" Elise wanted nothing to do with Nazi doctors. Then, in a softer tone, "No, thank you. I'm a nurse. I can take care of myself."

The driver opened the trunk. Fausten put in the suitcase, along with the flowers, then turned back to Elise.

"You'll see—this is much nicer than the S-Bahn," he said, motioning her inside, where it smelled like leather and pipe tobacco. When they were settled in the luxurious, plush warmth, the driver pulled away.

Elise had a moment of panic as she looked out the window. No one on the streets bothered to look up, let alone meet her gaze. *Anything could happen in here,* she realized. *Of course, anything could happen out there, too—and no one would lift a finger, either.*

"Welcome back to Berlin, Fräulein Hess. You will meet with

me tomorrow, nine A.M., at the Gestapo headquarters." It was not a request. "There is paperwork to be done."

Elise stared straight ahead. In front of her, the driver's thick neck looked like a raw red sausage. "My paperwork is in order, Captain Fausten."

He smiled once again. "I'm afraid I must insist."

Elise closed her eyes and gave a quiet sigh.

The sleek black car drove through Berlin, past grim-faced pedestrians who hid their eyes under hats and huddled into their coats, stalled cars giving off noxious exhaust fumes, rusty bicycles, and the occasional horse-drawn cart. It was, perhaps, not the most beautiful city in the world, especially now—but it was hers.

But Berlin had altered since she'd seen it last. In only a few months, old men were selling matchsticks on street corners. Gaunt women were searching the gutters for cigarette butts. In the Tiergarten, covered in dirty snow, shanties made from cardboard boxes shivered in the icy wind. Sullen women with too much makeup and hollow-eyed young boys beckoned from windows and alleys.

There was fear, too—Elise could smell it, metallic. It hung in the air like poisonous gas. No one met anyone else's gaze. Everyone walked as fast as he could. They all practiced the "Berlin look"—glancing to check each way before they entered and exited their apartment buildings.

They drove down Pariser Platz and under the Brandenburg Gate, covered in red Nazi flags and crowned by the triumphant Quadriga sculpture, which looked to Elise more like the Four Horsemen of the Apocalypse than the symbol of victory. As the Opel pulled up to the Adlon, a doorman in gold epaulets and white gloves opened the door. Another went to retrieve Elise's suitcase.

Fausten put a hand on Elise's arm. She started at the touch. "Fräulein Hess, I have read your files. I can see you're a good girl," he said. "A good German. An Aryan woman of the finest blood. I will do everything I can to help you."

Elise shook him off and got out of the car, waiting for the driver to bring her suitcase. Without warning, two Brownshirts in an alley across the street forced an old man into the back of an unmarked car behind them, its exhaust pipe choking out thick smoke as it sped away.

She stared at Fausten, who had rolled down the car window. "And I will pray for you," she told him.

Now the smile was gone. "Tomorrow. Nine A.M. Don't be late."

Elise passed through the entrance of the hotel and into the lobby, a bellhop following with her suitcase. It was like entering a dreamworld. With its palm court, fountain, and leather club chairs, the marble space was soaring and grand. Huge cut-glass vases of red roses and edelweiss—known to be the Führer's favorite flowers—adorned every gleaming surface. A harpist in the corner played over the genteel murmurings of the staff and guests.

Her father stood waiting for her in the petal-scented lobby. "*Engel,*" Miles Hess cried, opening his arms, oblivious to the stares of the other patrons.

Elise ran to him. "Papa," she gasped, burrowing her shorn head into his chest.

"Not too fast, *Engel,*" Miles Hess warned as she inhaled cheeses, meats, seeded bread with honey, and hard-boiled eggs. Elise hunched over, eating with her hands, like an animal.

Her father stared, then looked away. "Slowly, darling. I don't want you to get sick."

"I don't care," Elise mumbled through a swig of hot coffee—

real coffee—still chewing. "I don't think I'll ever be full again." She smeared bread with gooseberry jam before stuffing it into her mouth. She wrapped up all the food left in her napkin and hid it on her lap under the table when she was done. Her father pretended not to notice.

"I still can't get over how you look. . . ."

"I heard about Mutti." She took a gulp of coffee. "They told me at the camp."

Miles sat down next to her. Gently, he asked, "What did they tell you?"

"That she was killed defending the glory and honor of Nazi Germany." Elise gave a twisted smile. "My mother died a 'hero.'"

"Your mother . . ." Miles began. Then he put up one hand. "Wait."

He rose and walked over to a table with a Victrola and selected a record—a version of Mozart's *Don Giovanni* he himself had conducted. He turned up the volume, then came back to the table. He whispered into her ear, "Your mother isn't dead."

"What?" Elise's brain began to spin. She knew her mother had disappeared in the chaos, along with her half sister.

Miles put a finger to his lips to silence her. "She turned herself over to the British authorities. She's probably working with them as we speak, providing them with information only she knows from the Abwehr."

Elise tried to follow what her father was saying, but she was tired, she was so weary. . . . Once again the objects around her seemed unreal. *Bread*, she reminded herself of the words. *Knife. Cup.*

"Of course, the official Party line is she died in a great act of patriotism. We will, at some point, need to be photographed leaving flowers on her grave at Friedhof Heerstraße, in order to keep up the charade."

"But Mutti was a Nazi—she, she believed in all of their insanity!"

Miles gave her a warning look. Elise realized he was cautioning her—even with the loud music, the hotel suite was surely bugged. She needed to be extremely careful of what she said.

"And Margareta? Margaret Hope? My half sister?" Elise managed. She had not forgotten how she'd witnessed Maggie shooting the young German guard. And Maggie's using her and her connections for whatever undercover British mission she was on. Maggie had lied to her. All the while pretending to be her friend.

"She's back in Britain as well, as far as I know."

"I see." Elise felt nothing but disgust for her half sister.

"There will be a memorial service. We both must be there."

Elise tried to picture her mother in London, working against the Nazis, and came up blank.

"And you?" Elise looked around her. The suite was sumptuous. "You seem to be doing well."

"Well, they seized the house in Grunewald—for the Party's use, of course—but put me up here." Miles attempted a smile. "It's still advantageous to be a famous conductor. They can't kill me so easily or have me 'disappear' without an explanation. So they have created the public image of me as a bereaved widower, mourning for my beautiful patriot wife, who sacrificed herself in the line of duty. I bury my sorrow by conducting Wagner for Hitler.

"But let's concentrate on the good," Miles urged, taking Elise's thin hand and pressing it to his lips. "I have my beloved daughter back."

"For now."

"What do you mean?"

"This isn't a release—I'm on a nine-day leave."

"What?" Miles was incensed. "A leave? That is not my arrangement with Himmler—"

"I need to report to Gestapo headquarters at nine tomorrow," Elise told him, her voice low and even. "I believe my permanent release is contingent on my disavowing Father Licht, and recanting all the things we said publicly about the murder of children—the so-called compassionate death program."

"Which you will, of course. You will do exactly what you need to, in order to stay out of that place." Miles stared into his daughter's face, eyes dark. "In order to stay *alive*."

Elise gave a ghost of a smile. "I'll see what they want, first." She yawned, a huge gape she didn't bother to cover. "But first, bed."

When Philby left, Sarah and Hugh regarded each other. Hugh broke their gaze first and looked to the split logs in a rush basket by the fireplace. "I'll start a fire."

"Are you hungry? I can see what there is." Sarah went through an archway to the small kitchen and peered inside the icebox. "Two eggs, a little butter, some onions and potatoes, and a few shriveled little apples—I'll make an omelet. Oh, look, and they left us a loaf of bread and a bottle of cider!"

While Hugh built up the fire, Sarah made eggs, then brought plates, silverware, and glasses to the dining table.

"Looks lovely!"

"I'm no cook," Sarah confessed. "I can make the odd egg dish, but I'm not one of those domestic women. And—let me make this clear right now—Sabine isn't, either."

"Your French accent," Hugh said. "It's so patrician."

"While my English accent . . . is not?" Through her years in London, Sarah had kept her working-class Liverpudlian accent.

"Both of your accents are charming."

"All right, my husband—let's stay in character," Sarah admonished.

Hugh grinned. *"Oui, ma chéri."*

After they'd finished their meal, Sarah washed and dried the dishes while Hugh put on his coat and gloves and brought in more logs for the fire. Sarah threw on her coat, and together they went out the back door to the small garden, where a weathered wooden bench looked over the lake. The air was clear and crisp, the wind ruffling waves across the glassy slate surface of the water. As the pink and gold sunset faded, reflected by the lake, the three bright stars of Orion's belt rose in the sky.

Sarah leaned back and their knees touched. "All right, really now—just between you and me—how do you really know Maggie? Were you in love with her?"

In the violet dusk, Hugh put his arm around Sarah's shoulders. "Maggie? Who's Maggie?"

In the darkness, Sarah gave a catlike, satisfied smile. Together, they sat in a charged silence as more and more stars appeared, glittering like crushed diamonds in the night sky.

Chapter Seven

"I could have been in there with you two, you know," Maggie stated, setting her teacup down with a clink. "I know about 'cottaging.' The way pocket squares are folded, foot positions in the loo, so-called glory holes—all those sorts of things."

Mark's jaw dropped. "How the hell—I mean, how would a young lady like you know of such a thing?"

David can be quite candid when he has had a few drinks. "Never you mind."

Maggie and Mark had returned to MI-5 and gone up to Mark's office, eating pickled beet and margarine sandwiches, and sipping tea Frain's secretary had provided for them. A large clock ticked the seconds loudly.

Mark was pinning up what information and photographs he had on the corkboard along one wall. "Well, regardless of what you may or may not know about homosexuals, you realize Fishman wouldn't have been as forthcoming with a lady in the room, yes?"

Maggie arched an eyebrow. "I doubt it was *Fishman's* sensibilities we were sparing."

"Well, then next time, show a little leg."

"What?"

"A little more leg and unbutton a few more blouse buttons. That should do the trick." Then, "Joking! I'm just joking!"

"Mark! Really now." Maggie wanted nothing more than to change the subject. "How's your family? Your wife? Let's see, your daughter must be—what—two now? Two and a half? And didn't you say up in Edinburgh last fall there's another baby on the way?"

Mark didn't turn from the corkboard. "Frain didn't tell you?"

"Tell me what?"

"Bastard." When he spun on his heel to face her, Maggie could see the bleakness in his eyes. "They're dead. My wife and my daughter and my unborn child are all dead. They were killed in one of the bombing raids—while you and I were off chasing murderers in Scotland. They didn't tell me until I'd wrapped the case because, well, there was nothing to be done. They didn't want me—distracted."

"Mark!" Maggie was speechless from shock. Then, "Oh, Mark. I'm—I'm sorry. So very, very sorry for your loss."

In the corridor, someone paced by with a heavy tread.

"Do you—do you have a place to live?" she ventured. "You can always stay with me, if you need to. The place is big enough, and of course you're welcome. . . ."

"I'm staying in Hugh's flat while he's . . . away."

Maggie felt terrible. She'd never met Mark's wife and daughter, but she'd seen pictures and heard him speak proudly of the baby on the way. And now, dead. Those lives, that life—snuffed out. She stepped toward him.

He turned away. "I thank you for your offer," Mark managed in a strained voice. "But quite frankly, this subject is the last thing I want to talk about. In fact"—his eyes once again met hers, and she flinched at the shadows she saw in them—"while we're working together on this case, I'd prefer if you didn't mention it again."

There was a sharp rap at the door, then Durgin let himself in. "Hope I'm not interrupting anything," he said with his mad grin, shrugging off his coat and tossing it down. "Oh, tea!" he crowed, rubbing his hands together. "Is it still hot? Goody, goody, goody—let's get started then."

He flung himself down next to Maggie and crossed his legs, revealing brilliantly colored argyle socks. "Fancy digs," he allowed, taking in Mark's office while bouncing one knee. "Well, I have good news and bad news. While my men were able to pick up Mr. Fishman's, er, 'dance partner'—the posh fella in question swears he didn't see anything related to the disposal of a corpse, either. I didn't book either of them—we have their names and addresses, in case we need to question them again."

Maggie pushed away her sandwich; after Mark's revelation, she found it impossible to eat. She focused her attention back on the case. "In other words, a dead end."

"Lots of dead ends in this job, Miss Tiger. You may not know it from your cushy offices here, but at the Yard, we've been dealing with disappearing women for quite a while. There are women all over London who've gone missing in the chaos of the Blitz. Do you know how many letters from parents we've received, how many visits from private detectives we've had over the past year and a half? In case you're wondering why I've been assigned to this case, it's because at one point, half of London's detective force was investigating the disappearances of women. So the Chief formed a separate bureau, Mysterious Disappearances Department." He made a toast with his teacup. "And I'm the head."

Maggie was frowning. "So, many women have disappeared, but only two bodies have been found? Why the change now? Why the tribute to Jack the Ripper? Maybe he's keeping them. The girls, that is." The thought made Maggie's skin crawl. "You know, until he's ready. They could still be alive."

Durgin tapped his chin with one finger. "It's possible, of course. Anything's possible."

Two women had died in terrible, brutal circumstances. Maggie peered at Mark's and Durgin's faces. And yet, they seemed unconcerned. Didn't these men care? It wasn't just a case to be solved, the intellectual puzzle of a Ripper copycat. A knife and a madman had reduced at least two girls to stand-ins for other murdered women, separated by half a century. Was she the only person to remember these women had been living, breathing, vibrant women? Her stomach lurched as she realized she'd never heard back from Brynn. Where was she now? Was she all right?

"I have a friend," she said to Durgin, swallowing down dread. "Bronwyn Parry. She's from Wales, twenty-two, new to London, in town for a few formalities before taking on official duties. She was planning on staying at a women's hotel in the Baker Street area last night. And she didn't show up for her interview this morning at one of the SOE offices."

Durgin's face creased into a frown. "She fits the criteria."

"You don't think . . . ."

Durgin took a slurp of tea. "I can check for you."

"Thank you," she managed. "Now back to our victims. The dates . . ." She gestured to the board of photos.

"The Blackout Beast's dates don't match the original's dates," Mark stated. "Nor do they match the amount of time in between killings."

"*This* is what you two boffins have been working on while I was out? A time line?"

"Yes, we're working on a time line," Maggie explained, "comparing the so-called Blackout Beast's murders with the original Jack the Ripper killings." She pulled out index cards with names she'd written in thick blue ink and went to the corkboard.

1942. She pinned up the names *Joanna Metcalf* and *Doreen Leighton.*

And then, directly below and in parallel, *1888. Mary Ann Nichols* and *Annie Chapman.*

Then, in a neat row, the rest of the Ripper's victims: *Elizabeth Stride, Catherine Eddowes,* and *Mary Jane Kelly.* She then ran a line of brown string between the Blackout Beast's victims, and red connecting the original Jack the Ripper's murders. So far, Joanna Metcalf lined up with Mary Ann Nichols and Doreen Leighton lined up with Annie Chapman.

The rest of the line was ominously blank. Three to go. *Brynn . . .*

She turned to the chalkboard and wrote: SIMILARITIES AND DISSIMILARITIES OF VICTIMS, then made two columns.

"Both Jack the Ripper's and the Beast's victims are female," Mark said.

Durgin grimaced. "Thanks for the obvious."

"And the Ripper's victims were murdered over a period of twelve weeks," Maggie said. "The Beast's murders are much closer together."

"Usually there's what we call a 'cooling-off' period between murders." Durgin scowled at the chalkboard. "But if he wants the attention of the press . . . or his urge for killing is that strong . . . Usually these sorts of murderers stick to a longer pattern. If he's killing at short intervals, there might be something going on in his life, something new."

Maggie wrote, *New precipitating stressor?*

"And, the Ripper's victims were murdered outdoors, while ours were murdered inside, then moved," Mark offered.

Maggie wrote it all down on the board, chalk squeaking. "And don't forget the smell of gas on the victims' clothes."

Mark scratched his head. "Jack the Ripper's victims were prostitutes, while the Beast's are not."

"Not prostitutes, but professionals," Maggie clarified. "Independent women—with jobs outside the home. ATS, both of them."

Durgin groaned. "God help us all."

"But why Jack the Ripper?" Maggie mused. "And why now?"

"Shows a huge ego and decided lack of imagination," Durgin muttered.

"Wait—" Maggie said. "Not so fast. Jack the Ripper is a powerful symbol for violence against women. Look at the women this new killer has targeted—educated professionals, coming and going as they please. This war has turned everything topsy-turvy. Women are now challenging the status quo of nighttime London as a male-dominated space. What if invoking the specter of Jack the Ripper is intended to keep women scared and at home?"

"Is this what they're teaching you young ladies at boarding school these days?" Durgin's eyebrow lifted. "Because you might want to ask for your money back."

"No, wait—listen," Maggie insisted. "During the Victorian era, professional women who roamed London at night triggered fears of women's independence."

Durgin closed his eyes and pretended to snore.

Maggie ignored him. "The point of the Jack the Ripper killings was to frighten women into staying at home. What if that's the same cause now? What if someone doesn't like how women have more freedoms now? Working traditional men's jobs? Living alone? And so, invoking the mythical Jack the Ripper murders is a way to control women." She was thinking out loud. "Women are always in danger on the streets and in public spaces, but now even more so, as more women come to London for war work and lead independent lives."

She began to pace. "Our so-called Blackout Beast is drawing on these cultural fantasies we all share—our issues with the female body, about the dark labyrinthine city, the Minotaur, the madman." She was warming to the topic, remembering a paper she'd written for a Women in Victorian Novels class at college, drawing upon William Thomas Stead's book, *The Maiden Tribute of Modern Babylon*. "Our killer's continuing a long-running theme of male violence and women's helplessness against it. And so today's women are conditioned—reconditioned—to stay at home and not 'provoke' a man's violence. Well, sod that!"

"It's all very interesting, theoretically, but why now?" Durgin crossed his arms.

"Don't you see? Not only are women enjoying unprecedented freedoms, but London's wartime blackout has created the perfect cover for women to vanish. Thousands upon thousands of young women have come to London since the war broke out. It's a sea change in the way women are allowed to exist. In the context of history, it's huge! Enormous!"

Maggie spun on her heel. "All of these unmarried young women, released from the protection of their homes and permitted—*encouraged* even—to work and live without their families or a husband. Women who once would have gone straight from their father's home to their husband's are now living on their own or with flatmates. Don't you see? Women are *everywhere* in public life now—postwomen, bus drivers, tram conductors, dispatch riders on motorcycles, telegram messengers, Red Cross workers on bicycles . . ."

"You might be onto something, Miss Tiger," Durgin admitted. "There have always been disappearances in London, but there was a sharp uptick in the vanishings of young women with the blackout."

"Well, what do *you* have?" Maggie asked.

At his desk, Mark picked up a heavy tome, *The Complete History of Jack the Ripper*. "According to the author, who's allegedly an expert, injuries to the original Ripper's victims were crude, not made with any sort of surgical precision."

Maggie wrote *crude injuries* under the Jack the Ripper column. "But where the original Ripper's crimes were of passion, with rough slashes, the injuries to the Blackout Beast's victims are deliberate." In the other column, she wrote *precise*.

"Jack the Ripper—he had a need for control. Killing provided such a sexually satisfying"—Durgin looked to Maggie. "Sorry."

"Please continue."

"—sexually satisfying experience, he was compelled to repeat the fantasy with multiple victims."

"But there's no evidence of that," Mark pointed out.

"You're being literal," Durgin countered. "He might be using his scalpel as a stand-in."

"Charming," Maggie commented. "Impotence, plus sadism, plus need for control. Could that equal murder?"

"The links to sequential crimes are the sort of victim, the modus operandi, and the signature," Durgin explained. "So, here we have similar victims, consistent method of killing, and a quite literal signature—*Jack is back*. He may or may not have a criminal record. He's probably done any number of antisocial things, but if he's slick enough, or if his pater's powerful enough, he might have gotten away with them and not have a police record. He's most likely handsome, or at least inoffensive looking."

"Why do you think that?" Maggie asked.

"He didn't have to hurt them to get them to come with him—all of the injury was done later. His victims, at least initially, didn't see him as a threat. They trusted him."

Detective Durgin gazed off into space, as if picturing life through the eyes of the Blackout Beast. "He's a copycat killer, but he thinks he's better than the original Ripper—he's showing him up. That's why the injuries are the same, but more precise. He wants to be bigger than Jack the Ripper. Do the crimes better. Become even more famous. His ego—it's huge. And he's smart."

Mark's forehead creased. "How do you know?"

"No physical evidence. He knows about fingerprinting—enough to wear gloves. And I also suspect our man has a history of paranoia, which he may be able to hide quite well in public. Probably stems from some sort of childhood trauma—the early death of a parent, or witnessing a violent accident or crime. The kidnapping, the killing—it gives him back a sense of power. My hypothesis is he's trying to erase the memories of a brutal father, who may have abused him and his mother. A man contemptuous of women.

"Then the murderer's experiences of witnessing his mother's abuse and/or absence led him to feel victimized as he faced losses and rejections in his later life—while also unconsciously identifying with a violent masculinity that dominated women. He had issues with Mummy—and so now with all women. Or, at least, the women he sees as powerful—a threat."

"How can you possibly know—about his mother and father? Those are feelings, not facts. Guesses."

"*Hypotheses,*" Durgin corrected. "And I trust my gut. My gut's always right."

"A 'gut' can't possibly be right or wrong." *God help us,* thought Maggie, who preferred facts and science to feelings. She remembered a bad call she'd made trying to protect the Princess Elizabeth at Windsor Castle because of her dislike of one of the ladies-in-waiting. She'd sworn at the time never to let her personal feelings get in the way of solving a case again. "Your so-called gut is merely a collection of organs, connective tissue, and blood."

Durgin patted the starched shirt covering his lean midsection.

"Don't disparage the gut, Miss Tiger. It has almost twenty years of experience with killers, thieves, and the like."

"If I ever said I had a 'feeling' about something on a case, it would be labeled 'feminine intuition' and I'd be laughed at before I was kicked off," she retorted.

Mark looked up at the blank spaces. "With the way he's killing, we don't have much time."

"I know what you're thinking," Maggie said, "but those aren't places for murder victims to come—rather, those spots represent women we can save, opportunities for us to thwart our Beast. I think we should start with these books." She pointed to a few volumes about Jack the Ripper that Frain's secretary had left.

"At the Yard, we don't catch killers by reading books," Durgin stated, pouring himself more tea.

"Ah yes, you use the 'tummy tingles.'"

"I told you—the *gut*. Don't disrespect the gut."

"Forget the gut—what we have now is a lack of data. We need more evidence."

"You're not going to find it in books, Miss Tiger."

Maggie was undeterred. "But you see, our killer is using the same Ripper story we have here. But maybe there are more victims? There are the canonical Ripper murders, but what about the noncanonical victims—Martha Tabram, Annie Millwood, and Ada Wilson? We can look up those women, then check the morgues to see if any murder victims match the descriptions. And we'll need to check the hospitals, too—it's always possible our Ripper went after women inspired by the noncanonical murders. Maybe one or more of the present-day women survived."

Durgin jiggled his knee. "But there's a reason those particular murders are considered noncanonical—because Jack the Ripper *didn't* commit them."

"What you, or I, or the author of this book, or Jack the Ripper himself thinks—the only thing that matters is whether our Black-out Beast *thinks* Jack did them or not. And if the Beast *does* think Jack committed the noncanonical murders, and if he began this rampage with victims who match the noncanonical victims, as a sort of practice run, it would give us more data to work with."

"Martha Tabram may have been the Ripper's first victim. But she's not considered part of the canon because her throat wasn't cut. The murder of Martha Tabram doesn't fit the pattern," Mark told them.

"Patterns change," Maggie mused. "Evolve. Just as in nature. It's practically Darwinian. There would be practice victims, honing the craft, a development of technique. The murders our monster's taking credit for, they are what he considers his statement. But what if he had a few dress rehearsals? Or even more than a few?"

She picked up one of the dusty books on Mark's desk and paged through it. "Martha Tabram's throat wasn't cut, but she was stabbed thirty-nine times in her abdomen and neck. It's the kind of injury that would be relatively easy to track down."

Durgin exhaled. "All right, I'll see what I can do—call the Yard, check the hospitals and morgues." He looked up at the clock. "See if anyone has injuries matching those descriptions."

Mark sniffed. "Use the telephone in the office next door if you'd like."

As Durgin left, Maggie said, "I'll need a map of the area. I want to plot the points where the victims' bodies were left."

Mark rifled through his drawer and came up with a folded London map. "Perfect." Maggie pinned it to the corkboard, then pulled out two bright red tacks. "Joanna's body was left here," she said, piercing the map with one at Regent Park's Outer Circle, near the entrance to the Queen Mary Garden. "And Doreen's body here," she added, "at the intersection of Harley and New Cavendish streets."

"What does that tell us?"

"Well," Maggie admitted, "not much. Yet. But mathematics is the science of patterns. Plot the data and we just may learn something. Do you have another map? I'd like to keep one in my handbag as well."

As Mark handed her another, smaller map, she rolled her eyes heavenward. "His *gut*, can you believe it?" she murmured, tucking the map away in her purse. "As if his innards could speak. As if we were studying haruspicy, and could figure everything from the position of the liver. And people think women are erratic and emotional. . . . Mark?"

"What? Er, sorry."

"Oh, I don't know." It was late and Maggie suddenly realized she was exhausted. "I've never dealt with a serial killer before, of course—unless you count the Nazis, that is. There's a definite parallel with our Jack and the Nazis' need for domination, fear, and control by intimidation and violence—as well as issues with women. But what I do know is we need more *data*."

"Serial killer—"

Durgin called from the office next door: "'Sequential murderer' is what we call it at Scotland Yard!"

"These are killings in a series," Maggie called back. "Therefore, he is a 'serial killer'!"

Durgin's voice rang out. "Sequential! Murderer!"

"Is that what your *gut* said to call them? 'Sequential murderer'—fine," she muttered at Mark, who grimaced in reply.

Putting the map of London in her handbag reminded Maggie of the envelope Peter Frain had given her. She pulled it out. It was plain brown, and simply addressed. Inside was yet another envelope, this one ivory-colored, sealed with crimson wax. Maggie flipped it over, noting the embossed golden lion-and-unicorn insignia. "Do you have a letter opener?"

Mark handed her one that looked like an ancient dagger, and she slit open the envelope and pulled out the heavy cream card inside. It was engraved:

> *Her Majesty Queen Elizabeth*
> *Requests the pleasure of the company of*
> *Margaret Hope*
> *At an Afternoon Tea Party for Women in the Services*
> *On Monday, 30 of March 1942 from 15h30 to 17h30*
> *Buckingham Palace*
> *London*
> *Dress: uniform / day dress*
> *This Invitation Will Be Requested Upon Arrival*

Tomorrow, Maggie realized. *Of course, it's taken a while to get the invitation. . . .*

Durgin returned with a notepad, pencil behind one ear. "What's that?" he asked, taking in the fancy card.

Maggie smiled, dropping it back in her handbag. "Tea with the Queen, if you please."

"Oh, of course, Miss Tiger—or should it be *Lady* Tiger now? There's a Scottish tiger cat, you know—looks like a fluffy housecat, that is, until you get too close—then the claws come out." He blinked grayish eyes. "If you don't want to tell me, just say so. Besides, I have news—at the London Clinic, we have a female victim named Gladys Chorley, age twenty-two, with a massive lump on her head and thirty-nine—yes, exactly thirty-nine—stab wounds."

Maggie inhaled sharply. "We need to talk to her!"

"Now, hold on a tick, Lady Tiger—she's in a coma."

"We can talk to her doctor—"

"And he'll be in tomorrow morning at eight. We can all meet up at the hospital, in the lobby, at quarter to." Durgin was already on his way out the door.

He stopped and turned back, face serious. "By the way, I asked after your friend," he said to Maggie. "Bronwyn Parry."

Maggie's heart beat faster. "Yes?"

"No one with her name or fitting her description in any of the hospitals or morgues."

Maggie felt relief mixed with even sharper fear. "So, she might still be out there. He could have her—"

"Look, maybe she got cold feet is all," Durgin interrupted. "Maybe she missed her mum and went back home, or ran off with a particularly handsome Yank to Palm Beach, Florida." He shrugged and began to walk down the hall.

"Maybe." Maggie considered the tall figure walking away from her. "And what does your oracle-speaking *gut* tell you about her?" she called.

Durgin didn't turn around. "That she's still alive and she's out there. And that we'd damn well better find her."

The first night Brynn spent conscious in her underground cell, she lived through a wild, panicked fear. As she lay awake in the flickering candlelight, she tried to distract herself by studying the strangeness of her surroundings. Her bed was hard, and each time she turned over, she realized she could hear scratches and rustles through the walls, the occasional squeak.

Brynn had grown up with three older brothers, who teased her mercilessly, and she'd always refused to cry back then. Now she dropped her head on her arms and struggled not to burst into tears.

Crying was useless. Her throat constricted, as it always did at such moments, before she told herself sternly, *Be strong*. She started counting in her head, as she'd been taught at Beaulieu, to slow her breathing and heart rate. She needed a chance to think clearly. She was absolutely certain her life depended on it.

She drew the ragged quilt around her. "Other people have lived in worse places," she croaked, testing out her voice, which had been silent for so long. It was hoarse and rough, but she continued, finding the sound reassuring. "Right now, there are people in much worse places—in Ravensbrück, and Dachau, and Auschwitz. And I know they're being brave. People have spent years in the camps, enduring crueler conditions than this."

She looked over at her book on the table, *The Strange Case of Dr. Jekyll and Mr. Hyde*. She picked it up and turned to a random page: *"If he be Mr. Hyde,"* he had thought, she read, *"I shall be Mr. Seek."*

There was the odd smell—familiar now—and then Brynn fell back against the bed, her eyes closed.

Chapter Eight

The next morning, Elise had to wear the slippers to her appointment at the Reich Main Security Office. She stood in the snow on Prinz-Albrecht-Strasse, looking up at the massive gray stone building. Then, pulling her scarf firmly over her shaved head, she strode—head high—up the main steps and into the building's lobby.

The SS officer at the security desk raised his eyebrows at her appearance. "Papers?" he barked. Elise noted there was no *gnädiges Fräulein* here.

She handed them over to him. "I'm here to see Captain Alexander Fausten." Her voice echoed in the cavernous marble space. "We have a nine o'clock appointment."

"Regarding what, exactly?" The man's tone remained insolent.

"Condition of release," Elise told him, her voice not betraying the fear she felt.

The man thrust back her papers, scarcely glancing at them. "Up the stairs. To the right."

In the antechamber to Fausten's office, a buxom, blond, well-coiffed secretary sat at a large desk, her fingers striking the typewriter keys in sharp, precise movements. "You are Fräulein Hess?"

Elise nodded.

The secretary looked her up and down, taking in her scarf-covered bald head, her slippered feet. She pursed her lips. "One moment," she said, pressing down on the switch hook to clear the line, then pushing a red button under the telephone dial. "Elise Hess is here, sir." She replaced the receiver and thrust out her chin to indicate the heavy double doors. "Go in."

Elise knocked, then swung one of the doors open. The room was enormous, with red-and-gold wallpaper, and several small windows covered by heavy damask curtains.

"Come in!" Fausten called, smiling, rising behind his mahogany desk. There were death's-heads carved into the legs. "Good morning, Fräulein Hess!" And then he saluted. *"Heil Hitler!"*

Elise was taken aback by his energy, his—life force. No one at Ravensbrück was anywhere near as . . . animated. Fausten didn't seem to notice her shorn hair. Or her grossly swollen feet in her slippers. "Please," he requested, gesturing to a leather chair, "sit down."

She did as he asked.

"Did you sleep well, Fräulein Hess?"

"Yes," Elise managed. She was not about to thank him for his concern.

"I have met your father, Herr Miles Hess, one of my favorite conductors, of Wagner's *Ring Cycle* especially. He was here several times on your behalf."

Elise stared at him blankly.

"Well, your father went to Himmler himself about you. And your release. Your father was quite . . . persuasive, shall we say." He held out his hand. "Now, let me see your papers."

Elise handed them over. She knew what asking Himmler for her life must have cost her father, the anti-Fascist who'd hated Clara's Nazi cronies, who'd referred to Himmler in the past only as "the little chicken farmer."

Fausten dropped the papers on the desk in front of him, slipped on a pair of tortoiseshell spectacles, and read them over. As he did, he lit a cigarette and inhaled.

"I'm sorry," he said, looking up. "Where are my manners? Would you like one?"

Elise would have liked nothing better—it had been months since her last cigarette and she knew it would calm her nerves. But she shook her head. She would take nothing from this man.

He picked a piece of stray tobacco from his lip, then cast his eyes back down to the folder. "Here's what they say about you. *According to the findings of the State Police, Elise Hess endangers, through her conduct, the stability and security of the People and the State, in that she does egregious harm to the interests of the Reich through her subversive activities and collaboration with one of the most critical and harsh opponents of the National Socialist State.*"

He pushed the file away, taking a thoughtful drag on his cigarette. "So, you are released from Ravensbrück and are here in Berlin on a nine-day leave to attend the memorial of your mother, opera diva Clara Hess. You are staying in the care of your father, the great conductor Miles Hess. You were arrested for aiding Father Licht in his denunciation of Dr. Brandt and Operation Compassionate Death, correct?"

"Yes."

"And do you know our Führer has stopped the program?"

He's not my *Führer.* "Really." Elise didn't know this, but even if Hitler and his minions had deferred to the bishops and public opinion, she wasn't convinced the Nazis' murder of so-called defective children wasn't continuing in the shadows.

"He did." Fausten smiled. "This must please you."

Elise was silent. She looked down at her hands, knit gloves stretched tight over the swollen joints.

"Come now, Fräulein Hess," Fausten continued, his tone jocu-

lar. "You and I—we are friends, not enemies. Our common enemies are the Communists, the Bolsheviks, and the Jews."

Elise kept her face impassive but bit the inside of her cheek,
hard.

He rose and walked around his desk to sit on the leather chair
next to her. "Please see past the uniform, Fräulein Hess. I studied
law, you know—I didn't choose this career. It chose me.

"I have to ask you—how were you treated during your arrest,
interrogation, and incarceration?"

"As you must know, I signed a nondisclosure agreement." Elise
trained her eyes on the soot-stained window, where a shaft of light
had pierced through.

"Really. Tell me."

Elise met his gaze without flinching. "I've been hanged on a
cross, knocked to the ground, kicked and beaten, stripped naked,
put in solitary confinement, starved, and lunged at by snarling
dogs. We—they—we are *Stücke*. Things."

Fausten blinked impassively.

"Even fellow prisoners—some of whom have positions as
guards, policewomen, and barrack chiefs, can—with impunity—
insult and revile us, beat us, trample us underfoot, and yes, if the
whim strikes them, kill us.

"As far as anyone in the camp hierarchy is concerned, it's good
riddance—one less 'vermin' to deal with."

Fausten blinked again. "I see." He rose and went back behind
his desk, as if it offered him some fragile protection from the vile
things she had just told him. "I read in your file that, before your
incarceration, you were a nurse at Charité Hospital in Mitte. I also
read you were planning on taking vows to become a nun."

"Yes."

"Would you be surprised to know that when I was younger, I

myself wanted to be a priest? Yes, I am Catholic as well, Fräulein Hess. You see, we really are on the same side."

I highly doubt it, Elise thought.

"Jesus was a Jew, of course, but he rose up and overcame his disability," Fausten continued, crushing his cigarette in a heavy bronze ashtray. "The Aryans overcame Judaism. Overcoming it was, indeed, the work of the Lord. And now it is *our* work, Fräulein Hess."

"I judge not by race, but by character."

He looked at her sharply. "You must judge by *blood*."

"I am a nurse. And I can tell you, this is the truth—everyone's blood runs red."

He kept his gaze on her. "The Jews are different."

"And the Poles?"

He sighed. "The Poles are different yet again."

"Because I've seen what happens to Polish women in the camp." Elise couldn't stop herself, the words tumbling out one after another, hot and ugly. "Do you know what they call them at Ravensbrück? *Rabbits*. The Polish women are experimental animals, used for septic and antiseptic bone operations, and two types of surgeries on muscles. Incisions on legs filled with gravel, glass, germs, other matter to simulate war wounds. Various new drugs tested for efficacy. Sections of bone or muscle removed, nerve transplants. Without anesthesia and without aseptic treatment. They shout, 'Long live Poland!' as they're taken away to the operating theater."

Fausten tilted his head. "Why do they call them rabbits?"

"Because, after their operations, they hop around on their makeshift crutches. The youngest 'rabbit' was ten years old—we called her Bunny. She'd been cut open some half dozen times before she died. And the surgeries were done by a renowned Berlin university professor of medicine."

Fausten made a steeple of his fingers. "Yes, it sounds horrible. But please keep some perspective. We are in the midst of a holy war. It is God's will the Germans win."

"I find the words *holy* and *war* incompatible."

"But even Pope Pius disagrees. The Pope is no fool—he recognized the Bolshevik threat to Christianity. He signed the Concordat." Fausten pulled out a box of marzipan molded and painted to look like fruit and vegetables from his desk drawer, took off the lid, and slid the box toward her. "Would you like one?"

Elise's mouth watered. Marzipan was her favorite treat. But she would not be led into temptation. "No."

"We actually have the same aims, you and I." He picked up one of the candies from its ruffled paper. "We want you to play a role in reconciling the Reich and the Church. A German-Vatican dialogue." He popped the sweet into his mouth. Outside, a church bell tolled and a horn blared.

"Captain Fausten, your candy and your words fail to impress me."

He plucked out another marzipan, in the shape of a yellow peach. "Oh, you don't know what you're missing, Fräulein. . . ." Then, "Do you know where you'll end up? Do you really want to be a martyr?"

Elise remained silent, her face impassive.

"This is all we want." He lifted a piece of paper from his desk, fingers leaving a smudge of food dye. "We want you to renounce your role in the events at Charité Mitte hospital and exonerate Dr. Brandt. We want you not only to sign it but to take it to your bishop. And then you will be released. For good."

Elise held the paper up and read it, then put it down. She chose her words with care. "I will not be your Judas," she said finally.

"Jesus and Judas," Fausten mused. "Flip sides of the same coin, don't you think, Fräulein? Without Judas, we wouldn't have Jesus. We all have our roles to fill."

"You have no idea what my role is. And I have no desire to discuss theology with you."

He pushed the sheet of paper toward her. "Well, you have some time to think about it. Nine days to be exact." He smiled. "I'm here for you if you'd like to talk."

He rose and gestured to the door.

Elise struggled to rise, wincing in pain, leaving the paper behind on the desk. As he walked her to the door, he said in soft tones, "And know this—if you run away, we will shoot ten of your bunkmates in Ravensbrück. Please keep that in mind. I'll see you at your mother's memorial service," he told her, opening the door. "Oh, wait!"

He went back to his desk, picked up the paper she'd left, then chose another piece of marzipan. His hand hovered over the box, finally choosing a round red apple in its paper, dusted with sparkling sugar. "Here," he said as he walked back with his hand outstretched, holding both paper and apple. "Even if you don't want it now, take it with you. For later." The apple seemed to shimmer in front of her.

"No," Elise said. "No, I will not."

He tucked both in the pocket of her coat. "I hope you'll change your mind."

Numb, she turned and left, slowly picking her way back down the stairs. Outside, she took a greedy breath of icy cold air. Snow had fallen and children were playing in the street, the jumping game Heaven and Hell. The church bell chimed again, entwined with the sound of sirens.

———

Captain Fausten's superior, Heinz Gephardt, called him into his office. It was larger and even more imposing than Fausten's, but featured the same framed photo of Hitler.

Gephardt sat in a massive leather chair behind a desk carved with swastikas. He was a tall and trim man, almost sixty, with thin lips etched with deep vertical lines. "Did Fräulein Elise Hess show up?"

"Yes, sir. Right on time, sir."

"Good, good. Don't underestimate her importance. We're still having . . . trouble with the German bishops and certain parishes over this Operation Compassionate Death business. We need to mend fences—if only for appearances' sake."

"And the Pope?"

"Just last week sent greetings and addressed our Führer as 'esteemed gentleman.'" Gephardt shook his head dismissively. "I have no worries about the Pope."

"Elise Hess is a good Aryan girl. I hate to think of her back at Ravensbrück."

"Oh? She's being stubborn?"

Fausten shrugged.

"Let's raise the stakes, then. If you can't get her to sign this letter—you'll be sent to the Eastern Front." Gephardt smiled, letting the threat sink in. "No joke this time. And I hear it's still quite cold in Russia."

At the SOE training camp in Arisaig, Scotland, recruits were required to swim in Loch nan Ceall regardless of the weather. In London, Maggie had taken to early-morning swimming at the Ladies' Pond, an open-air pool off Millfield Lane, on the east side of Hampstead Heath in North London, open every day of the year. The water was freezing, but by swimming in it regularly, her body had become acclimated. She now found it invigorating exercise, as well as a way to clear her mind.

As she took a last tug on her bathing cap and buttoned the strap under her chin, she heard wolf whistling. Usually at this early hour she was swimming solo in the greenish water, or with one or two other stalwart women.

But a group of men, still drunk from the evening before, had wandered by to watch, beer bottles in hand. "Hey, nice ass!" one shouted, slurring his words.

Another bellowed, "Suck my dick!"

While the third leered and called, "Bottle of whiskey back in the trees—whattaya say, love? Come with us—we'll show you a good time."

Ignoring them, Maggie dove into the water, the shock of cold momentarily clearing her head and chilling her anger. She came up to the surface to hear their raucous laughter as they stumbled away. "I'd love to take a turn with that."

"Screw her till her nose bleeds," said another.

Maggie spat and began her laps with the crawl—but the peace she usually found under the wide sky eluded her. She knew why the men did it—they were asserting their power to her and also to themselves. They did it to remind her that she, as a woman, shouldn't forget her place in society—and any outing in public, especially in a bathing costume and alone, was dangerous.

Why can't we do something like go swimming, walk at night, cross the bloody street without constantly being reminded our bodies are merely things, ripe for insulting, leering at, and aggressive propositioning?

She flipped over and switched to the backstroke. Before Jack the Ripper's time, women were obliged to stay home, be the "angels of the house," with their only outings church or trips accompanied by men. Then, in Victorian times, women had more freedom—to go to the theater, to restaurants. But when the Ripper murders started, women were warned to stay inside. *I suppose we could post warnings to women now, to keep off the streets after dark, to walk in groups, to ask a man to be an escort.*

She gave a kick, her angry splash disturbing some nearby ducks. *But why should we have to?* Maggie thought. *Why shouldn't men have a curfew instead? Then we women could walk the streets— and swim the lakes—in peace.*

When her anger was spent, her limbs exhausted, and her lips blue, she climbed the dock's ladder to go back to the women's clubhouse to change.

Durgin was already in the lobby of Fitzroy Square Hospital when Maggie arrived, tapping one foot, running a hand through his unruly hair. They stood together, waiting for Mark, trying not to breathe too deeply of the air, reeking of alcohol. The pale blue walls were covered in propaganda posters. WOMEN OF BRITAIN— COME INTO THE FACTORIES! urged one poster, showing a woman in blue coveralls and a red head scarf, Spitfires flying high overhead. WOMEN ARE DOING THEIR BIT—LEARN TO MAKE MUNITIONS! boomed another, spotlighting a woman putting on a hairnet and smock. Yet another displayed a woman assembling a bomb: WOMEN IN THE WAR—WE CAN'T WIN WITHOUT THEM.

One in particular, however, made Maggie's lips twitch— Winston Churchill's head mounted on the body of an English bulldog against the Union Jack with the caption HOLDING THE LINE. *The P.M. did* not *personally approve that one,* she thought.

The waiting room was full of people slumped in hard wooden chairs, many pressing handkerchiefs against their mouths. There was such a cacophony of coughing and wailing babies it was hard to think. Maggie winced as she saw one woman pull away the cambric square she'd pressed to her lips. It was stained with bright-red blood.

As nurses in crisp white linen caps deferred to doctors with mustaches and large gold pocket watches, veterans in uniform— some in wheelchairs, some using crutches—tried to concentrate on their newspapers. Maggie could make out the *Times*'s headline, ALLIED POWERS REVEAL PLANS FOR SMASHING BLOWS AT HITLER AND GERMANY SOMETIME THIS YEAR.

She and Durgin both spied Mark at the same time. "Oh, goody—the gang's all here," Durgin muttered, making his way to the information desk. "We've come to see Dr. William McVite." He flashed his badge to a bright-eyed young nurse with freshly applied lipstick.

She checked a chart. "Dr. McVite's just arrived. You're welcome to go up and find him. Intensive care is—"

Durgin was off before she finished, the tails of his mackintosh flying behind him. "I know where it is," he rumbled, taking the stairs two at a time.

In the main second-floor corridor, Durgin spotted a short, gray-haired man in a long white coat, stethoscope looped around his neck.

"Dr. McVite," the DCI said without preamble, "we spoke last night, about your patient—the one with thirty-nine stab wounds."

"Ah, yes, Detective Durgin." The doctor reached out to shake hands. "I wish we could meet under better circumstances. And I would like to tell you there's been some sort of miraculous recovery—but I'm afraid Miss Chorley is still in critical condition."

"May we see her?"

"Of course." The doctor led the way to a small room, where a pale young woman with brown hair, a turned-up nose, and long, dark eyelashes lay with her eyes closed. "I know she looks as though she's sleeping, but she's in a coma. She's suffered severe head trauma."

"How long will she be in the coma?"

"There's no way to know."

"Her chances of recovery?"

"Impossible to say." Dr. McVite raised and dropped his shoulders. "She could wake up today—or she could spend the rest of her life the way she is now."

Maggie's heart skipped a beat as she realized the face was familiar. *Gladys Chorley,* she thought, her throat constricting. *Another of the SOE trainees—terrible shot, but the best at obstacle courses.* She blinked back tears. "Has anyone been to visit her?"

"No," the doctor said. "No family, no friends. No one's claimed her. She had a brother in the RAF—died in the Battle of Britain. And we've telephoned Miss Chorley's sister in Orkney, but she's a young widow with three children—unable to make the trip at the moment."

Maggie nodded, remembering Gladys's singsong Orkneyan lilt.

"Tea," Durgin muttered. "I need tea. They have excellent tea in the cafeteria," he announced, spinning on his heel. "We'll have tea and regroup."

Maggie stopped at the main doors. "I'll be right with you," she called after him and Mark. She walked to the nurse on duty. "Hello," she said, smiling. "I'm looking for information on Miss Gladys Chorley. Dr. McVite mentioned she hasn't had any visitors?"

"Chorley?" The nurse, a woman with thinning hair under her white linen cap, looked up from her charts. Her hazel eyes softened. "No, the poor thing's had visitors. *A* visitor, at least. Her boyfriend comes around regular—late at night, though. Second shift. A pilot, I think. Handsome devil."

Aha! "Do you know his name?"

"Something foreign. He spoke with an accent, I remember. Let me check the after-hours sign-in sheet." The nurse ruffled through some papers and came up with a clipboard. She ran a finger down a column of names and times. "Here he is—Captain Jakub Żak." She pursed her lips. "Sounds Polish, maybe?"

"You said he was handsome? What did he look like?"

"Dark hair and eyes. Straight part down the middle of his hair. A quiet, polite young man. Looked a bit like Tyrone Power in *Blood and Sand*. Never said much."

"Thank you, thank you so very much." Maggie would have hugged the nurse in gratitude if she could have. *Nurses run the hospitals of the world, just as secretaries run the offices.*

She raced to the cafeteria and sat down at Durgin and Mark's table with a triumphant smile. "Miss Chorley's boyfriend's been visiting," she announced.

Durgin blew on his tea. "Go on."

"His name's Captain Jakub Żak. A Pole fighting in the RAF. The nurse says he comes to see her after hours."

Durgin favored her with one of his mad grins. "Excellent work, Miss Tiger," he said, bolting the rest of his tea, then standing and clapping his wool hat back on his head. "I'll make a call and get an address. I need to testify in court today—so you two will pay a call on Captain Jakub Żak." He glared from beneath the hat brim. "*Don't* muddle it up."

"Don't blow a gasket!" Sarah was asleep when she heard the knocking, which was rapidly escalating into banging. She shrugged quickly into her red satin dressing gown and slippers, and padded downstairs to open the door. The fire had burned out during the night, and the morning air was frigid. "All right! All right! I'm coming! Don't get your knickers in a twist!"

She opened the cottage's front door, and there stood Kim Philby, impeccably dressed, smelling of shaving soap and lemon cologne. Behind him, the sky glowed. "Red sky in the morning, sailors take warning," he said.

"Please come in," she said, trying to smooth down her long dark hair.

"I know it's early," Philby declared, walking past her, "but we have a lot of work to do and very little time to do it. We're trying to get you out during this full moon, which is a little sooner than I'd like, but still manageable if we focus and work hard."

Hugh lay on the cottage's sofa, snoring. Philby shouted, "Thompson!" Then, with a poke to the younger man's shoulder, "Thompson!"

Hugh turned over, but the narrow sofa caused his broad frame to fall to the floor with a thud. He opened his eyes and saw Philby standing over him and Sarah trying unsuccessfully to smother a laugh. He bolted upright, blinking in bewilderment.

"Get dressed now, both of you, and come with me." Philby looked annoyed by their sloth.

They arrived at the former dining room of a high-ceilinged Georgian manor house, a brown water stain marring the egg-and-dart crown molding. "In addition to your ballet and cello rehearsals, you'll be expected to attend the other activities of F-Section trainees," Philby told them, their footsteps echoing on the scuffed parquet floor. "At this point, most of it is classroom work, but, believe me, not only is it difficult but the information you'll receive is vital."

Any carpets had been put into storage along with furniture. Military-issue metal folding chairs had been set up in rows. Sunlight streamed in through the taped windows.

"I have a meeting, but I'll be back," Philby informed the pair. "Wait for me when you're done."

More and more agents-in-training wearing civilian clothing drifted in as Sarah and Hugh took seats near the mullioned windows. A white-haired, pink-cheeked man shuffled in, leaning heavily on a carved hickory-stick cane. *"Bonjour, agents,"* he boomed.

"Bonjour, Monsieur Godfrey!" the students called back.

Godfrey gave Sarah and Hugh a shrewd look. "Ah, and here are our newcomers." He smiled in an avuncular way at the duo and said in English: "What are your names?"

"I'm Hugh Thompson and this is Sarah—"

Monsieur Godfrey's eyes blazed. *"Non, non, non!"* He switched back into French. "First of all, you must always speak in French. *Always.* Second, you must use your code names."

The rest of the class snickered.

"Sorry, Monsieur Godfrey," Hugh apologized in French. "I am Hubert Taillier. And this is Madame Sabine Severin."

"Good morning," Sarah offered, also in French.

"Well then, welcome, Monsieur Taillier and Madame Severin," Godfrey told them, still glaring. "As I was about to say, we of the SOE are not part of the conventional armed forces. Our mission is information gathering, disinformation spreading, and also sabotage and subversion. The P.M. charged us with the words 'Set Europe ablaze!' Our particular section of Europe is France, F-Section. Our ultimate goal is the liberation of the occupied territories of France."

"Will we be working with the Free French?" asked a young man with white-blond hair and a smattering of freckles.

"In theory, yes." The sarcasm in the teacher's tone hinted at the strain between the two organizations.

"Will there be an invasion? There will be an invasion of France, yes?"

"Yes, when?" others echoed in excitement.

"Now, now—let's not get ahead of ourselves." Monsieur Godfrey went to his military-issue desk. "You all think you know what a Nazi looks like," he declared, placing photographs mounted on poster board of different men in uniform on easels facing the class, "but it's not only the Gestapo you'll have to worry about in France. You'll need to distinguish differences in uniforms of the Gestapo, yes," he continued, pointing to each photograph in turn with his cane, "but also the Abwehr, German Army Intelligence, and the Milice—the French police collaborators."

"Filthy frogs," came a voice from the back.

"Stop!" Sarah retorted, turning. "Don't say that! My grandmother was French! She died a patriot!"

One of the fresh-faced young women in the front row raised her hand. "How do we determine their rank?"

Godfrey gave a grim smile. "The higher ranks of Gestapo and SS don't even wear uniforms—they're in plain clothing but have metal identification disks they can show when they want to identify themselves. So remember—even if someone isn't in uniform, he can still be a German, perhaps even higher-ranking than someone in regalia. Also, it's imperative to remember not all Frenchmen are on your side. A Frenchman doesn't need to be in a Milice uniform to be a collaborator. Many French are neutral, simply trying to get by. And even Resistance workers can turn if cornered. Remember that. And always be on your guard. *No one* is what they seem."

The lecture went on with questions and answers and then a quiz. After Sarah and Hugh had turned in their papers, the young woman who'd spoken earlier asked, "We're going out for a smoke—want to come?"

But before either could answer, Philby turned up behind them. "Alas, I'm afraid Madame Severin and Monsieur Taillier have a few other exercises they must do before they're off duty."

"Too bad." The girl sighed. "Hope to see you later," she added, flashing dimples and giving a significant look to Hugh.

"He's married!" Sarah shot back without thinking. When Hugh and Philby stared at her, surprised by her vehemence, she turned red. "Well, you *are*, Hubert," she muttered. "At least for the purposes of this mission."

Chapter Nine

Maggie and Mark took the Tube's Central Line to Northolt Junction, to the Royal Air Force's Northolt Aerodrome. After showing their identification to a round of guards, they were escorted to a conference room in the brick main building. The room was small and unheated. Loose glass panes rattled in the wind; they kept their coats and gloves on.

But before they had time to become truly chilled, a young man in a RAF uniform appeared at the doorway, his eyes wary. A Polish pilot flying with the RAF, on his cap was the Polish National Eagle in place of the British badge.

"Captain Żak?" Maggie asked, standing. "Captain Jakub Żak?"

"Yes," the man admitted in heavily accented English. "But my friends call me Kuba." He was as tall as Maggie, and his brilliantined black hair was combed back with a straight part. *Hmm, he does look a bit like Tyrone Power.*

"Captain Żak," Maggie said, preferring to keep things formal. "I'm Miss Hope and this is Agent Standish of MI-Five. We're here to talk to you about Gladys Chorley. Please, let's all sit down."

"Am I under arrest?" Żak joked, sitting and taking off his cap.

"No," Mark answered. "But we're interested in finding out everything you know about Gladys Chorley."

"Have you seen her?" Żak's dark eyes darted from one to the other. "How is she?"

Maggie shifted in her chair. "I'm afraid she's still in a coma."

"Is there anything new from the doctors?" he asked, voice eager.

"The doctor hopes she will recover and wake up," Maggie responded, "but as of now, there's no change in her condition."

"I'm sorry to hear that."

"How do you know Miss Chorley?" Maggie asked. "One of the nurses said you're her boyfriend, and the visitors' log shows you've visited seven times since she was admitted."

"Not her boyfriend," he clarified. "Just a friend. I trained with her brother—he died in the Battle of Britain. I promised him if anything happened to him I'd keep an eye on her. So I'd travel to London to see her when I had leave."

"Did she say what she was doing here in London?"

"Gladys was with the ATS. But she never spoke much about what she did. Claimed it was mostly typing and filing—you know, boring office work. She spent some time in Scotland, a month here and there. Last time I saw her, before—well—she'd recently gotten back from one of her trips. She told me she was in town for a few days, and then she was due to go on another."

"When was that? The last time you spoke with her?"

"Sometime at the end of January. We had drinks at the Criterion in Piccadilly Circus."

"How did you learn she was in hospital?"

"Gladys's sister called me. She told me Gladys had been in an accident."

"Where were you on the night of March twenty?" Maggie asked.

His face creased with concern. "I was here, on base."

"And on the night of March twenty-seventh? And March twenty-ninth?"

His hand rubbed at the back of his neck. "Here. On base."

"You don't mind if we verify those nights with your commanding officer?" Mark asked.

"No." Żak swallowed. "No, of course not."

"Do you know where Miss Chorley was living when she was in London?" asked Maggie.

"She was staying at a women's residence hotel in Marylebone," Żak replied. "I'd walk her to her door after we'd been out, and sometimes we'd talk in the lobby. But they didn't let men up, of course."

"Do you remember the name of the residence hotel?"

He closed his eyes, thinking. Then, "I'm sorry, I don't remember."

"Do you remember the address? Or anything nearby?"

"I'm sorry—I'm not familiar with London. It was near the Baker Street station, that much I know. A side street. Quiet and dark."

"Did she have any enemies whom you know of?" Mark asked. "A jealous ex-boyfriend, maybe?"

"No!" Żak exclaimed. "Gladys was a good girl. Hardworking. Didn't know too many people in London. Preferred to go to the cinema or a concert rather than any fancy parties."

"How would you describe her?"

Żak thought for a moment. "Strong, intelligent, athletic. Pretty. But stubborn. Very stubborn—just like her brother. A thoroughly modern girl. When we went out, I had the feeling that while she felt terrible about the war, she was glad for a chance to leave Scotland. She wanted to see more of the world."

"Is there anything you remember about the hotel?" Maggie asked.

"She stayed in a few, a different one each time. I remember they were all near Regent's Park and Baker Street, if it helps."

"It does."

"Thank you." Mark handed Żak one of his cards. "If you remember anything else—no matter how unimportant it may seem—please call."

"I will," Żak vowed, eyes serious. "I will."

After they checked out Żak's story with his commanding officer and it proved true, Maggie and Mark walked back to the Tube station. As they entered the train car, Mark sighed. "Another dead end."

"Maybe. But I'm glad to know the poor girl has someone visiting her. I wonder, if on some level, she knows. I do hope so." She chewed her lip, considering. "Mark, I have an idea."

Maggie turned to Mark when they reached the front door to the SOE offices. "Do you mind waiting while I run inside?" she asked.

They both ducked as a line of housewives in matching head scarves, on bicycles with wicker shopping baskets, pedaled down the street laughing and ringing their bells. When they were out of harm's way, Maggie explained, "They're understandably a bit edgy about people not associated with 'the Firm' skulking about."

"Of course not." Mark gestured at the café across the street. "I'll get a cup of whatever's passing for coffee. By the way, have you noticed how keen Durgin is on tea? I mean, I'm a fellow Englishman and even I find his zeal for it excessive."

"He does seem to enjoy it," Maggie agreed. "But I always find the Brits a bit odd when it comes to tea. Thanks—shouldn't be too long."

Upstairs, Maggie saw Miss Lynd making her way to the kitchen. "Wondering if you'd heard anything from Brynn Parry?"

"Afraid not, Miss Hope." The older blonde turned on the gas underneath the kettle. "You girls come and go so freely these days—speaking of which, where have *you* been, young lady?"

"Oh, a side job," Maggie responded, wanting to keep things simple. "And how is Agent Calvert?"

Miss Lynd examined her rings. "We haven't heard anything new from her. The communiqué you saw was the last she wrote."

"What?" Maggie was angry. No, furious. *Enraged.* "And what does Colonel Gaskell say about her radio silence?"

"He says she's fine and will contact us when she can. And that we shouldn't worry."

"Shouldn't worry?"

"I'm sure it's fine, Miss Hope," Miss Lynd said. But her eyes didn't meet Maggie's.

"Why didn't you listen to me? None of you have been over there on a mission—I have. And I knew something was wrong. I knew it. We're letting one of our own down."

"Miss Hope, please—not so dramatic. We're waiting for her to reach out to us."

"Well, what a bloody, bloody mess!" Maggie exploded.

"Miss Hope!"

Something had changed in Maggie. An agent's life was on the line. "No, I will *not* apologize for using profanity. If ever there was a time for some good, honest swearing, it's now, with an agent missing and perhaps dead! We've been trained to live on the land—if she's alive, she might be doing just that, in the Rouen area. But it's still winter—it's a hard time to be out. If I were her, I'd try to get to Paris somehow. Connect with some of the other agents. Try to get a message out."

Maggie thought back to Erica Calvert's files. "She has extended family in Paris. If she's on the run, I bet she'll try to go there and make contact. You need to get word to the Paris team she may be arriving," she said with authority.

"Y-yes," Miss Lynd agreed, accepting Maggie's direction.

Heading out of the kitchen, Maggie turned. "I need to use the telephone, in private. I trust I may use the one in your office?"

Miss Lynd blinked, still in shock at the abrupt turn of the tables. "Y-yes. Of course."

"Thank you."

Inside Miss Lynd's office, with the door closed, Maggie dialed SOE's main number at Beaulieu. "Hello, yes, I'm trying to reach a trainee named Sarah Sanderson. This is Margaret Hope with both SOE and MI-Five. It's important."

On the other end of the telephone line, there were crackles and splutters.

"Can you send someone to fetch her?" Maggie wrapped the black cord around her wrist. "Yes, I'm afraid it *is* urgent."

Sarah and Hugh were rehearsing. The ancient gray-stone Domus was part of the original Beaulieu Abbey, built in the year 1204, with high, beamed, sloping ceilings. As Hugh played scales in one corner, Sarah rested her hand on the ancient stone of the window-sill and went through her barre exercises.

It was not going well.

First, she was out of shape—out of ballet shape, at least.

Second, she had to master new French-made pointe shoes. Philby had procured a few pair from one J. Crait, the shoemaker for the Paris Opéra Ballet. Sarah wasn't used to the cut, shank, sole, or top of the box, and had to wet them down and crush them in a door before they were fit to use. And even then, she still felt odd without her usual Freeds. Furthermore, they were pale pink instead of peach satin, *quelle horreur!* "Well, if Yvette Chauviré can dance in them," she murmured, invoking the name of one of the Opéra Ballet's *danseuses étoiles*, "then so can I."

Sarah had seen the Paris Opéra Ballet perform in London after Serge Lifar had taken over the company, and she was familiar with the French style. Each country had its own ballet style. The Vic-Wells, where Sarah performed, was known for its softer and subtle arms, romantic arabesque placement, and serenity. Russian dancers had great drama, jumps, and upper-body movement. The Americans were fast, with flexibility and musicality. But French dancers were known by their impeccable turnout, their relaxed arms, strong backs, and chic, sophisticated, even witty elegance.

And so as Sarah went through her barre exercises, she worked on the clarity of her épaulement and port de bras, and the precision of her pointe work, especially petite batterie. She focused on cleanliness and clarity, and struggled with a tight fifth position. She still had her long, tapering legs, flexible feet, and musicality—even if she was frustrated with extensions that weren't as high as she was used to and falling out of pirouettes as she tried to remember how to place her weight.

Meanwhile, Hugh was also having problems, with his new cello. Philby had brought a Vuillaume, along with a Pajeot-tip bow. But even with a superb instrument, Hugh's scales were shaky and slow, with quavering tones and more than a few flat notes.

"I wish we had music," Sarah said, moving to the center for adagio.

Hugh looked pained. "I do know more than scales, you know. But I don't have any sheet music with me."

"Don't you know anything by heart?"

"Ah." Hugh thought for a moment. "Yes," he said finally. He straightened and placed his fingers on the strings, the bow hovering. "Are you ready?"

When Sarah nodded, the Domus was filled with the arpeggiated chords of the prelude of Bach's Suite No. 1 in D Major for unaccompanied cello. The instrument's rich tones filled the room, reverberating off the rough stone walls.

Sarah was familiar with the flowing Baroque étude. She closed her eyes, tried her best to forget her new pointe shoes, and began to move.

Together, the two worked through the piece with both technical control and spiritual abandon. Sarah made Hugh part of her dance, pirouetting around him and the cello, coming down to kneel in front of him in a lunge before rising to dance again. As the last notes hung in the air, Hugh was perfectly still, as was Sarah.

Somehow, together, they had made magic.

Hugh began to play again, this time, Scott Joplin's "Maple Leaf Rag." Sarah smiled and began to dance, not ballet exactly, but her own mix of classical, the Charleston, and swing, and included handstands, somersaults, and back bends. As the music ended and she landed in a split, breathing hard and covered in sweat, they couldn't contain their laughter.

"I'm so sorry to interrupt," came a woman's voice from the doorway. "I waited until you were done."

The dancer looked up, shocked at the intrusion into their intimate world. She blinked, coming back to reality. "Of course," Sarah said, going to her bag to get a towel and blotting her face.

"Miss Sanderson, you have a telephone call. From a Miss Margaret Hope. Miss Hope insists it's extremely urgent."

Sarah looked to Hugh, who was putting his cello back in its case, and felt a twinge of irritation at Maggie. She knew it was illogical, but she felt as if Maggie were deliberately following them, trailing after Hugh. She threw on a sweater and stepped into a skirt, then changed back into street shoes. "I'll only be a moment, Hubert," she called, hoisting her dance bag over her shoulder.

The dancer followed the woman past the budding magnolia

trees to the main SOE office, where she picked up the Bakelite phone receiver. She took a deep breath to quell her impatience. "Hello? Maggie? Is everything all right?"

"Sarah? I'm so sorry to bother you at Finishing School—"

"Not a bother at all, kitten."

"Sarah, when you first came to interview in London, did anyone here give you the names of any women's hotels, boarding-houses, that sort of thing?"

Sarah considered. "Yes, the woman at the front desk gave me a card."

Maggie's breath caught. "By any chance, do you still have it?"

"One moment." She opened her dance bag, rifling through soft leather slippers, more pointe shoes, a few extra pairs of tights, and several hair ribbons until she extricated her worn leather datebook. She flipped through the lined pages until she found the right date. "Alas, I don't have the card anymore, but here's a number I wrote down."

Maggie copied it onto a piece of scrap paper. "Thank you."

"Everything all right?"

Maggie gave a hiccup of a laugh. "Let's just say it's a good thing you stayed with us at the house the night before you left— and didn't go to a hotel."

"Maggie," Sarah asked. "Things really are over between you and Hugh. Yes?"

There was a long pause. "Did he ask after me?"

Sarah hung up the hand piece.

Hoping she and Sarah simply had a bad connection, Maggie called the number her friend had given her and found the hotel's name and address: The Castle Hotel for Women: Temporary Lodging for Ladies at 226 Ash Street, near the cross of Marylebone High Street and Paddington Street, and not too far from the SOE office on Baker Street.

When she and Mark arrived at the hotel, cold and breathless, no one was behind the reception desk.

Maggie pressed the doorbell a few times with a gloved finger.

As they were about to leave, the door across the lobby opened, and one middle-aged man let another out. "Thank you, Doctor," the first man said, clapping on his black bowler hat and tucking his umbrella under his arm.

"I'll see you next week, Mr. Finn."

The man opened the front door to leave, and Mark caught and held it, letting Maggie and himself in. The lobby was almost as cold as outside, the embers in the fireplace dying. They looked up at the man whom the other had called Doctor. A brass nameplate on the door read IAIN FRANK, M.D.

"You're Dr. Frank?" Maggie asked. The name sounded somehow familiar.

The doctor smiled, his pleasant face creasing. "The one and only." Dr. Frank was of average height and average build, in his early fifties, but his face seemed enormous, like a baby's, with pale, fat cheeks beginning their descent into jowls. He wore a rumpled Donegal tweed suit, his dark hair slicked back with Brylcreem, and he smelled of copious amounts of spicy cologne.

Mark peered into the office. "You don't have a receptionist?"

"I like to keep things simple—no receptionist, no bookkeeper. Usually my daughter keeps my appointments."

"Where is she today?"

"Are you checking in?" Frank asked. "I can help you. My daughter—who also works as a part-time receptionist—has taken today off, I'm afraid," he told them, extending a fleshy hand. There was a gold signet ring on his pinkie finger. "I have a medical office here and own the building, and a few others in the neighborhood."

"No, we're not checking in," Maggie replied. "But we would like to speak with you. I'm Maggie Hope. And this is Special Agent Standish from MI-Five."

"Please come in."

His office was a mess, with papers and books everywhere, framed medical diplomas including a doctorate of psychiatry askew on the walls. The heavy velvet curtains were drawn, and the fire had burned down to red embers. His enormous desk was overflowing with yellowing newspapers, dirty mugs, an ashtray full of butts. Papers spilled out of the trash bin.

When the doctor saw Maggie's look, he grimaced. "So sorry. Again, usually my daughter keeps me on a tight leash, but—" He shrugged and picked stacks of books off the chairs. "Please, sit down."

Mark took off his hat, but they kept their coats on. Upstairs, pounding and hammering began.

"Just some post-Blitz repairs." Dr. Frank smiled. "Now, how can I help you two?"

"Do you remember a woman named Joanna Metcalf, who may have stayed here in late March? And another young woman named Doreen Leighton? She might have checked in around the same time, maybe a day or two later?"

Dr. Frank shrugged. "I'm afraid I'm not on a first-name basis with all my guests."

"Miss Metcalf was found murdered on the twenty-seventh," Maggie said flatly. "And Miss Leighton on the twenty-ninth."

"Oh, dear, how terrible," Dr. Frank murmured, rubbing soft hands together.

"We want to confirm if either of them was staying here—and if and when they checked out," said Mark. "We're also interested in another possible guest, a Miss Gladys Chorley."

"And Brynn," Maggie added. "That is, Miss Bronwyn Parry."

"Oh, how I wish May were here," Dr. Frank complained. "She's the one who checks everyone in and out—plus she has a keen eye for detail."

"May we see the hotel's guestbook?"

"Of course!" Dr. Frank answered, rising. He went to the reception desk and took out a worn black leather volume. "Here we are," he said as he walked back, handing it to Maggie.

She paged through the entries. "Look, here's G. Chorley, signing in on March twentieth and then signing out again on the twenty-first. But the entries are in different handwriting."

"My daughter might have signed one or the other."

Maggie ran her gloved finger down the entries, not caring about ink stains. "Here's Joanna Metcalf, who signed in but not out. Same with Doreen Leighton." When she reached a particular line, she shivered with dread. "Brynn Parry also checked in on the twenty-eighth, but according to this, she never checked out."

"I must say," the doctor confided, leaning toward them, "I'm awfully glad you're here and asking about these matters. I can't tell you how many letters from parents I've received since this awful war started, asking if I know the whereabouts of their daughters. And every once in a while, a private investigator shows up." His fingers plucked at his tie, as if it were suddenly too tight. "Of course I'm happy to help them as best I can."

"Of course," Maggie agreed, although still shaken. "What sorts of questions do they ask?"

"They want information—the names of friends, forwarding addresses, suggestions on where to look next, that sort of thing. Sometimes May can tell them a little something about the girls."

"We'll need to cross-reference your guestbook with our missing persons list and list of the dead."

"Of course, of course, Miss Hope." Dr. Frank dipped his head.

"It's grieves me, truly grieves me, to hear these young women have gone missing. I often think of the parents and say a little prayer they've found their girls safe and sound. Maybe they've simply eloped. Or joined the women's services?"

Neither Maggie nor Mark responded; instead, Mark passed Frank his card. "If anything else should come to light, call us. We may need to bring you in for additional questioning."

"If I hear anything, anything at all, of course I'll let you know at once."

Maggie rose and went to look at his desk. There was a silver-framed photo of a woman in a smart hat with a young man—slight, with mousey hair and eyes. "Oh, that's my daughter, May, and her fiancé, Nicholas Reitter," Dr. Frank told her proudly. "He recently graduated with degrees in engineering and architecture. He's going to be surveying and making maps in the Middle East soon. We're lucky to have him—Nick's helped us out with a few repairs and some remodeling. He's fantastic not just with architecture, but the real mechanics of running a building as well, including the water and gas lines."

With the word *gas*, Maggie made the connection. "You're the man who also owned the building in Pimlico—the one that blew up due to a problem with the gas line."

Frank blanched. "It wasn't my fault. . . ."

Mark interjected, "The Met police are on it," he said, shooting Maggie a significant look. "We need to focus on *our* case."

Maggie nodded and looked down at the book. "It says here that Brynn Parry is staying in 745. May we see her room?"

"It's been cleaned any number of times. . . ."

"Why would it have been cleaned if Brynn Parry never checked out?" Maggie asked.

"We're not the most organized around here, as you may have guessed. . . ."

"We'd still like to see the room," Maggie insisted.

"Of course," Dr. Frank agreed, rising. "Please, follow me."

The doctor procured an enormous brass ring bristling with different-shaped keys from his desk drawer and set off. Maggie and Mark followed him into the rickety elevator, then through the hotel's winding passages.

Frank unlocked the door to room 745. The narrow bed was neatly made with a faded quilted coverlet.

Maggie and Mark examined the room and adjoining bath but found nothing. Maggie stopped at the windowsill. Down below, a horse-drawn cart proclaimed: MIKE'S GRINDING SERVICE—KNIVES, SCISSORS, GARDEN TOOLS—SHARPENED.

"What's that?" she asked, pointing across the way to a matching shabby red-brick building set off the street.

"Ah," Dr. Frank said, his round face creasing. "Our sister property. Brother property, really, as it's an all-male residence hotel. I own it as well."

Directly across was a window with the curtains open, a telescope pointed toward the room. *A voyeur. A Peeping Tom.* Maggie gestured to Mark. "Look," she urged, pointing at the telescope.

"Do you know who that particular room belongs to?" Mark asked the doctor.

"Yes, it belongs to one of our long-term residents, Mr. Leonard Roth." Frank lowered his voice. "He's a Jew, you know," he confided. "Not one of those Zionist ones, of course—a German Jew, one of the good ones. His family's lived a few generations in England—you can be sure I checked."

"We'd like to see his room," Maggie declared. "Now."

———

Across the street, in Leonard Roth's room, they found not only a telescope, its gaze fixed on the women's rooms across the way, but several charcoal drawings of women in various states of undress.

"Oh, dear," Frank murmured in distress. "You don't think—"

"We'll need to speak with Mr. Roth." Maggie handed the drawings to Mark to place in his briefcase. By the bed, they found a stack of writings by Jean Genet, Lawrence Durrell, and the Marquis de Sade.

"Look," Maggie said, picking up a book on the dresser: *The Fantasies of Mr. Seabrook,* with photographs by Man Ray. The cover showed a naked young woman bound in black leather and ropes, her mouth gagged.

In the nightstand, Mark found French pornographic magazines featuring women in collars and restraints. Maggie opened one of the dresser drawers: hoods, gags, several paddles, and a cat-o'-nine-tails. "Well, it seems our Mr. Roth is quite the libertine."

"I'm sorry you had to see this, Maggie." Mark's face was grave. "No lady should even know about this sort of thing."

Oh, please. "I've read *Lady Chatterley's Lover* and *Fanny Hill,* you know—I'm not a child." Then, of Frank, she asked, "Where does Roth work?"

"The BBC," the doctor answered, unable to tear his horrified gaze from their discoveries. "He's a wireless announcer."

"I'll make a call," Mark told Maggie. "Have him picked up."

She nodded. "And please ring Durgin to say we'll meet him at MI-Five."

Chapter Ten

Two undercover MI-5 officers were dispatched to the Broadcasting House, the home of the BBC on Langham Place, and brought back Leonard Roth. He was tall and slim and somewhere in his forties. He was a handsome man, in a slick, unctuous way, with too much sandalwood cologne and hair crème.

"All right, same as before," Durgin warned Maggie, eyes narrowing. "Mr. Standish and I will do the questioning—and you may watch through the mirrored glass."

"And, as before," Maggie countered, "I'd prefer to be in the room and contribute to the interrogation."

"Sorry, Miss Tiger," Durgin told her, not unkindly. "And I'm sorry you had to see the sorts of things you found in his apartment."

Oh, for heaven's sake. "So, let me get this straight—you're not worried about my seeing the corpses of murdered women, but you *are* worried about my seeing writings and photographs about sex? Sex trumps death? I'd say that's rather puritanical, Detective. And here I thought we Yanks had cornered the market on that."

"If Roth's our Blackout Beast, there will be stories disclosed you might not have the stomach for, Miss Tiger."

"If you hadn't noticed, Detective, I don't scare easily."

"And, as I've said before, there are facts he might not disclose in the presence of a young woman."

There were bigger battles to fight. "Fine."

———

In the interrogation room, Leonard Roth sat at a wooden table, drumming his fingers.

"I'd like to lodge a complaint against the agents who came for me at the BBC," he began in plummy tones. "Not only did they manhandle me, but they caused me undue embarrassment. How I'm going to explain this to my producer—"

"Looks like you enjoy a bit of manhandling," Durgin interrupted. He took the seat across from Roth. "Or is it that you like to do the manhandling yourself?"

"What the devil?" Roth exclaimed.

Mark took the charcoal sketches of the girls in various stages of undress from his briefcase. He set them on the table, fanning the papers out like a deck of cards. "How well did you know these women?"

Roth looked down at the drawings, then gave a short, strangled laugh. "This is a simple misunderstanding—I don't know them at all."

"You seem to know them quite . . . intimately," Durgin insisted.

Roth crossed his legs and leaned back in his chair. "Well, it's not my fault the girls don't close their blinds, now, is it?"

Mark leaned in. "It's not as if they're expecting someone across the way to have a bloody telescope!"

"If you ask me, if they left their curtains open, they wanted to be seen." Roth shrugged. "Probably enjoyed it."

"Where did you take them?" Durgin pressed. "When you met with these girls—where did you go?"

"I never met these girls—I never even spoke to them!" He tugged at his tie. "I know it might not look like it with everything you've seen in my room—but everything I do is, er, solo."

"Where were you on the nights of March twentieth, twenty-seventh, and twenty-ninth?"

There was a pause as Roth searched his memory. "I was at the studio," he managed. "I was on the air, live! I daresay you won't find a more airtight alibi than that."

"You could have recorded your voice and snuck out while it was playing."

"Gentlemen, I have a team of sound engineers, writers, and producers, as well as scores of adoring fans. Believe me, if I'd left the studio, it would have been noted!"

Durgin turned to Mark. "Confirm his story with the appropriate people at the BBC." He turned back to Roth. "We're releasing you," he told him, standing. "For now. Don't leave London."

The two men met Maggie back in the observation room.

"Well, so much for that," she said, disappointed. "Just because he's a Peeping Tom with distinctive taste in literature doesn't make him our murderer."

"Do you want to go with me to the BBC?" Mark asked. "Verify his alibi?"

"I told you yesterday," she chided, giving them both a mysterious smile. "This afternoon I have an appointment—tea with the Queen. But first I need to change."

"And how's your day going, young sir?" Maggie asked Griffin. From his bassinet fashioned from a dresser drawer lined with blankets on the kitchen table, the baby waved his chubby fists and drooled. "Ga!" he called.

"Yes, my sweet—'ga,'" Maggie answered, bending to kiss his head.

K rubbed his face against her ankles, and she reached down to pet him.

Chuck was heating up leftover Woolton pie. "Do you want some?"

"I'd love a piece," Maggie replied. "Skipped breakfast."

"From what I'm hearing," Chuck said, taking out silverware, plates, and napkins, "the explosion was absolutely preventable." Maggie noticed her hands were trembling. "The police found evidence someone was tapping the building's gas main—stealing it. Whoever did it used a hose attached to the gas line, to siphon it off." She set two places, keeping everything out of Griffin's reach. "Thank goodness most people were at work, but two mothers and three small children died. I only knew them by sight, but—" She faltered, unable to continue.

Oh, poor Chuck . . . Maggie got up and put her arms around her. "Shhhh . . . Now, why don't you sit down and rest—and I'll serve up that pie."

Dazed, Chuck obeyed, sitting at the table and reaching out to hold on to Griffin's bouncing foot. "We're lucky this little man didn't want to take his nap. And I was so angry, Maggie! You should have heard all I was saying as I packed him up in his pram. I was tired and just wanted a lie-down myself. The last thing I wanted to do was go to the park." She looked down at her gurgling baby in awe. "But he saved both of our lives."

"Thank goodness," Maggie said, using pot holders to take the pie out of the oven. "Will there be any funerals? Memorial services?"

"Yes," Chuck said. "Of course we're going." She rubbed at her eyes. "But I don't want to dwell on it. Tell me about you—what's going on in your life?"

"Oh, work," Maggie said, dishing up the pie, steam rising in curls. "Just paperwork, you know—answering the telephones and filing—boring things like that." She brought two plates over to the table.

"Any news on your sister?"

"Half sister. And not yet. But I *am* going somewhere rather exciting today."

"And where's that?"

"Buckingham Palace." Maggie grinned. "To take tea with the Queen."

Chuck dropped her fork. "Blimey O'Riley!" she exclaimed. "And here you are, keeping it so quiet. You could be a spy, you know! One of those Mata Hari secret agent types."

"Oh"—Maggie took a bite of pie, nearly burning her tongue—"don't be silly!"

"Well, Jesus H. Roosevelt Christ!" Chuck exclaimed, pressing her napkin to her mouth, her eyes aglow.

Maggie was glad to see her friend distracted.

"And now let's talk about the truly important things in life." Chuck took another forkful of pie and blew on it to cool it. "What are you going to wear?"

Maggie tried on dress after dress, as Chuck, Griffin, and K looked on.

Everything she owned was old, worn, and shabby. Most of her clothes were patched, some had holes from moths, while others had been made over using collars and cuffs from other outfits. "I could always wear my ATS uniform." Maggie pulled out her brown Auxiliary Territorial Service regalia.

Chuck crinkled her nose. "Er, no," she said. "No offense, but the Wrens have the best outfits. The ATS uniforms . . ."

Maggie sighed. "I know. They're not really flattering, are they? I love those black stockings the Wrens get to wear. We get only the loathed lisle."

"Why didn't you buy any clothes when you were in America?"

"I was busy with things like toothbrushes and soap. And silk stockings. And chocolate. I did buy a dress, but alas, it's a gown. I wore it to the New Year's ball."

"And books."

"And books," she admitted.

"You know," Chuck said, "I don't know how you'll feel about this, but there are other clothes here. I hope you don't mind, but I was having a poke around and found Paige's old things. I know you two used to share clothes. They're in her old room—well, Elise's new room, I suppose."

Maggie left her room for Elise's, with memories of her late friend and former flatmate, Paige, swirling about her, despite the new paint and construction. She walked to the closet of the yellow bedroom and opened the doors. There were all of Paige's clothes from the long-ago days before the war. They smelled faintly of mildew and a haunting touch of her Joy perfume. Maggie ran her hand over the pebbly bouclé fabric of a Chanel jacket. *Paige always did have wonderful taste. And plenty of money.*

Maggie pulled out a Schiaparelli suit. While the skirt was plain black silk, the jacket was black with a bright pink collar, embroidered with silk butterflies and demoiselles. In an instant, she made her decision. The suit was too beautiful not to wear.

"Do you think it's all right—to wear her old clothes?"

" 'There's a war on, you know.' " Chuck hugged her. "Carpe diem, my friend," she said. "Take it from me—carpe the fucking diem."

———

At the gates of Buckingham Palace, Maggie could see bomb damage to the Neoclassical façade. She smiled as she remembered David's critique of the palace's architecture—*Excruciatingly dull indeed—like a huge provincial Edwardian bank with the interior of a pretentious railway hotel*.

Looking closer, Maggie could see some of the broken windows had been boarded up. The ornate black iron fencing had been removed to make tanks and planes. And there were the huge craters in front of the main gates; workmen in coveralls were filling them in with wheelbarrows full of tar. Like the rest of London, the Palace had seen better days.

Despite the bomb damage, the targeting of Buckingham Palace by the Luftwaffe had resulted in only partial success. Physical damage was limited, and there had been no mass casualties. After one of the attacks, the Queen had expressed her solidarity with fellow Londoners, remarking, "I am glad we have been bombed. It makes me feel I can look the East End in the face."

Still, as Maggie eyed the balcony she was keenly aware this war would end in one of two ways: with the victorious King and Queen waving to crowds of their beloved people from above with the Union Jack waving proudly—or, instead, with them being hanged publicly from the same balcony, under red swastika banners.

Maggie showed her engraved invitation to the guard on duty and was directed beyond the façade to the inner quadrangle, decorated with symmetrical yellow stone panels, with oeils-de-boeuf, roses, garlands, and angels.

Another security check at the stairs of the entrance, and Maggie was escorted up the crimson carpet of the dramatic double staircase, then through the Grand Hall, with its gilt and mirrors.

Queen Elizabeth stood near the door of the Blue Drawing Room, flanked by ladies-in-waiting, greeting her guests. Petite yet commanding, Elizabeth wore a trademark Norman Hartnell—

designed dress in powder blue, light brown hair coiffed in perfect marcel waves with a wispy fringe of bangs. Her jewelry was her usual triple strand of graduated pearls, swaying teardrop earrings, and a diamond-and-pearl shell brooch. At her feet swirled a number of corgis, their eyes button-shiny and fur glossy.

Maggie tried not to startle, as she remembered one of those dogs had once given her hand a good chomp at Windsor Castle. The corgis appraised her, but didn't approach. *Well, that's a relief.*

"Good afternoon, Miss Hope," the Queen declared in her silvery, high-pitched voice. "Thank you so much for coming. It's delightful to see you again."

Maggie curtsied. "Your Majesty, thank you for inviting me. I'm honored to be here."

When the Queen extended her delicate gloved hand and gave Maggie's a gentle squeeze, the younger woman tried not to giggle at a sudden vision of the Queen eating Mrs. Roosevelt's proffered hot dogs at Hyde Park.

"The Princesses are here at the Palace today," the Queen told her.

"How are they, ma'am?"

A cloud passed over the Queen's face. "They're strong and resilient young women," she answered firmly. "The King and I are proud of them and all they're doing for the war effort. Although"—here the Queen leaned in, and Maggie detected the faint scent of lavender water—"between us, Lilibet's knitting is still rather lumpy."

Maggie repressed a smile. "It always was a bit, ma'am."

"However, there *is* some cheerful news," the Queen added with a proud smile. "Princess Elizabeth is to be Colonel of the Grenadier Guards!"

"Oh, how perfectly wonderful! Please convey my congratulations to the Princess."

"And speaking of women doing their all for the war effort, what are you doing these days, Miss Hope? Only what you're allowed to share, of course."

"I've recently returned from the White House, ma'am, where I worked for the Prime Minister during his trip to see President Roosevelt. And now I'm with SOE here in London, while waiting for the arrival of my sister—half sister."

The Queen clapped her hands together. "How wonderful! When I see how close Lilibet and Margaret are . . . Well, I think everyone should have a sister."

I only hope Elise and I will be that close. Maybe someday.

A line of guests was starting to grow behind Maggie, and the Queen took notice. "We'll chat more later, Miss Hope," she told her. "Enjoy the tea."

Maggie bobbed another curtsy. "Thank you, ma'am."

The Blue Drawing Room was ornamented in the Georgian style, in crimson and gilt. The walls were covered in cobalt flock wallpaper punctuated by tall columns painted to resemble onyx. Maggie suppressed another smile as she looked at the assorted curly, gold-legged furniture with sculpted backs, knowing David had called similar pieces "Ministry of Works Louis XIV." The tall windows overlooked private gardens, and Maggie could see the snow falling heavily now, collecting in the tufts of grass on the lawn.

The room was set up for afternoon tea, with silver urns, platters of sandwiches, scones, and cakes on a large plantation table, and armchairs with low side tables provided for informal seating. A harpist plucked arpeggios in a corner.

Upon closer inspection, Maggie saw little ivory cards with calligraphy that proclaimed the sandwiches beetroot and faux mayonnaise, liver pâté and celery with mustard, and cucumber and margarine. The scones were potato, with mock cream, and the cakes were eggless, made from carrots with spices. Forced yellow jonquils decorated the tables, and the china service for the austere meal, she was amused to see, was venerable Minton.

As she selected a few sandwiches and a scone, she heard a low voice behind her. "Ah, it's the infamous Spinster Tartlet!"

Maggie turned. "Mr. Thornton—good afternoon. I believe the last time we met I was throwing you out of my party."

Max Thornton made a low bow. "Forgive me, Miss Hope. I perhaps had too much to drink that evening." He used silver tongs with lions and unicorns to place a piece of cake on his plate.

"What brings you to Buckingham Palace, Mr. Thornton?" Maggie asked as they made their way down the table, selecting various tidbits. "I do hope you won't be turned out of here as well."

Max smiled. "I'm on the Women's Advisory Committee for Aviation."

Maggie tried not to gasp. "You?"

"Yes, I." He added in a low voice, "It's a wonderful way to meet pretty young ladies, you know." As they made their way to the delicate chairs, he asked, "May I sit with you, Miss Hope?"

"Suit yourself." As she took a bite of a beet sandwich, she was mortified to see red and white cat hair on Paige's skirt.

Their table was near a taped-up window looking out at the lawn, enormous urns empty and statuary stark and cold against the hazy gray sky. As the snow flew thicker and faster, Max took a sip of tea and looked around. "Rather flash, no?"

"I would call it . . . theatrical," Maggie countered, trying to be diplomatic. As they ate, they were surrounded by more guests, ladies of all ages in flowered dresses, hats, and waxy lipstick, and a few older men in well-worn Jermyn Street tweed suits.

When the crowd had finished their tea, the Queen, who'd been making the rounds, stopped in the front of the room, corgis at her feet. She drew the guests' collective attention and silence without having to say a word.

One of the corgis gave a huge yawn, then settled with his head on his paws and closed his eyes.

"I speak to you, the women—and yes, I see we have a few men here as well!—of the British Empire, who have been forced into war."

All attention was focused on the Queen. "Let us not forget those on whom the first cruel and shattering blows of war have fallen—the women of Poland," Elizabeth continued in her sing-song way. "Nor do we forget the gallant womanhood of France, who are called on to share with us again the hardships of war. War has at all times called for the fortitude of women.

"When it was an affair of the fighting forces only, wives and mothers at home suffered constant anxiety for their dear ones, and too often the misery of bereavement. They could do so little for the men at the Front. Now, this is all changed.

"For we, no less than the men, have real and vital work to do. To us also is given the proud privilege of serving our country in her hour of need. The tasks that you have undertaken are in every field of national service.

"I would like to thank you for giving your help in these trying times. When war is over we will continue to work for the continued well-being of all mankind."

She gifted them with a brilliant smile. "Thank you all."

When the applause had died down, Max told Maggie, "Of course, when the men come back from battle, it will be quite a different story."

"Yes," Maggie replied in kind, "they'll have a lot of changes to get used to, won't they?"

Max ignored the gibe. "Want to step out with a future RAF pilot?" he asked, using his handsome profile to great advantage.

"I used to step out with an *actual* RAF pilot." *Yes, and look how that turned out.*

"John Sterling. Yes, gone now—to make cartoons for Walt Disney. Not exactly men's work."

"Wartime propaganda," Maggie corrected, concealing her surprise at how much he knew. "Words and images—just as important as bombs these days, if not more so."

"You know," Max said, taking the last bite of cake, "before this war started I was studying to be a doctor."

"The military can always use doctors, of course."

"I was thinking, maybe instead of joining the RAF, about going back to finish medical school. Only a year left in my training . . . But the idea of flying a Spitfire is hard to shake off." He grinned.

"You won't continue to work for Mr. Churchill?"

Max shrugged. "The Boss knows I'm not going to be around forever. Although I feel sorry for him—losing all of the best and brightest young men to the services. Soon we'll be down to a few nearsighted Jews and women."

"Are you *trying* to be offensive, Mr. Thornton?" she asked, warning in her tone. "Or are you just stupid?"

It took a moment for her remark to register. "Sorry, sorry!" He laughed. "Don't be so spiky! Look, Maggie," he said, with his most earnest gaze. "We've obviously gotten off on the wrong foot. Let me make it up to you with dinner tonight—"

"Miss Hope!" The Queen stopped by their table, a trail of corgis following in her wake like ducklings.

Maggie and Max rose. "Yes, ma'am?"

"Walk with me, please, Miss Hope," the monarch commanded. "We didn't get to finish our conversation earlier."

Maggie shot a look at Max, then returned her gaze to Queen Elizabeth. "Of course, ma'am."

The corgis all waddled after the Queen as she led Maggie out of the drawing room. The massive oil paintings in the corridor had been removed for safekeeping, but the ornate Sansovino frames remained, works of art in themselves. Still, there were stains on the ceiling from water damage, and some of the plaster on the walls had been shaken loose, probably from bombing. Although there were a few guards in sight, Maggie and the Queen had relative privacy underneath the glittering chandeliers.

"It looks better at night," the Queen confided. Maggie noticed she was holding a glass of what looked—and smelled—like Dubonnet and gin. "And I must confess I prefer Windsor. I live for the weekends, when we can get back to our girls."

Maggie dared a look at the Queen's face. Her opalescent powder had settled in the creases around her eyes. She had aged in the last years. "It sounds challenging, ma'am."

The corgis' claws clicked on the gleaming wood not covered by the carpet, and a few had decided to start yapping. "Hush, darlings." The Queen opened her handbag and pulled out a small box of treats. She shook some onto the carpet, and the dogs dove, silent at last. *So* that's *what the Queen keeps in her handbag.*

One of the dogs looked up at Maggie, bared his sharp teeth, and growled low in his throat.

Oh, heaven help me. "Is that Dookie? I think he remembers me from Windsor." *And ruining my lovely leather gloves.*

"Of course he does! You remember Miss Hope, darling Dookie?"

Dookie the Corgi. My canine nemesis. But a loyal defender of the Princesses.

As Dookie took his biscuit, continuing to glare, the Queen turned back to Maggie. "Did you enjoy the tea?"

"Yes, ma'am, thank you. And your words were inspiring. It's wonderful you've taken the time to acknowledge and appreciate women's war work." Then, impulsively, she went on. "It's not al-

ways easy. You know. To be female in the professional world." She
took a breath. "I know Your Majesty has many concerns, but
women in the SOE—"

The chewing corgis all plopped themselves down on the carpet
with a collective sigh.

"Yes, Miss Hope?" the Queen prompted.

"They're doing the same job as the men, but not being paid the
same salary or receiving the same benefits. Not all of them return,
of course, from their missions—and their families are cheated out
of a pension."

"Hmmm . . ." The Queen pondered. "I'll look into it. I don't
know the details of what you actually do for the war effort, Miss
Hope, but I know—and Lilibet *certainly* knows!—all you have
done and how much you've sacrificed for the Royal Family. I can't
even imagine working in such a male-dominated profession—
which is why I want to say to you as a fellow Briton, a fellow
woman, and a grateful mother, if there's anything I can ever do to
help you—anything—please don't hesitate to ask."

Maggie felt the enormity of this offer. It was dizzying, as if she
were a knight having a Queen's token bestowed on her before battle. "Th-thank you, ma'am."

Once again, the Queen reached into her handbag. This time,
she pulled out a guilloche and gold card case, and removed a thick
white card, engraved with black lettering. "Should you ever need
to see me, dear—in an emergency—merely show this."

"Yes, ma'am." Maggie accepted the card with awe and gratitude. "Thank you, ma'am."

"And I'm very glad this is not goodbye; we will meet again tomorrow night."

"Ma'am?"

"For dinner! Just a small one, but the Princesses are here at

Buck House and they do so want to see you. What? You didn't receive that invitation? It's for you and a guest—"

"I've been traveling—and changing addresses, ma'am."

"Well, then, let me extend a personal invitation—come to Buckingham Palace tomorrow evening at seven-thirty, for dinner. Formal dress, of course."

Chapter Eleven

By the time Maggie passed back through Buckingham Palace's gates and into the dingy gray afternoon, the snow had stopped falling, but the slicing cold wind had once again picked up. The marble statue of Queen Victoria looked down worriedly at her subjects as the streets filled with people making their way through the slushy snow, desperate to get home before the sun set and blackout commenced. There was always an urgency at this time of day, to find safe haven.

"Ah, there you are!" Max approached, red-striped university scarf flapping. "This is a dangerous wind."

"You caught me, Mr. Thornton," Maggie said, her voice lost in the gusts. *And here I thought I was getting away.* . . .

"*Max*, please. And, again, I'd like to take you to dinner. To make up for my beastly behavior. Would you let me, Maggie?" He turned the full force of his charisma on her.

"Dinner, fine," she said loudly, almost shouting. "But it's going to have to be an early night."

They took a taxi to Covent Garden as the sun set, transforming London into an unfamiliar shadow world. "This place is one of my favorites," Max announced, seizing Maggie's arm in a viselike grip and steering her up the stairs of the Market's gray stone piazza to the Punch and Judy pub. As they walked, snow, leaves, newspaper pages, cigarette stubs eddied and swirled at their feet. She fought the urge to shake off his grasp. Her gut was telling her to. *But there is no "gut,"* she admonished. *Think like the mathematician you were trained to be. Aunt Edith would be appalled at the very idea of "the gut."*

And you don't want to be rude, after all.

The bright, bustling dining room of the pub seemed far removed from the dark, windy world outside, with its ornate gilded mirrors and shining brass chandeliers with frosted globe shades. The waxed, wooden walls glowed.

Maggie and Max checked their coats with a young woman with lank brown hair drawn back in a velvet snood, then maneuvered between the front tables near the bar, where diners sat with gas masks at their feet. Finally, they found a small table in the corner.

Beneath the high-beamed ceiling, framed posters of Punch and Judy shows through the years lined the walls, and puppets were displayed over the long oak bar. The mosaic floor was made of tiny black and red tiles, and the room thrummed with the clatter of metal against china, the clink of glasses, and the low rumble of conversation. It smelled of beer and cabbage. SOYA LINK SAUSAGES ONLY, warned the chalkboard menu.

"Would you like a drink?" Max asked her. "I find in these dark times, alcohol is often the solution."

"Actually," Maggie replied with a smile, trying to be gracious, "alcohol is not a solution—alcohol *plus* tonic is a solution." It was one of chemistry professor Aunt Edith's favorite quips.

He looked aghast. "There's certainly no tonic available now—"

Poor Max. He doesn't get it. "Actually, I'd prefer tea, please."

"Surely something a bit stronger!"

"No," Maggie countered. "I'd like tea. Thank you."

As Max went up to the crowded bar, she idly looked over to a dartboard. A game was in progress, with a cluster of white-haired men in the middle of a heated contest, their calls to one another growing more boisterous the more beer was consumed. Still, regardless of drink, they were good shots, and Maggie watched as player after player's darts hit the red bull's-eye, one flushed man in the corner keeping score.

"Fish and chips!" a gentleman in suspenders chortled as his three darts hit the 20, 1, and 5 for a total of 26. The rest of the group raised their glasses to him as he gave a toothy grin and took a deep bow. His friends applauded.

The dartboard reminded Maggie of the map they had at Mark's office with its red pushpins. *In darts, each player's trying to hit the bull's-eye or come as close as possible,* she mused. *But the Blackout Beast wanted to get the bodies as far away as possible from where the murders took place. He wouldn't leave a body too near the scene of the crime and/or his residence.*

Maggie watched as another man with wispy white hair and rolled-up checked shirtsleeves shot his three darts. They fell on the outer ring, and his friends taunted him with a chant of "Fish, fish! Fish!"

She chewed her lip, deep in thought. *While the dart player's goal is to hit the center, the serial—sequential murderer's is to create a protective zone. When the Blackout Beast dumps the bodies, he's going to want it to seem random—no evidence too close to him. But when someone's trying to do something at random, and not make a pattern—there's always an unconscious inherent design to it.*

A jolt of realization shot through her. *Could one create a formula that would point to where the killer was located, based on where the bodies are found?*

Max returned from the bar with two whiskeys. He sat in the chair opposite Maggie and put a glass in front of her while raising his own in a jocular salute.

"Thank you," she said, eyeing the whiskey, wishing for pen and paper to write down her dart-inspired revelation. "But I asked for tea."

"They're out of tea."

Maggie didn't believe him. As she left her drink untouched, she watched Max drain his glass in one thirsty gulp. He rolled the tumbler between his palms and held Maggie's eyes with his. She found his gaze disconcerting and looked back to the darts game.

"You know, I loved Punch and Judy as a child," he said, gesturing to a framed red-and-white striped poster on the wall near them, an enraged, hook-nosed Punch beating Judy over her head with his stick.

Maggie studied one of the Punch puppets above the bar: This one had a papier-mâché head with a red face, a sugarloaf hat, and a hunchbacked body clad in scarlet jester's motley with a tassel on his cap. He carried a huge black stick. "I didn't grow up with Punch and Judy." She imagined the beatings the Judy puppet must have endured over the years. "The show's not as popular in the States."

"Have you ever even seen a Punch show?"

"In passing, in the parks. It's a bit violent for my taste."

"Nonsense! It's great fun! Covent Garden is where it all started, you know."

"You seem to know a lot about it."

"I admit I had puppets when I was a child—and used to put on my own little shows. I had a pretty good swazzle, if I do say so myself—that's Punch's traditional voice." He cleared his throat. *"Hullo, Judy my girl. I want a little dance. What do you mean, you don't want to dance? I'll beat you silly and throw the baby out the window! What a piece of work about nothing!"* He smirked like a Cheshire cat. "I played a passable Devil, too."

"I don't like how Mr. Punch treats his wife." In most of the

performances Maggie had seen, Judy had been bludgeoned to
death, to the cheers of the audience.

"Oh, it's all in good fun. Besides, Judy's no angel herself. She
has it coming, really." Max laughed. "Why don't I get us some
food," he declared, more of a statement than a question.

"No." Maggie had lost her appetite. *I need to get home and work
on the formula. . . .* "I need to get home."

"Oh! Want to go somewhere quieter? More private? Do you
know anywhere around here where we can go? Air-raid shelter,
perhaps?" he added with a suggestive leer.

Maggie stood. "I'm leaving now."

"Are you a naughty girl?" he asked, mimicking Mr. Punch's
shrill tones. The effect was unsettling.

"No, I'm not. And stop using that ridiculous voice."

Max pulled out his wallet and opened it. He continued, still as
Punch, *"I have plenty of money, you know. Let me show you something."* He flashed a thick wad of bills.

"Put that away," Maggie hissed. "You'll be pickpocketed."

"I have about fifty pounds."

"Good for you," Maggie said. "I encourage you to use it to see
a psychoanalyst." She headed for the coat check and then the exit
without a backward glance into the windy darkness.

"Look," he called after her, following. "If you'd be kind enough
to have dinner with me, I promise I'll show you a good time." He
stepped in front of her. "Please."

"No."

"Let me at least get you home safely. It can be dangerous for
young ladies out there in the dark. I insist."

People were staring. Maggie saw no way of getting rid of him
without making a scene. "Fine."

They walked side by side toward the Tube station. Beyond the
blacked-out windows and blank façades, people's voices could

be heard, enjoying the evening. Happy noise in the darkness of the blackout always struck a strange chord with Maggie, the disembodied voices seeming somehow macabre. After turning down James Street, Max said to her, "Do you know I've had my Mr. Punch moments, too? I hit a girl once. Knocked her out."

What? "And why would you do that?"

Once again, he began to speak in Punch's squeaky tones. *"Because her old man didn't like me, you see. So I kicked him in the privates and then knocked him out."*

Maggie realized there seemed to be no point to this strange admission and continued to walk, faster now. The pavement, covered in the afternoon's snow, now turning to ice, was slippery. And in Paige's tight Schiaparelli skirt and heels, she couldn't walk as fast as she would have liked.

Max kept up with her easily. "Did you know there's a drug you can give to dogs to prevent them barking during air raids? It is called Calm Doggie, and you can buy it at any chemist's—I admit to using a few myself during the Blitz. Slept like a baby through everything."

Calm Doggie. Maggie had heard of the pills you could grind up and put in dog food. *Could it work to knock women out before they were murdered? Was there any way Mr. Collins could test for it being in the women's blood?*

In the heavy darkness, she found it increasingly difficult to find her way and reached into her purse for a small electric flashlight, with regulation blackout shutters. She turned it on and shone the weak beam on the ground as she picked her way forward in the gusts.

Again, Max stepped in front of her. "You don't want to use that," he told her, taking the flashlight from her and switching it off. He tossed it into an alley.

"Hey!" Maggie was angry. "That's mine!"

"But you have me, my dear, you have me!"

"I'll take it from here on my own."

"But I want to kiss you good night. There's an air-raid shelter not far from here. It will be empty, I promise." Punch's voice in the darkness made her flinch.

"No." Maggie was adamant. "I've had quite enough of your cheek, Mr. Thornton. Goodbye."

"You must call me Max." He pulled her into a doorway off the street.

"I said *goodbye!*"

Max tried to kiss her, putting his hands on her waist, then moving them lower.

"Stop it!" Maggie hissed, shoving him away.

He pinned her against the wall to block any escape and took her face between his hands. As Maggie opened her mouth to scream, his fingers wrapped around her throat. When he squeezed, she gasped frantically. But the more she struggled, the tighter his grip became. His fingers dug deeper into the flesh of her neck.

Her throat began to close and her arms grew heavy. A thick gurgling noise was the only sound escaping her mouth—but she could hear another sound, too—him, moaning in pleasure as he rubbed against her.

Her SOE training kicked in and she kneed him in the groin. While he cried out in pain and clutched at himself, she grabbed his head with both hands, pulling it down so she could slam it against her rising knee, hard. She heard a satisfying *crack*.

He slumped to the top stair of the doorway, hands to his face. "Bitch!" he screamed into the shadows. "You broke my nose!"

As Maggie backed away, she could see the blood dripping down his upper lip, black in the dim light. He spat out a loose tooth, looking shocked, almost offended. "How am I going to explain all this at Number Ten? I can't work for the Prime Minister looking like this!"

"Not my problem." Maggie shrugged, turning to walk away. "Maybe it's time to join the RAF."

"You whore!" he spat. "Dirty slut!"

"No," Maggie said, her voice calm and her senses sharp despite the pulse pounding in her ears. "If you want a prostitute, go to Hyde Park and use your money. But I'm not for sale. And never yours for the taking."

He rocked back and forth in pain, pinching the bridge of his nose to stanch the flow of blood. "You're all for sale, all of you bitches . . ." he moaned. "You let me buy you whiskey, you smiled at me, you liked it. . . ."

"I was merely being polite. My mistake." *Lord, good manners just might get women raped—or worse.* Giving him one last look of disgust, she ran off into the darkness.

Lungs burning, heart thudding, Maggie opened the front door to her house with a heavy iron key.

"Hello?" she called, pushing the door in with trembling hands. She slammed the door behind her, then bolted it. "Chuck? Mr. K?" She heard padding footsteps and then felt soft fur swirling around her shins. "Ah, there you are, K," she exclaimed, reaching down to rub his head. "And how's our Home Guard doing this evening?"

Somewhere upstairs, a light was on. "Chuck?" she called, instantly wary. Her heart lurched with fear. *Had the doors all been locked? Could anyone have gotten in? Could Max have gotten here first—he knows where I live, after all. . . .* "Chuck, are you all right?"

Maggie took the stairs two at a time in the chill air, K behind her. Chuck's door was ajar, with light spilling out onto the hall's rug. "Chuck?" Maggie called, heart racing, rapping at the door. "Are you there?"

There was the sound of footsteps, then Chuck stepped out into the hall, closing the door firmly behind her. "Jesus H. Roosevelt Christ, girl!" she whispered. "I just got His Nibs to sleep and now you come in yelling and pounding on doors. . . . All right, it *is* your house and all, but—"

"No, no—I'm sorry," Maggie countered, laying a hand on her friend's arm. "Not used to babies, I'm afraid. And I was worried. This place has quite a history—plus with what's going on out there . . ."

"Let's go to your room so we can talk."

Maggie led the way, pulling the blackout curtains closed, then turning on a bedside lamp. K had followed closely at her heels. She went into the bathroom and turned on the water in the tub. "It's been a long day," she called out to Chuck. "A very, very long day."

"How was tea with the Queen?"

"Lovely," Maggie answered, coming back to the doorway. "The palace is . . . ornate."

"How was the food? Were there lots of delicious things to eat?"

"Alas, no—the Royal Family believes in keeping to the same strict rations as the rest of us. But it was well presented—served on the very best china."

"Well, that's no fun."

"Tell me about it."

Chuck looked at her closely. "No offense, Mags, but you look like shite."

"As I said, long day."

Chuck walked to Maggie and turned her around. "Bloody hell, woman! What happened to your throat?"

"A man—he got a bit frisky."

"Frisky? *Frisky?*" Chuck, a pediatric nurse before she'd had Griffin, began to do a cursory examination. "If that's frisky, I'll eat my garters. No," she said, her fingers cold but gentle on Maggie's bruised neck. "That's *evil*, is what it is."

"A bad date is all," Maggie said, turning and changing out of her borrowed finery, then slipping on her robe.

"I'll let you take your bath, but after you finish, come downstairs so I can take a better look at your neck and put some ice on it."

"Fine," Maggie agreed wearily. "Thank you. You're a lifesaver."

"Are you going to report him to the police?"

"No, I don't think that's necessary." Maggie remembered the blood dripping from Max's nose and the lost tooth. "He's learned his lesson."

Chuck shook her head in disapproval. "I'd have him hanged by his pretentious university scarf. Oh, and I'm so sorry to have to tell you this, but there's no hot water."

"*What?*"

"I took the liberty of checking the furnace today. We're completely out of coal. And while there's some coke left, it's not enough to last us to the next delivery. So—if it's all right with you—we're doing hot water on an alternating-day basis. This happens to be a 'cold' day, but I found some hot water bottles and left you one on your bed. We can boil water in the kettle and fill them up tonight."

Bloody hell. Bloody, bloody hell.

"I'll heat you up something for supper," Chuck continued. "I made a veggie mash—all right, it's mostly all turnips and cauliflower with margarine and some bread crumbs, but it's not half bad, really. . . ." She left the room, heading for the stairs.

"Sounds perfect." She'd postpone the bath for another day. One with hot water. "I'm just going to wash up at the sink and come downstairs. And then you can tell me about *your* day."

"And I can treat your neck!" she called from the stairwell. "I don't like the look of those bruises!"

K was still winding around her ankles, and as Maggie washed her face, trying to rinse off the horrible evening, he jumped up on the closed lid of the toilet to keep watch. "Bold little thing, aren't you?" she scolded, and he gave her slow blinks. Her hands went to her neck as she peered at it in the mirror. The marks were red and growing darker.

K began to purr.

Maggie met her own eyes in the mirror. *You were afraid,* she realized. *But not afraid of him—afraid of being rude. Rude! Afraid of trusting your gut. How many women are raped and worse because they've—we've—been taught to be pleasant, to be a good girl, to keep the men happy?*

She gave her reflection a grim parody of a smile. *Never again,* she vowed, splashing cold water on her face and darkening bruises. "I do solemnly swear I will trust my instincts—my 'gut'—from now on," she told the cat. "No matter how unscientific it may seem."

It was slightly warmer down in the kitchen and smelled of mashed potatoes; the wireless was on, playing "Chattanooga Choo Choo."

"Well, your breathing's fine, your eyes are fine, and your voice is fine," Chuck reported once she'd examined Maggie. "Here," she said, going to the icebox. "I got some snow and wrapped it in a tea towel. Wrap that around your neck. It will take down the swelling."

Maggie did as she was told, then began eating the vegetable

mash Chuck put in front of her. It was plain, but hot. And she was unexpectedly starving.

Chuck pulled down the bottle of Jameson whiskey David had procured for her the night of the party. "Saving it for a special occasion—but I think this might be it." She poured both Maggie and herself a glass. "What the devil's this world coming to?" She pointed to the newspaper. "You probably haven't had time to read the paper yet—what with tea with the Queen and the attempted strangulation and all that—but there's more news from the East about the Jewish camps."

"Heaven help us," Maggie said, taking a sip.

"We don't have the details yet, but whatever's going on over there, it's evil incarnate," Chuck said, taking a swig of her whiskey. "Look—'Extinction Feared by Jews in Poland'—Henry Shoskes says the monthly average of those dying is ten thousand. Ongoing! I'm a nurse and I've seen dead bodies. Then I try to imagine one body times ten thousand—and that's just a month—and my mind simply can't do it."

Maggie tipped her head back and gulped the remains of her whiskey.

Chuck looked to her friend. "Sorry. I know you've had a bad day."

"Mr. Churchill once gave a speech and he changed 'dark times' to 'stern times,'" Maggie said softly. "But sometimes I think he should have left it that way—these really are dark times, aren't they, Chuck?"

"More whiskey?"

"Yes." Maggie held out her glass, trying to hold back thoughts of Brynn, and Calm Doggie, and the dead women in the morgue. "Yes, please."

Brynn slept on and off, increasingly disoriented and unaware of time, of day and night, of days passing. The only markers she had were the meal trays left while she was asleep, usually toast with margarine, and tea, and the occasional sandwich and small, wrinkled apple.

Brynn was sure she was being drugged, but she couldn't taste it in the food. Still, she ate sparingly, and drank the tea only to soothe her parched throat. Despite her precautions, her hands had tremors and she couldn't shake the disoriented, foggy feeling that kept her in bed, or the waves of nausea rolling incessantly through her.

What was most disturbing, however, was how someone had access to her room, someone was coming in and going out, and she was unconscious when it happened. It was more than disconcerting. It was terrifying.

Still, she sat up and breathed, calming her heartbeat, giving her brain oxygen, clearing her mind. As she did, she became aware of a sound piercing through the heavy door and thick walls.

It was faint, but still distinct.

The sound of a woman screaming.

Chapter Twelve

The phone rang at five A.M.

Maggie scrambled out of bed and ran down the hall to answer it, shaking off a headache. "Yes?" she said, disoriented and out of breath. "Hello?"

"There's been another murder," Durgin stated without greeting or preamble.

Maggie was instantly wide awake. *Work. Yes, work is what I need.* "I'll meet you and Mark at the coroner's."

"Just what I was thinking." He hung up without saying goodbye.

DCI Durgin stood next to Mr. Collins, hands clasped behind his back, eyebrows drawn together, as he watched the autopsy. "The recent murder of Miss Olivia Sutherland is an exact reenactment of Jack the Ripper's killing of noncanonical victim Emma Elizabeth Smith in 1887," Durgin announced to Maggie as she walked in.

"Good morning, Detective, Mr. Collins." She had wrapped a flowered Liberty of London silk scarf around her bruised throat.

She stopped short when she saw the body of the young woman. *Oh God, poor Olivia Sutherland.* She had a sudden urge to run out of there, run as fast as she could. Go back to bed, hide under the covers, and weep for Olivia—for all of them who'd ended up on a coroner's table.

But instead, she bit the inside of her cheek and then asked, "Where's Mr. Standish?"

"He called in sick." Durgin looked disgusted. "Sick! Wouldn't catch a Yard copper calling in sick. Ever. Not even with plague."

"Sick?" Maggie had never known Mark to take a day off. As Durgin shrugged and rolled his eyes heavenward, she said, "Never mind. Where was Miss Sutherland's body found?"

"Cross of Gloucester Road and York Street."

With a deep sigh, she pulled the map of London that Mark had given her from her handbag and marked off the newest location with a red X. The Xs were making a loose circle, a hangman's noose. She bit her lip. If her theory was correct, it was growing ever tighter around the place the Blackout murderer was holding and killing his victims.

"What's that?" Durgin asked, approaching to peer over her shoulder.

"It's—it's something I'm working on. A map of the places the bodies were found. I'm working on a mathematical formula—it's an idea I had while I was watching a darts game last night—"

"Oh, that reminds me—how was tea with the Queen?"

At this, Collins looked up from the corpse and gave Maggie a sour glare.

Maggie was in no mood to engage. "Her Majesty sends regards. Any witnesses?"

Durgin turned back to the body. "My men are doing the usual appeal now. And we've had press sniffing around. Can't let them get hold of it—or we'll have a panic on our hands."

"Might not be the worst thing," Collins interjected. "Maybe the young ladies will stay home at night for a change. They should all be under curfew—at least until this bastard's been caught."

Maggie's hand crept to her bruised neck and worried at her scarf. "And why should the young ladies have to stay at home and off the street, Mr. Collins?" she asked in a preternaturally calm voice. "*They* certainly haven't done anything wrong. Perhaps it's the men who should be under curfew—they're the ones committing these horrible crimes, after all." Then, "Is there any way to test if the women were given a calming medication, such as a tranquilizer?"

Collins gave her a curious look, then frowned. "Unfortunately, no. Someday, I hope we'll be able to test for what, if any, drugs are in the bloodstream, but for now, if it's not in the stomach and recognizable, we don't know."

"Find any fingerprints?" Maggie asked.

"No." Durgin was still staring at her. "Still nothing. You know, I'm considered to be rather an expert on fingerprinting—and the cheeky bastard's not leaving any."

Maggie circled the woman's body lying on the gurney. "In the original Jack the Ripper killings, the police examined the eyes of those killed—they believed the victims' retinas might have somehow retained an image of the killer. . . ."

"I already checked her eyes," Collins snapped. "You think I don't know how to do me job? Of *course* I checked her eyes. I checked the eyes of all the girls."

Maggie had an odd feeling in her stomach. *Could this be "the gut"?* "No, no," she clarified, "not the eyelids. The eye*balls*."

"There's no way in hell she could have fingerprints on her eyeballs! In all my days of working on the dead—"

Maggie dug her fingernails into the palms of her hands.

"Shut up, Collins," Durgin interrupted. "Did you check?"

"Well, no—"

"Then, I'm going to dust her eyeballs for prints," Durgin declared. He went to the metal counter and took out a feather brush and a glass jar filled with dark gray powder, as well as a small paper printed with the words ADHESIVE STRIPS and a blank leather-bound notebook. Dabbing the brush into the powder, he approached the corpse. "Would you do the honors?" he asked Collins.

"Sir! Yes, sir!" Collins responded, still aggrieved. He went to the body and pried open the left eyelid, then gestured theatrically to the detective.

Maggie's stomach churned, and she was suddenly glad all she'd had that morning was tea.

As Durgin gently brushed the powder over the exposed eyeball, an image began to appear. Maggie moved closer to watch, mourning the murdered woman, disgusted by the physicality, but also undeniably and irresistibly fascinated by the science.

Durgin continued to move his wrist with delicate grace and guide the brush with his fingers. More and more lines began to emerge, like a photograph developing in its chemical bath. "The chemical composition of fingerprint powders can vary," he murmured, "but they all basically work the same way. Latent prints are created by the natural secretion of sweat and oils from the skin that leave behind an outline of the ridges found on one's fingers. A person's fingerprints remain constant from womb to grave. Only damage to the skin of the finger can alter the print. So each print is wholly unique—even the prints of identical twins differ."

The Detective Chief Inspector tapped his brush back into the powder and began again. Faint swirls began to take shape on the eyeball.

"My goodness," Maggie breathed.

"I'll be damned," Collins muttered. "The murdering devil *did* leave a print on her eyeball. Deliberate, I'd say. Like a bloody calling card."

Durgin selected an adhesive strip and placed it on the powdery eyeball. He waited, peeled the strip off, then pressed it to a blank white page in his notebook. There it was. A fingerprint, as distinctive as a snowflake.

"Good job, Miss Hope. What I'm using," Durgin told Maggie, "is Henry Faulds's classic method of recovering prints from a crime scene."

Through a magnifying glass, he examined the print in the book. "It's a good one," he assured them. "So we can take it back to the Yard and see if we have a match.

"You were right this time, Miss Tiger," he said, straightening. "Good on you. But don't get your hopes up. First of all, there are hundreds of thousands of prints and no way to match them, except going through all of them one by one. And we have limited manpower. And, even if we *could* go through all of them, there's no guarantee there'll be a match in our records. And, even if there is a match, a positive latent match doesn't guarantee a conviction."

"Still, when we catch our Blackout Beast, we'll have solid evidence for his arrest and conviction," Maggie mused. "Detective, you did say serial killers—er, sequential murderers—have the same sorts of victims, the same ways of murder, and always a calling card? We thought the Ripper graffiti was his calling card—but here's a far more personal one."

"Glad to see you've been paying attention," Collins muttered.

"Collins," Durgin said. "You'll check the eyeballs of the other Blackout Beast's victims for prints, yes?" It was not a question.

"Oh, the things I do for lurve . . ." the shorter man grumbled, but went to pull on gloves nonetheless.

Durgin peeled off his, tossed them into a garbage bin, then scrubbed his hands with soap and water in the sink. "Good job, Miss Tiger."

Maggie tamped down her surge of pride—she didn't want the

men to see any emotion, good or bad, in her expression. No smiles. No reactions. *To exist in a man's world, you need a face like a poker player's.*

Durgin dried his hands and picked up the notebook with the print. "And now let's head to the Yard. Maybe we'll get lucky and this devil's print will match something in our books."

The New Scotland Yard, on the Victoria Embankment, was housed in respectable-looking large red-brick Romanesque-style buildings, slashed by thick horizontal bands of white Portland stone. As Durgin led Maggie through a maze of poorly lit corridors inside, she couldn't help but wonder: How many murders had he worked since the outbreak of war? Too many, probably—and how sad and ironic. How many air raids had the people survived? How many nights had they been dragged from the warmth of their beds by the wailing of sirens? To survive the Luftwaffe bombs—only to be murdered by a fellow Briton . . . She shuddered.

"The governing principle of forensic science, as laid down by Edmond Locard at the beginning of the last century, is 'every contact leaves a trace.' " Durgin was speaking as swiftly as he walked. The peeling painted walls they passed bore posters: *DO YOU KNOW THIS MAN? City of London Police—Murder of Police Officers—REWARD!* And *ENLIST NOW—YOUR KING NEEDS YOU.* "There are eight basic fingerprint patterns of arches, loops, and whorls. And every human finger fits into one of these categories in its own unique way."

Maggie nodded, listening intently. This was a science she didn't know—it was intriguing.

They reached a door marked EVIDENCE ROOM. Durgin opened it and led them in. The room was large, with towering pigeonhole cabinets lining all four walls. "We have about ninety thousand finger- and thumbprints on file here," Durgin said, going to a cabinet and pulling down binders. The middle of the room was stacked with boxes upon boxes, marked ROPE AND TWINE BINDINGS, TORN AND STAINED CLOTHING, and DEATHBED SHEETS. Maggie walked around them. Exactly what horrific tale had each box to tell, what mysteries could each solve—if only there were enough time and manpower to devote to them all?

Durgin gestured for her to follow him. "Now we have to see if our Blackout Beast's prints match any we have here." They reached a large room of desks, and Durgin went to one by a large window overlooking the Thames. The river glimmered coppery green in the gray light, and curved like a snake. "Have a seat," he said as he put down the books of prints. "I'll get us some tea and then we'll begin."

Tea? Made for me? Maggie tried not to smile as she took off her coat and sat opposite his desk. It was chilly in the vast room, despite a few portable radiators glowing orange dotting the perimeter, and she left her gloves on. Stacked around each desk were boxes and boxes of files, again marked EVIDENCE. It would take an army to get through them all in any sort of timely way, and even so, more and more cases were pouring in. The staggering amount of information, each box representing a dead person, made her head spin.

"He doesn't have to work these cases, you know." At the desk next to Durgin's, a broad man with carroty hair streaked with white looked over as Maggie arranged her scarf to make sure it covered her bruised neck. His nameplate read GEORGE STAUNTON. "He's of senior rank, but he insists on working murder scenes himself."

"Really?" Maggie realized how little she knew of the DCI.

"Oh, Durgin's probably sent—let's see now—hundreds of murderers to the gallows over the years. He's too modest to say, but he's our own Sherlock Holmes, he is. He hates that it's on the wall, but you should read it." Staunton jerked a thumb at a framed *Time* magazine cover that read HIS MAJESTY'S GOVERNMENT'S REAL-LIFE SHERLOCK HOLMES, with a picture of a younger Durgin with his magnifying glass.

He was handsome, Maggie thought. *Still is, really.*

She walked over to read the smaller print. The caption said: *Detective James Durgin is far more human than the great fictional sleuth, and the cases he handles are of a bloodier nature.*

"I framed it for him, just to tick him off—he hates it. He hates any kind of publicity. But he'd be a fool not to take on the Beast," the orange-haired Staunton continued. "It's a career maker, it is. Did you see this morning's latest?" He handed a newspaper to Maggie. The headline screamed, HUNT IS ON FOR THE BLACKOUT BEAST!

The article described the gruesome slayings and Scotland Yard's search for a maniac, written with lavish speculation and very little accuracy. *Well, if our Blackout Beast is looking for attention, he's certainly got it now,* she thought grimly.

Maggie looked over Durgin's desk. No photographs. No books. Nothing personal at all, except for his nameplate and, tucked in one corner, a worn postcard of Simberg's *Wounded Angel.*

Durgin returned and set down the tea tray on the desk. "Grand, just grand," he groaned, seeing the headline.

"Do you want me to be mother?" Maggie asked, out of habit.

"No, you're our guest. I'll pour."

Well, this is getting better and better.

Durgin grimaced. "Afraid the milk's powdered."

"I simply adore powdered milk. It's what the Queen serves at Buckingham Palace, I'll have you know."

Staunton glanced over. "I wouldn't mind a cuppa, old man."

"Well, get your lazy arse up and get your own mug, you sorry blighter!"

Maggie hid a giggle behind one hand.

"Er, sorry, Miss Hope," Durgin said. "We're a bit informal here. Not used to ladies around."

"It's fine. Comradely, in fact."

The DCI handed her a mug of steaming tea. "I'll wager you've heard worse."

"Indeed."

Staunton passed a stack of messages to Durgin. "Questions from the press."

"Oh, my favorite part of the job." Durgin rolled his eyes and began to flip through them.

"They keep asking if the women are"—Staunton looked sideways at Maggie and lowered his voice to a stage whisper—"*virgins.*"

"Oh, good grief." Durgin ran a hand through his hair.

"They want to know if the girls were, you know, good girls," the other detective continued, "or if they, you know, got around."

Double standard. They would never ask that of a male victim. . . .

Durgin shook his head. "We're telling them nothing."

"The press do like to divide women into virgins and whores, don't they?" Maggie said. "And if the victim was a virgin, then it's 'oh, poor thing!' and if she wasn't, then there's the insinuation 'she got what she deserved.'"

"It's not relevant either way." Durgin pushed the message slips away and picked up his mug.

"Showed your Miss Hope the magazine cover," Staunton teased.

"Hate that damn thing!" The tips of Durgin's ears turned pink.

"Don't believe a word of this malarkey," he said to Maggie. "They only framed it to torture me."

"You're quite the legend, Detective Durgin," she declared, sipping her tea. "Mr. Frain told us a bit about you when we started, but certainly not the whole story." She now appreciated the depth and breadth of Durgin's experience—and understood his arrogance and impatience with outsiders. Forensics was a science, a complicated and relatively young one—she didn't know the half of it. Yet.

"So what's your take on all of this?" she said, pointing to the Blackout Beast headline.

Durgin gulped from his mug. "What makes our case unique, in my opinion, is the speed with which the murders are taking place." He poured himself another cup. "In all my years, I've never seen a murderer repeatedly strike with such brutality in such a short span of time. Our Beast is going at it awfully fast. Something's going on in his life—something's troubling him, a catalyst. And killing—well, that relieves some of the pressure. But not enough. So he has to do it again. And again."

"Do you think it's stress from the war?" Maggie asked. "He's a veteran? Injuries to the brain? What they call 'shell shock'?"

"Maybe, maybe not. My gut still tells me he's younger. Everything's changed with the war, but, then again, lots of things are still the same. There are the same barroom brawls, petty thefts, rapes, assaults, and murders—maybe even more now. And we have new immigrants—the Poles, the Canadians, and now the Yanks— coming in and not always on their best behavior. Ironically, the Blitz has given the perfect cover for our own killers to hide their evidence—strangling or beating their victims, then hiding the bodies in the wreckage of a shattered building. Who knows how many people, allegedly victims of the Blitz, were actually murdered? The sheer number of bodies we've retrieved since this war's started has made it impossible for us to autopsy all of them."

He shook his head. "But our Blackout Beast—he's a narcissist. Cocky—which is why I'm hypothesizing he's young. He's far too brazen to hide his deeds in the mess left by the Germans. He wants us to find them, he's practically gift-wrapping the bodies. He has some nerve, he does. Still"—Durgin tapped at the side of his nose—"he's not new at any of this—his work shows too much experience. Too much control. He's not an amateur, but he still wants to show off. He must be loving the attention from the newspapers."

Staunton left, after muttering something about "getting my own damn tea," and Maggie noted how much she liked being with Durgin, despite the circumstances that brought them together. She had never heard Durgin so loquacious and decided to press on, to try to learn something about the man himself. "Why did you become a detective?"

"Books."

Maggie wasn't about to be put off by his short answer. "Which books? *The Adventures of Sherlock Holmes*?"

"No, actually." He drained the last of his tea. "As a young lad, I was an aficionado of the literary adventures of Detective Sexton Blake by George Mann. Detective Blake's the anti–Sherlock Holmes. Whereas Holmes pontificates and theorizes, Blake's a man of action. Do you know, there were times as a boy where I'd go to my room to read Blake's latest adventure, only to find the comic gone?"

He laughed. "I'd conduct my own 'investigation,' which would always end at my father's chair. And, underneath the seat cushion, I'd always find the missing magazine." He sat back in his leather desk chair and grinned. "My father wouldn't admit to reading such a thing, of course, so he'd say he was screening it to make sure it was appropriate for an impressionable young lad such as myself. Yes, as if I'd believe that!"

"So, you always wanted to be a detective?"

"I loved Sexton Blake, but I didn't think detective work was something real people did. Police work, yes—detective work, no. But then I eventually left Glasgow for Oxford, I had what the doctors call a cervical rib"—he pointed to the right side of his rib cage—"a protrusion of bone from the seventh cervical vertebra, near the neck, pushed against a nerve, causing a lot of pain. I was admitted to hospital for surgery and, during recovery, my roommate happened to be a former officer of the Metropolitan Police Department. He'd been shot in the face, can you believe? While trying to apprehend a suspect, of course. He was in hospital to preserve the sight in one of his eyes. So I was bored, and he was bored, and pretty soon I had him talking about all of his adventures on the force—and it brought back the memory of all those Sexton Blake stories."

"How do you do it?" Maggie asked, sincerely. "Work as a detective? And keep on doing it?"

Durgin refilled his mug. "Many, *many* cups of tea, obviously."

"No, really. How?"

"You're thinking about becoming a detective?"

"I just want to do my bit to help win the war."

"Fair enough." He rubbed his hands through his hair. "The men I hunt are evil. I believe in Satan. I believe in his power. I believe he can work through us if given half a chance. These men I pursue, like Satan, they target the weakest among us, usually women and children. I like nothing more than to catch them and throw them to the courts. It gives me immense satisfaction. There's nothing like it."

Durgin took a breath. "It's taken its toll, obviously—you can't witness the mutilation of children and violent murder in its infinite forms without it corroding your soul. But I continue to fight. It's all about the fight for good over evil, God over the Devil." Then, as if realizing how much he'd said, "But enough about me—back to work!" He handed Maggie a book with cataloged fingerprints. "Let's try to find ourselves a match, shall we?"

She was glad to see the maniacal glee was back in his eyes.

In her feather bed at the Adlon, Elise had nightmares of Ravensbrück. In her dreams, she was on a witness stand in a cavernous courtroom, run by impassive judges with blank faces. She was asked to describe her experiences—and the words wouldn't come. When they did, they came slowly, painfully, with gaps and long stretches of lost memory.

She looked down at the defendant—a man made up of crawling black flies. She knew instantly he was Satan. She needed to bear witness against Satan.

It's important. Think.

She woke up panicked and feeling powerless. *Someday I will testify.* She stretched her body, feeling for all the painful places. She pointed and flexed her feet. They were slowly healing.

"Elise, are you awake? You have a delivery!" her father called.

Elise rose and slipped into one of her father's dressing gowns, which he had given her.

The package on the dining room table was from the KaDeWe department store. Elise knew the luxury store well, from the days before the war.

"Well, open it!"

Inside, wrapped in lavender-scented tissue paper, were an abundance of clothes: tights, wool dresses, sweaters, underthings, nightgowns and bed jackets, fur-lined boots, and, yes, a wig. She gasped, then impulsively pulled it over her scalp. "What do you think?"

Her father clapped and beamed. "A film star! Ingrid Bergman!"

Elise stepped to the large mirror in the hall. She saw herself with long golden waves once again and repressed a gasp. Then she reached out a hand to touch the locks. It was hair, yes—real human hair—and she suddenly had a good idea of how it had come to be a wig. She blanched and ripped it off, throwing it on the floor.

Still, it's not his fault, she thought, struggling to control her breath. "Thank you, Papa," she said, picking up the wig and giving her father a hug.

"I wish I could take credit, but it's not from me."

"Then who—?"

"Perhaps there's a card?"

Left in the box was a heavy envelope with her name handwritten on it in old-fashioned Fraktur script.

> *Dear Fräulein Hess,*
>   *I have taken the liberty of asking my sister to put together some items a young lady might need at this time of year.*
>   *Yours sincerely,*
>   *Alexander Fausten*

"Completely inappropriate!" She backed away from the box as if it were a bomb. "Throw it out," she declared. "Wait—give it to the poor. I won't wear anything from *him*."

Hess's eyes blazed. "Who? Who sent you these things?"

"Captain Alexander Fausten. The man I met with yesterday at the Gestapo."

Hess's demeanor changed from angry to beaten. "I didn't want to ask you yesterday, because you looked so tired," he ventured, "but how did it go? With"—he couldn't say the words—"them?"

Elise began to pace. "Captain Fausten wants me to sign a paper exonerating Dr. Brandt and incriminating Father Licht."

"How is Father Licht?"

"Dead."

"They killed him?"

"The official story is he suffered a heart attack on the train trip to Dachau."

"Ah." Then, "If you sign this paper, what happens?"

"Then I can stay here, in Berlin."

"And if not?"

"I go back to Ravensbrück."

Elise's father was silent for an agonizing moment. "How long do you have to decide?"

"I must give them my answer next week."

Her father was silent. Then he placed his large, warm hand over hers, tears welling in his eyes. "Think carefully, my darling. Think very, very carefully."

Mass at St. Hedwig's was a somber affair, with Nazi banners hung from the soaring arches and a gold-framed picture of Hitler on the altar. When it was over, Elise waited in line to speak with the new priest, Father Ulrich Kappler.

"Thank you for a wonderful mass, Father Kappler," she said as the crowd dissipated.

The priest took in her shorn head and scarf and took an involuntary step back. "Thank you, Fräulein," he murmured, recovering. "May the peace of Christ be with you."

"And also with you, Father Kappler. It is I—Elise Hess. I worked closely with Father Licht—"

The priest glanced around to make sure no one had overheard. "We do not speak his name here," he whispered.

"Why not? He was a good man. A great man. A great priest."
People were beginning to stare, and Elise ignored them. "We
should be celebrating Father Licht's life and raising our voices in
protest against his death—"

Father Kappler looked to a few Brownshirts at the church
doors. At his glance and the sound of a rising voice, they began to
walk over.

But before they reached Elise, Captain Fausten appeared at her
side. "Thank you, Father," he stated, pulling Elise's arm through
his. "Fräulein Hess isn't feeling well. I'm sure you'll understand if
I take her home now."

Father Kappler's worried eyes took in his SS uniform and rank.
"Of course, Captain. Heil Hitler!"

"Heil Hitler!"

"Are you insane?" Fausten hissed as they walked down the front
steps.

"St. Hedwig's is my church. My home. My sanctuary." Where
once tears would have flowed, now Elise's eyes were dry. "Father
Licht, my priest—my hero—is dead after being taken away to
Dachau—and I'm not supposed to even acknowledge his existence? I'm not supposed to speak his name?"

"No." Fausten's face was shuttered like a Wannssee villa closed
for the winter. "He is now considered a traitor to the Reich, and
the less you say about him—the less you think about him—the
better."

"He will be sainted."

"Maybe." Fausten exhaled. "Someday."

"Years from now, we will pray to Saint Licht. And the Father
Kapplers of the world will be either reviled or forgotten."

"In the meantime, Fräulein, I strongly advise you to keep quiet."

As they walked down Behrenstrasse, their breath made white mist in the frigid air. The church bells rang, their silvery music cutting through the chill. But even though Elise was physically home, in the city where she grew up and lived all her life, she felt incredibly alone.

Who are these people? What have they done with everything I've ever known and loved about my city—my country? And her heart was filled with longing. For kindness, for peace on earth, for goodwill toward man. *Where has it gone? How did it disappear so fast? Will it ever return?* She looked up to the cloudy gray sky, searching for some sort of answer. There was nothing.

Elise gave Fausten a sideways glance. "What are you doing?"

"I'm walking you back to the Adlon."

"Why? Am I under surveillance?"

He smiled. "No, I am a proper German gentleman. I will see you home." They walked together in silence. "I had no choice, you know," Fausten offered. "I didn't choose this way of life. I went to law school, before I was conscripted. I wanted to be a lawyer. But not for the rich—to defend the poor."

"So, you're educated. That fact makes it even worse. For it makes you not only arrogant but also willfully ignorant. You should have known better. You should know better now."

Fausten stopped her. "I'm not your enemy, Fräulein Hess."

Elise gave a bitter laugh. "Of course you are."

He rubbed at the back of his neck. "No, you don't understand—I am Alexander Fausten. My favorite book is *The Magic Mountain*. My favorite composer is Bach, especially the *Brandenburg Concertos*. My favorite opera is *The Magic Flute*. I love mountain climbing and *Pfannkuchen* filled with plum jam. I love playing the violin but have no sense of pitch. I don't always believe in God, but I go to church and try, every single Sunday. My mother, I'll have you know, loves me and thinks I'm a great catch for any young German woman. I'm a person. I want you to see me as a person, not this uniform."

"Not like a Jew? Not like a Pole? Not like a 'rabbit'? Of course your mother loves you. I'm sure Hitler's mother loved him. But— let me ask you this—how can you believe in God, at least try, and do what you're doing?"

"I am many things and one of them is honest, Fräulein. Blunt, even. And I will tell you now, in all honesty, that in these times you must learn to be quiet and play the game—or else you'll end up back at Ravensbrück."

"Would it be the worst thing?" Elise turned away.

Fausten caught up with her easily. "Well, yes. Your chances of survival there are low, despite your Aryan blood."

"Would it be worth betraying Father Licht? All those dead children? All those parents who grieve now, whose children are dust in the wind or lying in unmarked graves?"

"Would Father Licht really want to see you die?"

"Why doesn't the Pope protest about the roundups and the camps, do you think? It's been bothering me—why doesn't he speak out?" Snowflakes began to swirl, catching on Elise's eyelashes.

Fausten looked everywhere but her eyes. "His Holiness pro-tested the deportation of non-Aryan Christians in the Netherlands— and forty thousand were rounded up and sent to concentration camps. Every time he speaks out, more die. What if he protests again? Does he want that on his conscience?"

"The Nazis have been the worst thing possible for our country. Tell me somewhere deep down inside, you know. You *know* we as a people are better than this."

Fausten looked around. But no one was in hearing distance as they walked past the wooded edge of the Tiergarten; there was only the sound of the occasional car and horse-drawn cart passing. "I am but one man. What can I do?" They crossed Unter der Linden, the snowflakes falling thicker and faster.

"You could desert," said Elise. "Go into hiding."

"I have no wish to hide, like an animal, never having a moment's peace." Fausten brushed snow from his coat. "And I know what the camps are like. I have no wish to end up there. And neither should you."

"What did you see in the concentration camp?" Elise asked, spotting a chink in his armor. "What did you do?"

"I—I did what I was told," he said curtly. "And I was rewarded with my current position here in Berlin." There was silence as Elise realized what he must have been part of.

He went on, "Please . . . Renounce your Father Licht for the sake of your survival! Then you can stay here. To go back to Ravensbrück is certain death for you, you must realize. We should obey orders—to hate the deviants and the Jews."

"So, you don't really hate them? The so-called deviants and the Jews?"

Fausten took a breath. "I loved a Jewish girl once. She was taken away—Dachau, probably. I pray, for her sake, she is dead."

"Ah, so you do have a heart! And, possibly, a soul."

"Villains are never the villains to themselves, Fräulein. Remember, to my mother, I am a hero. She would say, 'My son, he was an excellent student, graduated first in his class. He plays the violin badly, but I'm deaf in one ear and just turn away. He was going to become a lawyer before the war.' She is proud.

"Then one day I was conscripted. Sent to training camp, taught how to kill. I had no choice. Now she is proud because I wear a uniform that brings our family respect. I do a job that gives me enough money to take care of her."

"There is always a choice."

"No. There isn't!" Fausten's eyes flashed with anger. Elise could feel it radiate off him, like heat. "Not all of us are willing to die for our ideals! *I* am not willing to die! I'm not willing to see my mother rounded up and sent to a camp. I want to be a part of the Germany that rebuilds itself. Eventually. See past the uniform, Elise. I didn't choose it."

They had reached the entrance of the Adlon. The doorman touched his hand to his cap. "Let me take you to the cinema," Fausten said.

"Is that an order?" Elise asked.

"No." He looked pained. "It is your choice. I respect your free will."

Elise was silent.

"I will be at the Ufa-Palast am Zoo for the two o'clock matinee. I will stand outside the theater with two tickets. And I hope you will come and meet me."

The hotel lobby's warm, perfumed air seeped out toward her. Inside, concierges in gold braid whispered assurances to guests and rang tiny brass bells. Bellhops pushed Rimowa suitcases and Louis Vuitton trunks over the polished marble floors. *It's so easy, this world,* Elise thought. *So protected.*

"Good day, Fräulein Hess," Fausten said.

She waited for him to salute and say the seemingly inevitable "Heil Hitler!"

He didn't.

Chapter Thirteen

Miss Lynd of Baker Street had arrived in Beaulieu wrapped in furs and scented with Jicky.

She knew Sarah and Hugh—Madame Sabine Severin and Monsieur Hubert Taillier—had been busy. Agents at the Finishing School learned evasion techniques by being shadowed by instructors around local towns such as Bournemouth, Southampton, and Portsmouth. They had also practiced shadowing other trainees, in and out of department stores and shops in the towns.

Miss Lynd settled herself in Kim Philby's office, with a view of three shaggy ponies chewing on the grass lawn, and waited until the two trainees knocked at the door. "Come in!" she called. She continued in French, "I'm pleased to say all of your instructors have given you excellent reports. How are you two feeling?"

"It's all a bit unreal," Sarah confided, as they both took seats. "But thank goodness muscle memory is helping. And for Hugh, as well."

Miss Lynd nodded. "It will be real soon enough. You've been cleared to go during this full moon. Everyone feels you're ready. And you're needed in Paris."

Sarah leaned forward. "Can you tell us anything more about our mission?"

"I'm sorry," Miss Lynd said, not sounding sorry at all, "but you'll have to wait until you arrive in France. Your SOE liaison there will have further instructions for you." She studied them, her eyes kind. "As we've been saying from the beginning, it's a dangerous mission. You have time to change your mind—and we won't hold it against you."

"Of course we're going!" Sarah exclaimed. "We've worked too long and hard not to!"

"Indeed," echoed Hugh.

"All right then, it's settled—you're going to Paris." Miss Lynd gave a half smile. "Oh, and there's one more thing we need to take care of, before you go. Your codes. Mr. Philby tells me he's gone over it with you and you know your codes will be given to you on silk. You'll use each one once and then burn it. If you can't remember the code, they can't get it out of you."

The unspoken word *torture* hung in the air.

"And, in case you've had to destroy your silks, you've both chosen poems to memorize. But remember, if the Nazis can't find any codes on you, they will know you have destroyed them. They know about the memorized poems, and they'll do everything in their power to get you to tell them. And it's imperative you do not. Remember, if they learn your poem, they can transmit back here as you. Such an ability compromises us and all the agents coming into Paris after you. You'll need to hold out for at least forty-eight hours. That will give your network time to scramble."

"One of the reasons we have our cyanide pills, I gather." Hugh said it quietly.

"Madame Severin," Miss Lynd said, "I will now need to you to tell me your poem."

"I've chosen William Butler Yeats's 'Among School Children.' "

"Well." Miss Lynd raised a plump, ringed hand. "Let's hear it, my dear."

Sarah closed her eyes and recited the poem, stiff at first, but then warming up, until she reached the last stanza:

> *"O body swayed to music, O brightening glance,*
> *How can we know the dancer from the dance?"*

There was a moment of silence, and then Miss Lynd sniffed, her eyes moist. "Quite appropriate. And you, Monsieur Taillier?"

Hugh looked out the office window, the breeze stirring the bare black branches, took a breath, and began Wordsworth's "I Wandered Lonely as a Cloud":

> *"They flash upon that inward eye*
> *Which is the bliss of solitude;*
> *And then my heart with pleasure fills,*
> *And dances with the daffodils."*

There was a loud sniff. "Well, that's done then." Miss Lynd rose. "I'll be seeing you both soon, to take you to the aerodrome."

She smiled, a kind one this time, and genuine. "And I do believe there's a dance at the Domus tonight. Why don't you two take a break from all"—she fluttered a hand—"this . . . and go have some fun?"

At Scotland Yard, Maggie and Durgin went through book after book of fingerprints on cards, but they found no matches to the one he'd lifted from Olivia Sutherland's eyeball. Still, they'd covered only a small fraction of the fingerprints in the books. "I'll get some men on this," Durgin said at last, closing the one in front of him. "But there are walls of these books. What you saw in the evidence room is really the tip of the proverbial iceberg. And we just don't have the manpower right now."

"And even if every single record is checked, he might not have committed a crime?"

"I'm sure he's committed any number of crimes," Durgin replied gruffly. "But either he's been smart enough to get away with them, or he's posh enough to talk himself—or buy himself—out of an arrest." His expression was one of utter disgust. "Our august British class system at work."

"Although if—when—we catch the Blackout Beast and fingerprint him, the evidence linking him to all the murders will be absolute." Maggie took a sip of tea, long grown cold. "You know, regarding the original Jack the Ripper case, there were all sorts of conspiracy theories: that Jack was a Mason, that he was a Royal, that he was related to Queen Victoria. Some theorize Jack could have been a woman. If we can only figure out what narrative our Beast's using . . ."

She sighed. "But theorizing isn't going to help. Would Sherlock Holmes have theorized? No, he would have stuck to the evidence. The facts." She looked up from the book to Durgin. "He would have loved your fingerprinting system."

"Holmes is a fictional character."

"Yes," Maggie agreed, "but Holmes—or rather A. C. Doyle— changed the way we look at and treat evidence."

"As you know, I'm more of a Detective Blake man."

"Isn't it funny," Maggie mused, pulling at her scarf, loosening it, "how Jack the Ripper was a real person and Sherlock Holmes wasn't—and yet we talk about them the same way? In some ways they both feel simultaneously real and fictional."

"When I talk about my gut, you know, I'm not talking about emotion—I'm using years of experience. And, of course, the facts." As he spoke, Durgin took in the bruises on Maggie's neck.

"I understand. I just don't have that experience—and until I do, I think it's best to stick with the facts. I will be Holmesian."

Durgin stared her in the eye. "All right, Miss Tiger—now tell me what happened to your neck—go a round with the Queen?"

Maggie put a hand to her scarf. She didn't want to talk about it, certainly not with Durgin, who might start to worry for her safety and take her off the case. "It's nothing. Really."

The detective quirked an unruly eyebrow. "Do I need to take you to the interrogation room?" He smiled to let her know he was joking—mostly.

"Last night," Maggie admitted, "after tea . . . with the Queen—I went to a pub with an acquaintance. He got a little . . . handsy on the walk home. So I had to put him in his place. He, I promise you, looks far worse than I do."

"Really?" The detective's stormy look brightened. "What did you do?"

"Broke his nose, I think." Maggie tried not to look pleased and failed. "And knocked out a tooth. I'm sure he'll have some explaining to do at work today."

"Good girl!" The telephone on Durgin's desk warbled, and he picked up the receiver. "Yes? Which hospital?" He scribbled on a scrap of paper, then hung up.

"Our Blackout Beast has claimed another, but not only did this girl survive—she's awake and able to talk."

Maggie and Detective Durgin caught a black cab to Fitzroy Square Hospital, where the latest Blackout Beast victim had been taken by ambulance.

With a jolt, Maggie realized the hospital was familiar—and not because of any of the Blackout Beast's victims. "When we're done," she told Durgin, "there's someone else I'd like to visit here." Across the street, the cinema's marquee announced the new film *The Wolf Man* in tall red capital letters. Rows of posters on each side showed actor Lon Chaney, Jr., made up with fangs and fur.

"Of course."

"The Beast's on a roll," Maggie mused as they walked up the front steps of the hospital together, taking them two at a time.

"Almost through with his run, if he's still following the Ripper murders. There's still the double murder—Elizabeth Stride and Catherine Eddowes—and then the final murder—the most violent of them all—Mary Jane Kelly."

"Then what?" Maggie's voice was bleak, thinking of Brynn and the murdered women. "Will he keep on killing?"

"If we don't catch him, he's made his name for the history books, and most likely goes back to murdering women and disposing of their bodies in private. Or he keeps going as the Blackout Beast, charting new territory. He creates a new legend. Regardless . . ."

"Regardless, we need to catch him."

They went to the reception desk and then sprinted up the stairs. Huge taped windows looked out over the street, while the stone faces of winged cherubs watched as the wind whipped through the naked branches, snowflakes spinning down from the sky.

As they traversed the shining floor of the corridor, Maggie's heels clattered. A doctor, a stocky, graying man with a large watch and fat fingers—one encircled in a thick gold wedding band—looked up from a chart as they approached. "You must be Detective Chief Inspector Durgin." He and Durgin shook hands. "Miss Plunket's awake," he told them, snapping the chart closed. "But she's extremely fragile. She can't talk for long."

"What are her injuries?" Maggie asked. "How badly is she hurt?" She bit her lip, fearing the answer.

The doctor looked down his nose at Maggie, as if just noticing her presence. "And you are?"

"Waiting for your answer to her questions," Durgin said. "As am I."

The doctor shot him a look. "Her throat was cut, severing her left carotid artery. There were no other incisions or injuries."

She looked to Durgin. "Just like Elizabeth Stride, Jack the Ripper's third canonical victim."

Durgin's face was grim. "With all due respect, Doctor, we're trying to save women's lives. There's a killer out there—the press is calling him the Blackout Beast. He might have gotten to Miss Plunket."

"I've heard of this Beast, but I can give you five minutes only. She's extremely weak. With all due respect, *Detective*, I'm trying to save a woman's life."

"Before we go in," Maggie interjected, "what can you tell us about her? In Jack the Ripper's day, his victim Elizabeth Stride died. What made the difference for Miss Plunket?"

"We were able to get to her before she bled out. And we now have better medical care than in the Victorian era."

Durgin crossed himself. "Thank God."

"You might want to thank modern medicine," Maggie countered.

The doctor, leaving a trail of lime-scented cologne, led them to Daphne Plunket's room and then left them. "Five minutes," he admonished. "And then I'll be back to throw you both out if you aren't gone."

A petite woman lay in a narrow bed. She looked out the window at the falling snow, her eyes unblinking, her fingers worrying at a blanket's silk-covered hem, which was pulled up to her chin. She had unwashed wavy strawberry-blond hair that fell to her shoulders and acne scars on her sunken cheeks.

"Miss Plunket," Maggie began gently, "I'm Maggie Hope and this is Detective Chief Inspector Durgin. We're so glad to see you're, well, awake now. We—we'd like to ask you some questions about what happened." She shivered, wishing she could spare the blonde any further pain. But she had a job to do. "I know it might not be pleasant, but we're trying to catch whoever did this to you—and stop him from doing it to anyone else. Whatever you can tell us is of utmost importance."

Daphne turned her head toward them and gave a weak smile which seemed to come at great cost. Maggie could see Durgin hanging back. *He's letting me take the lead on this one,* she realized. *He thinks she'll respond better to a woman.*

Maggie poured a glass of water from the pitcher on the bedside table, held it to Daphne's lips, and waited until she took a sip. Then, she steeled herself. "Do you remember anything at all about how you were abducted?"

"He . . . knew a lot about me."

Maggie was careful to keep her voice mild. "Did you know him?"

"No. . . . He wore a mask."

A mask—good God. It must have been absolutely terrifying. "Do you remember anything about him? His hands? His hair? His scent, perhaps? Any small detail could be important."

"He wore gloves," the injured girl managed. "Black leather gloves." She pulled the blanket even higher, as if to hide from the memory.

"Do you live here in London?"

"No, from Cornwall. Interview . . ." Daphne took a raspy gulp of air. "Special Operations Executive."

"The SOE?" Maggie's eyes met Durgin's. He was thinking the exact same thing she was. "And where were you staying?"

"Some . . . hotel. Women's hotel, near Baker Street—don't remember the name. Oh, why didn't he kill me?" she moaned.

"It wasn't about you," Maggie said, stroking the woman's hair. "Whoever did this thinks only about power and hatred and control." Then, "Did he speak to you at all?"

"I don't remember—I'm . . ." She took a tremulous breath. "I tried to be strong. But I shut my eyes. I pretended it wasn't happening. But now, when I shut my eyes, I see him. All I see is him. . . ."

"Shhhh . . ." Maggie opened her handbag and took out a clean handkerchief. She used it to dab the tears away from Daphne's cheeks. As the woman released her viselike grip on the blanket, it slipped to reveal indigo bruises on her neck. "Daphne, did the man in the mask try to choke you?"

"No. I was on a date, going out to dinner, before the man in the mask . . . There were Punch and Judy puppets and posters everywhere. We went somewhere in Covent Garden."

Maggie's heart skipped a beat. "Daphne, what was the name of the man you were with? Do you remember?"

"Max . . . Max something. Handsome man, but got a bit rough when I wouldn't go to an air-raid shelter with him and—you know . . ."

Could Max be the Blackout Beast? He certainly had the temperament for it. "Could this Max be the man in the mask?"

The girl stared at her. Terror flared in her eyes. "I don't know," she said, her voice rising in pitch. "I remember he tried to choke me, but I got back to the hotel. I thought I was safe. I thought I was safe there. *I thought I was safe! I thought I was safe!*"

Durgin called into the hall. "Nurse!"

The nurse, in a white winged linen cap, held Daphne down while murmuring comforting words, then gave her an injection to calm her. When the girl quieted, she sank back into the pillow. Her eyes slipped shut.

"She'll still have to wake up and deal with the trauma," the nurse told them. "But for now she needs sleep."

Maggie looked to Durgin. "This Max is a man named Max Thornton, who likes to take women to the Punch and Judy—I'm certain of it. He's the one who gave me my souvenir." She pointed to her neck.

"The little . . ." Durgin's unspoken profanity hung in the air between them. "Well, then—let's arrest him for assault. You know this Max Thornton? Who the devil is he?"

"He's a private secretary for Mr. Churchill at Number Ten."

"Well, I'm about to get a few officers, go cuff him, and bring him in. I don't suppose you'd like to come and watch?"

Maggie thought of how deliciously satisfying it would be, to see the look on Max's face as he was led off in handcuffs in front of David, Mr. Snodgrass, and Mrs. Tinsley—maybe even the P.M. himself—from Number 10 Downing Street. But she had something to do first.

"I'll leave that task to you, Detective," she said regretfully. "As I mentioned, there's someone else here, another patient, I need to visit. I'll meet you back at Mark's office at MI-Five later. Happy hunting."

Maggie knocked at Edmund Hope's hospital room door. "Hello," she called, always unsure of what to call him. *Dad? Father?* It was almost laughable. *Edmund? Professor Hope? No.*

He had gingery hair like Maggie's, but dusted with gray. His skin was dull and papery. When he looked up from his book, she saw his eyes were threaded with red veins. "Margaret. You're here."

"I am." There was an awkward silence as she tried not to look at the place on the bed where his legs would have been. "You're looking well. I mean," she said hurriedly, "your face has a bit more color, I think."

Edmund blinked.

Well, this is going well, she thought. "So, how are you feeling?"

"Better now," he said. "It was hard at first, but things are improving. And it's been weeks since I had my last drink."

Maggie perched on the visitor's chair. "I have a colleague who stopped drinking. He takes a lot of tea now. Seems to work for him."

The awkward silence returned. "What are you reading?" Maggie asked, desperate to fill it.

He held up the book, its cover featuring a figure caught in transition between man and beast. "*The Werewolf of Paris*. Guy Endore."

"Don't know it, I'm afraid."

"It's set in the nineteenth century—the story of a woman who's raped by a priest and then delivers the baby, named Bertrand, on Christmas Eve. He's a werewolf—born with two souls, one of a man and one of a beast. And, occasionally, the beast's soul takes over and turns him into a wolf, on the prowl for blood."

Inside, Maggie grimaced. The novel seemed to parallel her father's own eerie behavior of the past winter—two souls. "Do you think maybe it's a bit much? I could bring you something lighter? *Blithe Spirit*, perhaps?"

"Life can't be fixed with a book. Or even a play."

"No, I suppose not."

"And, as we get older, making amends isn't so simple, either."

"True," Maggie said carefully, knowing they were on thin ice. Whatever he wanted to say, she wasn't sure if she wanted to hear it.

"I've realized you can't merely say things—you have to mean

them. When we met back in the summer of 'forty, I made a lot of promises to you, and I didn't keep them—"

"Well, as they say, 'There's a war on, you know.'"

"But sometimes there's just too much damage," Edmund pressed. "I know early on in your life I abandoned you. I thought at the time it was for good reasons, or at least important reasons, but now as I look back"—his eyes dropped to the book in his hands—"I have my doubts. I was young and heartbroken and completely unprepared to take care of a child—and so I abdicated my responsibility to Edith. But it wasn't right, Margaret. And you suffered for my passivity and cowardice."

Pain pierced her heart, but Maggie ignored it. "You, er, had a lot going on in your life."

"Yes, but then when you came to London as an adult, we had a second chance. And once again I've disappointed you, let you down."

Maggie was not able to absorb the words, true as they were. "It's—you know—the war. Things are complicated."

"Your Aunt Edith did her best, I know."

"I mentioned I saw her in Washington in December. Do you remember that? You were on some pretty powerful drugs at the time. She's well and sends her regards, too."

"I've caught bits and pieces of your conversations, here and there. I'm glad to hear Edith's well." Edmund looked up to the ceiling fan. "I don't deserve your forgiveness. But I hope you'll give me the opportunity to prove myself."

"Er, thank you." Maggie rose, feeling flustered and confused. Who was this man, really? And how much did she owe him? "I really have to get back to the office now. Big case to solve. Interrogation to get to. Oh, I forgot—Peter Frain sends his regards. By the way, I'm not sure if you know, but Elise is coming to London."

"Elise?" he asked, momentarily confused.

"Clara Hess's daughter with Miles Hess. My younger half sister."

"Ah." A shadow crossed his face.

All Maggie wanted to do was leave. "Well, congratulations again on your sobriety," she said. "Good luck!" she called, forcing her mouth into a smile and trying to sound enthused.

He raised one hand from the book as she left. "Good luck to you, too, Margaret."

When the nurse's aide came in, Edmund barely glanced at her, immersed once again in his book. She was wearing the uniform of a volunteer—a light blue dress with a white cap and apron, each with a thick red cross. They were often in and out of his room. "And how are you doing, Mr. Hope?" came a resonant and smoky voice. "Do you need an extra pillow?"

At the sound of the voice, Edmund looked up in shock. The nurse had dull brown hair pulled back in a tight bun, not cascades of glossy blond waves. And instead of the fashionable made-up look befitting a German opera diva, her face was bare. And she looked older, with lines around her mouth, and a deep slash between her eyebrows.

But he'd know that voice anywhere. It haunted his dreams. "Clara," he whispered, putting up his hands, as though for protection.

"Our daughter's looking well," she said matter-of-factly, nodding in the direction Maggie had exited. "She's the one thing you ever got right."

"*Clara* . . ."

"If she's yours, of course. I have my doubts." She closed the door and locked it. "You tried to kill me, Edmund," she said sweetly, walking over to his bedside. "But, as usual, you bungled it. Just like you always bungled everything. Apparently, nothing changes. Not even after twenty-seven years."

"Who told you?" he said, eyes wild. "Peter? Peter Frain? How did you survive the fire? How did you get here?"

Clara leaned over him with the pillow, looking deep into his eyes and baring even white teeth in a smile before covering his face with it. She pressed it down, hard, making sure he couldn't breathe. "You never wanted me to sing, Edmund," she said as he struggled. "Do you know how gorgeous my voice is? In Europe, the elite threw me bouquets. But you didn't even like me to sing to the wireless around the house.

"Goodbye, Edmund."

When at last his body stilled, and she was certain he was dead, she straightened and tucked the pillow back under her arm. With her free hand, she smoothed back wisps of brown hair that had come free. "See you in hell, darling."

Chapter Fourteen

Elise met Fausten at the Ufa-Palast am Zoo on Auguste-Viktoria-Platz in Charlottenburg. He was standing in front of the enormous classical theater, redesigned by Albert Speer. Passersby gave him and his uniform anxious looks. "I didn't think you'd come," he said, as she approached.

"I didn't think so either. But here I am."

He nodded and opened the door for her, handing their tickets to the usherette.

Inside the cavernous theater, the plush velvet seats smelled of cigarette smoke and wet wool. It was frigid. The newsreel was playing the *Ufa-Tonwoche*, the propaganda short that always ran before the main film.

Elise and Fausten slid into their seats by the flickering light of the glowing screen. Silver light shimmered through the darkness as the film *Jud Süß*, about Karl Alexander, the Duke of Württemberg, who borrows money from a Jew, ruining his city, his court, and ultimately himself, began.

"The Jews are coming into town," the narrator's voice, a deep booming bass, intoned. *"They cross our land like snails. Keep in mind, dear Christian, a real Jew is your worst enemy."*

Elise pulled her coat tighter around her.

"I advise you to burn their synagogues and schools," the voice

continued. *"Get rid of their teachings, which are full of lies. Pray to your God. . . ."*

Elise stood. "I'm leaving."

"It's just started . . ." Fausten whispered.

"I'm not going to sit through this—" she said, making her way up the aisle.

Fausten followed, took her arm and steered her to the door to the lobby. "Shhhh . . ." he warned.

"—cheap propaganda," she finished on the frost-covered pavement outside.

"Cheap?" Fausten retorted. "That film cost two million Reichsmarks!"

Ignoring him, Elise began to walk.

"Veit Harlan really is an excellent director," Fausten added, catching up with her.

"But have you read Lion Feuchtwanger? This film is nothing like the book. Jews have been persecuted throughout history! And this is thousands of years of anti-Semitism distilled into pure . . . hatred. But I have a few other, more pungent words in mind."

Fausten shook his head. "No, the Jews have brought misfortune upon themselves."

"No! That's stupid, lying propaganda—teaching us all to think of them as animals or lower—as things—to kill them more easily."

"It *is* true! And a lesson for us all."

"Not the Jews I know. *Knew.*"

Fausten sighed. "Yes, there is always one good Jew, isn't there? And even this *one* didn't seem so bad, at first—but then look what happened. . . ."

"You don't have to be like this, you know." Elise kept walking. "I know you don't really believe all of these lies. You don't have to be one of them."

"And yet I do, as I'm quite fond of this thing we call life. And I must advise you to be a good Aryan woman now as well. The brutal reality is if you don't denounce Father Licht by the end of your leave, you'll be sent back to the camp."

"I know." The words and their meaning hung in the air.

"So," Fausten said, "what are you going to do?"

A long black saloon car pulled up, then stopped short with a squeal of brakes.

The back door swung open. "Get in the car," came a man's voice from the shadows inside.

"What?" Elise looked confused.

"Get in," the man in the car repeated.

"Now, see here—" Fausten began.

There was the click of a gun's safety catch. "If you know what's good for you, you'll let her go, Nazi pig."

Then, in a lower voice, "We're with the Resistance, Elise. We're helping you escape, don't you see? We're getting you out of here. But first you must get in the car."

"No!" Elise cried. "No, I can't!"

The man in the shadows of the car's interior sighed. "This is not the time to be a hero."

"This is *exactly* the time to be a hero," Elise turned to Fausten. "Aren't you going to do anything? Arrest them?"

Fausten looked at her, eyes grave. "I think you should go with them," he said slowly. "Leave here."

"What?"

"Go. You are too good for this part of the world."

"And that's why I need to go back to Ravensbrück!"

"No, you would be wasted there. You would die."

Fausten's eyes locked with those of the man in the car. Without another word, he took Elise's arm and guided her inside.

"No!" she cried, shaking him off. She tried to run, but she slipped and fell on one knee, crying out as the pain ricocheted through her body. Fausten caught up with her easily as the car inched forward; he clamped his hand over her mouth while the man in the car grabbed at her waist and pulled her in.

"No!" Elise cried after Fausten. "Come on, arrest me! Arrest me, you Nazi bastard! If you let me escape, they'll send *you* to the Eastern Front!"

Fausten turned on the heel of his gleaming black boot and stalked away, a black figure against the dazzling snow.

"Let me go," Elise sobbed. "I need to go back. Do you know what they'll do to my father if I go missing?"

Her captor was silent a moment, as if considering how much to tell her. "We're working *with* your father. He was instrumental in setting up this escape."

"What? They'll kill him!"

"They might," the man agreed bluntly. "Then again, they might send him to a camp. Or perhaps they'll leave him be. As Hitler's favorite conductor, he still wields power." He clamped a wet handkerchief over her mouth and nose. She fought for a moment, then slumped down in the seat, eyes closed, breathing deep, still at last.

"Good God, who is this girl?" demanded the man behind the wheel. "And why's she so fucking important?"

The man in back shrugged. "I don't know, but the orders for her come from London—and they're straight from the Prime Minister himself."

Brynn was groggy, but she was sure she had heard something—and cracked open her eyes to see the door close; then she heard the sound of it being locked from the outside.

She tried to move, but her limbs resisted. She'd been drugged again. That must be it. Her heart was racing; she could hear her pulse drum in her ears.

Every sense alert, she stayed perfectly still, waiting. When her heart had stopped pounding, she sat up, carefully, slowly. Everything ached. Her head throbbed. She could swear there was some sort of smell in the room—a lingering odor she half-recognized.

Brynn looked around, not knowing if it was morning, noon, or night. The chamber pot had been replaced by a clean one. The candle had been lit.

She made her way over to the dressing table, the stone floor damp under her bare feet. On it was a tray with a pot of tea, a mug, and a plate of cold toast. *Well, at least I won't starve. And if it's drugged, at least I won't die hungry.* She drank the tea straight from the pot. It was lukewarm and dribbled down her chin, but she didn't care. When she had drunk her fill, she crammed toast into her mouth, margarine smeared across her lips.

Only when she was sated did she realize there was a note underneath the tray. She plucked at it with trembling hands. It was typed.

> *Dear Miss Parry,*
>> *You must not call out. You must not try to escape.*
>>> *The Blackout Beast*

The *"Blackout Beast"? Is this some sort of horrible joke?*

Wiping at her face with her sleeve, Brynn began to pace back and forth in the small room, her feet and the hem of her gown becoming dirtier as she did.

You must not try to escape, the note had warned.

Well, bugger that, Brynn decided. She ran to the door, flung herself against it, pounding it with her fists. Nothing happened; it didn't budge.

Her knees buckled and she slid down the length of the door.

People will be worried, she reminded herself. *They must be looking for me.* But she'd told her mother and sister she was going off on a mission and they wouldn't hear from her for a while. She didn't really know anyone in London. She'd missed her appointment at SOE, but they probably wrote it off as nerves or last-minute panic and desertion. Who would be looking for her? She was a fool to think so.

She felt light-headed once again, a tinny buzz in her ears. *Must think.* The walls were made of rough stone. Methodically, she pushed on each and every stone to see if any would give. No. She threw herself back on the bed, refusing to let herself cry. *Think, think.* She squeezed her eyes shut, frantic.

She opened them again, staring up at the ceiling. It was low and plaster. Was that a small, nearly imperceptible opening in one corner? She was too short to reach it, but she dragged the bed over, scrambled onto it, then reached up. The opening was well camouflaged, but it was a pipe, a copper pipe. The pipe was how she was being drugged, she realized. She was being gassed.

She ripped the flounce from the hem of her nightgown and stuffed it inside the pipe.

No more Sleeping Beauty now. Next time you come, you Beast—or whoever you are—I'll be ready.

After taking leave of her father, and cheering herself up with a cup of tea and hot soup in the cafeteria, Maggie used the public telephone in the hospital's lobby to call in to Durgin at MI-5.

"We've booked Max Thornton and brought him in," he told her, "but the devil's still being processed. If you need to go to the

SOE office, do it. Take your time. I'm going to let him stew in a very small cell."

Maggie took the Tube to the Baker Street stop, then went to the SOE office to see if there was any news of Agent Calvert and to go over Brynn's files once more. As usual, the air in the offices was freezing. She could hear other people, but the reception room at least was empty. Out of the corner of her eye, she caught a scrawled message: *DAVID GREENE AT NO. 10. TELEPHONED. PLEASE RETURN CALL.*

Is this about Max? She dialed the number and waited to be put through. When she finally reached David, he sounded relieved. "You're a hard woman to get ahold of, Mags," he scolded her.

"So I hear," she said, thinking of the Queen. "It's been a rather busy time. Are you all right?"

"Well, this isn't a personal call. Well, it is in a way, but—I want to let you know, on behalf of the P.M., our agents in Berlin have your sister. They're bringing her to Paris and from there to Free France, and then to Madrid and Lisbon and finally to London. Of course I'll keep you apprised as things go forward."

Maggie slumped back in her chair, flooded with relief. "She's out," she murmured. "She's really out of that hell. David." She blinked back tears. "Thank you. And please thank Mr. Churchill for me, too."

"Will do."

Maggie wanted to ask if he'd witnessed Max's arrest, but bit her tongue. As she replaced the receiver in the cradle, she realized it was quiet in the office. Too quiet. Then she heard faint voices spilling out through the high transom window. There was a meeting going on in the conference room.

The SOE staff was discussing one of F-Section's Paris networks, code-named Prosper.

"The rules are changing," she heard Miss Lynd drawl. "Since

the laws changed, all young men in France are liable to be arrested. They're not classified as 'essential workers.'"

"What happens to them?" Maggie heard Brody say.

"They're sent to Germany as forced laborers—and we all know what that really means. Women, however, can invent any number of cover stories to travel and arouse little suspicion. I suggest we begin training even more women to be sent over, as our male agents are sitting ducks. Even with the proper paperwork, they raise suspicions."

"Miss Lynd, I asked you to solve the so-called woman problem, not make it worse," Colonel Gaskell cautioned.

"Colonel," she replied crisply, "you asked me for my help and this is it. I know you're not pleased with seeing women in combat, but the reality is, right now in France, women can accomplish things far more easily, and in more relative safety, than men."

"Fine," Gaskell retorted, obviously displeased. "For now, at least. What else do we have on the agenda today?"

"We have two new agents going into Paris with the full moon," Miss Lynd explained. "Sarah Sanderson, who is now Madame Sabine Severin, and Hugh Thompson, code-named Hubert Taillier."

As if reading Maggie's mind, Brody asked, "Any news on Erica Calvert?"

"Reports say she's been spotted in Paris. But it's hard to get any confirmed information," Gaskell admitted.

"So our agent's in Paris, without the benefit of a network?" Miss Lynd asked, her voice sharpening. "We need to get her out!"

"Calm yourself, Miss Lynd! These two new agents—Severin and Taillier—can get us a better picture."

"I'm not comfortable with two inexperienced agents being sent in blind," Miss Lynd insisted.

This is Sarah and Hugh they're talking about! Suddenly Maggie knew what Durgin meant about his "gut." *Something is very, very wrong.*

Miss Lynd continued, "My feeling is we should keep Severin and Taillier here until we have a better picture of how Prosper's faring. And we must make plans for an extraction of Agent Calvert. The materials she has are vital to the war effort. *To see a world in a grain of sand*—I don't know the exact nature of her mission, of course, but if it's to do with the geology of France's northwest coastline, it must be of vital importance to those planning the invasion."

Listening to make sure the meeting was still going on, Maggie picked up the telephone receiver again and dialed Beaulieu, waiting impatiently for the dial to stop clicking. "Yes, I need to get a message to Sarah Sanderson. It's Maggie Hope. Yes, please ask her to call me. And yes, it's an emergency." If Sarah and Hugh were really still being sent to France, they deserved to know the whole story before they left. There were definitely problems in the Prosper network.

A niggling worry wouldn't leave her in anything resembling peace. She took out Erica Calvert's folder and looked once more at the message:

.... . . - .. . -..—- # / . ...- . .-.-.—-.... .. -.-. . /—.—-—-
-.. /.... . .- . . .-.-. /.-. ..- ..- / .-.—- .- .. .-..- / .—.
.-.. ..-... ./ .-. .—.—-... . .-. /—-- -.... . .-. # ... / -.... .
-. -.... -.. . - -.—.-.-. /—.. ... . —- -. /—.—- .. .-—. /
—. .-.. .-..-.-. / . .-. .. .-.. .-./ -.-. .- -.. ..- .-. .-.-

And, once more, she translated the Morse code into plain text:

Hello!
Everything good here. Left Rouen. Please remember
mother's birthday with gift. Mission going well.
Erica Calvert

Something was off, she knew it. *Is it your "gut," Hope?* She chewed absently on a pencil eraser. *No,* she thought. *It's years of experience with codes and working as an agent behind enemy lines myself.*

She squinted at the sentences, taking them one by one.

Hello!
Everything good here.
Left Rouen.
Please remember mother's birthday with gift.
Mission going well.
Erica Calvert

The first letter of every sentence, taken together, spelled out *HELP ME.*

The message was a call for help. It was there, in code—and, once unbroken, plain as day. Her heart began to race. *HELP ME*— God only knew what was happening to Erica now.

The door opened and the group filed out. "Ah, Meggie, you're back," Gaskell muttered. "Terrific. Fetch me a cuppa, would you? Thank you, dear girl."

"Colonel Gaskell," she said, paper with the broken code in hand, "I've gone over Erica Calvert's last message to us again. There's a hidden message. In code."

"We've been over her messages already."

"Colonel Gaskell!" She pushed the paper with the broken code closer to his face. "H-E-L-P M-E. HELP ME. She's begging for help!"

"That's no code." Gaskell blinked pale eyes. "Coincidence, nothing more."

"Excuse me, sir. But with everything—her not giving her security checks, the mention of a gift for a dead mother, and now HELP ME . . ."

"Coincidence," he rumbled. His eyes flashed, and suddenly Maggie felt a stab of fear. *He* looked as though he wanted to strangle her. She'd always seen Gaskell as a bumbling, incompetent manager—now she realized he definitely had a more dangerous side as well.

He shoved the folder back at her, then turned, revealing a black *X* made by the crossed suspenders on his back. "You're still working with MI-Five?"

"Yes, sir," she said, taking a few steps back in alarm.

"Well, then I suggest you return to them—and get the hell out of here."

"Hello?" Maggie called as she took off her coat, hat, and gloves, and set down her handbag on the front hall's walnut console table, trying to quell her fear and outrage before seeing Chuck and Griffin.

She could smell the odor of burning bread, and followed it to the kitchen to find Chuck, making toast. Of course she couldn't say anything to Chuck about Agent Calvert and the SOE's refusal to take her disappearance seriously or her concerns about Sarah being sent to Paris, and the secret gnawed at her insides. She crossed to one of the high-backed chairs and sat, pressing her curled fist against her lips. *Erica. Brynn. Countless other women . . .*

"I was able to speak with Nigel last night," Chuck began before Maggie could say anything. "Honestly, I don't like to worry him—if it wasn't for the change of address and telephone number, I might not have even told him. Poor dear has enough to worry about."

Griffin lay in his makeshift bassinet on the table, his chubby little arms and legs waving as he babbled. "Well, hello, sweetie," Maggie cooed, reaching over to kiss his bald head, where fine, wispy hairs were beginning to grow in. He smelled of soap and innocence, and grace—and he had absolutely no knowledge of war and undercover agents and murdered women. "You're so yummy," she cooed. The simple joy of having Griffin wrap his pudgy fingers around her thumb could almost—almost—keep her fears for the safety of Erica and Brynn at bay.

"Isn't baby head smell the most wonderful smell in the entire world?" his mother mused. "I take big whiffs all the time. To me, he smells like Scottish shortbread—although all my Irish ancestors are probably turning in their respective graves at that."

Maggie heard a string of loud *meh*s and spun to see K padding into the room, his claws clicking on the tiles. He rubbed up against her, purring loudly. As she reached down to scratch him under the chin, he flopped down, showing his belly.

"He's missed you," Chuck observed as K prowled to his food bowl. "Cheeky little bugger. Do you know he's caught any number of mice—but won't eat them? Leaves quite the collection at the foot of your bed. I've been burying them in the back garden."

"Lovely." *All this and dead mice, too?*

"Meanwhile, to get tins of cat food, I have to wait in yet *another* queue. With all the crazy cat ladies. The 'crazy cat lady queue.' These are dark times, indeed."

She placed a plate of toast and margarine on the table in front of Maggie, then sat down with one for herself. "There's some coffee, if you'd like. It's mostly water, but it's brown, at least. And hot. And it *smells* like coffee, even if it is chicory and has no bloody flavor."

"You're a miracle worker, Chuck," Maggie said. Still, she only sipped at the coffee, leaving the toast untouched.

"Well, it's the least I can do, with your letting us stay here and letting me use your coupons." Chuck glared down at K, who had settled at Maggie's feet. "I only wish the moggy would show a lit-tle gratitude."

"Gratitude? From a cat?" Maggie tried her best to smile. "Oh, I think you'll be waiting quite a long time."

Chuck finally took a good long look at her friend. "What hap-pened to you? You look bloody terrible."

"Goodness, thanks." Maggie shrugged. "Just—just another rough day at work."

"By the way . . ." Chuck licked crumbs off her fingers. "Two packages came for you, while you were gone. I left them in your room."

"Thanks. I'm going to wash up and then call in to the office."

"Don't you ever get a day off?"

"Maybe when the war's over . . ." Maggie called from the stairs.

K followed close behind, meowing impatiently. "Hush, you," she told him as she reached her bedroom.

After washing her face with cold water and brushing her teeth with powder from a tin, she went back to the bedroom. With cold fingers, she opened the first package, recognizing not only the rows of U.S. stamps but also the elegant handwriting. It was from Aunt Edith, and filled with tins of pineapple and raspberries, blue cans of Spam, and several thick, heavenly chocolate bars.

Maggie smiled, a real one this time. Their last meeting in Wash-ington hadn't been perfect, but she and her aunt were both doing their best to bridge the distance. Maggie laughed when she saw the final item, at the bottom of the package: an issue of *American Phys-ical Society Journal*, with a lead article by J. R. Oppenheimer. *Of course—to Aunt Edith intellectual sustenance counts as much, or more, as physical.*

K had jumped up on her dresser and was madly scratching at the other package. Wrapped in brown paper and tied with heavy twine, it had the name MARGARET HOPE written across it in heavy

black, block letters. There were no stamps—it must have been
hand-delivered. "Well, what have we here?" Maggie murmured,
thankful for the distraction.

K stared up at her without blinking. *"Meh!"*

Maggie picked up the package; it was heavier than she'd expected. She froze. A red stain seeped from one corner, soaking the
brown wrapping paper. It was blood—she knew the musty tang all
too well.

She felt as though she were about to be sick, but took a shallow
breath. She reached for the sterling silver letter opener on her desk,
then sliced through the twine.

She pierced through the brown wrapping paper and tore it
open, then lifted off the cardboard lid. Inside, there was a sheet
of folded paper. This, too, was stained with blood. And then—
something—wrapped in waxed paper that had parted wide enough
to reveal its glistening red contents. It gave off a strong meaty
smell, and K tried to stick his head into the box to get a better sniff.

"No!" Maggie screamed in horror, her cry echoing in the
sparely furnished room.

She backed away, unable to tear her eyes from the bloody
organ, smothering the howl she wanted to make by clamping her
hands over her mouth. Realizing K was trying to investigate the
obscene object, she scooped him up, then set him on the floor, none
too gently. K jumped silently up onto the bed to regard her, and the
package, with inscrutable eyes.

Maggie swallowed hard and with shaking hands lifted the letter.
She unfolded it, staring at the spidery handwriting.

Dear Miss Hope:
As you may have deduced by now, I have decided to send
the working women, who have always ruined my life, to their
Maker (or to the Devil, as the case may be).

Even though I've taken on the legacy of Jack the Ripper, in homage to his killing of whores, I consider myself a rational and erudite man. However, the so-called modern woman enrages me.

You want to keep the advantages of being women, while stealing the strengths of men.

You are intent on transforming our patriarchy into a matriarchy, which denies the intrinsic worth of Englishmen.

And so the once proud, virile, and impregnable British Empire has been turned into a woman, one who is submitting to the rape of the Nazis.

I may sound like a madman, but I am but a rational, intelligent English gentleman who has been driven to murderous insanity by modern women.

Do you want to know who's to blame for the Blackout Beast killings?

Look in the mirror, Miss Hope.

It is you, and the rest of your modern sisterhood, who are at fault.

You did this.

And I will annihilate you all.

Chapter Fifteen

"This!" Maggie tossed the grisly box, which she'd wrapped in a white pillowcase, onto the low table in front of Durgin. "*This* package came today. It was left. At my house. My *house!*" She crossed her arms tightly across her chest, hugging herself, heart thudding.

Durgin looked up from a stack of papers. "And what do we have here?"

"See the viscous red liquid leaking out of said package?" Maggie fumed. "Well, it's *blood*. Blood from a kidney, if I'm not mistaken. And a human one at that, if I'm to believe the accompanying note!"

Durgin put down his tea and peered closer, opening the pillowcase, his eyes widening at the sight of the bloody box. He squinted down at it, as if it were Pandora's and contained all the horrors of man—then back up at Maggie, seeing the stricken look in her eyes.

"Do you think—do you think it could be . . . Brynn's?" she managed.

"There's no way to know." His expression of sympathy was the last straw. She ran out of the room, pressing her hand against her mouth to stifle her weeping.

In the ladies' W.C., she retched into the toilet, bringing up the bad coffee. Finally, when she was done, she made her way to the sink to wash her face. As she spat water into the sink, she looked at her reflection. *Look in the mirror, Miss Hope,* the letter had read. She waited until the urge to vomit again had passed. Then she dried her hands and did what she could with her hair before exiting.

Durgin was in the hall, waiting for her. "I asked the secretary, Mrs. What's-her-name, to make you tea."

Maggie nodded. "At least I didn't vomit on a crime scene," she tried to joke as she walked unsteadily back to their shared office. His hand closed on her upper arm as he guided her steps. She didn't shrug him away. Human touch felt terribly important at that moment.

Durgin walked her away from the grisly package and to the far sofa. "Where did you find it?"

She turned her face from the package. "In my bedroom."

He perched on the sofa arm beside her. "Did you see who delivered it?"

"No. My flatmate found the package on the doorstep and brought it upstairs."

"All right, I'm going to call the Yard and have someone investigate if there are any witnesses to who may have left it." As he rose, he gave her shoulder an awkward pat. "And I'll see where the blasted tea is. . . ."

As he went to the desk and made the telephone call, she picked at a loose thread on the cuff of her sweater, her heart drumming. *Someone left me a kidney. Whose was it? Brynn's? That of another woman working with SOE? One murdered by the Blackout Beast?*

She continued to pick at the fraying cuff as she listened to Durgin speak to an officer at the Yard, then place another call, this one within MI-5, requesting a photographer.

When he was done, Maggie began speaking, the words pouring

from her. "I have a friend who's a mother staying with me, with her child. A *baby*! I can't have"—she fumbled for a word—"*offal* delivered to my home! And the letter—"

She put her hand to her mouth, covering it as though she could force the words back in; she couldn't speak them aloud. *If that's her kidney, then where's the rest of her? Oh, Brynn . . .* She dropped her hands to her lap, and underneath the tabletop, curled them into fists, nails digging deep into her palms, making angry red crescents.

"Miss Hope," Durgin said, gently. "Maggie. I'm now going to ask you—with all due respect—to take a deep breath."

She did.

The detective put on a pair of rubber gloves. He moved back to the package, lifting it from the pillowcase. "It's addressed to you—by name."

Maggie nodded, mute with misery and fury. She watched as he parted the brown butcher's paper. Using the tips of his fingers, he pulled out the note, then peered inside. "That's half a kidney, all right," he said as the unpleasant odor permeated the office. "Can't tell if it's human or not." He looked over to her. "Please go into my bag and get my powder and brush. I'm going to dust for prints."

Maggie did as he asked.

He dipped his brush into the powder. "Did you touch it?"

"No. Of course not," she snapped. "Oh, goodness—I touched the letter! I didn't know what it was when I did—"

"It's all right," Durgin allowed, unexpectedly gentle. After dusting the package, notes, and kidney itself, he picked something up with his tweezers. "What's this?"

"A hair?"

"A *cat* hair," Durgin specified. "Marmalade tabby, I'm guessing."

"It's mine." Maggie groaned and dropped her head into her hands. "I mean, it's from my cat."

"It's always best, on the whole, Miss Hope, not to allow animals to contaminate crime scenes. Whenever possible, of course."

Maggie's head shot up. "Well, tell that to *him*, living on rationed cat food and smelling a nice raw kidney!"

He gazed at her a moment before replying. "Well, we have no fingerprints, no insects, and no fibers—beyond the hair of one red tabby cat. But the letter . . ." He shook his head. "The letter gives us quite a lot of information on our Beast and the way he thinks."

An MI-5 agent came to the door with a heavy black camera, and Durgin waved him in. As the photographer, a walrus of a man with an elaborate white handlebar mustache, began snapping pictures from every conceivable angle, Maggie asked, "Do you really think the Beast ate the other half, the way Jack the Ripper allegedly did? We're now dealing with cannibalism?"

"Maggie, come walk with me." Durgin picked up their coats. "Let's let this man do his job." He held Maggie's for her as she put it on, then put on his own.

Outside, the pavement was slick and wet, and more snow was falling. For the moment, the wind had died down. *The perfect time to light up,* Maggie thought, suddenly desperately craving a cigarette. "Do you smoke?"

"No, I quit that habit, along with the whiskey, back in the day. You?"

"I stopped, too. Bad for the lungs, I believe."

"Absolutely right—and I've seen enough autopsies on smokers' lungs to know."

There was a low wooden bench outside a chemist's shop, protected by a striped awning. Durgin stopped and took a seat. "Do you mind?" he asked, looking up at Maggie.

"Thank you," she said, realizing why he'd brought her out. "The fresh air *is* helping."

"Well, it's not every day you get home delivery from the so-called Blackout Beast. Along with a manifesto of hatred."

They sat, watching the snow spiral down, the white flakes melting on the black, wet street, the sky overhead a milky gray. Their arms brushed and both stiffened and drew apart.

"How did you meet Frain?" he asked. "What's your connection with MI-Five?"

"Frain?" Maggie was desperately glad to talk about anything but the package. "Peter Frain and I worked together on a case when the war had just started and I was working as Mr. Churchill's secretary. He found I was good at codes and things, and then he recruited me. Even though I'm technically with the ATS and employed by the SOE, I do the odd job for MI-Five, too." She gave a harsh laugh. "Which, I suppose, is what makes me one of those 'professional women' our Beast hates so much."

"We're up to his penultimate victim now. If he follows the pace he's set, it won't be long."

"I know." Maggie knew all too well what victim they were up to—Catherine Eddowes, victim number four. If they didn't catch the Blackout Beast, he'd not only kill doppelgängers of Catherine Eddowes and then Mary Jane Kelly but, just as Jack the Ripper had, never be caught, never pay for his crimes. Like the original Jack, he'd vanish, leaving London in confusion and terror.

"Come, let's get you that cup of tea."

"I'd rather have a medicinal brandy, if you please."

"Not sure if there's any left in the city, but we can try."

They walked to the nearest pub, the Golden Dragon, where Maggie sat and Durgin ordered for them at the bar. He returned with a mug of tea and a small glass filled with amber liquid. "They didn't have any brandy—this is fairly ancient sherry, but I didn't think you'd mind."

Maggie sipped the sweet liquid gratefully. It stung her lips and felt hot going down her throat. As she sipped, Durgin watched her face with concern.

Maggie finished her sherry without speaking, then put down her glass. There was nothing to say. She had been sent half a kidney by a sequential murderer, as a warning. It was all so horrific, so shocking, that silence seemed the only sane option.

And so they sat, until Durgin's tea turned cold. "Do you want me to take you home?" he asked finally.

Her head snapped up. "Certainly not!" Then, "I'm not going to be frightened off."

"Maggie, this is no time for false bravado. Whoever our Beast is, he's telling us he knows a lot about you—he knows your name and where you live."

"Do you really think my going home will keep me safer than working at MI-Five? My home is where he delivered the package, after all!"

"I've assigned plainclothes officers to keep a twenty-four-hour watch on your house," Durgin countered.

"I'm staying," Maggie said. The set of her jaw made it clear there would be no argument. "Brynn is . . . well, I hope she's still out there. And I'm not going to rest until we find her."

"Well, then—are you ready to question Max Thornton? I think we've let him sulk behind bars long enough."

Maggie stood, still shaky. But she squared her shoulders and lifted her chin. "Why, James Durgin—what a delightful way to spend the evening."

———

"My name is Hubert Taillier," Hugh was saying once again in French, scowling down at his snarled tie. "We met in Monte Carlo, at the ballet. I was playing cello in the orchestra and you were performing your first *Les Sylphides*."

Sarah peered over his shoulder in the bathroom mirror and dabbed on the last of a well-worn pink lipstick, then she turned and expertly tied his tie. "We married in the south of France, Côte d'Azur, after a whirlwind courtship."

"At the church of Saint Jean-Baptiste, in a small ceremony. I wore a blue suit—"

"—and carried pink silk roses—"

"—that I'd sprayed with perfume!"

"And made me sneeze all through the ceremony!"

Sarah and Hugh had been practicing their background as diligently as they'd been studying spycraft, ballet, and cello at the SOE's Finishing School at Beaulieu.

"You look beautiful, darling," Hugh said to her, unable to tear his gaze away from Sarah in her plum-colored silk dress.

"And you look handsome as well," she replied, her eyes locked on his.

"Shall we go?" He offered his arm. "One last dance before the madness begins in earnest?"

Together, they walked in the twilight, their hands brushing, then their fingers entwining.

"I just learned a great French expression," Sarah told him. "*Mi chien mi loup,* which means dusk, but literally translates to 'between dog and wolf.'" She squeezed his hand. "Shall we continue our stories again?"

Hugh began. "Of course we have no children—"

"Because of my career."

This time, Hugh squeezed her hand. "No children *yet*, anyway."

"Oooh, I do think we finally found something to argue about, darling."

As they walked closer to the imposing gray-stone Abbey, they could hear the band playing jazz. "After you," Hugh said, opening the heavy wooden door for Sarah, who glowed.

Hugh and Sarah had rehearsed in the Domus of Beaulieu's Abbey, and it had always been empty, an almost mystical place. Now the ancient lay brothers' dormitory was full of men and women jitterbugging to Tubby Jackson and the Jackson Band, as a banner hung over the stage pronounced. Several of the musicians playing were colored, and Sarah was surprised to see one of the trombone players was a colored woman, somewhere in her twenties, wearing a shimmering evening gown and pearls.

Against one ancient stone wall was a table with several punch bowls and tiny cups, and plates piled high with sandwiches. The air was hot from the press of bodies and smelled of perfume, brilliantine, and cigarette smoke. Sarah heard a young man next to her say, "Look at the blackbird up there—she's not too bad, really."

"Especially not with her lips around that horn," his friend replied. "Oh, the things I can picture her doing. . . ."

A third behind them added: "Why is it, outside of a few sepia females, there are aren't women musicians capable of 'sending' anyone—at least sending them farther than the nearest exit?"

The first sniffed. "Only God can make a tree, and only men can play jazz, what ho?"

But before Sarah could say anything, she and Hugh were swept up into the crowd of their fellow agents-in-training, Lindy-hopping to one of their favorites, "Eight to the Bar." When it was over, everyone in the high-ceilinged room was struggling for breath. They laughed and clapped, kissing cheeks.

"Miss Lynd!" Sarah called, waving to a blonde in a corner. *"Bonne soir!"*

"Madame," Miss Lynd answered as they walked over, hand in hand. "Monsieur." She gave a rare smile as she ladled out punch. "I hope you're having fun," she said in French, pressing glasses into their hands. "Cheers!"

"Miss Lynd—" Hugh put down his glass and offered his hand. "Would you like to dance?"

But as the band segued into the slow and dreamy "I'll Be Seeing You," and the lights dimmed, Miss Lynd gave a cryptic smile. "Actually, Monsieur Taillier," she suggested, "why don't you dance with your wife?"

Hugh offered Sarah his arm, and she took it. He led her to the middle of the dance floor. Onstage, a woman with glowing ebony skin in a fuchsia satin dress and rhinestone earrings that shone and sparkled under the stage lights took a deep breath and began to sing in a resonant alto.

Sarah and Hugh danced together well, as if they really had been married for years. "What we do for the war effort," Sarah complained softly into Hugh's ear.

"Even if all of this is pretend," Hugh replied, spinning her around and then holding her in close, "that doesn't mean my feelings for you aren't real."

They danced until they were the last couple on the stone floor. When it was finally time to go, Hugh snagged one of the bottles that had been brought up from Beaulieu's cellars.

"Nettle wine," Sarah exclaimed, stumbling in her high heels on the flagstone path, "oooh la la." She lifted the bottle and took a sip.

"Easy there," Hugh warned, taking the bottle back. "Don't twist an ankle now. We've come too far."

She giggled and clutched his arm. "Heaven forbid."

At their storybook cottage, they both stumbled in the door, laughing. "I must take these heels off, darling Hubert—my feet are killing me." She limped to the sofa and began to undo first one tiny buckle, then the other, slipping her feet out and wiggling her toes with a noisy sigh of relief.

Hugh shrugged off his jacket and sat next to her. "That was fun."

"Yes, it really was."

"We're going to Paris."

"Yes, we really are."

Suddenly, they were both serious. Then Sarah sighed again. She turned. Winding her arms around Hugh's neck, she kissed him on the mouth, gently at first, then more passionately. They both wanted to stop thinking, to escape from the endless limbo before actually landing on French soil.

Hugh wrestled off his tie. When he tried to unbutton his shirt, Sarah tore at it, buttons popping and rolling everywhere. Together they fell backward, entwined on the narrow sofa, desperate to free themselves from the tension of the last few months.

Afterward, they lay back, panting and sweating.

"Well, that was quite the send-off," Hugh managed, trying to catch his breath.

Sarah was still breathless, too. "I hope you don't think I used you."

Hugh kissed the top of her head. "Anytime. I'm your husband, after all."

"I need to take my mind off of everything. I'm not scared exactly, but . . ."

Hugh began to kiss her neck, working his way down. "Why, madame," he murmured between nips, "I'm happy to distract you all night, if that's what you desire."

Maggie peered through the mirrored window at Max Thornton, sitting at the scarred wooden table, his hands cuffed in front of him, his nose covered in white gauze and surgical tape. When Durgin took in the state of Max's face, he whistled. "You weren't kidding about your skill set, Miss Hope."

Maggie shrugged, the image of the kidney before her again. She refused to dwell on it and refocused on Max. She was filled with a primitive and passionate hatred for him. He'd tried to strangle and rape her—just as he'd tried to strangle and rape Daphne Plunket. And who knew how many other women he'd preyed upon and victimized? *He deserves his bloody nose—and so much more. But did he send the kidney? Is he responsible for murder?*

"So, I'll wait here," Maggie said, expecting the usual, "while you question him, right?"

Durgin astonished her. "Actually, Miss Hope, if you're up to it, you're leading the interrogation today." He handed her the case file.

"I?" She was gobsmacked. "I'm definitely up to it—though I don't know how objective I'll be. . . ." But she took the file.

"Nonsense. You will be a consummate professional and rattle him hard enough to shake a confession out of him. Understand?" He walked to her and loosened her scarf, so the bruises on her neck were exposed. "Perfect. Absolutely perfect."

Maggie raised one hand and rubbed absently at the purple marks. She was torn between her feelings—on the one hand, wanting to run and hide, and on the other, wanting to intimidate Max the way he'd attempted to terrify her. She decided cool professionalism was in everyone's best interest, including her own.

Maggie and Durgin entered together. Max looked up from the table. "You!" he rasped when he recognized Maggie. "What are *you* doing here?" he demanded, revealing a missing front tooth.

"And imagine my surprise at finding *you* here, Mr. Thornton," Maggie replied coolly as she took a seat. "But when we saw Miss Daphne Plunket's injuries and she identified you as her attacker—

after a drink at the Punch and Judy pub, of all places—I knew we had to ask you a few questions." She opened the file. "For the record, I am Miss Margaret Hope, with MI-Five. My colleague is Detective Chief Inspector James Durgin, of Scotland Yard."

"You're the lead on this, right?" Max looked to Durgin. "You're the man, I can talk to you. You can tell her to leave, right?"

"Oh no, Mr. Thornton," Durgin answered placidly. "Perish the thought! I assure you Miss Hope is running this investigation."

Max tried to fold his hands, but couldn't. They twitched in his lap. "I want my solicitor!"

"I'm sure you do," responded Durgin impassively.

Maggie went through the file. "Daphne Plunket was choked and nearly raped—and has identified you as her attacker. What happened that night?"

"We went out to a pub, then things got—a bit out of hand." Max looked to Durgin, muttering, "*You* know how it goes. Women."

"Miss Plunket was nearly strangled, Mr. Thornton," Maggie reminded him. "That's not 'out of hand,' that's assault and attempted murder."

"I want my solicitor," he repeated.

"And then she was nearly murdered, with her left carotid artery severed. Why did you try to kill her, Mr. Thornton?"

His mouth gaped open in shock. "But I *didn't*! She ran away and I went back to Number Ten. Mr. Greene was there. He's my witness."

"And what about the dates of—" Maggie knew them by heart. "March twentieth, twenty-seventh, and twenty-ninth?"

"Nothing to do with me." He shrugged, looking unconcerned, but his hands would not keep still.

"What do you know about Brynn Parry?"

"Who? Look, I want my solicitor."

"Brynn Parry, ATS officer. From Wales."

"I have no idea who you're talking about. And I'm sure I have alibis for all of those as well. I'll say it one last time, I want my solicitor."

Maggie knew they were at an impasse. "Guards!" she called, not without a certain satisfaction. Two burly men in uniform appeared. "Please take Mr. Thornton back to his cell—to await his lawyer."

Max gave Maggie a vicious look as he left. She met his cold eyes, unflinching.

When the sound of footsteps had quieted, Durgin asked, "Getting hungry? I can run out and get us some fish and chips? Or, at least, what's passing for fish these days?"

"No!" Maggie cried, appalled. Even through her interview with Max, she hadn't forgotten the package and its bloody contents.

"Sorry." Durgin frowned. "Do you want to go home? I can have one of my men—"

"No," Maggie answered, her tone not inviting opposition. "I'm staying."

"Very well, then—but you really should eat something. We have a lot of work in front of us."

"Coffee," she decided. It had been a long day. She couldn't bear the thought of food, but surely she could manage coffee. "I don't care how bad it is, as long as it's hot and caffeinated."

"Coffee, check," Durgin said, rising and reaching for her coat, helping her into it. "Ah, the glamour—the long hours, the bad pay, the dead ends . . . But it'll all be worth it when we catch the Beast."

The man in the smudged sunglasses leaned against the wall of the building opposite New Scotland Yard on Victoria Street, hat pulled down over his eyes, a newspaper obscuring his face. But he wasn't interested in the day's lead story, about Nazis losing even more ground in Russia. He was waiting for the redhead to appear. She'd been there all day. He knew after his little gift she'd go running to her DCI. Yes, and there she was, her red hair like a beacon, walking swiftly, her shoulders hunched over, her head down. Submissive, good. That was the way he liked them. Had she shrieked when she'd opened the package? Had she cried? Had she felt frightened and alone? As he watched the whore walk down the stairs with the detective, he hoped so, he really did.

Once again, as in the park, she turned and looked at him, looked straight through him—almost as if she could read his thoughts.

He turned away and tucked the newspaper under his arm and walked on, cursing under his breath.

After having a few bites of toast and sips of coffee at a nearby café, Maggie went back to what she now thought of as their—Mark's, Durgin's and her—shared office to work, sitting down at Mark's desk to use the telephone. According to David Greene, Max Thornton had indeed been in the office at the estimated times of the murders. And Chuck had neither seen nor heard anything about the package; she had merely found it at the back door. Maggie leaned on the desk in exhaustion. *Two more dead ends,* she thought wearily. *And two more murders to go.* Once again, the image of the bloody kidney in its waxed paper came back to her, unbidden, relentless. She wondered when she would stop thinking about it. *If* she would *ever* stop thinking about it.

As the door opened, she started. "Ah, Mark," she exclaimed, relieved. "You scared me!"

"Sorry," he said.

"Are you feeling better today?" Maggie inquired as he hung up his coat and hat.

"Glad to see you've made yourself at home." Mark sat on the sofa, his eyes not meeting hers.

"Oh," Maggie said, rising. "I needed to make a few calls in private—didn't think you'd mind."

"No, no." He waved his hand at the desk. "It's yours now. Obviously Frain's going to see the work you've done and promote you. I'll be working back down in the basement before long, most likely."

Maggie could see the tension and exhaustion on his face. "Mark, you know that's not true. You're doing an excellent job during a stern time." She appraised their corkboard and the map. "We're all on the same team."

She squinted at the map and the red pushpins. "Two to go." She remembered her dream of the man of numbers and flies. *Mathematics,* she thought. *Patterns. Logic. Math . . .*

Mark pulled out a silver flask from his breast pocket. "Want some?"

"No, thank you."

Mark took a gulp before saying, "Sometimes I need a drink."

"Mark, how much have you had today?"

He took another long swallow, then looked at her sideways. "None of your damn business." Then, gentler, "Remember, this is England—we drink our feelings."

Well, not much to say to that, is there?

"*This* is all I have now," Mark continued, raising his flask. "No wife, no children, no home. This"—he looked around the office, gesturing with the flask and spilling a bit—"is all I have left. And I'm mucking it all up."

"We're all doing our best," Maggie reminded him, her voice low. His misery distressed her. "*You're* doing your best, Mark."

"Do you think so?" He turned to face her. "Do you really think so?"

Maggie saw the look in his eyes, the way they burned with need and desperation. "Mark, no."

"Please, Maggie." He leaned in closer, breath stinking of whiskey. "Just once. What harm can it do? I need to forget everything that's happened, everything that keeps happening. . . ." He reached for her, trying to bring her mouth to his.

She stiffened as his hand met bruised flesh. "No," she insisted, trying to be gentle, but still pushing him away. "No, Mark."

"Please, Maggie . . ." He was nearly sobbing as he forced his mouth on hers. "I just need to forget. . . ."

"I said *no*."

His eyes narrowed, cruel. "You gave it up for Hugh. Oh yes, do you think he didn't tell me all about it? And you gave it up for your RAF pilot. So what's one more time, with one more man? As you keep pointing out, it's not as if you're some blushing virgin. . . ."

"You're drunk, Mark. Leave. Now."

He toasted her with his flask. "Bitch! Frigid bitch!"

"Get out." She stared at him until he edged to the door.

The furious glitter was back in his eyes. "You spread your legs for Hugh. . . ."

"Get. Out."

After a long moment, he picked up his coat and hat and strode out.

When he was gone, she went to the door, slammed it shut, and locked it. Then she leaned against it, heart pounding, waiting for the sound of his echoing footsteps in the hall to cease.

And now she was crying, weeping, really—for the first time since she had opened the package, since she'd seen Joanna Metcalf's mutilated body in the park, really since she'd left John in Washington.

She crossed back to the sofa and dropped down on it, her shoulders shaking and her chest heaving, her hands pressed over her wet face as she tried to muffle her sobs. *The kidney,* she thought. *The kidney most likely belonged to a woman who'd died in terrible, brutal circumstances. A sharp knife had reduced a woman to a lump of meat, a re-creation of a Ripper victim, a numbered murder case to be solved. But she wasn't just that—she'd been a living, breathing human being. . . .* After a few minutes of tears, Maggie went to her handbag and dug out a cambric handkerchief, wiping at her eyes and then her nose. She gave a sniffle and then a noisy blow. *There now. Stiff upper lip. What would Mrs. Vera Baines say?*

But she was grateful she'd had a few moments to be alone, to not have to look brave or efficient or professional, to not have to talk or explain, to not be judged according to her sex by her male colleagues.

There was a knock at the door—*shave and a haircut, two bits!* Maggie jumped up, startled. "Who is it?" she called, her voice pitched higher than usual. *Is it Mark? Is he back?*

"Durgin."

She blinked away tears and pressed at her wet cheek with the cuff of her sleeve before she opened the door.

His eyebrows shot up as he took in her red eyes and nose. "Everything all right?"

"Perfectly fine," Maggie answered in clipped tones. Durgin placed steaming newspapers smelling of fried fish and potatoes on the desk. Her stomach lurched. "Mr. Standish was here. He is . . . still not well . . . and I convinced him to take a few more days off."

"Hmmmph." Durgin gave a suspicious look, then took off his coat and hat. He came back to the table, opening up the grease-stained papers. "Only thing newspapers are good for, in my opinion," he declared, grabbing for a chip. "At least we've been able to keep most of the details on this case from Fleet Street."

Maggie ignored the food. She walked to the map, running her fingers over the pushpins that indicated each victim found: *Joanna Metcalf—Mary Ann Nichols,* and *Doreen Leighton—Annie Chapman. Gladys Chorley—Martha Tabram, Olivia Sutherland—Elizabeth Stride.* There were two ominous spaces left underneath *Catherine Eddowes—*and *Mary Jane Kelly . . .*

When she saw Buckingham Palace on the map, Maggie gasped, remembering. It was the night of the Queen's dinner. "I'm supposed to be somewhere tonight—but I'll cancel, of course."

"I think you should go. Take a break, and get your mind off things. Come back refreshed. Quite frankly, I'd advise it. You've had one hell of a day." Durgin took a bite of chip. "Where are you off to?"

"Dinner with the Royal Family at Buckingham Palace, actually." As she patted back loose tendrils of red-gold hair, she flashed a sudden smile. "Why, DCI Durgin—would you care to join me?"

Chapter Sixteen

"I can't believe I let you talk me into this," Durgin muttered under his breath to Maggie as servants soundlessly cleared away china and crystal in Buckingham Palace's Chinese Dining Room. It was decorated in flamboyant gold and jade-green papers, red silks, and chinoiserie panels originally bought by George IV for the Brighton Pavilion. The storybook oriental splendor—golden dragons, enamel pagodas, and shining lacquerwork—all illuminated by tall beeswax candles, was a universe away from the cold and dreary and dangerous London outside the palace walls.

Maggie and Durgin were seated at a table set for ten, who included King George and Queen Elizabeth, as well as various high-ranking government officials, their wives, and a few lesser royals. Dinner had been cream of barley à la reine soup, matelote of eels, and cutlets made from mutton purée Maggie decided tasted like old socks. Dessert was Tarte de Pommes.

From behind the blackout shades and rich crimson draperies, the windows rattled in their frames. "A storm's brewing," intoned an ancient duchess, her black, arched eyebrows painted on like two commas, her heavy emerald earrings swaying.

"The wind's picking up," the Queen said, her voice rising over the rattle. She was wearing a sapphire-blue silk gown and dripping in diamonds. Maggie was amused to see that none of the other women were in blue, a nod to the Queen's authority that she'd learned during her days at Windsor—*only the Queen wears blue*. Maggie herself was in a long white gown she'd bought in Washington, D.C., which she'd worn only once before, to a New Year's ball at the White House. And Durgin, seated next to her, was in his Scotland Yard dress uniform. He'd been quiet all evening. Maggie was disappointed none of the other guests had gone out of their way to make him feel welcome. It wasn't that they'd been rude; they'd simply ignored him. And Maggie and Durgin were seated too far from the King and Queen for them to ask him any questions.

"And I daresay the temperature's dropping. Shall we retire to the anteroom?" The Queen stood, and her guests scrambled to their feet. "There's a lovely fire there. And the Princesses will meet us. They're quite keen to reenact one of their pantomimes for you all!"

Durgin offered his arm, and Maggie took it; it was strong and solid. She felt better since they'd reached the palace. It was only a temporary respite, she knew. But it felt as if they were suddenly miles away from London, the case, and everything else going on.

They followed the rest of the group into the drawing room. The Queen was correct. A huge roaring fire had been lit and a tea service had been set up. The ladies' jewels—rubies, diamonds, and sapphires set in gold and platinum—sparked and glowed in the flickering light.

Suddenly, there was the sound of running footsteps. "Miss Hope! Miss Hope!" Maggie heard. It was Princess Margaret, with her creamy cheeks and mischievous grin.

Behind her, walking more sedately, was Princess Elizabeth, her gentian eyes clear and bright. "Welcome, Miss Hope," the older princess said. "It's lovely to see you again."

"This is Detective Chief Inspector James Durgin," Maggie told the two girls as around her people poured tea from a silver urn and took seats. Durgin bowed gravely, while the Princesses greeted him and giggled. Then, to Durgin, Maggie said, "And these young ladies are the Princesses Elizabeth and Margaret. They let me teach them mathematics at Windsor Castle, two years ago."

"Was Miss Hope a good teacher?" Durgin asked, quite serious.

"Well . . ." Princess Margaret began, weighing her opinion.

"Miss Hope was an excellent maths teacher," Princess Elizabeth stated, brooking no discussion. "And she also taught us secret codes and cryptology." Maggie and Elizabeth exchanged a significant look, remembering how using code had saved the young princess's life.

"What did the grown-ups get for dinner?" Margaret interrupted. "We were stuck with mock mutton cutlets. They're the worst—taste like old, dirty laundry."

"Margaret!" Elizabeth warned.

Maggie giggled. "We had the same, if it makes you feel better."

"Oh, I do miss sausages," Elizabeth sighed.

"I personally miss chocolates most," Margaret confided, taking Maggie's hand and leading her to a low divan near the fire.

Durgin followed, and Princess Elizabeth went to get the tea. At the piano in the corner, a man in a dinner jacket began to play Cole Porter's "You'd Be So Easy to Love."

"Hello," Maggie said to a woman seated in a wing chair across from her, Princess Margaret, and Durgin. She was not much older than Maggie, in a scarlet dress showing off her delicate collarbones and a long, slim neck encircled by a choker of pearls. She was the younger wife of one of the officers, and hadn't said much during the dinner. Her husband was standing and chatting with the King and the other men, and Maggie thought she looked a bit lonely.

Elizabeth set down Maggie's and Durgin's teacups and smiled as she also took a seat. "Lady Westfield is an expert Tarot card reader," the Princess informed them.

"Hardly," the woman in scarlet said. "But I did pick up some cards in France a few years back. And I enjoy doing readings for friends."

"Would you read Miss Hope's cards, Lady Westfield? Please?" said Elizabeth.

"Oh yes," Margaret agreed. "You *must* read her cards."

Lady Westfield went to her beaded evening bag and opened it, pulling out a box wrapped in a silk scarf. The leather box was engraved with the lettering B. P. GRIMAUD, ANCIEN TAROT DE PARIS, and a gold triangle in a circle.

Margaret's eyes were wide as she looked up at Maggie. "Do you believe in the Tarot, Miss Hope?"

"Well," replied Maggie, trying to be diplomatic. "I prefer math, science, and provable facts. However," she said, winking at Durgin, "I *have* become more interested in instincts and the unconscious of late."

Lady Westfield placed the scarf and the box on a low rosewood table, then passed the deck to Maggie. "Please shuffle," she instructed.

Maggie did as she was bid, enjoying the cards' elaborate illustrations. "Don't look!" Margaret warned. "You mustn't look."

"All right," Maggie acquiesced—she had nothing against Tarot cards as an amusing parlor game but didn't take the idea of a reading seriously. When she was satisfied, she handed the deck back to Lady Westfield.

As the lady took them, she said, "Before we begin, you must tap the deck three times."

Maggie felt a rush of impatience but realized this action was part of the act. *Well, Lady Westfield certainly does put on a good show*, she thought.

"Tarot cards can be a window to ancient wisdom, to truths

we've become alienated from in these modern times," Lady West-field said, pressing the deck in her hands. "The cards are a book of life, can answer the deepest questions, and sometimes can be a means to warn of imminent danger."

Beside Maggie, Princess Margaret gave a melodramatic shiver.

"They represent challenges and tests, twists of fate. They move from terror and loss to unexpected good fortune—and out of darkness, hope is born."

She laid out three cards from the top of the deck, facedown.

Maggie felt a prickle of expectation. *It's only good theater,* she reminded herself.

The first card showed a naked woman and a naked man. They stood in a field with a mountain peak in the distance, over which an angel with wings and a purple cloak hovered.

"Ooooh!" Margaret gave Maggie and Durgin a significant look, and Maggie, despite her best efforts, felt herself blush. *We're just sitting too close to the fire,* she thought, unable to look at Durgin.

"Hush, Margaret," Elizabeth scolded.

But Lady Westfield was focused on the card. "The Lovers represent perfection—harmony. There is mutual attraction, yes, but it's their trust in one another that gives them the strength and confidence to overcome the obstacles in life. The bond between them is incredibly strong—not necessarily marriage, but still a powerful connection."

"Weren't you stepping out with Hugh Thompson when you were with us?" Margaret interjected, giving Durgin a sideways look. "We rather liked Mr. Thompson, didn't we, Lilibet?"

Maggie smiled at the use of Elizabeth's childhood nickname. "That was a long time ago," she said, remembering how Hugh had once taken a bullet to the leg to save the Princess from a kidnapper.

Lady Westfield put the card down. "The Lovers card also represents choices on a grand scale. A dilemma may be presented to you in the near future that demands an action or a decision—and you'll need to make the right choice."

Lady Westfield gazed at Maggie. "Something is going to happen, something big, that will change the course of your experience—something that may seem negative at first, but will later prove to be a blessing in disguise.

"If you find yourself at a crossroads where you must choose between taking the moral high ground or low, then you need to consider all consequences before acting. The Lovers card tells you your own values will be challenged, and you must make a definite decision."

"All right, then!" Maggie said with a breeziness she didn't quite feel. *Nothing more than a parlor game . . .*

Lady Westfield looked concerned. "Are you all right, Miss Hope? Would you like me to stop?"

"No, no—go on. Please."

The second card Lady Westfield turned over was the Priestess. The illustration was of a seated woman in midnight-blue robes, her feet resting on a golden crescent, a smaller crescent adorning her brow, and a silver cross at her throat. She was sitting in front of a tree, holding a book in her hands.

The card was upside down.

"Interesting," Lady Westfield mused. "The reverse Priestess. The High Priestess sits at the gate of great Mystery, as indicated by the Tree of Life. She sits between the darkness and the light, represented by the pillars of Solomon's temple, which suggests she will mediate a passage between life and death. In her lap, she holds the half-revealed and half-concealed Torah, representative of the exoteric and the esoteric teachings and higher knowledge. The moon under her left foot shows her dominion over pure intuition."

"Why is she upside down?" Maggie asked, trying not to let her voice betray her growing apprehension. "What does that mean?"

"The High Priestess reversed can signify you don't hear your inner voice. Your intuition's calling out to you, but for some reason you won't listen. You may be a highly intuitive person, but also someone who's lost the connection at some point." Her eyes met Maggie's. "You need to get that connection back."

"I told you," Durgin said, leaning back behind Princess Margaret to whisper in her ear, "you have to pay attention to the gut."

"Oh, please," Maggie protested, but she didn't pull away from him. She tried to brush off the feeling that, somehow, Lady Westfield might be right.

Lady Westfield turned over the third card. It was the Devil.

The illustration showed the Devil with the face and torso of a man, but the horns of a goat and the legs of a bull. *The Blackout Beast,* Maggie thought. The feelings of comfort she'd felt in the protection of Buckingham Palace vanished. She had a sudden vision of Brynn dancing with the Beast.

As Princess Margaret gasped, a tree branch banged at the glass of the window and they all froze. Lilibet gave a small laugh, then put a hand over her mouth.

Lady Westfield was undisturbed. "If you notice, the Devil has the wings of a vampire bat, an animal that sucks the lifeblood out of its prey. Above him is an inverted pentagram, signifying the darker side of magic and occultism.

"At the foot of the Devil stand a man and a woman, both naked and chained to the podium on which the Devil sits. They appear to be held here, against their will, but closer observation reveals that the chains around their necks are loose and could be easily removed. The dark and doorless cave implies the Devil dwells in the most inaccessible realm of the unconscious, and only crisis can break through the walls. There's a great confrontation coming—"

Elizabeth noticed Maggie's pallor. She poked at her sister's shoulder. "Margaret, why don't we do our pantomime scene for the guests? That might be fun."

"Oh, Lilibet, I don't want to—I want to know more about this Devil! I don't even remember all my lines—"

"We'll do *Sleeping Beauty* then. You're sleeping the whole scene and don't have any lines. Come." Princess Elizabeth's voice was commanding.

As the young royals performed their scene, Durgin slid over to sit closer to Maggie. "Are you all right?"

"Of course," she whispered back, her knee brushing his. "It's all superstitious nonsense."

"Whatever you say."

When the Princesses were done, there was applause. The older woman with the heavy makeup went to the piano and began to play Purcell.

Two of the officers ambled over and pretended to listen to the music. Then, "You're not serving in the military?" one asked, taking in Durgin's police uniform.

"I was too old for the original call to arms—and I find more than enough battles to fight to keep people safe from harm here in London."

The first officer raised his eyebrows at Durgin's accent, and the second leaned in. "But you have to admit, the Nazis are pure evil. What goes on in London can hardly compare."

Maggie could see a muscle in Durgin's jaw begin to twitch. "Unfortunately, there's plenty of malevolence thriving in London."

The first man reached over and, with fake joviality, clapped Durgin on the shoulder. "Why don't you do something for us, Detective? Can you play the piano? Recite a poem?"

Maggie hated, truly hated, the English aristocracy in that moment. "You don't have to—" she began.

"Oh no. I'm delighted," Durgin said in a tone that sounded anything but.

When he walked to the fireplace and turned to face his audience, there was silence. He swallowed. Then, taking a deep breath, he began to sing in a rich baritone:

> "Oh, the summertime is coming
> And the trees are sweetly blooming
> And the wild mountain thyme
> Grows around the blooming heather
> Will ye go, lassie, go?
>
> "And we'll all go together
> To pluck wild mountain thyme
> All around the blooming heather
> Will ye go, lassie, go?"

As he sang, the Queen, originally from Angus in Scotland, leaned forward, her eyes shining. When he began to sing the refrain, she joined him, her voice silvery but strong:

> "Oh, the summertime is coming
> And the trees are sweetly blooming
> And the wild mountain thyme
> Grows around the blooming heather
> Will ye go, lassie, go?"

There was silence, then enthusiastic applause. The Queen walked over to Durgin to thank him for the song. "That was my favorite when I was younger," she told him. "And a perfect song for a winter night such as tonight. Thank you, Detective Chief Inspector, for the gift of your beautiful voice."

Durgin gave a shy smile. "Thank you, Your Majesty. Er, ma'am."

Once again, a branch thumped at the window and a stiff wind rattled the panes. The Queen moved to the blackout curtains and peeked out. "Why, it's a blizzard out there!" she exclaimed. "There's no visibility whatsoever!"

The King cleared his throat. "A b-b-blizzard in a b-blackout!"

The Queen put a dainty hand to her ample, jewel-covered bosom. "The King's right," she said. "London in both a storm *and* the blackout will be a veritable labyrinth. You all *must* stay. I insist." She walked to her husband and took his hand. "We insist."

"Huzzah!" cried Margaret. "Miss Hope will stay!"

"Really," Maggie demurred, "I don't live that far. . . ."

"And then there's that Blackout Beast we've all been reading about in the papers," one of the officers said. "Nasty bit of work."

"We've heard of him," Durgin said drily.

"And of course we have plenty of bedchambers," said the Queen. "Fifty-two, I believe. I'll have the servants make up rooms." As she yanked on a needlepoint pull, she said with a smile, "You *must* stay. After all, it's a royal decree!"

The room Maggie was given was decorated in soothing tones of rose and fawn, with a large canopied bed and a small sitting area with a wide, long damask sofa and two wing chairs in front of a recently lit fire. The room was still freezing, and Maggie was grateful when there was a knock at the door and a maid stood there, offering a hot water bottle. "Please let me know if you need anything else, miss. The pull's on the right-hand side of the bed."

"Thank you," Maggie replied, wrapping her hands around the heat of the rubber bottle covered in soft wool. "Good night!"

As she explored the suite, she was amused to see a five-inch water line in the bathtub. *Even in Buckingham Palace* . . . she thought. There was also a lace nightgown and peignoir in dark blue velvet lined in silk and quilted satin slippers laid out on the bench at the foot of the bed.

Just as Maggie had finished washing up and changing, there was a knock at the door. She opened it. "Thank you, but I'm fine—" she began.

But it wasn't the maid, it was Durgin. "Don't ever open a door without asking who it is!" he fumed.

"Keep your voice down!" Maggie whispered. "Get in before someone sees you!"

He was still in his uniform. Maggie flushed pink and pulled the belt of the robe tighter. "Well, what is it?"

"There's a maniac out there," he said, locking and chaining the door. "I wanted to make sure you're all right."

"The snowstorm's given us a bit of a reprieve."

Durgin roamed the room, checking the closets and the locks on the windows. "Nowhere is safe."

Maggie's face darkened. "Not for Brynn, certainly."

"And since you received that package, not for you, either." He rubbed the back of his neck. "I'm serious, Maggie. I don't think you're safe here."

She gave a laugh halfway between a bark and a snort. "It's Buckingham Palace, for heaven's sake!"

"They've learned to protect themselves against falling bombs, but not a serial killer."

She smiled. "Oh, and here I'd gotten used to 'sequential murderer.'"

"I'm staying," he announced flatly. "I'll sleep on the sofa."

"It's much, much too short for you. You take the bed, I'll take the sofa."

"I won't hear of it."

"Well, I'm not tired anyway. Look, they've left us an electric kettle. Would you like some tea? There are even biscuits—Scottish shortbread. Although judging by the gray appearance and the oil on the doily, made with national flour and margarine. We can work."

"Work?" Durgin sat gingerly on the edge of a pink silk wing chair.

As Maggie bustled about, filling the kettle and plugging it in, she told him, "I've had a few ideas and I want to discuss them with you."

When the tea had been poured and shortbread laid out on the low table, Maggie went to her handbag and took out the map of London that Mark had given her. She'd kept track of all the places the women's bodies had been left with dots of red ink. "Look," she said, pushing it over to Durgin and sitting cross-legged on the carpet in front of the fire.

"A map of London. With the body dump sites marked. Yes, we have the same map back at the office."

But Maggie was thinking. "I saw a darts game the other evening."

"Maggie, we have a murderer to catch," he said gently. "Do you really have time for darts?"

"No, listen to me," she insisted. "You said that sequential murderers had certain patterns."

He took a sip of tea. "But yes, that's the right idea. No murderer is going to leave a body too near the scene of the crime or their residence."

"So there's a, a—let's call it a defense area," Maggie explained. "Now, when our Blackout Ripper dumps the bodies, he's going to want it to seem random—no evidence too close to him or where he lives. But according to math, even when someone's trying to do something at random and not make a pattern—there's always an inherent subconscious design."

"Not sure I'm following you, Maggie."

She closed her eyes. *Mathematics, cool and elegant,* she thought. Math had always been her savior, her calm, her respite. Even her joy. Math would help. It always did. She took a deep sigh and tried to make sense of the patterns she was seeing emerge. "Look, the Ripper's victim's bodies are located at specific coordinates, around the defense area. We can express this in a formula. I need paper!"

"Can't help you, I'm afraid."

Maggie stood and went to a small desk. Inside was ivory letterhead engraved with BUCKINGHAM PALACE and matching envelopes. And several gold-capped Parker pens. She took an envelope back to the low table and sat down again in front of the crackling fire.

She wrote out a formula with Xs and Ys, subscripts, brackets, and parentheses, and a variety of Greek letters and algebraic symbols.

Durgin watched, eyebrows pulled together.

"Look, the summation in the formula consists of two terms— the first describes the idea of decreasing probability with increasing distance. The second deals with the concept of a so-called shield area. The main idea of the formula is the probability of crimes first increases as one moves through the shield area, away from the place where the murders were committed, but then decreases."

Durgin set his cup down. "And if you'd say all that in the King's English, I'd be most obliged."

Maggie sat back to look at the formula. "The idea is—the probability of crimes increases as one moves through the shield area, away from the murder area, but then decreases afterwards.

And while the killer is trying to place the bodies randomly, he's not. He doesn't want them too far or too near to him, or to each other. Basically, what he's doing is creating a circle around where the murders are taking place. It's like a reverse bull's-eye."

She realized he wasn't following. "In other words, it's a non-pattern that really is a pattern. I could work it out mathematically, with this formula, but we just don't have the time or the manpower. Er, womanpower."

"I still don't understand."

"It's like . . . an accident of probability theory. With enough data points, patterns will emerge that point to the place where the murders took place." She gave a maniacal grin that rivaled the best of Durgin's. "The problem is that math is elegant and humans are . . . not. This is an ugly equation for ugly behavior."

He gave a crooked smile. "Are you telling me you have a *gut* feeling?"

She took one last look at the formula, then looked at the map. "Absolutely not. My absolutely logic-based and mathematically worked out *hypothesis* is that our Beast is committing his murders right"—she made a black circle on the map, approximately in the middle of all the red marks—"here."

She leaned in and squinted, looking at the maze of crossing streets. Her eyes widened. "That's practically Ash Street, the address of the Castle Hotel for Women—"

"But we've always suspected the Castle Hotel."

"Suspected, yes—but now we have actual mathematical proof. There's a connection between the murder of SOE women and the Castle Hotel for Women. Someone left the Castle's cards there, to give to prospective agents. . . ."

"So we're still where we started."

"Not entirely." Maggie took a sip of cooling tea. "It occurred to me that we've all done a great job keeping the real details of the

Blackout Beast case out of the papers," she said, "but now I'm thinking—maybe we can use the press."

"How so?"

"You said our Beast is young and arrogant. Dangerously arrogant. Well, coverage in the press is only going to inflate his ego, yes? He must be following the story. How could he not?"

"And?"

"*And,*" Maggie continued, animated by the thrilling new use of math, "we can use it to our advantage. We use the press to taunt him, to draw him out of the underbrush where he's hiding."

"That's a terrible idea," Durgin said, biting into a crumbly gray biscuit. "We can't risk a possible victim."

"But he's going to choose a victim anyway. So, this time, let's *help* him choose." Maggie sat down on the sofa with her cup and saucer. "We mock the killer about the kidney. Or, rather, *I* do. At a press conference. I've already thought it out."

"No. Absolutely not."

"I speak at the press conference, identify myself as someone working on the case, and then leave myself open, as bait. I can check in to the Castle Hotel, just like the other victims. Meanwhile, you and the rest of your men move in for the capture."

"Are ye daft, woman?" Durgin exploded. "That's the looniest idea I've ever heard of! We don't use humans as live bait! This isn't some Highland huntin' party!"

Maggie suddenly remembered a snippet from her dream. *Am I the hunter? Or the hunted?* she'd asked. *Both, apparently.* "We're nearly up to Jack the Ripper's last victim, Mary Ann Kelly. Between my being a 'working woman' and the red hair . . ."

Durgin considered. "If we hold a press conference—"

"*When* we hold a press conference—" She tucked her feet under her. "We taunt him with the ultimate next victim—me."

"It's not a bad idea," he relented. "But I'll have every man at my disposal watching over you. The bastard won't touch a hair on yer wee pretty head. . . ."

They stared at each other for a heartbeat.

"You're sounding most Scottish tonight," Maggie said finally, breaking the silence.

"It happens when I get angry. The idea of you in danger makes me livid."

"The song you sang was beautiful. You have a remarkable voice."

"My Gaelic heritage." He looked around the room, then sighed. "Never thought I'd sleep in Buckingham Palace."

"It's my first time, too. Here, at least. I've stayed at Windsor, as the girls told you." Only the dancing orange blaze illuminated the room. She gave a wide fake yawn and rose to her feet. "I'm *exhausted*."

Durgin put down his cup and stood as well. "I still don't like the idea of this press conference," he said, taking a step toward her. "I don't like the idea of your speaking publicly as a way to lure this bastard closer."

Just like in North and South, *when the heroine speaks in public, in front of an angry mob, only to be struck by a stone.* "You don't have to like it."

Another step. "I'd never forgive myself if anything happened to you."

Maggie's heart skipped a beat. Then she said, "I'm sure you say that to all your colleagues. Mr. Collins from the morgue, especially."

Durgin took her hand, and interlaced his fingers in hers. "Collins especially, yes."

As their fingers entwined, Maggie felt a fierce and giddy joy in her chest. Impulsively, she leaned forward and kissed him on his stern mouth.

When they both finally drew back, Durgin pushed her tumbled hair from her eyes. "When this is all over, and we're not working together anymore, I'd like to do this properly. Ask you to dinner and a film, that sort of thing."

"I'd like that."

"In the meantime, since I've agreed to this press conference idea, I'll take the couch. You take the bed. Be gracious in victory, lass."

Maggie made her way to the bed as Durgin tried his best to settle in on the sofa. "I do try."

"Bronwyn Parry," the voice droned as the door swung open. "Miss Parry! It's *time!*"

A man stepped into the room. He was wearing a black Victorian costume, complete with vest, cloak, jabot, and gloves. He had a silk top hat under one arm, and his face was hidden by a white mask with holes cut for the eyes and mouth.

Brynn was already awake and alert, unaffected by the stupor-inducing gas since she'd plugged the copper pipe. Every fiber of her being was focused on the man standing in front of her. Her captor. Her jailer. Her killer.

"I know what you did with the pipe, Miss Parry," he purred. "Naughty, naughty, naughty! A naughty girl. None of the others thought of that."

"H-how do you know?"

"Peepholes!" he said with glee. "But that's unimportant. This is a special evening. A date, if you will—or an outing, you might say." Behind the mask, he chuckled. " 'Out'-ing? Good, isn't it? Do you catch it? No? Well, you will soon."

He dove at her, his gloved hand pressing over her mouth and nose, his weight forcing her into the corner, pinning her down.

She struggled to stay clear and focused. *Think, Brynn, think!* She realized the glove was damp, with that same familiar odor. It squeezed against her face, suffocating her.

When he saw her eyes close, the man swept her into his arms and carried her to the main room of the stone-walled cellar. It was cavernous, windowless, and dank. "I'm not a violent man," he said to himself in a mild voice as he set Brynn's limp body down on an operating table in the center of the room. "Not by nature, at least.

"But if you poke at a lion in a cage with a stick, over and over and over again, the lion is going to roar. No, that lion is going to *bite*. And once the lion realizes the cage is but imaginary, the lion is going to kill everyone who ever tried to poke him, ever."

He leaned down to Brynn, his masked face close to her ear. "I'm not just Jack the Ripper, Miss Parry, or the so-called Blackout Beast—I'm a *crusader*. A crusader for the rights of the English gentleman, which have been trampled by you modern women. The female manipulation of males during the last decades—the feminized men in Britain and Europe. So I need to send a message."

Brynn began to regain consciousness. She had been trained by the SOE to fight, using any and all weapons she had at her disposal, and instinctively, her eyes flicked around the room as he bound her hands and ankles to posts built into the table with leather shackles. In the shadows, she could just make out a grotesque contraption in the corner that appeared to be a medieval torture rack. There was a shelf of organs in formaldehyde, a medical cabinet full of amber bottles, and a steel tray displaying surgical instruments.

He noticed her eyes were open and finished binding her hands and feet. "I see my job, during this insane war, is to reestablish the patriarchy," he continued. "How else can we win the war? And still keep our heads up when it's over? It's not your fault," he continued, musing. "Women after you will see the bodies and they'll be warned. Once again, they'll know their place."

She blinked and fought to escape the shackles. But she was still drugged, and the shackles were too strong.

He slapped her across the face, and she whimpered. "Look over there." He seized her chin in one gloved hand and pointed her face toward the wall. "My kiln—made of firebrick. If I turn on an oil jet atomized with steam, the entire kiln's filled with a flame so hot it can melt iron." He laughed. "I told them it was because I was interested in researching glass bending. No one even questioned how large it was. But as soon as I get a body inside, close the door, and turn on both the oil and the steam—not even the bones remain."

"Did you get it from Hitler and his camps?" she managed. "Is that what you're going to do to me?" Her whole body felt stiff, anesthetized.

"No, Miss Parry," he said, looking over his surgical instruments. "You are going to be immortalized as I am. You're not Bronwyn Parry anymore. Tonight, you will be playing the role of Catherine Eddowes in my tribute to Jack the Ripper. Tonight we will be performing yet another act of a morality play I've created, to warn the whores of the world what's to come if they don't behave.

"It's time," he told her, his eyes gleaming behind the mask. "For your out-ing."

She fought against the restraints.

"Be loud as you'd like, Miss Parry," he urged, finally choosing a ten-inch scalpel. He turned back to her, blade in hand. "This cellar is soundproof. No one will hear you scream."

Chapter Seventeen

"Thank you all for coming, especially on such short notice," Durgin was saying from a podium set up in a large conference room in Scotland Yard's offices. The windows offered a view of the slanting afternoon light over the gray-green Thames, but everyone's attention remained focused intently on the Detective Chief Inspector, dressed in uniform. A forest of microphones poised to catch every word—BBC, CBC, and even a few from Australia and the United States—surrounded him. Photographers, with their heavy black cameras and huge flashbulbs, were standing close, ready to take aim. "But today we have breaking news in the search for the sequential murderer whom the press has dubbed the 'Blackout Beast.'"

A murmur rippled through the restless crowd. Flashbulbs popped and exploded. The unexpected bright lights made Maggie, standing behind Durgin with a few of the Scotland Yard officers, wince and shield her eyes. Blinking to dispel momentary blindness, she stared at the crowd, going over each individual man in turn. In their dark suits and ties, they all looked perfectly respectable—serious and sober, as befitted the situation. *What did you expect, Hope? Devil's horns? Glowing red eyes? Cloven hooves?*

And what did the Beast expect from her?

Maggie wore a tweed suit with thick shoulder pads, a scarf to hide her fading bruises, her pearl earrings, and a fresh pair of silk stockings she'd bought in Washington. She'd dabbed on lipstick and her red hair was swept back into a tight bun. Her goal was to look professional. The sort of competent woman the Beast hated most.

"The Blackout Beast has been specifically targeting patriotic young women, working for the Government," Durgin continued, leaving out any specific mention of SOE. "Three women have been killed and their bodies displayed in ways reminiscent of Jack the Ripper. But today, Scotland Yard has a new lead in the search for this killer."

More flashbulbs popped.

Durgin gestured to Maggie to come forward. "Today, I have a colleague with me—Miss Margaret Hope. Miss Hope has been assisting us with the investigation."

The crowd's murmurs increased.

Maggie raised her head and pressed her lips together to disguise their trembling as she stepped toward the podium. When she reached the copse of microphones, Durgin shook her hand—a perfect photo opportunity. Another explosion of flashbulbs ignited, and she tried not to wince at the bright lights and dizzying cacophony.

Then she turned to face the crowd, straightening her shoulders and raising her chin. "Thank you, Detective Chief Inspector," she said, unsmiling. She swept her gaze over the assembled men. "I can tell you the man we're looking for, the so-called Blackout Beast, has a specific type of victim. His ideal is female, in her twenties, and involved with Government work. Typically she's in London for only a short while, meeting with higher-ups before beginning her war-related job. Because she's not from London, and may not have family and friends here, she may stay at a women's residence hotel. These are women just like me," she said, scanning the pale faces of the men in front of her, "young, professional, trying to serve our country as best we can. So, for me, his attacks are personal. As will be his capture."

Gauntlet thrown! Maggie looked past the microphones, the cameras, and into the crowd. He was there, she knew it. A hot rush of anger quelled her nerves. "This killer drugs the women, so he can control them." Maggie felt strength course through her, as she imagined the Beast taking in her words. "But now he's beginning to slip up, to make mistakes. One of his victims, whose name we're protecting for privacy, survived his attack. And she's been able to give us details, crucial details—details that will ultimately lead to the Blackout Beast's capture and arrest."

Durgin joined her before the microphones. "We hope to bring this murderer to justice as soon as possible," he said, wrapping things up. "Thank you for coming."

Again, flashbulbs exploded as reporters shouted questions. Durgin and Maggie ignored them. Walking out of the room, Maggie decided it had gone fairly well, considering they hadn't given any real news. *Not that the press will complain.* The press conference was merely like a javelin grazing the Beast's side—enough to wound his pride, to rouse his bloodlust—to make her his primary target.

As she and Durgin walked together to a squad car in full view of the throng, she kept her spine ramrod straight. *Follow me, you bastard. You know you want to. Follow me and tonight we'll catch ourselves a beast.*

"Excuse me, sir." The voice came from an officer with white hair who'd cut his chin while shaving that morning, leaving an angry red mark. "But I'm afraid another body's been found."

When Maggie and Durgin reached the crime scene, again in Regent's Park, dark clouds were rolling in. The wind had picked up, and branches of the oak, ash, and beech trees were black against the overcast sky and the snow-covered ground. The police were putting up another tent, so the Yard's staff could keep out both drifting snow and interlopers as the doctor worked. Entering the tent, Maggie flinched. It stank of blood, now an all-too-familiar scent. Mrs. Vera Baines, with her silver-handled walking stick, sat in one dim corner, arms wrapped tightly around herself as though to keep pieces from flying off.

Maggie took a deep breath and looked to the body laid out on the tarp. She started when she saw the young woman's face.

Brynn.

The dead girl was Brynn.

She swallowed hard as she blinked back scalding tears.

"Just like Catherine Eddowes," she could hear the doctor saying to Durgin, as though underwater. "The report shows the details."

"She was your friend, wasn't she?" Durgin said to Maggie, his voice gentle. "The one you asked after?"

"Yes," Maggie managed. She flipped up the collar of her coat. "Excuse me, I need some air."

She left, walking a few paces away from the tent, then sagged against the brick wall enclosing the misty park. The afternoon was oddly quiet. All she could hear was the occasional distant hum of a car engine, the rattle of bare branches in the frosty east wind.

Brynn was dead, slaughtered the same way Jack the Ripper's victim Catherine Eddowes had been. Another brave woman of the SOE, dead before she could even begin her mission. Before she could even begin her life.

Maggie felt rage rising inside of her. There was one murder left—the doppelgänger of redheaded Mary Jane Kelly—one more chance to stop the Blackout Beast. *I'm going to catch you, you monster. And I'm going to stop you. You'll never do this to any of us, ever again.*

She unpinned her hat and shook out her hair from its tortoise-shell clip, so it swirled around her shoulders and down her back. It was red, like Red Riding Hood's cloak. Red as any matador's cape. *Tonight I'll be playing the role of my fellow redhead Mary Jane Kelly,* Maggie thought. *Between the press conference and the hair, I should be damn well irresistible.*

As she looked around the ghostly park, wondering if he was there, she thought, *Come on, you bastard, you son of a bitch. Come at me, then—like the Minotaur you are, coming for the maiden in the labyrinth.*

Come on, you Devil—I dare you.

The man with the smudged green sunglasses smiled as he tracked Maggie and Durgin from the Scotland Yard press conference to where he'd dumped the body in Regent's Park. He watched from his usual bench, throwing crumbs for a few pigeons into the snow. He watched as Maggie left the tent, looking queasy. Would she vomit? No—too bad. She saw him then, saw him and held his gaze, watching him watch her. He couldn't move. And then she unpinned her red hair, shaking it down to her shoulders, eyes flashing.

Very well then, Miss Hope. Challenge accepted.

"We can still call this off," Durgin said as Maggie checked in with May, the young blonde with the port-wine stain and gray front tooth at the desk at the Castle Hotel.

"No," Maggie told him. Then, to the girl, "No, I *don't* have any luggage, actually." She was trying to modulate her voice, which kept creeping higher in pitch. After she signed her name in flowing black ink, she looked around her. A number of women in uniforms or brightly colored dresses under wool coats were going out for the evening. The lobby was emptying out, the fire dying. It was quiet, but he was there, she was certain of it. She felt his presence. *Come on, you Beast. Come and get me.*

"Well, please let me know if you need anything." May's face was troubled.

Dr. Frank came out from his office, hand extended. "Ah, Miss Hope! How are you?"

Maggie ignored his question. "This is DCI James Durgin," she said, gesturing.

"Why, hello! Hello! How do you do, Detective."

Durgin's face was stone. "We spoke earlier today on the telephone."

"Of course, of course! Right this way!"

In the privacy of his office, Dr. Frank asked, "How's the investigation going? Any news? I certainly hope so—those poor, poor women. And I'm happy for you to make use of the Castle Hotel, in any way you need."

The plan Maggie and Durgin had devised was for her to check in to the Castle Hotel, where the Beast, incensed by her appearance at the press conference, would make his move. Durgin and his officers would be outside in an unmarked car, watching the front entrance. There would be another unmarked police car at the back. A plainclothes officer would be in the hotel's lobby, pretending to wait for one of the guests. If Maggie were to be in any danger, she would take off the blackout curtains in her room, to let the light spill out into the darkness. Then they'd know she'd been approached.

"I'll have May escort you to your room." The doctor was all concern.

"You don't have to do this," Durgin said, taking her hand. "We can call this off, here and now."

Maggie wanted nothing more than to run from the building, run away from London, from the war, from everything. But instead she took a shaky breath. "No, I'm staying."

As Durgin glared, Dr. Frank dialed zero on the telephone. "Yes, Miss Hope is ready to be shown her room, darling."

When May entered, she asked, "Anything else, Daddy?"

"No, my sister. This is Miss Margaret Hope, the woman I spoke with you about—"

"Yes, we met when she signed the book—"

"—and DCI Durgin. After you take Miss Hope to her room, I want you to exit the hotel, as we discussed. The police officers will take care of you."

"Daddy—" May protested.

"Your father's right," Durgin said. "It's for your own safety, Miss Frank."

May smiled. "Of course. Whatever you say."

"May!" came a deep, resonant voice, the sort movie stars used. It belonged to a young man opening the door; however, the voice didn't match his looks. The man was short and slight, boyish-looking, despite his smart double-breasted, pin-striped suit and camel-hair coat. His eyes were a striking hazel. Skin tags dotted his face, and his upper front teeth overlapped, one with a significant chip.

"DCI Durgin and Miss Hope, this is Nicholas Reitter," May told them. She'd blushed hotly as the young man entered.

"You're May's fiancé," Maggie stated.

Nicholas smiled. "Why yes. She mentioned that, did she?"

"She's wearing an engagement ring and your photograph is on her desk."

He looked at her strangely. "You look familiar, Miss Hope. Have we met before?"

Maggie felt a prickle of recognition, but couldn't quite place him. "I don't think so."

May fluttered her eyelashes. "Nicholas couldn't serve because of a congenital heart defect," she explained, "but he's off to the Middle East soon—surveying and mapmaking and all sorts of things I don't really understand." She twisted at her ring. "We'll be married during his first leave."

Durgin looked to Maggie. "Are you ready?"

"As I'll ever be."

May touched the redhead's shoulder. "Come, let me show you to your room."

Faux-gas lamps at haphazard intervals along the corridor left long shadows as Maggie and May walked past.

May opened the door to the room Brynn had stayed in, then handed Maggie the key. "Here you go. Is there anything else you need?"

"No, thank you, though."

"I'll leave you to it, then."

Inside her cramped room, Maggie tossed her handbag on the dresser and slipped off her coat. She sat down on the bed.

And waited.

The chamber was furnished and comfortable enough. Its windows were blocked by blackout curtains, and the only sounds she heard were the low rumble of traffic and a faint wailing siren. Maggie stared up at the ceiling, heart beating, doing breathing exercises.

Then she heard a scratching at the door.

She froze, her heart pounding.

As the door opened, she called, "Yes?"

But no one was there. *Must have been the wind.*

———

Hours later, well after midnight, Maggie knew it was time to go. The Blackout Beast—if he was even there—wasn't making his move in the hotel, at least that night.

Feeling equally disappointed and relieved, Maggie took the aging elevator down to the ground floor and nodded to the officer working the lobby. She exited and walked through the moonlight in the biting cold wind to the unmarked van where she knew Durgin and his officers were waiting, along with May.

"He's not going to show," Maggie told Durgin. "I want to leave."

Durgin gave an explosive exhale. "Well, we gave it a shot," he said. "I can't say I'm sorry this has all come to naught. Let's get you home. Do you want a lift back to your house?"

Maggie nodded. "Yes, thank you."

"You'll be safe there. I'll have my men in place by the time you arrive. There will be one inside the house to greet you—George Staunton, you've met him at the Yard—and then leave. And then the rest in the shrubbery, waiting." Durgin turned to May. "And you, you'll be all right?"

"I'll be fine," she assured him, pulling her coat around her. "I'll make sure everything's in order and then lock up."

As Maggie and Durgin drove off, May walked into the hotel and went directly to the front desk, picking up the telephone receiver. She dialed the numbers of the public call box and waited until the connection was established, looking around to make sure none of the officers were still there.

"Yes, she just left for her house," May whispered to the person on the other end of the line.

Chapter Eighteen

Locking her front door behind her, Maggie flipped on the lights and shrugged off her coat as she walked toward the closet, looking for Detective George Staunton. *Well, at least I'm not blindfolded this time,* she thought grimly, ignoring the tension in her neck and jaw. *And at least Chuck and Griffin are safe.* Chuck and her baby had been evacuated, and were spending the night at the Savoy Hotel, with Scotland Yard guards right outside their door. Even K had been evacuated. The thought of her cat enjoying the Savoy almost—*almost*—made Maggie smile. She glanced around the shadowy foyer, expecting to see Staunton.

But instead, Mark stepped out of the shadows. *Mark? He's not part of the plan.* Maggie hadn't even seen him since he'd gotten drunk and, well—

"You?" Maggie managed, her voice sounding overly loud in the eerie quiet of the deserted house. "Where's Staunton?"

"Plans change." Mark's breath was hot and reeked of alcohol. *Has he been drinking again?* Maggie took a step back. "And he's only a Met officer. I'm MI-Five." Mark reached behind him to pull out a gun from the waist of his trousers. "You're better off with me."

Then, "This is some place you have. It's all yours?"

"Yes," Maggie said, in no mood for conversation. "Inheritance. Long story."

"Still, it's awfully big for an unmarried woman, alone."

"I have flatmates."

He saw how her eyes darted up the stairs and into the shadows. "I've already checked it out, cellar to attic. There's no one here. And the Beast won't get past the officers stationed outside—we'll get him before he gets you."

Maggie drew in a trembling breath. At the front door, Mark turned back at the last second, as if he were going to say something. Instead, he shook his head and opened the door, letting the light shine out, letting his voice carry, and making a big show of leaving.

Using her as bait in her own house was their backup plan if the Beast didn't come to the hotel. If he followed her, which is what they all hoped, the Met police would get him before he even set foot inside.

And so, with any luck—if that was the word—the killer was watching Mark leave, too.

When he was gone, Maggie fumbled with the locks, which slid into place with loud, echoing *clicks*. She hooked the chain on the door. Now there was nothing to do but wait.

She wandered the rooms, flipping on lights, looking in closets and behind furniture. Why wasn't the telephone ringing? Why wasn't Durgin calling to tell her they'd arrested him, that she was safe now? She sat down on a wing chair in the library, waiting, tensed, listening to every creak and scrape the old house made, sounds like trolls under a bridge.

She decided to go upstairs, to her bedroom—she'd lock the door and feel safe there. With one last look around her empty library, she stood. She checked the lock on the back door and rechecked the front. Then she maneuvered up the steep steps in the darkness.

In her bedroom, Maggie pulled open the blackout curtains, and looked out into the night. The moon was glorious—full, bright, and almost blue against the night sky. Where were the surveillance officers? She knew they were probably hiding in the shrubbery, maybe even in one of the tall trees, but still. She couldn't see them.

What if the Blackout Beast had killed them?

No, of course not. She shut the drapes. But even with the blackout curtains in place, the moon was dazzling enough to sneak slivers of light into the room through the cracks.

She sat on the bed and leaned back against the headboard, knowing it could be a long wait.

The officers were out there, circled around the house. The Beast couldn't get past them. But in her heart of hearts, doubts lingered. After all, she'd publicly mocked him. A tremor shot through her body. *Ring me,* Maggie willed Durgin. *Tell me you caught him.* But the telephone remained silent.

Then the back of her neck prickled. A gloved hand clamped implacably over her mouth, holding a handkerchief doused with something strong and foul.

As Maggie struggled to turn to face her attacker, he climbed on top of her, hand with the cloth pressed against her mouth and nose. She knew he wanted to kill her, but first, she also knew, he would rape, torture, and mutilate her. Like Mary Jane Kelly, Jack the Ripper's final victim, the one with the red hair. He would be satisfied with nothing less.

As she struggled under the cloth, unable to see, he spoke, his voice warm and resonant. "In case you're wondering where your team is, they're all dead."

Oh, God. The men were dead. George Staunton was dead. *Mark* was dead. And back at Scotland Yard, Durgin didn't even know. She was alone.

Her vision blurred as she slid off the bed, hitting her head on the parquet floor. The breath went out of her lungs with a gasp.

A jumble of pictures spun in her brain, stories girls had whispered—of attacks on unprotected women, throat cuttings, rapes, molestation. Her first terrified impulse was to hide in the closet, crawl under the bed, fly down the back stairs and run screaming into the relative safety of the blackout—anything to escape him. But then she remembered Brynn.

I'm still alive, she thought through the haze of drugs. *I still have a chance to get him. For Brynn. For all of us.*

Maggie's breath came back to her, suddenly and painfully. *I'm in the labyrinth,* she realized. She forced her eyes open, then struggled to her feet, stumbling and staggering, her drugged mind playing tricks on her. Confusing images came and went—the man of crawling flies, the devils of Doré's etchings, Brynn's white face, her vacant eyes staring heavenward.

Maggie forced herself to climb down the wooden stairway. She had a sudden memory of the men at the swimming pond who'd shouted obscenities at her. What if they, too, were waiting for her? As she fought waves of dizziness and nausea, the stairs seemed to twist and turn. Were they moving? Like snakes and ladders? Who was there? Mark, mocking her, telling her to spread her legs like she had for Hugh? Hadn't she just come up these stairs? Or was she going down?

She couldn't remember. She couldn't remember anything now. She was hopelessly bewildered, dizzy from whatever drug the Beast had given her.

She stopped and listened, sniffing at the air like a terrified doe. She didn't hear anything. Surely he was coming after her? Was he on the stairs behind her right now? Blood roared in her ears. She caught herself on the stair railing, and then she fell.

At the foot of the staircase, she lay crumpled, panting harshly, pain exploding through her body. In her haze, she wasn't sure if the monster's claws on the hall table's legs were real or imaginary.

She crawled forward, and pulled herself up onto a chair, using every remaining scrap of strength she possessed. She heard footsteps, heavy on the stairs. She tried to stand, but couldn't. Couldn't move at all.

There, looming in front of her, was Max, who turned into the red-faced puppet Punch. Then the figure was the violinist in the park, playing *Symphonie fantastique,* devil horns on his head. And then Mark, reeking of alcohol. And then the Blackout Beast, his blade glittering as he savaged Brynn's body.

"Come on!" she heard him bellow, shaking her back into consciousness. The man in the green sunglasses.

She looked up and realized who it was—Nicholas Reitter, the architect. May's fiancé. She blinked, realizing too late. He was also the man in the park, the man with the green sunglasses. The one who'd always been there, in the background. The one she'd never consciously registered, but must have noted, all the same.

She could hear his breath rasping in the shadows, and then the safety on a gun being released. "Let's have a game of Hide and Seek, shall we, Miss Hope? You're *it!*"

Maggie forced herself up. She wavered as she made her way forward, to get to the front door.

"I'll count down from ten and give you a head start? Ten. Nine. Eight . . ."

Maggie tripped and fell again. *He has a gun.* Excruciating pain shot through her right ankle, but she pushed herself up again, sticky, warm rivulets of blood running down her shin. *Keep going.*

Nicholas Reitter was the Blackout Beast.

She was going to die.

A small part of her wanted to laugh, if only because Nicholas was so short, so slender, his hair was so very mousy brown. *This, this is the dread Beast?* And then she did laugh, in a series of breathy exclamations, halfway between a snort and a scream.

"Why—" She heard his resonant voice as though from far, far away. "I've found you!" As he grabbed at her with gloved hands, Maggie could feel his heat. *He's enjoying this,* she realized, shuddering. He was feeding on her fear, her blind panic, her abject terror.

"I've been watching you," he told her as he grabbed her by the armpits. "Meddling bitch."

"You killed them," Maggie said slowly. "They were going to go off to war—brave women, doing their duty—but instead, you killed them."

"Women," he stated, his eyes rolling like a rearing warhorse's, "should *not* be going off to war. Should *not* be doing a man's job. That's the *problem.* Why won't you understand? Can't you see what a laughingstock we Englishmen will be if anyone finds out? 'Oh, the British men can't do it themselves, have to get a bunch of girls to step in. . . .'"

The word *laughingstock* rang in Maggie's ears. *Laughingstock,* she thought. *You're terrified of being a laughingstock,* she realized. *Not of being attacked or raped or murdered as we women are, but of being laughed at, found wanting. Terrified of being laughed at. How droll,* she thought. *And how drolly horrible and horribly droll.* The revelation cleared her head.

"What happened to you?" she asked, as he picked up a ball of twine for wrapping packages, then sliced it with a letter opener. "What happened when you were a little boy?"

"Shut up," he snarled.

Despite the headache piercing her skull, the throbbing in her ankle, and the blood dripping down her shin, she persisted. "What you're doing"—she shrugged—"it's just misogyny, age-old male violence against women. There's nothing heroic about it—it's not some noble crusade. You're not Jack the Ripper. Not even a Blackout Beast. You're a terrified young man, scared of being sent off to war, with a horrible bedtime story you want to tell."

"Women's place is in the home, yes. Mothers are the angels of the hearth." His pupils were pinpoints of concentrated hatred. "For years, I've been treated like a mouse, not a man. Now I'm a god and you women are the animals. And I'll slaughter you all like animals—a god exacting my retribution. For the crime of living a better life than I can have. If I can't stop you, I'll destroy you."

His voice was rising in volume, and his tongue flicked out like a snake's. "You denied me happiness, and so now I'll deny you life—it's only fair. And when I'm finished, there will be mountains of skulls and rivers of blood—and rightfully so. You all deserve to be annihilated. I'll give you whores exactly what you deserve—eradication."

Despite her fear, her gut was telling her things. Interesting things. "Your mother—" Maggie managed. What had Durgin said about the Blackout Beast after Doreen Leighton's murder? Something about the murderer's mother. *Abandonment. That's it.* "Did she die? Or did she leave you?" His breath caught and she knew she was on to something. "How old were you?"

He didn't answer. In a flash of empathy, his childhood torment raged through her, terrifying and bitterly cold.

"I'm sorry," she said, as he twisted the length of twine, binding her hands together. "I'm sorry you didn't have parents who cared for you and protected you. I'm sorry you didn't have a mother— for whatever reason."

He didn't stop.

"It wasn't fair for you—you were just a child," she persisted, "and I'm so sorry. I wish things could have been different for you. Mothers are not supposed to cause pain, they're supposed to love you and defend you. And fathers are supposed to protect you— not attack you." The ironic parallels to the relationships in her own life weren't lost on her.

"But you can't take away your pain by blaming someone else. You can't blame this generation of women. You can't take away the pain by hurting us. It makes you as bad and as hurtful as your own parents were."

Something flickered in the depths of his eyes, something nasty. "Shut. Up. You. Ungrateful. Bitch!" The blow to her face sent the room spinning.

Maggie pulled herself together through sheer force of will. "You have a choice. You can stop this madness."

He slapped her across the face again. Harder this time. *"Shut up!!"* he roared. His eyes were red and bestial. And when he leaned into her, she used the opportunity to slam her forehead into his. As he staggered back in shock, she shook off the twine and ran.

All she could see were sparks and shooting stars. A door. She pulled hard on the knob. It wouldn't open.

She was sure she could hear footsteps behind her, although she couldn't see anything in the darkness. She twisted frantically at the doorknob, slamming her shoulder into the door. There was a *ping* of metal as the dead bolt snapped and fell to the floor. When the door opened, she fell into another room. *Where am I? The drugs . . . is this how Brynn felt?*

The library. There were large plate-glass windows, all obscured by blackout curtains. On her hands and knees, she crawled to them, ripping the heavy black fabric down. Then she flipped on every switch and lit every lamp she could see, dragging them into the windows. *Light,* she thought. *Light will save me.*

Then the world kaleidoscoped, patterns swirling. She spun and tumbled helplessly into the darkness. When she recovered, she saw ancient stone walls. *A maze,* she realized. *The labyrinth.*

That's when she heard Brynn's voice. "I met the Beast in the labyrinth, too. I tried to get away, but he killed me." Brynn walked to Maggie.

"What?" Maggie couldn't process what was happening. *"Brynn?"*

"Before the first village was built on the marshes of the Thames, there was a labyrinth here. And a Beast. There's *always* been a Beast here."

"Jack the Ripper," Maggie murmured.

Brynn shook her head. "Much, much older than him. Jack was only one of his more recent disguises. There have been so many others. And now he's the Blackout Beast."

"I've dreamed of the Beast," Maggie said. *Brynn. It's so strange to see Brynn. Does this mean I'm dying?*

She knew, with the certainty of dreams, that somewhere in the labyrinth lurked the Beast, biding its time, waiting to come for her. She could hear it as it pawed the ground, snorting.

Then in the dream, or hallucination, or whatever it was—it charged. She couldn't see it clearly in the dimness, couldn't see if it was a boar, or an ox, or some kind of prehistoric mammoth. But it was gigantic, with scarlet eyes in a goat's face, flaring nostrils, and sweating flanks. The body of a man and the legs of a bull. A Minotaur. The Beast.

As it charged her, Maggie rolled away at the last moment. It galloped past, red eyes smoldering. Hidden once again in shadows, it threw back its head and howled.

Maggie struggled to her feet and waited, knowing the Beast was biding its time.

Are you the hunter or the hunted? Maggie heard Brynn call. As time expanded and contracted, Maggie felt hundreds of years come and go in a few breaths.

In the shadows, she could hear it snorting and growling, cloven hooves pawing at the ground.

Once again, it charged her. Maggie waited until the last possible moment, then somersaulted to one side—but not before grabbing and ripping out a knife from the Beast's hide. It felt cold in her hand. Solid. Heavy.

The Beast turned and bellowed, its goat eyes shining with pure hatred. Blood trickled from its side.

Maggie had the prickly déjà vu feeling of taking part in an age-old dance. She stood, stance wide.

With a deep bellow, the Beast charged once more.

She felt cold to the bone. She lifted the knife she'd pulled, then realized it was a gun.

The kaleidoscope turned once again, and Nicholas Reitter stood in front of her, on the blood-spattered carpet of the library, a long stiletto in hand. He looked up at her, eyes glazed with hatred. She stared as his face changed from naked anger to a contemptuous smile.

When she saw his lips lift in that parody of a smile, she felt nothing but overpowering fury. *It would be easy, so easy, to shoot him*, taunted a voice inside her. *It would feel so good, so satisfying, to watch him die.*

She thought of all the dead bodies of women she'd seen, of Brynn's lifeless face, of all the violence that the Beast had done. That Reitter had done. Rage and hatred coursed through her veins, making her want to hurt back. To kill. *Just pull the trigger. Pull it. Get a bit of your own back—*

But no. She lowered the gun, hands shaking, and took a step away. *No*, she thought. *No*.

He leered as he screamed, "Fucking whore." Then he lunged.

I will not *let you kill me.* Maggie aimed at his head and pulled the trigger. *I will* not *die for you.* The kick of the gun made her stagger backwards, hands smarting, as the roar of the explosion filled her ears, and the acrid smoke burned her lungs.

Reitter fell backwards to the floor with a violent crash, legs and arms akimbo.

Maggie stood over him, gazing down into what was left of his jaw. A pool of blood began to spread on the carpet.

She stood there, the gun still hot in her hand, watching him bleed. Her mind was blank with shock, the thud of her heart like a drumbeat in her ears, the air of the library cold on her face.

She'd struck a blow of revenge for Brynn. For all the murdered women. For herself. She wasn't proud—but she wasn't ashamed, either. It was kill or be killed. The hunter or the hunted. And she had made the decision to kill—in order to live.

She stood over the body, gun still pointed down, breathing heavily.

There was banging at the front door, then a deafening crash as the Metropolitan Police officers broke it down. Maggie looked up and saw Durgin in the lead, his own pistol drawn.

"I shot him," she told him, in a voice that sounded surprisingly normal. She could only watch as he and the officers took in the fallen body, the widening circle of red on the carpet, and then her own blood-flecked face.

One of the men knelt down to take Reitter's pulse. "He's alive," he told them. "We need to get him to hospital."

As the men carried Reitter out, Maggie reached up to wipe at a tear rolling down her face. But when her fingers came away red, she stared down at them, transfixed by the sight of Reitter's blood.

"You're safe now," Durgin said, putting an arm around her as they watched the men carrying Reitter leave. "You're all right."

Somehow in that moment, Maggie knew exactly what to do. She took her fingers and smeared a line of blood across one cheek, then the other, then her forehead. She was now a hunter.

Chapter Nineteen

As early morning sunlight streamed through the windows, Sarah yawned and stretched in bed. "May I make you a cup of tea, darling?" she said in perfect French, tracing the line of his jaw with one finger.

Hugh beamed. "Thank you, dearest. That would be lovely," he replied, stroking her dark, silky hair.

The leggy brunette slipped into her red silk robe and went down to the kitchen. "It's a bit like playing house, isn't it?" she called to Hugh, who'd followed behind. She began to rummage through the cupboards to find the tea things and bread and jam for breakfast.

As the kettle began to whistle, Sarah turned off the gas and used a pot holder to pour the hot water into the teapot she'd prepared. She assembled everything on a tray and carried it to the table, which Hugh had set.

Sitting down, she reached for the creamer to pour a splash into Hugh's mug. "No!" he cried, reaching over to grab her wrist in midair. "Remember—in France it's tea first, then milk, not the other way around! Something even as small as that could give us away to the Gestapo!"

Sarah set the creamer down and picked up the teapot instead, realizing not only her error but what a mistake like that could cost them in France. "Sorry. I'm so, so sorry."

Hugh released her hand, but kept his eyes on hers. "We're a team now," he reminded her. "Whatever comes, we'll get through it together. I'll cover for you—you'll cover for me. But it's best if we keep our wits about us."

The telephone rang and Hugh rose to answer it. "Yes," he said, looking back at Sarah. "Yes, of course. We'll come to the office right away."

Next to the pristine white hospital bed, a pot of forced pink hyacinth blossoms on a table gave off a pungent sweet scent. Durgin slumped in the chair next to the bed, asleep, snoring softly.

Maggie was already awake and sitting up in the white enamel bed, reading a tattered and dated issue of *Vogue* one of the nurses had given her. She couldn't stop staring at an advert of an enraged man towering over a redheaded woman. The caption read: *Is it always illegal to kill a woman?* There was the company logo and then the response: *Show her it's a man's world.* She dropped the magazine and it fell to the floor.

She tried to move again. She was bruised, yes, bloodied, a bit—but felt no serious damage beyond the remnants of a horrific headache. Then she thought back to the events of the last few days, yesterday, last night . . . to Brynn.

Brynn. Brynn and all the other SOE women who'd been killed. Murdered. Gone, destroyed. What had Reitter said? *It wasn't fair.* Well, Maggie was old enough, and had seen enough, to have given up any hope of life being fair long ago, but it seemed the women's deaths had ripped a dreadful and forever unmendable hole in the fabric of life.

Slowly, memories began to trickle back. The press conference. The desperate struggle in her house. Her visions of Brynn and the

Minotaur. Shooting the Blackout Beast—Nicholas Reitter, May Frank's fiancé. She reached up to touch the blood on her face, but someone had washed it off. Her fingers came away clean.

Durgin opened his eyes. She'd always thought they were gray, but in this light, they looked forget-me-not blue. He sat up, surreptitiously wiping at his mouth to see if he'd drooled. "Morning," he said. "How do you feel?"

"I'll live."

Maggie's hands went to her head. It was covered in bandages, and she could feel a large and painful lump on the crown.

"The visions I had . . . They were . . . insane." Maggie pinched the bridge of her nose. "And now I have a god-awful headache."

"I'm not surprised." Durgin reached out to clasp her hand. Their fingers interlaced. "You'd been given drugs and hit your head, hard." He appraised her, then asked gently, "Do you remember anything?"

"If you're asking if I remember shooting Reitter, the answer is yes."

"The shot you fired missed his brain, but took off most of his jaw." He poured water from a carafe into a glass and handed it to her. "He's still alive, Maggie. It will take some time, but eventually we'll put him on trial. Justice will prevail." He brought her hand to his lips and kissed it. "But, darling," he warned. "You need to be careful."

"I know, I know." Maggie grimaced. "When you stare into the abyss—"

"—the abyss stares back at you. Yes, believe it or not, this humble DCI has read Nietzsche, too."

They sat together in silence, then Maggie asked, "Who is he? Nicholas Reitter?"

Durgin's eyes narrowed. "My men put together a profile for

me, earlier this morning. Reitter went to the Oxford College of Engineering, and studied architecture. Didn't graduate, though. Despite the fact his professors all said he was one of the most gifted students they'd ever met, he apparently had problems with authority figures—left the program. When the war broke out, he enlisted in the Army. And he was dismissed for what his records show were 'issues with superior officers.' "

"I see."

"Here's something interesting—he interviewed for SOE after being discharged from the Army. He has a good command of French—and made it to the first round of training in Scotland."

"They do take all sorts."

"But he had authority issues there, as well—and he was asked to leave before making it any further in the program. He came to London and somehow met Dr. Frank, who owns a number of properties in the Marylebone area. Because he didn't have a degree, he'd recently been drafted to—what he considered—a substandard post in the Middle East—that's what we think the catalyst was for the murders—his terror at the idea of being shipped off."

"So—why re-create the Ripper murders?"

"He'd been killing women in private, one every six months or so, and disposing of them in a large kiln in the basement of the Castle Hotel. But when he was called up, his anxiety increased. He wanted to do something more public, make a statement. The pace of his killings also increased, as his date of departure loomed."

Maggie chewed on her lip. "So, that's where the anger and rage came from—the women of the SOE—who were succeeding where he'd failed."

"More than that, I'm afraid. We still have to connect the dots, but it seems he'd already started abducting and killing young women from St. Hilda's at Oxford, even before the war. There's no telling how many women he's killed. We do know his mother abandoned him when he was three. According to police reports, his father was abusive—made him and his brother beat each other with belts for sport."

"He has a brother?"

"The brother's institutionalized now. And from what our psychologist said of Nicholas Reitter, working women remind him of his mother. And so, by murdering SOE women, he could be punishing his mother over and over again for leaving, for living a public life, for working. In his eyes, for abandoning him."

"How did he manage it?" Maggie felt a wave of nausea. "Did he have a contact at SOE?"

"Thankfully, no. But he was engaged to the daughter of the hotel's manager."

"May?" Maggie did remember the young blonde. Remembered how May had shown her to her room that night, must have shown Brynn to the same room . . . "*May* knew of the murders?"

"Worse than that—May helped Nicholas set the women up to be captured and killed. She and Reitter met and fell in love when her father had to rebuild the hotel. She became his accomplice, leaving the cards for the Castle Hotel at the SOE offices—Reitter knew where they were, of course, because he'd interviewed there himself. She always asked women who arrived how they found out about the hotel, and if they said SOE, she was sure to put them in rooms fitted with gas pipes, then let Reitter know they were there. She helped him give food to the women, helped move the bodies, too."

Mind-boggling. "But *why?*"

"We don't know." Durgin crossed himself. "Love, probably. Or, at least, what she thinks of as love. But she's in custody as well, for her part."

"My God." Maggie blinked. "A woman—a woman involved with all this . . . A woman helping to kill other women . . ." Then she startled. "Gas pipes?"

"Yes, that's how he—they—kept their victims quiet."

"Dr. Frank also owned the building in Pimlico that exploded. The newspaper said it had something to do with the gas pipe." Maggie put the pieces together. "It's probable Reitter had something to do with that, too, isn't it?"

Durgin gave a deep sigh. "You may be right. I'll get my men on the connection—and all of Dr. Frank's other properties, as well," he said with a grim nod. "Look, I don't want to push you—but you're going to have to give your statement to the police."

"Well, *you're* the police, aren't you?" She tried to force the corners of her mouth up into a smile, but it hurt too much.

"It's a bit more formal than that. The infamous endless paperwork, I'm afraid."

"Yes, paperwork—I know how much you love paperwork." She grimaced. "Just one more question—how did you know your men had been killed and I was alone there with him?"

"The redoubtable Mrs. Baines. Thank goodness for her! She saw all the light pouring out from the window you'd opened and rang me. I knew then that something had gone terribly, terribly wrong."

"Well, remind me to thank Mrs. Baines."

"Last night you brought down evil, Maggie. Pure evil."

"Evil actually can't be scientifically defined." Maggie tried to fix the bandages on her head, then gave up. "Evil's nothing more than an illusory moral concept linked to religion and mythology."

"I know evil," Durgin insisted. "I've seen it. Fought it. And last night—that was the real thing."

"You should know now," Maggie told him, "before we go out to dinner, that while I have a great respect and affection for many religions—and a particular affection for the Jesuits for reasons I can't go into—I'm not a believer myself."

Durgin's eyebrows shot up to his hairline. "You're *not?*"

"I'd rather concentrate on the here and now. I choose to act as though God does exist—and, who knows? It is possible. Even as a mathematician and scientist I'm aware there are mysteries we can't begin to know. I take on many of the traditional morals not because of reward and punishment, but because I feel they help me live a better life and it's the right thing to do. 'Love your neighbor as yourself'—it's quite beautiful—and common sense, really."

Durgin shook his head. "Nicholas Reitter—we found where he was keeping and killing the women, his victims. It looked like something out of the *Inferno.*"

"Reitter was a man—but not a devil. And certainly not a beast." She shuddered as a vague memory of something, something gigantic with knife-sharp horns, flashed through her mind. Then she dismissed it. "The belief in a supernatural source of evil isn't at all necessary. Men alone are quite capable of it." She took a sip of water. "It's interesting Dr. Frank's a psychoanalyst—maybe at some point they'll be able to isolate what we think of as 'evil' and perhaps even cure it. But it might take a while—despite Freud's writings on the unconscious and Jung's on the shadow self."

Durgin shook his head. "I still believe evil is real. And a force to be reckoned with."

Maggie remembered her own hatred, standing over Reitter with her gun, his blood splattered on her face. Once again, she rubbed at her cheek. "But if we kill those who are evil—do we become evil ourselves?"

"I think," Durgin said, "that you did what you had to, in the line of duty. I think you saved the lives of countless women. And I think—while it's always preferable to apprehend a suspect without bloodshed—that last night, the Blackout Beast got what he deserved."

The day was cold but beautiful, with a dazzling blue sky and puffy white clouds. The air smelled of sun-warmed seaweed and mud from Hatchett Pond as Hugh and Sarah strolled hand in hand through the gardens of Beaulieu. "Spring is coming," she announced, as a gentle breeze blew.

"Technically, it's still winter."

"Maybe according to the calendar, but spring's in the air." The grounds of the estate looked almost like the Garden of Eden with their apple trees, stone fruit orchards, and black earth dug up in anticipation of spring Victory Garden planting. At the edge of a field showing the first tips of green snowdrop shoots, an ancient oak towered over the land. It was gnarled and battered by the winter's storms, but it held firm. England. Britain. *What we're fighting for,* Sarah thought. *Why we're going to Paris.*

Hugh cocked his head. "If you look at that tree from the right angle, it rather looks like Churchill, don't you think?"

They entered the manor house. Miss Lynd was still using Kim Philby's office, which had a view of bare treetops from wavy greenish glass windows. "You two will obviously be working at the Palais Garnier and the environs, reporting to ballet master Serge Lifar. Your contact at the Paris Opéra will provide housing for you. A radio contact has been established. You'll receive that information after you arrive—"

Kim Philby opened the door. "Hope I'm not interrupting."

"Not at all, Mr. Philby," Miss Lynd replied. "We're just wrapping up." She looked to the duo.

"The moon is full and we have good weather. We'd like you to go tonight. We have a plane in place," Philby said.

Miss Lynd gave a smile, a genuine one. "We're taking you to the aerodrome before midnight."

"Midnight," Sarah mused, her eyes locking with Hugh's.

"By the way, this telephone message was left for you." Miss Lynd passed Sarah a note. It was from Maggie, asking her to return her call and saying that it was urgent she do so.

"What is it?" Hugh asked her.

Her jealousy was irrational, Sarah knew, but it was hot and strong nonetheless. She had no desire to bring up the topic of Maggie and no desire to return her call. "Nothing that can't wait until we get back from France."

Elise and her captors had made it to a safe house just outside Paris. The SOE agents took Elise inside with them and had her sit in a corner of a small old-fashioned kitchen while they spoke in rapid French to the men there, other SOE agents and Free French, she realized, translating in her head. It was a modest house, with a pump at the sink, a fireplace to one side. One of the men from the house gazed at Elise, then went upstairs to alert their radio operator the subject had arrived safely.

"Are you hungry?" one asked, pulling out coarse bread and purple fig jam, and pouring steaming milk into cups.

"We'll untie you if you promise not to do anything stupid," said another.

"Why are you fighting us, anyway?" asked her original captor. "We're all on the same side, you know."

Elise forced her lips into a smile. "I need to use the toilet. Please."

"Of course," the man who'd driven replied. "We didn't mean to scare you, you know. We're the heroes! Here to save the day!"

The other man dipped his bread into the steaming milk and

began to chew hungrily. "You certainly have friends in high places." He shook his head. "Downing Street."

"How far are we from Paris?" Elise asked. She could see woods and fields through the open windows.

"Not far. About seven or eight kilometers, I think."

"The toilet?" she repeated. She smiled. "I promise I'll be good."

"Outhouse is back there," the driver said with a jab of his thumb. "Pump's right by the back door."

"Thank you," she said. "Sorry I was so much trouble. Thank you for everything."

When she reached the outhouse, she turned to look through the kitchen's window. The four men were all enjoying their breakfast, talking and laughing, clapping each other on their backs, congratulating themselves on a job well done. They weren't watching her.

Elise turned and began to run through the woods as fast as she could on her damaged feet, not looking back.

When Maggie had finished writing her statement, was discharged by her doctor, and had arranged a scarf around her neck to hide her fading bruises, Durgin was waiting to take her home.

She opened the door, and there stood Chuck, Griffin in her arms, David at her side. "Maggie! Thank God you're all right!" Chuck embraced Maggie with her free arm, then nodded at Durgin. "Who's he?"

"Detective Chief Inspector James Durgin. He's a . . . friend."

"Good enough for me." Chuck bounced the gurgling baby on her hip. "Bring him to the library and I'll make us all some tea."

David shook Durgin's hand. "How do you do, Detective Chief Inspector."

"Durgin will do just fine."

"Meh!" K proclaimed, rubbing his face against her, then flopping on the carpet, showing his ginger belly. Maggie scooped him up. "Well, hello, Fur Face," she said. "Good to see you, too."

As Chuck bustled about the kitchen getting the tea ready, Maggie sat down next to David on the library's sofa. Durgin took a wing chair.

"What happened to the rug?" David asked. "That's antique, you know."

Maggie remembered all the blood. "I, er, need to get it cleaned."

"I know you've had a lot going on recently," David said, "and that's quite the understatement."

Maggie caught Durgin's eye. "You have no idea."

"I thought about whether to tell you or not, but in the end, I decided it's best you know, and as soon as possible."

Oh no, what now?

David patted her hand. "Elise was picked up by SOE agents in Berlin. She was supposed to be taken to Lisbon—but she escaped from our men. She's on the run now. Just outside Paris."

Maggie couldn't believe what she was hearing. "Why would she run away from the SOE? They're *saving* her, for goodness' sake! Doesn't she understand that?"

"Apparently, she wasn't particularly happy to be saved."

"What?"

"Her father—er, your stepfather—er, Miles Hess—was working with our agents, and through his own contacts, he arranged things so she would be released from Ravensbrück. The problem is the Gestapo made her release dependent on her renouncing the priest she'd been working with. They also threatened her fellow prisoners if she didn't return."

"Our saving her life may have cost her friends theirs," Maggie said, suddenly understanding why Elise wouldn't want to leave Berlin.

"From what I understand," David continued, "she's quite familiar with Paris, as her parents—er, your mother and stepfather—keep a flat there."

"What do you think she intends to do? She has nothing—no French identification, no papers, no ration card. . . ." Maggie's eyes widened. "The nuns. The nuns will take her in and hide her." She was standing, with no memory of having risen. "I need to go to Paris!" she exclaimed.

"You can't just 'go to Paris.' . . . "

"It's not only Elise—there's an SOE agent who was sent into a hostile situation and left for dead, despite coded messages for help. I think she might be in Paris now"—Maggie's thoughts clicked into place, and she swayed a bit as more information crowded into her brain, buzzing and urgent—"which is where they're also sending Sarah and Hugh. But the Paris network is in trouble. SOE may be sending them into a death trap—and they don't even know!"

Chuck walked in with the tea tray. "Who wants to be mother?"

All three of them froze and stared at her without speaking.

"What?" Chuck demanded, exasperated, as she set down the tray. "Do I have something on my face?"

The three were silent. While David and Durgin were cleared for a high level of security, Chuck wasn't.

Chuck shot David a warning look. "I'm not going to ask you anything," she said, "and I'm not going to tell you anything. But if anything happens to Maggie, anything at all—"

From the kitchen came Griffin's wails. "Mummy's coming, love!" Chuck called, mumbling "clingy blighter" as she left the room.

"I need to change," Maggie said. "And pack."

"This is utterly ridiculous!" David said, following her. "Even for *you*. And despite your brilliant background in maths, you often defy all logic. What are you going to do for papers?"

But instead of going to her own bedroom, Maggie went to Paige's old one, where she selected a smart Chanel suit and all of the accompanying accessories. *What's more French than Chanel?*

"Easy enough to conjure a fake French identity." Maggie threw things into a bag. "For me, at least. I've done it for dozens of other agents."

"Well, then how are you going to get there? It's not as if you can simply swim the Channel. Or flap your wings and fly."

"Silly David," Maggie said, looking up at him with affection. "As you well know, there are ways, if you know the right people—"

"Come now, even the P.M. wouldn't—"

From downstairs Chuck called, "I'm sorry I don't have anything sweet, but I do have some bread and margarine—"

Maggie came down the stairs with a bag and suitcase, David trailing behind her, still protesting. At the bottom, she kissed Chuck, and then both of Griffin's cheeks. "I'm sorry, but I have to run," she said. "By the way, Chuck, I believe it's quite possible a young man named Nicholas Reitter is responsible for tampering with the gas lines of your building and the resulting explosion. He worked for your landlord, Dr. Iain Frank."

Chuck's mouth hung open in a perfect circle. "How do you know? And where is he now?"

"He's in police custody," Maggie said matter-of-factly. "Charged with multiple homicides. Look, I'll be in touch as soon as I can," she added, giving David a hug.

"Maggie, this is madness," he protested.

"And you—" She dropped to her knees. "Be good for Chuck and Griffin, K, promise? I'm counting on you," she said, rubbing his head. The orange cat began to purr. "I'll be back as soon as I can."

"You're leaving?" Chuck exclaimed. "What? Now? Wait—where? Why?"

Maggie was pulling on her coat. "I'll be back as soon as possible. Please hold down the fort while I'm away."

She looked to Durgin. "Let's go." As the door closed behind her, David, Chuck, Griffin, and even K all stared at one another in shock.

"Well," David muttered. "At least she's wearing a *particularly* lovely Chanel suit."

Chapter Twenty

The art-deco apartment's rooms were fashionable, but dusty and unused—the way the Hess family had left them the last time they'd visited—a strange time capsule. The sun was setting, casting an orange glow over the walls.

Elise went to the room that had been used as her father's study and located a particular bookcase. She pulled on one of the leather-bound volumes, Voltaire's *Candide*.

Nothing happened.

Then she gave one side of the bookcase a push.

It spun, revealing a small secret room, complete with a low bed, a desk, and a chair. She walked inside. Closing the bookcase behind her, she turned the succession of locks.

Sitting on the bed, she pulled out the rosary from her dress pocket and began to pray.

At Beaulieu, Sarah and Hugh were being treated to a special meal: rare pink roast beef and golden Yorkshire pudding, with all the trimmings. They dined alongside Miss Lynd, Philby, and some of the agents to be dropped into other Nazi-occupied countries that night. There was even wine, champagne and then an excellent Bordeaux, from Lord Montagu's Beaulieu estate cellars.

The couple had just finished their coffee when a courier burst into the dining room. "They're ready for you."

"It's time," Miss Lynd said.

Maggie raised her hand for a taxi as Durgin held on to her valise.

A black cab pulled up. "Where to?" asked the driver, a large bald man with the broken and scarred face of an ex-boxer.

As Durgin put her case in the trunk, Maggie settled herself in the backseat. "Buckingham Palace, please." To Durgin she said, "Come on!"

While the cab moved out into traffic, the driver began to hold forth in a broad Cockney accent—on Winston Churchill, on Anthony Eden, on Franklin D. Roosevelt. He continued with the problems with rationing and the black market, following up with exactly what was wrong with films these days.

"Yes, yes, of course," Maggie answered absently, her mind on other things.

"American, 're you?" he asked. "What're you doin' 'ere, love? Bit of sightseeing? Come to see the 'oles and the rubble?"

"No," Maggie replied, taking a dented tube of lipstick from her handbag and pressing some on her lips. "I'm going to see the Queen."

"Ah, o' course you are, miss." The driver lifted his cap and whistled. "Whate'er you say, miss."

He let the two passengers out at the gates of Buckingham Palace. The workmen were still repairing the craters left by the bombs.

Maggie walked to the entrance. "Miss Margaret Hope and Detective Chief Inspector Durgin for the Queen," she declared, standing tall.

The guard on duty, a lanky man with gray-streaked chestnut

hair and a small paunch, began to laugh. "I'm sorry, miss. But to see the Queen, you need an appointment."

"I have this." Maggie drew a card from her handbag. It was the one Queen Elizabeth had given to her at the tea. "Her Majesty said to show this card if I ever needed to see her in an emergency. And we must see her. Now."

Queen Elizabeth's private sitting room was much smaller, plainer, and less formal than the Blue Drawing Room, with glowing fringed lamps and silver-framed photographs of family and dogs on every surface. The corgis were all asleep in a large basket by the fire, snoring noisily, and the Queen was knitting a soldier's sock.

"Miss Hope!" she called out in surprise as the butler led Maggie inside. The Queen put her knitting to one side. "To what do I owe this pleasure?"

"Your Majesty." Maggie curtsied. Durgin made a stiff bow. "You said if I ever needed anything—"

"Yes, yes, of course." She nodded. "Give us the room," she told her butler.

"Yes, ma'am," he said, walking out backwards.

When the double doors had clicked shut, Maggie began. "Ma'am, I know this is last-minute and quite extraordinary—"

"We do happen to live in extraordinary times, Miss Hope."

"Well, ma'am, you see—I need to go to Paris. On a matter of national security, as well as a personal emergency. It's a full moon, and I know there's an SOE flight scheduled to leave sometime around midnight. Would it be possible for you to get me on it?"

The Queen blinked. "Of course," she said, standing. "Where does this flight leave from?"

"Tangmere Aerodrome, ma'am. In Tangmere village, about three miles east of Chichester in West Sussex."

The Queen rang an embroidered pull cord, and in moments her butler reappeared. "Yes, ma'am?"

"I'll need a car and driver," she announced. "Miss Hope and I—and Detective Durgin—will be going to the Tangmere Aerodrome in West Sussex."

The butler looked perplexed. "Er, tonight, ma'am?"

"Yes, tonight. Immediately, in fact." There was no brooking disagreement with the Queen.

"Yes, ma'am." He backed away. "Very good, ma'am."

The Queen looked to Maggie. "Miss Hope," she said, walking to the door, "you will explain everything to me in the car."

Maggie and Durgin exchanged glances.

"That's—that's it?" Maggie asked, trailing after the Queen somewhat like a lost corgi puppy. "You don't have any questions? Concerns?"

"Of course I do," the Queen replied. "But there's no need for dramatics. I trust you when you say this is important, and I'm sure we can manage to get you on that flight. Not only do I owe you for saving my daughter, but"—she looked to Maggie with her deep blue eyes and gave a conspiratorial, and quite unroyal, wink—"we women need to stick together."

Maggie finally had a chance to catch her breath and think as the Queen's Bentley wended its way to the aerodrome through the dark. Sitting pressed against Durgin, she had told her long and convoluted story, and the Queen had listened. And now Her Majesty was leaning her head back on her seat's embroidered doily, had closed her eyes, and was snoring lightly.

Maggie rested her head on Durgin's shoulder and looked out into the shadows. *Is there such a thing as evil? Or is "evil" a disease? Is Nicholas Reitter evil? Is Hitler evil? Or are they sick, mentally ill? Are they curable? Or, in spiritual terms, can they be "saved"?*

Why even try to understand? But then, that was nihilism. Wasn't it better to struggle for some glimmer of understanding than to flounder in total darkness? Wasn't it better to hope than to be cynical?

I can't fight everything, Maggie realized. *But I can do some things. And those I'll do to the best of my ability and strength.*

As she looked up at the silvery moon and the dusting of stars across the violet sky, she remembered some lines from a Dante class she had taken:

> *We mounted up, he first and I the second,*
> *Till I beheld through a round aperture*
> *Some of the beauteous things that Heaven doth bear;*
> *Thence we came forth to rebehold the stars.*

It was good to see the stars again.

Sarah and Hugh arrived at the aerodrome. The hangar was enormous, and they shivered as they walked to a large table that had been set up in preparation for their departure. "Before you leave," Miss Lynd was saying to the pair, "we need to know your wishes in regard to your families."

"We've already made our wills," Sarah reminded her.

"No, I mean in terms of communication while you're away," Miss Lynd clarified. "Obviously, you won't be able to communicate with them, but is there anything I can do?"

"If you could send a postcard to my mum, letting her know I'm all right, that would be lovely," Sarah answered steadily.

Miss Lynd affected nonchalance. "Of course."

"My mother's birthday is in two weeks," Hugh realized. "Would you be able to send a card to her from me?"

"Should I go missing," Sarah said slowly, "I'd like to avoid worrying anyone as much as possible."

"How would you like me to handle things, dear?"

"I don't want you to worry my mother unnecessarily. Only tell her anything if—if the worst happens."

"Yes, same for me," agreed Hugh, jaw clenched.

"And of course that's *not* going to happen," replied Miss Lynd with false bravado, "but I do like to have all wishes and requests on file."

Philby arrived and walked up to the group. "Remember," he said, pulling Hugh aside, pressing something into his hand, "you need to work closely with the French Communists. We're all on the same team now. Give this to a stagehand named Jean Paul Dunois, will you? He works at the Palais Garnier."

Hugh looked down at the covered wooden bowl in his hand. "What is it? Soap?"

"That's prewar, triple-milled French shaving soap, my friend." Philby smirked. "And if you unscrew the false wooden bottom, you'll find a note inside. That's what I want you to pass to Monsieur Dunois."

Hugh brought it up to his nose to sniff. "It smells like violets," he said slowly, as if flooded by memories. "Maggie used to smell like violets."

"Your girl?" Philby asked

"Ex-girl." Hugh placed the bowl in his rucksack.

As Philby went to speak to the pilot, Miss Lynd once more inspected their pockets, checked clothing labels and laundry tags. She also went through their bags and suitcases, examining every article they were bringing for any signs that would betray them as British. They were given the requisite identification, ration cards, clothing coupons, and 50,000 French francs. "You each have your cyanide tablet?" she asked.

Sarah and Hugh nodded.

"And your wedding rings?"

They held out their left hands, gold bands glinting in the overhead fluorescent light.

"All right then—let's get on with it." She completed their disguises with a packet of French cigarettes for Hugh, and a recent French newspaper for Sarah.

Sarah took a trembling breath. "Are you all right, dear?" the older woman asked.

"Excited, mostly," Sarah answered, dark eyes sparkling. "I'm sorry we're not jumping—those three terrifying jumps in parachute school, for naught!"

"We ordered a landing to save your pretty ankles for dancing. And wear and tear on Monsieur's cello."

Hugh glanced up from his papers. "Good to know my cello's considered more valuable than I in the grand scheme of things," he deadpanned. Miss Lynd favored him with a rare smile.

Sarah looked to the brooch on Miss Lynd's lapel, a graceful gold iris set with sapphires, amethysts, and emeralds. "You're so clever, Miss Lynd. Even though we're at war, you always make sure to wear something pretty. It does help with morale."

Miss Lynd responded by unpinning it. "The iris is the national flower of France," she said, offering it to Sarah. "The *fleur-de-lis*. May it bring you luck." She pinned it on the younger woman's lapel.

A large Army station wagon arrived at the hangar, and the party was driven out to the tarmac in the bright moonlight, where the Lysander waited, casting shadows.

The group got out of the car and huddled together, backs to the icy wind. As Philby reiterated takeoff procedures, their luggage was stowed under hinged wooden seats. When Philby was finished, Miss Lynd moved forward. She embraced Sarah and shook Hugh's hand. She gave a loud sniff, blinked hard, then took several paces back as the pilot signaled for Sarah and Hugh to climb into the plane.

"This is it," Hugh told Sarah. "Are you ready?"

She smiled. "Let's give those bloody Nazis some Wellie, shall we?"

They climbed the ladder into the plane. The engines started and were left ticking over for several minutes. As the pilots carried out their checks, they briefly opened up to full throttle, then returned to fine pitch. Miss Lynd, motionless on the tarmac, looked up toward the windows, her eyes inscrutable.

Before the workmen could remove the ladder and close the plane's door, there was a blaring of horns and the blink of headlights.

"What on earth?" fumed Miss Lynd, glaring at the driver. The car in question was a black and burgundy Bentley with no license plate. Instead of the Bentley's usual Flying B bonnet ornament, there was a silver figurine of St. George on a horse, preparing to fight the dragon.

As the car screeched to a stop, a door flew open. Maggie emerged, resplendent in Chanel.

Miss Lynd's jaw dropped, a singular occurrence. "Miss Hope!" she squeaked. "What are *you* doing here?"

Maggie gave her a Mona Lisa smile. "Room for one more?"

"Certainly not," Miss Lynd said, drawing herself up to her full, imperious height.

The car's driver walked around to open the other passenger door.

He extended his hand and out, onto the tarmac, stepped the Queen, Durgin behind her.

Miss Lynd went pale. "Your Majesty," she murmured, bobbing a curtsy. "I—I . . ." It was the first time Maggie had ever seen Miss Lynd at a loss for words.

"Good evening, Miss Lynd—it *is* Miss Lynd, isn't it?" the Queen asked as if she were at a garden party, not on freezing cold tarmac in the dead of night. "I already know a bit about you and your organization."

"Yes, er, yes, ma'am," Miss Lynd managed.

"And now Miss Margaret Hope has important business—Royal business, top secret, of course—in Paris." She fixed clear blue eyes on Miss Lynd. "And it is imperative she take this flight."

"Your Majesty," Miss Lynd began, "this is highly—"

"—unusual, yes, of course," the Queen interrupted with a wave of her plump gloved hand. "However, this is wartime—and extraordinary circumstances seem to abound these days, don't they?" She looked to Maggie. "Well, go on then, Miss Hope."

"Thank you, Your Majesty." Maggie gave a deep curtsy. Then she turned to Durgin. "Thank you—for everything."

"You promised you'd go to dinner with me," he said, stepping forward, hugging Maggie tight. "I'm going to hold you to that, when you get back."

She kissed his cheek. "It's a date." Maggie picked up her suit-case, then turned to the plane.

"By the way, Miss Lynd," the Queen declared, her voice rising above the noise of the engines. "I had an interesting discussion with Miss Hope about female agents and their pay and pensions. I understand you're the person with whom to follow up? I'd like to see some of these issues sorted, and sooner rather than later." Her lips pursed. "We shall have a meeting."

"Y-yes, ma'am."

Maggie took the stairs two by two, thinking of both Erica Calvert and her half sister Elise. She stopped at the top rung and turned back, calling into the wind, *"Vive la France!"*

Acknowledgments

Thank you to Noel MacNeal and Matthew MacNeal for their support and patience.

Thanks to editor extraordinaire Kate Miciak at Penguin Random House, as well as Julia Maguire, Allyson Lord, Maggie Oberrender, Kim Hovey, Victoria Allen, Vincent La Scala, and Dana Blanchette, a.k.a. Team Maggie. Special thanks to deputy copy chief Dennis Ambrose. I am, as always, grateful to the intrepid Penguin Random House sales force.

I'm always appreciative of Victoria "Agent V" Skurnick, Lindsay Edgecombe, and Stephanie Rostan at Levine Greenberg Rosten Literary Agency.

Special thanks to readers Idria Barone Knecht; Scott Cameron; historian Ronald Granieri; Meredith Norris, M.D.; police officer Rick Peach; and Blitz-suvivor Phyllis Brooks Schafer. As well as Rebecca Danos and Michael T. Feeley for probability theory and Rossmo's formula. Thanks to Caitlin Sims for the French and Tom Gold for ballet help. A special thanks to Lily Peta for knowledge of pointe shoes.

And cheers to fellow Jungle Red Writers: Rhys Bowen, Lucy Burdette, Deborah Crombie, Hallie Ephron, Julia Spencer Fleming, Hank Phillipi Ryan. Thanks to you all.

Sources

One tool . . . men and women have for displaying power is some degree of control over the narratives about sex and gender.

—CATHERINE R. STIMPSON, FOREWORD TO *CITY OF DREADFUL NIGHT: NARRATIVES OF SEXUAL DANGER IN LATE-VICTORIAN LONDON*, BY JUDITH R. WALKOWITZ

Alas, I didn't have to go far to find "inspiration" for a misogynistic murderer, even today. (Especially today?) If you'd like to know more, look up Anders Behring Breivik, Marc Lépine, Elliot Rodger, the anonymous posters of "Gamergate"—all fearful of women and women's increasing public power.

There really was a serial killer (sequential murderer) in London during the Blackout. His story is different from that of Nicholas Reitter and May Frank, but you can read about it in Simon Read's *In the Dark: The True Story of the Blackout Ripper.*

Books consulted on Queen Elizabeth, the Queen Mother:

Behind Palace Doors: My True Adventures as the Queen Mother's Equerry, by Colin Burgess, with Paul Carter

Elizabeth: The Queen Mother: A Twentieth Century Life, by Grania Forbes

My Darling Buffy: The Early Life of the Queen Mother, by Grania Forbes

H.M. Queen Elizabeth the Queen Mother, by Ian A. Morrison

The Queen Mother, by Ann Morrow

Queen Mother, by Penelope Mortimer

The Private Life of the Queen: By a Member of the Royal Household, by C. Arthur Pearson

Backstairs Billy: The Life of William Tallon, the Queen Mother's Most Devoted Servant, by Tom Quinn

Counting One's Blessings: The Selected Letters of Queen Elizabeth the Queen Mother, edited by William Shawcross

The Queen Mother: The Official Biography, by William Shawcross

Books about crime, forensics, and serial killers:

The Invention of Murder: How the Victorians Revelled in Death and Detection and Created Modern Crime, by Judith Flanders

Death in the City of Light: The Serial Killer of Nazi-Occupied Paris, by David King

Dr. H. H. Holmes and the Whitechapel Ripper, by Dane Ladwig

The Devil in the White City: Murder, Magic, and Madness at the Fair That Changed America, by Erik Larson

Forensics: What Bugs, Burns, Prints, DNA and More Tell Us About Crime, by Val McDermid

A Serial Killer in Nazi Berlin: The Chilling True Story of the S-Bahn Murderer, by Scott Andrew Selby

The Complete History of Jack the Ripper, by Philip Sugden

City of Dreadful Delight: Narratives of Sexual Danger in Late-Victorian London, by Judith R. Walkowitz

SOE Books:

Women Heroes of World War II: Twenty-six Stories of Espionage, Sabotage, Resistance, and Rescue, by Kathryn J. Atwood

The Women Who Lived for Danger: The Agents of the Special Operations Executive, by Marcus Binney

Nancy Wake: SOE's Greatest Heroine, by Russell Braddon

SOE Agent: Churchill's Secret Warriors, by Terry Crowdy

The Beaulieu Finishing School for Secret Agents, by Cyril Cunningham

*SOE in France: An Account of the Work of the British Special
    Operations Executive in France 1940–1944,* by M. R. D. Foot

A Life in Secrets: Vera Atkins and the Missing Agents of WWII,
    by Sarah Helm

*Flames in the Field: The Story of Four SOE Agents in Occupied
    France,* by Rita Kramer

Christine: SOE Agent and Churchill's Favourite Spy, by Madeleine
    Masson

*A Cool and Lonely Courage: The Untold Story of Sister Spies in
    Occupied France,* by Susan Ottaway

Violette Szabo: The Life That I Have, by Susan Ottaway

My Silent War: The Autobiography of a Spy, by Kim Philby

How to Be a Spy: The World War II SOE Training Manual, by
    Denis Rigden

Odette: World War Two's Darling Spy, by Penny Starns

*Spymistress: The Life of Vera Atkins, the Greatest Female Secret
    Agent of World War II,* by William Stevenson

Odette: The Story of a British Agent, by Jerrard Tickell

About World War II Germany and Ravensbrück camp:

Priestblock 25487: A Memoir of Dachau, by Jean Bernard;
    translated by Deborah Lucas Schneider

*The Blessed Abyss: Inmate #6582 in Ravensbrück Concentration
    Camp for Women,* by Nanda Herbermann; edited by Hester
    Baer and Elizabeth R. Baer; translated by Hester Baer

The Dawn of Hope: A Memoir of Ravensbrück, by Geneviève De
    Gaulle Anthonioz; translated by Richard Seaver

Four Women from Ravensbrück: Five Stories from the Shoa, by
    Roberta Kalechofsky

Berlin at War, by Roger Moorhouse

What Was It Like in the Concentration Camp at Dachau? An Attempt to Come Closer to the Truth, by Johannes Neuhäusler

Books about London during World War II:

The Love-charm of Bombs: Restless Lives in the Second World War, by Lara Feigel

Few Eggs and No Oranges: The Diaries of Vere Hodgson 1940–45, by Vere Hodgson; preface by Jenny Hartley

Inside Buckingham Palace, by Andrew Morton

Buckingham Palace: The Official Illustrated History, by John Martin Robinson

Fashion on the Ration: Style in the Second World War, by Julie Summers

Exhibits:

Beaulieu Abbey, Beaulieu, England

Beaulieu Estate, Beaulieu, England

Imperial War Museums exhibit, "Fashion on the Ration," London, England

Wellcome Collection's "Forensics: The Anatomy of Crime," London, England

"Women's Land Army at Exbury," New Forest National Park, Beaulieu, England

Documentaries:

H. H. Holmes: America's First Serial Killer

How Sherlock Changed the World

Secrets of Scotland Yard

If you enjoyed *The Queen's Accomplice*, you won't want
to miss the next suspenseful novel in the Maggie Hope series.

Read on for an exciting preview of

THE PARIS SPY

by Susan Elia MacNeal

Coming soon from Bantam Books

Prologue

Only a single small sparrow, hiding in the branches of a budding chestnut tree on Avenue Fochs, dared to pierce the street's eerie silence with her chirps and trills.

Even though it was midafternoon, there was no traffic on Baron Haussmann's grand neoclassical boulevard, which linked the Arc de Triomphe to the Bois de Boulogne. The vélo-taxis avoided the wide street itself, while pedestrians and bicyclists sidestepped its *contre-allée*—the inner road separated from the boulevard by a green ribbon of verdant lawn, dotted with blooming forsythia bushes and budding irises.

There were few cars in Paris in the spring of 1942, and the large black Citroëns and Mercedes favored by the Gestapo that dared to make their way down Avenue Fochs seemed to glide silently. Without traffic, the air on Avenue Fochs was unexpectedly sweet and fresh.

The ornate cream-colored Lutetian limestone façades, with their wrought-iron balconies, tall windows, and mansard roofs, were considered the height of Parisian elegance. However, there was a more ominous factor behind Haussmann's design—some of the architect's critics opined that the real purpose of his grand boulevards was to make it easier for the military and police to maneuver, and to suppress armed uprisings. They argued that the small number of large, open intersections allowed easy control by a minimal force. In addition, buildings set back from the street could not be used so easily as fortifications.

The distinctive Haussmannian architecture had also made it easier for the Nazis to invade Paris during the Battle of France in June 1940.

On the section of Avenue Fochs closer to Porte Dauphine stood several anonymous buildings that gave the street its chilling reputation, which resulted in its isolation. Nos. 82 and 84 housed the Paris headquarters of the Gestapo—the abbreviation for *Geheime Staatspolizei*, or secret state police, founded in 1933 by Hermann Goering and controlled by Heinrich Himmler. The Gestapo leaders had chosen Avenue Fochs deliberately for their headquarters of terror: it was named after the French general Marshall Fochs, to whom the Germans surrendered in November 1918.

Inside No. 84, in a large office on the first floor with high ceilings, elaborate crown moldings, and a glittering cage chandelier, light refracting through its spear- and point-cut crystals. A large reproduction of Nicolas Poussin's *Rape of the Sabine Women* hung on one wall. Obersturmbannführer Wolfgang von Waltz's ears pricked at the low growl of a car piercing the silence of the street. From his desk, he looked out the window over Avenue Fochs to see a gleaming black Benz pull up to the curb. Two SS officers in black emerged with a young brunette in handcuffs.

Obersturmbannführer von Waltz was in his early forties, handsome and immaculately groomed, with golden-blond hair and silvery sideburns. Only his middling height and a pointed, jutting chin kept him from looking like the Nordic gods of Nazi propaganda posters. Despite his SS rank, he wore a double-breasted gray-striped suit, silk Hermès tie and pocket square, and handmade alligator shoes. He wore civilian clothes on purpose—to disarm and put at ease prisoners. He left the actual torture to the SS henchmen in No. 84's soundproofed basement.

Von Waltz was the chief for France's section IV Counter-espionage division and of the Sicherheitsdienst, the German security service, answering directly to Himmler himself. Technically, he was the third-ranking Nazi officer in Paris, overseeing the task of arresting and interrogating foreign agents. Before the war, he'd received his doctorate in Romance languages and had been a professor at the University of Vienna. He'd volunteered as the conductor for the St. Stephen's Cathedral boys choir and was known for his graceful dancing, especially the fox-trot.

He lifted the heavy black Bakelite telephone receiver with immaculately manicured hands and dialed his secretary. "Frau Schmidt," he crooned in honeyed tones, "our guest has arrived from the Rouen office. Please put on coffee for our meeting." Coffee—real coffee—not the ersatz coffee made from chicory or roasted acorns, was as precious as gold or diamonds in occupied Paris.

Hertha Schmidt did as she was told, but she didn't like it, not one bit. A German woman in her twenties, she relished the many luxuries, such as coffee and chocolates, that working for the SS in Paris afforded her. *"Terroristen,"* she muttered as she measured out the ground beans, resentful that the enemy would be treated to a cup of the office's precious brew. *"Englisch Terroristen."*

As von Waltz heard the heavy iron courtyard gate clank shut, he looked up from the file in front of him, sent to him by motorcycle courier, containing all the information gathered on the captured agent. He heard footsteps on the staircase, then a rap at his office door. He smiled, eyes shining. "Come in!" he called in Austrian-inflected French.

The two SS officers who opened the door looked grotesquely large, towering over their captive. The petite woman trembled violently and looked as if she might faint.

Von Waltz rose, clicked his heels, and bowed. "Please sit down,

Mademoiselle," he said in gentle tones, indicating a fragile gilt chair. "Would you like a drink? Coffee is on the way, but I can get you something stronger if you'd like. You look as if you could use it."

He gestured to the two men. "Take those off," he ordered, indicating the heavy cuffs shackling the woman's delicate wrists. Once they did as they were told, he dismissed them.

"That's better now, isn't it?" Von Waltz took the seat across from the woman instead of returning to his desk chair. Her face was swollen beyond recognition; eyes slits in the battered flesh. Impassively, he noted her matted and dirty hair, the bruises on her neck, and the stench of sweat and urine. Three of her fingernails had been torn off. Her stained and ripped dress concealed whatever else she'd endured. She moved slowly to rub some life back into her hands.

He clicked his tongue against his teeth. "I see you've shown the poor judgment to resist in Rouen. I do trust you will do better here. Ah, coffee!" he cried as Frau Schmidt entered bearing a silver tray piled with a silver sugar bowl, creamer, and plate with pastries. "I do love the ones with the hazelnut crème filling," he confided as the secretary set it on the table between the Obersturmbannführer and his prisoner. "Of course, German pastry is the best, but there is something special about Parisian pastry that makes it a very close second."

"Would you like me to pour, sir?"

"Thank you, but no, no. I'm sure we can manage, yes?" As he reached for the coffeepot, he watched the prisoner take in his office. There was the mandatory portrait of Hitler over the marble fireplace, topped with a mounted Degen SS saber with an ebony grip. On the mantel was an antique Jean Gille unglazed bisque porcelain figure, with enamel and gilt, of a beautiful woman in

repose—*The Sleeping Beauty.* Next to it stood a Sèvres vase of violet hyacinths. The blossoms gave off a sweet and almost narcotic
scent.

A beechwood fire had been lit earlier in the day against the
damp spring air, and although the logs had burned down consider-
ably it still crackled. There were red Nazi flags on both sides of the
hearth. On a rosewood table, a marble chessboard was set up with
a game in progress.

"Would you prefer I call you by your code name?" he asked as
he poured steaming coffee with graceful movements. "Or by your
real name—Erica Calvert?"

He watched for her reaction. "And do you take sugar or cream?
Or both?"

Erica shook her head; von Waltz dropped two sugar cubes and
a generous pour of cream into a cup for himself. "Well then, I shall
call you Mademoiselle Calvert."

He blew on his coffee before taking a sip. "You are Erica Grace
Calvert, one of Winston Churchill's secret army of undercover
agents, known as the SOE or Special Operations Executive, recruited to 'set Europe ablaze.' "

Erica avoided his direct gaze.

"You were captured in Rouen and held for questioning."

The agent remained silent.

"And you're so tiny!" he exclaimed, studying her. "I had no
idea when I read your file that you'd be such a tiny little thing—
and so young, as well." From his jacket pocket, he took out a silver
case. "Cigarette?"

Erica made a sound halfway between a snort and a mew.

"My colleagues, unfortunately, were not able to obtain any sat-
isfactory answers from you. And so you have been sent to Paris, to
me." He left the case open, placing it on the table between them. "I

will ask the questions now, and, as you can see, we can make this a civilized exchange. It is up to you." He set down his cup and saucer beside the cigarette case. "What were you doing in Rouen, Mademoiselle Calvert?"

"I can't say," she managed through bruised lips.

"Plans for sabotage?" von Waltz suggested.

Erica shook her head.

"To whom were you reporting?"

"I can't say."

"With whom were you working?"

"I can't say."

"Where are the secret stashes of arms and explosives you and your colleagues are bringing over here?"

"I can't say."

Von Waltz smiled as he leaned back in his chair and crossed one slim leg over the other. "And how did you enjoy your stay at Arisaig House? I hear the Scottish Highlands are quite beautiful, especially in the autumn."

Erica's breathing stilled. There was no way he could know that location—the location of the SOE's paramilitary training—or that she had trained there in September and October.

"You did quite well with your parachute training at Ringway. And how did you enjoy your time at Beaulieu?" The Obersturmbannführer pronounced it correctly, the English way, *bew-lee*. Beaulieu was the SOE's so-called finishing school, where chosen agents were sent for their final round of training. "I hear even in winter, the weather there in the south of England is surprisingly mild."

"How—how—" Erica stammered.

"We know a lot about you, my darling girl. For instance, how you've been leaving off your security checks, hoping your London office will notice and realize you've been captured." He smiled.

"Meanwhile, the Baker Street agents *have* noted your lack of security checks—but scolded that in the future you must be more careful with your coding."

"I don't believe you."

Von Waltz rose and crossed to his massive desk, flipping through pages of her file, picking one out. Walking back, he handed it to her. " 'Your 5735 security check acknowledged,' " he recited from memory, taking his seat. " 'You forgot your double security check. Next time be more careful.' "

He studied her face, relishing her expression of abject shock. "You, Mademoiselle Erica Calvert, are in the SOE, specifically in F-Section, prepared for work in France. Specifically, you are part of the Prosper Network, whose leader is Major Francis Alfred Suthill."

She flinched.

"Ah yes, we have an eye on Major Suthill here in Paris. We haven't picked him up yet—but we will."

Not only had she been betrayed, Erika realized, but there was a mole somewhere in SOE. But who? In France? Or in London?

Von Waltz continued. "We have picked up any number of your fellow SOE agents, and we are using them, and their radios, in a little game we are playing with England. *Das Englandspiel,* as we say in German." His voice still gentle, he added, "We know how scared you are, Mademoiselle Calvert. You've been confessing your fears in your letters home to your father."

Erica gasped. "How can you know that? There's no way you can know that!"

Von Waltz ignored her outburst. "Fear in wartime, Mademoiselle—well, it's nothing to be ashamed of. But I must speak frankly. Your superior, Colonel Harry Gaskell, has sent you, a woman, here, in direct violation of the Geneva Convention and all the rules of gentlemanly warfare."

Despite her shock and fear, Erica let out a snort at the Nazi's hypocrisy.

"You have been sent here against all the rules of war," the Obersturmbannführer continued. "A woman. In civilian clothes. As a secret agent. To commit acts of terrorism against us. You know what the penalty for that is, yes?"

Erica didn't reply. Of course she knew. *Execution*. By firing squad or noose.

"But I am a gentleman. I don't want you, a woman—a *lady*—to be sacrificed for the stupidity and rash decisions of your superiors. Your Colonel Gaskell dropped you into a trap—and then stupidly failed to recognize his own security checks, checks his own people had put into place to keep you safe, that were being left off as a warning you'd been captured."

He stood, crossing the plush Persian carpet. "They think on Baker Street and Orchard Court that we're bungling, ham-handed Nazi fools." At his desk, he picked up another file and pulled out another piece of paper.

It was a chart of the SOE hierarchy in London, every name correct. When he handed it to Erica and she realized what it was and how much sensitive information it contained, she felt tears sting her eyes.

"I know you told your little cover story ad nauseam to the SS officers in Rouen, but let's dispense with it here, shall we, Mademoiselle? I can't promise you everything, but I can tell you I can save your life. Instead of being executed, you'll stay here. You will share all the information you know, then work with us on our English radio games. And when the war is over, you will find out who betrayed you—and get your revenge."

Erica was struggling to process everything von Waltz was throwing at her. His men had captured her in Rouen, but they still didn't know she'd come ashore on the west coast of France. He didn't know she had been trained in geology and that she'd been sent to the beaches of Normandy to obtain sand and soil samples.

If he learned the truth, the Nazis would know Normandy was being a considered a possible invasion site. And while the Germans would of course consider Normandy a possible landing point, Calais was the more obvious choice. A soil sample, which would help the engineers know what sort of equipment and tanks to send on whenever the Allies invaded, would be a red flag to the possibility of the Allies using Normandy, shattering the advantage of surprise. They didn't know and they couldn't know—not because of her. *As long as I can keep that from him. . . .*

Von Waltz sat and regarded her smugly. "A terrorist, against the Geneva Conventions—out of uniform, behind enemy lines, seeking to sow seeds of fear and unrest. A girl terrorist at that. How badly things must be going in England for them to send little girls! They should not have made you come."

She blinked up at him. "I wanted to come."

"They should not have let you."

Like all other SOE agents, Erica had been issued a cyanide capsule, in case of situations such as this. But hers was concealed in a fountain pen in her handbag, which had been confiscated.

"You know there is nothing you won't tell me when we're through, Mademoiselle. Save some time—and your beautiful face—and tell us everything you know."

Erica stared at him in despair, then slumped over in submission.

His smile was cryptic. "Yes, we know everything. Look—give us the location of the British arms and explosives and we'll forget the rest. Those arrested as a result will be interred until the end of the war. This is an agreement we will make—you and I."

Erica was silent, broken.

"If this does not happen, the villages around where we think the depots are will be burned. And all of the inhabitants, including your fellow agents, will be killed.

"We are all afraid in this war, Mademoiselle. But now you can free yourself of fears. There's nothing dishonorable in it. Help us! Give us the location of your agents, weapons, explosives, safe houses. And no one will be hurt. I give you my word, as an officer of the Third Reich."

Erica peered up at him. "I think I'll have that drink now," she whispered.

He clapped his hands together with delight. "Good, good!" he exclaimed, rising and going to the bar cart. He poured two fingers of scotch into a glass, then handed her the heavy tumbler.

She downed it in one gulp, then shuddered. "I will talk to you," she told him. "I will tell you everything I know. But I'm exhausted. I need to wash. Change my clothes. To eat."

"Of course."

"And I'd like my handbag—I have a compact in there. And some lipstick."

"I'm afraid that's not permitted. But we can show you to a place where you can freshen up. And I will have a plate prepared for you, for when you are ready, and some good French wine. And after that, we will chat."

"Yes," she said, struggling to her feet.

"You've made the right decision." He opened the door and gestured to the two guards outside. "Please take Mademoiselle Calvert to the prisoners' lavatory and allow her to freshen up. When she is finished, bring her back here."

The fifth-floor servants' quarters had a shared bath. The guards admitted her, then stationed themselves outside the closed door. Erica looked around. There was a dirty tub and a ragged towel on a hook. Over the chipped enamel sink was a mirrored medicine chest. She looked inside—nothing but rust on the shelves.

Grimly, she looked at her reflection in the mirror. Her bruised face grimaced back.

She could break the glass and try to slit her carotid artery—but the guards would hear the crash, and they would stop her before she could achieve her goal. She had already been through days of torture and deprivation. No, she couldn't take much more. She would break, she knew it. Slowly, she went to the window, opened the curtains, and looked out. From the fifth floor, it was a long drop to the pavement below. No one could survive such a fall.

Striking while her courage still held, she opened the window and crawled out, finding footing on a rain gutter. If she killed herself, the secret of the Normandy sands and soil would die with her. The planned invasion would have a chance. She had confronted death back in Rouen and made her peace with it. She knew what she had to do. Only one thing tormented her: Who was the mole in the SOE? Who'd betrayed her?

The sound she made as her body struck the pavement was swallowed by von Waltz's bellow of frustrated rage.

SUSAN ELIA MACNEAL is the *New York Times* and *USA Today* bestselling author of the Maggie Hope mystery series. She is the winner of the Barry Award and was shortlisted for the Edgar, Macavity, Agatha, Dilys, Bruce Alexander Memorial Historical Mystery, and Sue Feder Historical Memorial awards. She lives in Park Slope, Brooklyn, with her husband and son.

www.susaneliamacneal.com
Facebook.com/MrChurchillsSecretary
Twitter: @susanmacneal